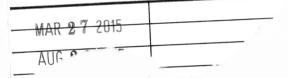

MICHAEL GRANT

BZRK
APOCALYPSE

EGMONT
USA
NEW YORK

EGMONT

We bring stories to life

First published in the United Kingdom by Egmont UK Limited, 2014
First published in the United States of America by Egmont USA, 2014
443 Park Avenue South, Suite 806
New York, NY 10016

1 3 5 7 9 8 6 4 2

www.egmontusa.com

Library of Congress Cataloging-in-Publication Data

Grant, Michael, 1954-
BZRK apocalypse / Michael Grant.
pages cm
Sequel to: BZRK reloaded.
Summary: In the concluding book in the BZRK trilogy, war is again being
waged in the macro and the nano, and Lear's identity is finally uncovered.
ISBN 978-1-60684-408-3 (hardcover) -- ISBN 978-1-60684-409-0 (eBook) [1.
Utopias--Fiction. 2. Nanotechnology--Fiction. 3. Conjoined twins--Fiction. 4.
Twins--Fiction. 5. Science fiction.] I. Title.
PZ7.G7671Bzs 2014
[Fic]--dc23
2014002442

Printed in the United States of America

For Katherine, Jake, and Julia

APOCALYPSE

ONE

Sandra Piper was having dinner with friends when it started.

She was eating chilled lobster on the teak deck of a producer friend's Malibu home, along with a former costar named Wade Talon (a ridiculous screen name in Sandra's opinion), her current director (Quentin—no last name necessary), a very rich and rather magnificently tattooed woman named Lystra Reid who had an odd vocal tic that added "Yeah" to random sentences, and an extraordinarily fit, tall, and broad-shouldered man whose name she kept forgetting but who might have been named Noble, or something very close to that.

The Noble creature was listening, rapt, while the more famous folk discussed work and mutual friends and more work. In fact, in one way or another it was all work.

 Sandra had been nominated: Best Actress. Very tough competition. The oddsmakers called her a long shot at six to one. Long but not impossible. And despite the fact that Sandra Piper was a mother of two, a down-to-earth thirtyish woman with a masters in economics who had smoked pot exactly twice in her life and never drank more than two glasses of wine, she was thinking of seducing young Mr. Shoulders. Mr. Shy Grin. Mr. Large-But-Sensitive Hands.

1

Because he was definitely interested, and she had been divorced for two years and had dated no one in that time. And she was exhausted from long days on the current shoot, plus her son, Quarle (three years old), had just gotten over a two-week-long bout of the flu.

And really, what the hell was the point of being America's Sweetheart if you couldn't even get laid? Would a male actor in the same situation even hesitate? Well, some, sure. But lots wouldn't. So why should she? Wasn't that why Quentin had invited Noble . . . ? No, wait, now she remembered. His name was Nolan. Whatever. Wasn't he there for her, um . . . amusement?

Unless. Oh, had he come with the Lystra person? Was he here for *her*? She would be closer to his age, not a beauty but attractive enough, given that she was not Hollywood at all but some sort of health-care billionaire.

No. No, young Mr. Body of Steel was not eyeing Lystra. He was eyeing the next winner of the Academy Award for Best Actress. *Uh-huh.*

But the idea sighed inside her and deflated like a balloon with a slow leak. She shook her head, a tiny movement not intended for anyone else, and took a deep breath. She had to help Quinn (seven years old) with her stupid California Mission project, due tomorrow.

God, she was boring. Boring and responsible and definitely America's Sweetheart, except that when it came right down to it, she was Mommy.

Suddenly her hand jerked and she tipped her wineglass over. The last ounce of white wine drained onto the wood surface, alarming no one.

"Sorry. I just—"

Sandra frowned. Shook her head.

"What's the matter, Sandy?" Wade asked.

"I'm just . . ." She shook her head again. Frowned, despite the fact that frowning would crease her ageless forehead. "Oh my God, is there something in the wine? I'm . . . I'm seeing something."

Nolan looked at her from beneath lashes that would probably have tickled her cheeks (and other places, too, if she'd just said the word) and asked, "Are you feeling ill?"

"It's . . ." She laughed. "This is going to sound crazy. It's like I can see something that isn't there. I'm . . ." She looked away from them, stared out toward the black Pacific Ocean, wondering if somehow what she was seeing was a reflection off the wineglasses.

But no. It was still there. It was as if she had a second set of eyes, and they opened onto a small TV screen in a corner of her *own* eyes.

"I'm seeing, like, like . . . just flat, but weird." Then, a sudden, sharp gasp. "Oh my God, a second one. Like another window in my head."

"Maybe you should lie down," Nolan suggested.

"Or have another glass of wine," Quentin said, and laughed. But now he, too, was staring at her sideways, with concern on his face.

"There's two . . . Oh! Oh! Oh! There's a giant insect. I'm going nuts. Maybe I'm having a stroke."

"I'm calling nine one one," Nolan said, and pulled out his phone.

"Jesus Christ! It's a huge bug. I can see it! It's turning, it's coming toward me. . . . Oh, oh God, I think I'm moving it! I think I'm making it move!"

She pushed back hard from the table. Glassware clattered and toppled. Wade leapt to his feet and caught her arm as she lurched away from the table.

"It has eyes! It has eyes! Oh, God. Oh, God. My face! My eyes! Those are *my* eyes!"

She pushed Wade aside violently, then, abashed, shocked by her own behavior, she tried on a fleeting smile, reached out a reassuring hand and said, "I think I need help. I think I'd better see a doctor."

"That would be best," Lystra Reid said coolly, then added, as if an afterthought, "Yeah." She had moved to place her back against the railing and was watching with detached interest. At least she wasn't taking a picture to tweet later.

"Ambulance is on the way," Nolan reported.

And Sandra thought, *Well, he certainly won't sleep with me now.* But that thought came and left in a heartbeat, because something else was happening on that eerie picture-in-picture view in her head. She was seeing a falling drop of liquid that must have been a million gallons. It was far bigger than the terrifying bugs with her face smeared across them, her eyes; those nightmare insects with *her own damned eyes.*

The drop landed. It swept around the two bugs, engulfing them. And instantly it began to eat away those insect legs. It chewed burning holes into those insect carapaces. It burned away those distorted reflections of her own face like an old-time filmstrip jammed in a projector that bubbles and caramelizes and is gone.

The picture frames in her head blinked out.

They were gone as fast as they had come.

Sandra stood now, seeing only through her own eyes, seeing only what was real.

She laughed. "Hah-hah-hah-hah. Hahahahahahahah!"

And then she screamed. "Ahhhh! Aaaaaahhhh! You're devils! Devils!"

Nolan moved to grab her because she was climbing awkwardly onto the table. She slipped, skinned her knee against the edge, stared down at the blood, and shrieked, shrieked like a mad thing.

She snatched up a knife. Not a very big knife, just a dinner knife with a point and modest serrations. She stabbed it into Nolan's thick bicep.

The strong man screamed, a more feminine sound than one might have expected.

"Hah! Hah, devil!" Sandra yelled, happy at the sight of his blood, fascinated.

Wade and Quentin backpedaled, making sure to keep the table between themselves and the long shot for Best Actress.

In Sandra's eyes they were not backing away, they were coming for her, with their fangs out, and claws for fingers, and liquid fire dripping from their eyeballs—it was all about the eyeballs, it was there, in the eyes, the demons.

Sandra Piper turned the knife around and stabbed it into her belly. It didn't go far. It drew blood, but just a stain the size of a quarter.

"Hey, hey, hey!" Quentin yelled.

"No, no, stop that, stop that this instant," Wade said.

Nolan made another move—this time wary—to take the knife from her.

Sandra spit at him. "Hah!" she yelled, and stabbed the knife into her own eye. Her left eye. Pulled it out bloody and clotted with viscous goo.

Cries of horror, and now even she could see that they were backing away, the devils. It was working. *Hah! Run, devils, run!*

She then stabbed the knife into her other eye and pushed it through cracking bone, pushed it until the hilt was stopped. Then she twisted the knife around as if she was trying to churn her own brain.

Her knees gave way. The knife dropped from her hand.

"Stupid Mission project," she said. Then fell onto her back, laughing and howling, laughing and howling. "Devils! Dev—"

It was Lystra Reid who took the knife from her. And Lystra who placed a napkin over the bloody craters in her face.

Not that Sandra Piper could see that.

TWO

Her name was Sadie McLure. She had indifferently styled brown hair and smart, skeptical brown eyes that could take on golden highlights and even suggestions of green in certain lights. She had freckles on her cheeks and across the bridge of her nose. She'd never liked the freckles—they seemed to be accompanied by the word *cute* and she didn't like people thinking of her as cute. Cute was a belittling word.

The cute freckles had a second outpost on her chest, and a lesser presence on her shoulders. But all her freckles were now almost hidden by a rich, deep tan.

Her name was Sadie McLure, but in certain company she called herself Plath, after the great and tragically suicidal poet.

It was her nom de guerre. Her BZRK name. The name that defiantly acknowledged that there were only two possible fates in her future as a member of BZRK: death or madness.

She had a net worth expressed in billions of dollars. She had a small but effective private army in the form of McLure Labs security under a Mr. Stern. (She must have heard his first name at some point, but what had stuck was the Mr. and the Stern.)

She had seen terrible things, Sadie had. As Plath she had *done* terrible things, too, and had terrible things done to her.

She was sixteen years old.

A month had passed since that bizarre and fateful day when the *Doll Ship* had burned down much of the Hong Kong harbor waterfront. A month since the president of the United States had blown her own brains out on nationwide TV after being (correctly) suspected of murdering her husband.

A month since Sadie as Plath had sent her biots into Vincent's brain, one armed with acid to burn the biot-death madness from him. The great advantage of biots over their mechanical competitors, the nanobots, was the closeness of the connection between twitcher and biot. That was also the greatest disadvantage because that same connection meant that the loss of a biot sent its creator on a downward spiral into madness.

Vincent had spiraled following the loss of one biot and serious injury to a second.

From a desperate desire to save Vincent, Sadie had undertaken a grim mission to cauterize parts of his brain. But at this moment that terrible day was compartmentalized if not forgotten, and Sadie was doing something that was not at all terrible. She was on a white-sand beach beneath palm trees. A picnic was laid out on a woven mat of the kind the locals used. There was cold fried chicken, cold lobster, and a bowl of vanilla-spiked fruit in the local Madagascar style.

There was also a bottle of white wine, now empty, and a bottle of vodka, now partly empty.

And there was a boy.

He was naked as Sadie. His name was Noah, though like Sadie he sometimes used a nom de guerre: Keats.

Whether they were Plath and Keats or Sadie and Noah, she was on top and he was inside her. They were both smiling because the ash from the joint in Sadie's mouth had landed on the very tip of Noah's nose, and when she blew it away it made him sneeze. Which struck them both as funny, so they laughed, and that physical convulsion had interesting side effects.

"Laugh again," Noah said.

"Not yet," Sadie said.

"You're torturing me."

"I'm teaching you endurance," she said, voice slurring.

"I'm standing right at the very edge of a cliff," he said, and his eyes closed and his smile became dreamier. "If you laugh . . . or even move at all . . . or even breathe deeply, I'll go right . . . *mmmm* . . . over . . . the edge."

"You're going with a cliff metaphor?" she asked, and giggled.

Which was all it took.

She watched his face while his body arched and thrust and shuddered and finally subsided. His expression was more animal than human in the first seconds, and the sounds he made were definitely not witty banter. Or even half-drunk and quite stoned banter. But then that feral look softened into an expression like you'd see on the face of a saint in a Renaissance painting.

And then he laughed, too.

And opened his blue, blue eyes and said, "Don't go yet."

He remained inside her, in more ways than one. He was also

inside her brain, and not metaphorically. A tiny creature smaller than the period at the end of a sentence—a creature that was built from an exotic stew of DNA that included Noah's own—was deep within Sadie's brain. This was a *biot*. One of *his*, Noah's biots, because biots were nothing if not unique to their creator. It was designated K2. Keats 2. His other biot, K1, was in a tiny vial stuck in the buttoned pocket of his shorts, which were . . . he looked around . . . over there, somewhere.

K2 had the job of maintaining the fragile latticework painstakingly built around a bulge in an artery in Sadie's brain. Left alone, the aneurysm might never pop. Then again it might pop at any moment, which would almost certainly kill Sadie, perhaps over the course of pain-filled hours.

Noah had worked with scarcely a break over this last month to strengthen the Teflon casing around the deadly bulge. It was tedious work. Fibers had to be carried through Sadie's eye, down the optic nerve, up and down the soggy hills and deep valleys of her brain— quite a long trip for a biot—then carefully threaded in place. Basket weaving.

All the while a sort of picture-in-picture was open in Noah's own mind, an artificially color-enhanced but grainy picture. Imagine a 3D special-effects movie but with the color flattened out and stripped of nuance, all shot through a dirty lens.

Noah knew Sadie with an intimacy that was impossible for people who did not travel *down in the meat*. When she became aroused, he could feel the artery beneath his biot's six legs pumping faster, harder. But it was not just the relatively monotonous, liquid-encased surface of the brain that he had seen up close. He had at various times, in the course of more than one desperate mission, crawled across her eyes, her lips, her tongue.

She kissed his mouth and then the place just beside his mouth and then his neck. Then she rolled off onto the blanket and looked toward the food.

"You didn't . . . ," he said.

"No." She struggled to find the right tone. Unconcerned but not indifferent. Nonchalant, not like it mattered. Then tried switching to a sexy purr. "But I loved every minute. That's not the only thing in the world, you know."

"It's not?" he asked, trying to be funny.

"Want some lobster?" she asked, deflecting him. She didn't like talking about sex. The effects of weed and wine were ebbing, leaving her tired and groggy. She could be cranky in a minute if she let herself.

There were things nagging at her, distractions. She wanted to keep pushing them away, but self-medication had its limits and all those niggling worries would resurface, frequency and intensity increasing. She had pushed it all away for a month and now "it" was pushing back.

"I do want some lobster, I absolutely do," Noah said.

"Then trot on over there and get me some, too."

He sighed. "It's always something with you. *Undress me. Make love to me. Feed me lobster.* You are so demanding." He stood up, and she saw that half his hard, lean behind was coated with sand. She lay back, head resting on one hand, enjoying that particular sight, and the view beyond. They were in a secluded lagoon on the western edge of the island, facing the much larger island of Madagascar, which was a blur of green ten miles off.

A quarter mile to both north and south, armed men—fashionably attired in white Tommy Bahama shirts and automatic rifles—watched for any threat to their privacy. Just out of sight behind a rocky point, a yacht crewed by ex-soldiers rolled in the gentle swell and kept a radar lookout over the area.

Noah brought her pieces of lobster on a small china plate.

"We're out of wine," he said.

"Good. Time to sober up, anyway."

"Is it?" he asked. "Why?"

She sat up and reached for her T-shirt. He interrupted her with a kiss and gently stroked her breasts as if saying good-bye to them. "I quite like these," he said.

"I guessed that. Can I put on my shirt now?"

"I suppose." He started to dress as well: shorts, a T-shirt, sandals. He reached down and pulled her to her feet.

"I'll call for our cab," Sadie said. She pressed the talk button on a handheld radio—there was no cell-phone reception this far up-island.

Five minutes later, as they packed up the picnic, a glittering white cabin cruiser appeared around the point.

The captain gave a little *toot-toot* on the horn, and the boat blew up.

It took a few seconds for the flat *crump!* of the explosion to reach them. It took a bit longer for the debris to splash into the water.

And just like that Sadie and Noah were Plath and Keats once

again, running now, food and blanket forgotten. McLure security men were tearing along the beach from north and south, assault rifles in their hands, yelling, "Get under cover, get under cover!"

The boat burned for a while—there was no possibility of anyone having survived—and then it slipped beneath gentle waves that were a very similar color to Noah's eyes. The pillar of black smoke was smothered. A black smudge rose until it was caught by a breeze and blown away over the island.

Vacation was over. The war for the human race was back on.

THREE

The roll that had begun was accelerating. The ship's ballast had shifted decisively. It rolled onto its side, sending the flames shooting hundreds of feet into the air.

The inside of Benjaminia *was a slaughterhouse—dead Marines, many more dead residents hung from bloody catwalks. The sphere turned on its axis, and floors became walls. Bodies fell through the air.*

Like the turning drum of a dryer, the sphere rolled on, and now people clinging to desperate handholds fell screaming and crashed into the painted mural of the Great Souls.

Water rushed in through the opened segments.

The blowtorch submerged but burned on and turned the water to steam as the Doll Ship *sank, and settled on the harbor floor.*

When the *Doll Ship* sank, the Armstrong Twins had found themselves in Hong Kong's Victoria harbor.

They could not swim. With some effort, and if they felt in a cooperative mood, they could manage to walk, dragging the useless third leg. But swim?

It was Ling who had saved their lives. Tiny, ancient, birdlike Ling. She had cupped her hand beneath their chin and churned the filthy water with her legs. She'd sunk beneath the waves repeatedly, rising each time to gasp in a single breath mixed with salt water, to cough and gag, and yet to keep her legs churning, until a fishing boat had come to the rescue.

They would find a way to reward Ling. They vowed that. She had saved their lives and very nearly died herself.

The Armstrong Twins had made their way from Victoria harbor to Vietnam, where they had financial interests and owned a small but useful number of local government officials. From there they'd made their way to Malaysia, to the Sarawak state on the island of Borneo.

The Armstrong facility there was involved in mining rare earths. And it did a bit of logging, as well, all very eco-friendly, with careful replanting programs and all of that. Whatever it took to avoid too much scrutiny. The Armstrongs were good corporate citizens out of self-interest.

But this facility was not strictly about mining or logging. It was built of three elements: there were two identical buildings, each a crescent, facing each other across an elongated oval that formed an enchanting tropical garden, a sort of tamed version of the surrounding rain forest.

There were trees and flowers, streams full of fish and waterfowl, pink gravel pathways leading to benches, and seating areas where the white-collar employees could take their lunches alfresco.

At the top of the oval, connecting the two crescents, was a stumpy tower topped by a domed observatory. There was an impressive optical telescope that profited from the profound darkness of the surrounding countryside.

No one was using the telescope at the moment because it was pouring rain. It often poured rain here. And when it poured it was unlike anything Charles Armstrong had ever known in New York. It came down not in drops but in sheets. The heavens did not sprinkle on Sarawak, they emptied buckets and bathtubs and swimming pools.

Charles watched a lizard climbing up the glass side of the dome, pushing against the stream of water. Sarawak had lizards. It had lizards and snakes and birds in abundance.

"I would have thought the rain would wash it off," Charles said.

His brother, Benjamin, was less interested by the lizard or the rain, but of course could see both since it was impossible for the twins not to face in the same direction. Their individual eyes could roam this way or that, focus independently under the direction of their separate brains, but they did not have separate heads, rather two heads melded together.

This gave them two mouths, one nose, and three eyes. The middle eye was a bit smaller than the other two and often had an unfocused, glazed quality. It could see, but its focus was not consciously directed by either Charles or Benjamin. Rather it often seemed to have a mind of its own and would focus where it willed, suddenly granting depth perception to one or the other twin, but never both at once.

They were large, the twins were, tall but even more broad, with shoulders capable of carrying the unusual weight of their doubled head. Two arms, neither muscular; two fully developed legs; and a third, stunted leg.

At the moment they were sitting in a modified electric wheel-chair. It was far more capable than the usual motorized wheelchairs and had been given an almost dashing, exotic look with burgundy velvet trim, two side panels that likely concealed weapons, and wheels that looked more racetrack than hospital, but it remained, in the end, a wheelchair.

The observatory was their haunt for now. There was a bedroom down a ramp, and a specially outfitted bathroom. But the bedroom had only conventional windows. All their lives had been spent indoors, and they craved the openness of the observatory, even when all they could see was water sheeting down the glass and a lizard struggling against that tide.

"Looking at lizards," Benjamin said, disgusted.

They had both been depressed since the sinking of the *Doll Ship*. The *Doll Ship* had been their happy place, the place they could think about when life became too gloomy or the pressure too intense. Now it was gone. All those poor people, the people who worshipped them, who saw beauty in their deformity, all of them gone.

"Fish food," Charles said, knowing where his brother's thoughts had wandered. "And we still don't know how it happened."

"A Swedish intelligence officer and a British admiral."

"But how?"

"Many questions, brother."

They turned the wheelchair to face the large monitor that hung above a touch-screen desktop. The monitor was divided into twenty-four smaller frames. Three were tuned to various news outlets. The rest were clearly surveillance cameras. An empty room with desks. A break room with one woman making coffee. A lab with two people in white coats moving to some unheard music while they tapped on keyboards. A puzzling view of what might be a warehouse.

One by one the video tiles flipped to be replaced by different views. Every corner of the Armstrong empire.

They could see everything, but what could they control? They weren't even sure they could return to New York. London, too, might be out of bounds.

"We are hiding like rats from a cat," Benjamin said.

"We're foxes at the very least," Charles said, trying to make it sound like a good thing, trying not to think about the way fox hunts usually ended with dogs tearing at the cornered animal. "System: locate Burnofsky."

A larger picture appeared, in the center of the monitor. The object of their search had his back to them. He was hunched over a terminal.

"There's our Karl," Charles said, steel in his voice.

"Ours?"

Charles sighed. "Either he hit bottom on some grand, final bender and decided to turn his life around. Or—"

"Or BZRK wired him," Benjamin said.

"Ling!" Charles yelled. "It's dinnertime, and I find I would enjoy a drink."

They shared a digestive tract, despite having two mouths. It took consent from both for either to drink alcohol. Or to eat, though they tried to be tolerant on that. Benjamin liked to snack on a bowl of Chex Mix sometimes, and Charles preferred fresh fruit. Apricots. He loved a perfect apricot, though a really good one was hard to find.

"A drink, yes," Benjamin said. "And maybe more than one apiece."

Ling appeared, moving with a gliding speed that belied her advanced years.

"Ah, our friend and hero, Ling. I shall have a glass of wine," Charles told her. "A Cabernet, I think."

"I'll have a Cognac," Benjamin said. "You know what I like."

They sat glumly watching the video frames opening and closing around Burnofsky as the system cycled randomly through the hundreds of surveillance cameras. Here was a woman making copies. There a man staring blankly into space. A couple putting on coats ready to go home. Jet-lag-dulled shoppers at the Twins' O'Hare Airport store. Two men debating something, both pointing at tablets.

At the bottom of each window was a small tag giving the location. Athens. Newport News. Tierra del Fuego. Johnson City. AFGC—the Armstrong Fancy Gifts Corporation—had locations all over the world, even without counting the shops in virtually every airport.

"We have not lost, brother," Charles said softly, with what he hoped was an undertone of iron resolve.

"Yet we're in hiding."

"We have not *lost*. We are not *beaten*. We have the Hounds. We can rebuild the twitcher corps. We can start again. And we have Floor Thirty-Four."

"Floor Thirty-Four's a losing tactic," Benjamin snorted. "Defensive. It takes down BZRK. But it does not give us back the president we lost, or the premier we lost, goddammit! God *damn* it!" He slammed his fist down on the desk, making Charles's glass of wine jump. "Or Bug Man. Or the *Doll Ship*." He moaned. "What we have lost! What we have *lost*!" He drained the snifter of Cognac in a single long swallow.

"When Floor Thirty-Four is ready, we take down BZRK and all they have within weeks. It spreads, brother; it will find them in all their hiding places. And when it has done its work, we will be without enemies, we—"

"Without enemies? You think BZRK is our only enemy? Don't you know the Chinese are dissecting every body they fish out of Hong Kong harbor? They know. They *know*! And if the Americans and Europeans don't know yet, they will soon."

"What is it you want, Benjamin? To unleash the gray goo?"

The *gray goo*, a ridiculous name for a deadly threat: self-replicating nanobots. Nanobots building more nanobots with whatever material they found at hand. Going from thousands to millions and billions and trillions in mere days, consuming every last atom of carbon and a good many other elements as well. Everything that lived or had lived on the surface of planet Earth. Everything that made life possible.

Nanobots were the mechanical answer to biots. Just as small, but without the eerie and inexplicable link that connected a biot to its maker. Nanobots had to be run through a game controller. They were somewhat less capable, but they had a huge advantage: it was nothing to lose a nanobot. But to lose a biot? Well, that way madness lay.

Benjamin gestured at the screen. He happened to be focused on a family at one of the AFGC shops, this one at Airport Schiphol in the Netherlands. A family. Man, woman, blond child, poring over souvenirs. "I hate them sometimes. I hate them enough to do it."

Charles intuited which frame his brother was focusing on. "Yes, but imagine them as *ours*, brother. Imagine them united with us. Imagine them happy to look at us. Imagine what we can make them into with our nanotechnology and our friends from Nexus Humanus."

"Nexus Humanus," Benjamin snorted. It was a cult they had financed as a way to recruit twitchers to control nanobots, and other useful folk. But it had lost steam, like bargain-basement Scientology. "We had it, the world we seek. The *Doll Ship*." A tear welled in Benjamin's eye, swelled, and went rushing down his cheek.

"Nonsense, brother, it was only a *model* of the world we seek."

"A world united," Benjamin said, bitterly wondering at his own naivety. Weeping, figuratively at least, for the benighted human race that was being deprived of the utopia he saw so clearly. "One vast interconnectedness, with us at the nexus."

"It can still be. It can. But not if we unleash the SRNs. Not the gray goo, not that final act of Götterdämmerung. The lesser tack, though . . ." Charles was offering a sacrifice to the god of Benjamin's rage. A step short of apocalypse.

"Massed preprogrammed attack," Benjamin said, accenting the final word. Nanobots could be programmed to carry out simple commands autonomously. Large numbers of them, so long as the task was simple. Millions of them if necessary. They could be programmed to destroy all in their reach for a certain period of time and then turned off, a sort of localized, small-scale gray goo.

"If it's true that the intelligence agencies either know or will soon, then we won't be safe, even here. But if we disrupt . . . If we launch mass releases. Washington. London. Beijing. Give them something to keep them very busy. And at the same time use the Floor Thirty-Four weapon to take out BZRK . . ."

"There he goes. Burnofsky. He's doing it again." Benjamin had spotted it. He gave the voice command to expand the screen. Burnofsky's image pushed all the others aside.

In the image—high-def, no grainy monochrome—Burnofsky had lit a cigarette. He took a few puffs. Sat, staring at nothing. Took another drag on the cigarette.

"Here it comes," Benjamin said.

Burnofsky slid a desk drawer open. He drew out a framed photograph of a young girl.

"The daughter," Charles said. "He's never gotten over it."

Burnofsky looked at the picture and puffed his cigarette so that now the smoke partially obscured the image, swirling up around the hidden camera. They could see only the side of the man's face, but the smile was huge, ear to ear. The smile and a silent laugh.

"Volume up," Charles ordered.

Burnofsky was making a chortling sound, a private, gleeful, somehow greedy sound. Like a miser counting his money.

"Bugs in your brain, baby," he said, laughing happily. "Bugs in your brain."

"System: zoom in on Burnofsky's face," Benjamin ordered. The camera zoomed. "He's crying as he laughs. Crying and laughing. Here it comes."

Burnofsky lifted his shirt up off his corpse-white concave belly. They had a poor angle on this, just barely able to see.

Burnofsky sucked hard on the cigarette, and holding the smoke in his lungs, stabbed the lit end of it against his belly.

They heard the sizzle.

He held it there; held it, held it, held it . . . and then, with a cry of pain that caused smoke to explode from his mouth, Burnofsky at last pulled the cigarette away.

"Karl, Karl, Karl," Charles said.

"Exercising, eating well, no more drugs, far less alcohol." Benjamin recited the relevant facts. "Seemingly less depressed. And this self-mutilation is the price, somehow. You know it's BZRK, brother. You must *know* that. He's wired. They've taken our genius from us."

Charles sipped his wine. He had to take it slow if Benjamin was going to be swigging brandy. "I don't *know* it. But, do I suspect it?"

He let the question hang.

"We must return home. Home to the Tulip."

"Back to the Tulip?" Charles's voice was troubled. "Even now that will be dangerous."

"I've spent—*we've* spent—our lives skulking and hiding, brother. Is there not, finally, a time to stand up and be seen and counted?"

Charles didn't argue. He knew it would be pointless. Benjamin would have his own *Götterdämmerung*. Charles felt sick inside. He did not want this to end in apocalypse. He had never wanted anything, really, but for all the world to be happy. And to accept him for what he was. And if only he could be allowed to wire the entire human race with his nanobot forces that beautiful vision would be realized. A world of peace. A world free from want and hate and fear and pain because every human being would be brother, sister, father, mother to every other human being. *One vast interconnectedness.*

"We hit back," Benjamin was saying. Over and over. "We hit back!"

Charles closed his eye and heard the voice of his brother, so many years ago, so long ago, before they understood. Before they came to accept their isolation and loneliness. The voice of the child Benjamin was the voice of the grown man now.

Hit back, hit back, hit back.

On the screen Burnofsky was giggling and crying.

FOUR

Sadie and Noah were bundled into a Land Rover and driven straight, without packing, without ceremony, without time to breathe, to a privately owned airstrip and practically shoved aboard a Gulfstream.

The pilot filed a flight plan for the relatively short hop to Sambava Airport on the main island of Madagascar. But that would be the expected route, and if the enemy had gone to the trouble of blowing up a boat, would they hesitate at an airport assassination?

So the Gulfstream flew on, took on fuel in Kenya, and made the long haul to Madeira to prepare for the final leg to New York's Teterboro.

At Madeira the security men let them off the plane. Plath and Keats took a taxi into the whitewashed city of Funchal, where they ate voraciously at a café that smelled of garlic, red wine, and cedar, and served cod and prawns and good, doughy bread in a sky-blue stucco dining room. The Gulfstream had left in too great a hurry to take on food, and despite their picnic lunch hours earlier, they were starving.

"So what do we do now?" Keats asked. He had the sense that this might be the last time they could speak freely. There was a single weary McLure security guy outside on the street, gun out of view but not out of reach, but no one was watching or listening in the restaurant and the clatter of cutlery on pottery and china would have obscured their words in any case.

"Back to New York," she said with a shrug.

"And then?"

"Then we do whatever Lear tells us to do." It sounded bitter. It was.

Keats tore at a piece of bread then used it to sop up some gravy. "That's not proper, is it? Proper table manners, I mean."

"Yeah, that's what I care about," Plath said. "Table manners." She offered him a smile and put her hand on his.

"It doesn't make sense, that's the thing," Keats said.

"Manners?"

"Blowing up the boat."

One of Plath's continuing joys in her relationship with Keats came from the fact that in just about every case where she wondered if he was understanding things, he was. He might look a bit like the naïve dreamboat guy, but those too-blue eyes and sensuous mouth were deceptive. There was a sharp, observant brain there as well.

When am I going to stop underestimating you, Noah? She asked herself this silently, and in her mind he was firmly Noah still, not Keats. Keats was work. Noah was . . . well, what? Love?

He loved *her.* Did she love *him*?

Was it a class thing? The fact that she came from money and his family had never risen to middle class? Was she really that shallow? She wouldn't have thought so, would have angrily denied it. But at the same time, coming into her inheritance had without doubt added just a bit of swagger to her worldview.

She was rich. Very rich. He was very much not. Was that why she still held something back from him? That would be shameful. Or was it simply that she had seen him in ways no young woman is meant to see a young man? She knew too much and had memories that were far too vivid and intrusive. She knew what his lips looked like in the micro-subjective.

She knew that down there, where distances were measured in microns, those full lips were crusted parchment. She knew that his fingertips looked like arid, plowed fields. She knew that his tongue was serried ranks of pink hoods, and that trapped between the rows were bright false-color bacteria.

She knew that living things crawled in his eyelashes, tiny things, unless you were down in the meat and saw them m-sub. Then they didn't look so small. M-sub fleas looked like spiky, punk versions of the armored oliphaunts from the *Lord of the Rings* movies, except that they could jump a thousand times their own height.

She knew, above all, that all the intelligence and charm and wit, all of his readiness to commit, all the love he was so ready to express, was nothing but minute electrical charges firing along neurons in the wet folds of his brain.

She had not just seen these things on an image captured from a scanning electron microscope. She had *been* there in her biots. She had seen them all with biot eyes that were as real to her as her own.

Even now she knew that Noah was seeing the same with her. One of his biots was in her brain right now. All three of hers—P1, P2, P3—were in the vial she wore on a chain around her neck for safekeeping, but she was still seeing through their eyes, seeing a long, rainbow-hued glass wall. Three distinct windows were open inside her visual field. And if they ever began to go dark . . . then would come the madness she defied by taking the name Plath.

Down in the meat.

Once you had gone down in the meat, the images could not simply be set aside and ignored. And after memories came imagination, so that she would picture things she had not seen through biot eyes as they would look at m-sub.

She would see the micro detail of his lips and her own; she would see the rough furrows of his fingertips as they brushed her nipples; and she could imagine the billion tail-whipping sperm cells as he ejaculated.

It was all, at the very least, distracting. Though somehow it never seemed to distract *him—*

Keats waved his hand up and down in front of her face.

"Sorry," Plath said, and snapped back to reality. "I was considering. The boat. Yeah, it was both crude and ineffectual."

"Armstrong wouldn't come at us that way," he said. "If they knew where we were, they'd deploy nanobots. There have been servants in and out of the house, we had a doctor in when I got food poisoning; there were opportunities for infestation."

"Or they could have targeted some of Stern's people and bounced the nanobots to us from them. I mean, if you know where two members of BZRK are, you try to *wire* them, you don't try to kill them." She glanced over her shoulder upon saying the word *BZRK*, pronounced with vowels intact: "Berserk."

Keats nodded, tore off another piece of bread, sopped up more gravy, and popped it in his mouth. Plath could imagine the scene down at the m-sub. The teeth would be impossibly huge, scaly not smooth, massive mountainous gray boulders dropping from the sky and rising from below to crush and—

I have to stop this. I have to get control of my thoughts.

Too easy to let that consciousness of another universe take over her mind. Too easy to go from distraction to revulsion. She had to be able to be with another human being without always picturing that other, stranger reality.

"Maybe it was something totally different," Noah suggested. "Maybe there was a fuel leak on the boat. Maybe we're just overreacting."

"Maybe," Plath said. "But our time in the Garden of Eden had to end eventually. We had to go back. We're supposed to be running things."

Keats met her gaze and shook his head slowly. "No, not we. You, Sadie." Then with a wry smile he corrected himself. "You, *Plath*."

She could have said that they were partners. She could have said that obviously he was as important as she was.

But she had not told him about the message from Lear telling her to get back in the game. The message she had ignored for days.

She wondered if she should tell him now.

But instead she copied him and mopped up some gravy. She didn't have time to worry about tending to Keats's ego. Her mind was filling with the implications of the suspicion that they were being shepherded.

Driven.

Manipulated.

. . .

Anthony Elder, who had once used the name Bug Man, was shopping for onions at Tesco. Not just onions, there were other things on the list, too. But it was onions that somehow irritated him.

Nutella
Beans
Bread
Pasta (store brand, nothing fancy)
Mushrooms (fresh, button, 1/2 pound)
Cheerios
2 oranges
3 onions (the white kind)

Three onions. The white kind.

This was his life. Again. His mother was already on him about going back to school. To *school*!

"You don't want to go on neglecting your education, Anthony. That's most likely why you were let go."

Let go.

Well, no, Mum, I wasn't exactly let go. I ran for my life—flew for it, actually, all the way back to England—after my mistakes caused the American president to blow her brains out in front of the whole world. It wasn't because I couldn't conjugate French verbs or recall the date of the Battle of Hastings.

He didn't say that to his mother, of course.

He walked down the cereal aisle searching for Cheerios,

maneuvering around a woman who was pushing both a baby buggy and a shopping cart. He found the cereal, puzzled for a moment over what size box he should be getting. His mother would chide him no matter what he chose.

Small, then. Easier to carry home. Less chance of catching some smart remarks from passing thugs.

He'd been on top of the world. Now he was self-conscious about being seen by others his age, struggling with plastic bags of pasta and Nutella and onions. The white kind.

A pretty girl coming toward him looked right through him as if he was invisible.

He'd had the most beautiful girl in the world. Jessica. She'd been a slave to him. A slave. The memories made him ache inside. He would never get within conversational range of a girl like that again.

Top of the world, that's where he'd been. But all that was gone now. All that gone and now he was invisible to women and girls. He was a moderately attractive black teenage boy with no obvious signs of wealth or future prospects. Why *would* they look at him?

He rounded a corner, walked glumly past aisles of this and that, entirely forgetting the pasta, ignoring the plastic-wrapped slabs of meat to one side, heading to onions.

He felt rather than saw that something had changed.

Instinct. Some sense that was not quite sight—sound, smell, or touch. The certainty that he was being watched. Without turning to look he knew he was being followed. His speed was being matched.

He walked slower, stopped, pretended to admire the lamb; but the presence did not pass him by.

He moved suddenly toward the produce department, walking too fast, and he felt his pursuer keep pace.

Well.

Well. Ah. So. So was it cops or killers?

His heart was heavy in his chest. His feet dragged a bit, just the toes scraping on the tile. Shit, he'd just started to think maybe he was out of it, that maybe the Armstrongs would let him go. He'd given them a lot of good work, after all.

If not some hitman for the Armstrongs, was it police? Or even MI5?

He stopped in front of a bin of oranges and rested his hand on one, just feeling it. He liked oranges. Was this the last one he would see for a long while? Or the last one ever?

He turned, resigned, not seeing the point really in continuing to pretend. And there was his pursuer.

Now surely *that* was not a cop or MI5.

The man was well dressed, almost like a banker. Far too elegant looking to be a cop. He was a black man, tall, thin, with glasses, and when he met Anthony's eyes he smiled. Like an old friend. At first Bug Man felt himself relaxing, but no, no, that was a bad idea. A smile meant nothing.

"You want something?" Bug Man asked. His voice was ragged. Maybe the expensive suit hadn't noticed.

"Anthony Elder?"

He nodded. What would be the point in lying?

What about running? He could surely outrun this man.

"Are you here to kill me?"

The man was not surprised by the question. "Not at this time." He smiled. "But you will be taken for questioning by this time tomorrow."

"Haven't done anything."

"Oh, come now, you know better than that. People of our particular skin tone don't need to be guilty of anything to be questioned by the police, now, do we?"

Bug Man moved a step sideways, edging along the oranges. He spotted the onions. The white ones.

"Met police will pick you up tomorrow, but of course it's not really for themselves. They'll turn you over to the Security Service, to MI5, for questioning."

The man moved closer so he could speak more quietly. He smelled of sandalwood and spearmint. Bug Man liked the cologne, didn't like the man belonging to it. He had a ridiculous urge to ask him whether it was available for sale here at Tesco.

"They will detain you on a secret warrant, and in all likelihood you will be given a chance to plead guilty so as to avoid a public trial. They'll put out a statement accusing you of something like embezzlement. Something safe for public consumption. They'll promise to let you out in a few years, and they would, really they *would*. Except that you'll have been gutted by some hardened lifer in your cell long before that. They'll make sure of that. If they don't, their cousins will—the Americans."

Bug Man licked his lips. This was a threat, but not just a threat. This was the beginning of an offer.

"Whatever they want, the Twins, whatever they want, I'm still the

33

best; I'm still fucking *Bug Man*."

"The Twins?" The man made a crestfallen face, an act, a little show that he was putting on. Bug Man wanted to punch him. "Oh, yes, the *Twins*. Well, Anthony, this is not really about them. I'm not able to tell you anything, really, but I can tell you that I don't work for the Twins."

Bug Man took a breath. He'd forgotten to do that. "Who are you, then?"

"My name is George. George William Frederick."

He said it as if it should mean something to Bug Man. And it did ping some distant, dusty strand of memory. But nothing meaningful. It was a name out of a different time, Bug Man felt.

"You slept through history, didn't you?" George William Frederick said. "That's a shame. History is everything important, really. In any case, I'm here because the surveillance team that has been on you for every minute of the last month is outside, in the parking lot, drinking coffee in paper cups and eating HobNobs, confident that you will soon emerge with your groceries. They'll follow you home, as per their orders, log your movements, and go off shift at eight p.m. They won't bother with physical surveillance after that; they'll be watching on the cameras they have in your home. Yes. So, as it happens, this would actually be an opportune time for you to follow me, out of the back of the store, to a waiting car."

Bug Man immediately ran through some of the more embarrassing things that would have been observed by cameras in his home. But he was mostly over the concept of privacy. The Twins had had cameras on him from the start of his employment by them.

"And then?" Bug Man asked.

George-With-Three-Names shrugged. "All I can tell you is that an Armstrong hit team is also looking for the right moment to shoot you, and tomorrow MI5 will bundle you off to prison where they or the Americans will do for you, and the third alternative, the one I'm offering you, is preferable."

Bug Man knew the man was speaking the truth. Or at least believed himself to be telling the truth.

George-With-Three-Names. George William Frederick. The penny dropped.

George III.

The mad king.

"You're BZRK."

"Think what you like," George said with a self-satisfied smile. "I'm your way out."

"You *are* going to kill me." Bug Man was proud that he managed to get the words out with only a minor tremor in his voice.

George tapped his waist. There was something there that was no belt buckle. "If that were my instruction, you'd never know about it. By the way, you're not Roman Catholic, are you?"

"What? Church of England, I guess. But—"

"Good."

Bug Man let it go. The point was, this wasn't an assassination. "Will I have time to say good-bye to my mother?"

George shook his head.

"Good," Bug Man said. He nodded, smiled for himself alone, and thought, *Okay then: back in the game.*

[ARTIFACT]

An exchange of texts

Plath: Back in NYC. What is our mission?

Lear: Destroy AFGC.

Plath: What does that mean?

Lear: Find and kill the Twins. Destroy all AFGC records. Kill or wire all AFGC scientists and engineers. Their technology must be obliterated.

Plath: I'm to do this with 7 people?

Lear: You had your vacation. Besides there is an 8th.

Plath: Caligula?

Lear: I've always found him very useful.

[Long pause]

Lear: Time is short, Plath.

Plath: Short why?

Lear: AFGC very close to developing remote biot killer. Nature unspecified. Days not weeks until it is weaponized. You must strike before then. Ticktock. Death or madness.

ELAPSED TIME

The Gateway Hotel could not be repaired or rebuilt. The blowtorch heat of the burning LNG carrier ship had burned everything capable of burning. Natural gas burns at temperatures ranging from 3,000 to 3,6000 degrees Fahrenheit, and that's enough to incinerate furniture, carpet, and paint. It's also enough to melt glass and soften structural steel. A human body is a marshmallow.

The Gateway was a black, bent, crumpled horror that reminded some observers of a very old woman, bent by arthritis, in the act of falling to her knees.

Buildings on either side had burned as well. Buildings farther back in Kowloon, where the gas had rolled through the streets before catching fire, were burned. Some had exploded, simply popped open like rotting fruit. Kowloon Park was a field of ash.

The Chinese government had not been able to conceal the extent of the disaster. It was visible from satellites and from the decks of passing ferries and cruise ships. This was Hong Kong, not some provincial outpost. The whole world passed through Hong Kong.

The government had kept a faithful account of the dead and presumed dead. Now over a thousand. The "presumed dead" included those so badly burned that no more than a few bones with the marrow boiled away had survived and could not be identified.

Divers were still pulling bodies out of the blistered and twisted hulk of the liquid natural gas carrier—the ship dubbed the *Doll Ship*—that lay at the bottom of Hong Kong harbor. The Chinese government was nowhere near as forthcoming on this part. The official story was that it had been simple error on the part of the ship's captain. He was dead: he wasn't going to argue.

No one spoke openly of the bodies of children found blown apart. No one spoke of the fact that one of the ship's spheres, and possibly a second one as well (it was hard to tell), had never contained LNG but had instead been something very much like a human zoo.

Crewmen who had managed to jump ship were picked up and spirited away to a camp in far-off Qinghai Province. A small number of British Royal Marines were held there as well. And twenty-four civilians, neither crew nor soldiers—inmates on the *Doll Ship*—were being held at a small local hospital that had been taken over by the Ministry of State Security. The MSS had drafted a dozen radiologists, neurosurgeons, and pathologists, snatched them up from cities all over China and bundled them off to Qinghai.

Interrogations were under way.

Medical investigations were under way.

Neither was terribly gentle.

Chinese premier Ts'ai attempted to shut down the camp, ordered all survivors to be executed and their bodies cremated. Which would have worked had not the governor of Qinghai Province slow-walked that order. He smelled a rat.

Two weeks after the Hong Kong disaster, the MSS briefed certain members of the Central Committee on their findings from the survivors. And on Ts'ai's unusual and very out-of-channels effort to shut down the investigation.

Twenty-four hours later the Chinese official news agency reported that Premier Ts'ai had suffered a stroke. He was getting the best care available, but doctors were not hopeful.

In fact, the top of the premier's head had already been sawed off. His brain had been carefully scooped out of his skull, flattened and stretched, frozen, cut into handy one-centimeter sections, and was now being examined minutely under a scanning electron microscope.

They found numerous strands of extremely fine wire—nanowire— in segments as long as three centimeters, and a dozen tiny pins.

Similar wire had been found in the brains of survivors of the *Doll Ship*.

A careful—but less drastic—autopsy of President Helen Falkenhym Morales found no evidence of brain abnormality. Then again, the single nine-millimeter bullet she had fired into her own head had bounced around a bit inside her skull and made a mess of the soft tissue.

The FBI director, a man who would not have fared well himself if his brain had been carefully examined under an electron microscope, pushed for the conclusion that the suicide was a result of depression following the death of her husband.

FBI forensic experts produced a report stating that the videotape purported to have been taken (by means unknown) directly *through the president's eye*—the videotape that seemed to suggest that President Morales had beaten her husband to death—was a clever fake.

There was obviously no way for the images to be real. Presidents did not commit murder.

Then again, they didn't make a habit of committing suicide, either. But that undeniably happened.

In a bit of historic irony, the authoritarian state of China discovered the truth, while the American democracy had thus far missed it.

But there were other investigations under way. A joint committee of Congress. An independent blue-ribbon panel featuring a former secretary of defense, a former senator from Maine, and the chairman, a former president of the United States.

Only one of them had thus far been compromised by busy little creatures laying wire.

Minako McGrath, who had been kidnapped and taken aboard the *Doll Ship*, was one of the few to escape entirely. With the help of an ex-marine, former gunnery sergeant Silver, who'd been aboard that floating horror show, she made her way back from Hong Kong to Toguchi, Okinawa, one step ahead of the Hong Kong authorities.

But she found some changes when she finally reached her home. Her Facebook and Twitter accounts were closed. Her Internet access— in fact her whole family's Internet access—was blocked.

Then her mother was called in to see the commander of the local base where Minako's father—himself a U.S. marine—had been stationed before he was sent to Afghanistan and killed. She was told quite simply that if she could keep her daughter quiet, her family would be safe and her late husband's official military service record would remain unblemished.

There was no direct threat. Just that promise. Just the carrot. The stick was only implied. The general looked sick to his stomach going even that far, but marines obey orders, and it was clear that he was passing on an order that came from very high up the chain of command.

Having been saved by one marine, and honoring the memory of her father, upon hearing the ultimatum Minako nodded solemnly and raised a hand in salute.

"Semper fi," she said.

A week later Minako's mother, the police chief of their little town, was offered a civilian contract to work in security on the base, at a seven-hundred-dollar-a-month increase in pay.

Minako got a Vespa motor scooter.

And from that point on Minako discussed the *Doll Ship* only with her marines-supplied therapist, who duly shredded all records of her visits and prescribed Prozac.

Despite the separate efforts of the Chinese and U.S. governments, Google searches for various conspiracies were up in the last month.

Way, way up.

Possible suspects included the Illuminati, the Church of Scientology, Anonymous, the Freemasons, the Roman Catholic Church, the Bilderberg Group, Iran, China, the CIA, the NSA, the DEA, MI5 and MI6, Mossad, Agência Brasileira de Inteligência, Direction Centrale du Renseignement Intérieur, the Russian Federal Security Service, and, of course, space aliens.

With far fewer searches: the Armstrong Fancy Gifts Corporation.

And with only a handful of searches, most as a result of accidental misspellings: BZRK.

There was no change whatsoever in searches for "Lear."

FIVE

Plath. That was her name again. Plath, not Sadie.

She'd been back in New York for just thirty-six hours, sleeping the first half of that.

Plath was provided by the weather with a perfect disguise to move about the streets of New York. It was freezing and the faux-fur-lined hood of her coat along with superfluous glasses and her newly blonde hair made it very unlikely that anyone would recognize her.

She had taken a cab to the Tulip. The Armstrong headquarters was not a place where she could take any, even slight, risks of being recognized.

But she had gotten out and walked the last block to the Freedom Tower. It soared up into low-hanging clouds. One hundred and four stories of defiance to replace the lost World Trade Center towers.

She had not yet been born when the towers fell, but she had seen the video. They'd had a unit on terrorism in school.

The Tulip was not as tall as either the World Trade Center or the Freedom Tower.

She had distinct memories of the videos of that day, September 11, 2001. Funny that she recalled them so clearly. But there it was, playing over and over in her mind.

The jets.

The initial explosions.

The spreading horror of billowing smoke.

Two hundred people leaping to their deaths rather than die more slowly of smoke and flame.

The awe-inspiring, horrific collapse as the melted, hollowed-out building fell.

Find and kill the twins. Destroy all AFGC records. Kill or wire all AFGC scientists and engineers. Their technology must be obliterated.

It was all in the Tulip. The technology, the records, the scientists. The Twins. Up there at the top floors, what, sixty-seven? Sixty-eight? She'd been rather distracted the last time she was in the Tulip, hard to recall the exact floors where the Twins lived and looked out over the concrete and haze of the city.

A single skyscraper in Midtown Manhattan.

Her breath came out in a cloud of ice crystals. She looked around, feeling obscurely guilty, but no one in the sparse crowd of tourists or the crew at work around a steaming manhole was looking at her.

Under her breath, Plath made a sound. It was the sound of a slow-motion explosion.

Lystra Reid watched Plath as she looked up at the Freedom Tower and knew exactly what she was thinking. Exactly. She was contemplating destruction, *yeah, yeah, yeah.* Destruction. She was envisioning it already.

That was quick. But then, if you want great results, hire great people. Even if they are a wee bit nuts.

Lystra had a Starbucks latte in her hand. One of the things she would miss, she supposed: convenient and at least somewhat drinkable coffee. There were things about this game space, this paradigm, that she would regret losing. But it was never good to become complacent.

Time for the 2.0. As there was a Grand Theft Auto 6, there must inevitably come a day when GTA 6 was done and a GTA 7 must be born. Even the greatest game was eventually played out. When you had squeezed all the fun out of Portal you needed a Portal 2, 3, 4 . . .

"Yeah. Yeah."

She shivered—it was cold—and tossed the cup into a trash can. Her newest tattoo was itching, and she scratched her rib cage discreetly. She was just thirty feet or so from Plath. Plath was, what, fifteen years her junior? But they could have been sisters, perhaps, in a different world. Maybe, come to think of it, they *would be,* in this new game Lystra was creating.

She acknowledged her own loneliness. Emotional honesty did not frighten her. There had been a price to pay for becoming what she was: rich, successful, powerful beyond what anyone would guess. Arguably at this point, the most powerful person on Earth.

No, the truth never scared Lystra.

Lonely? True. Strange? True, yeah. Yeah. Crazy? Well, once upon a time, yeah, but no longer.

She closed her eyes and replayed the memory of seeing madness overtake Sandra Piper. God, that had been intense. The eye-stabbing thing, wow, that was the kind of detail you got only from seeing things firsthand.

She remembered a girl trying to strangle herself with a bedsheet. Crazy people did crazy things. *Back in the day, back in the old days, yeah.* But never anything to match the weirdness of watching a famous actress stabbing her own eyes. Now *that* was crazy.

Sad to think that she would have to retreat soon and watch the endgame play out from a distance. But not yet. There would be many rich, visceral experiences to come before she headed south.

And then?

And then she would play the new game and win that as well. Or not. She might not master the new game. She might even lose.

The idea made her smile. Her father had taught her to understand that life was a walk on a tightrope and death was the ground. Sooner or later, no matter how agile you were, the ground would claim you.

He'd been full of gloomy pronouncements back in the old days, sitting in lawn chairs outside their trailer as the carnival shut down for the night. They would sit there, the two of them, the man and the child, as the lights went out on the Mad Mouse and the Ferris wheel. They would sit and sip their drinks—bourbon for her father, unsweetened iced tea for her—and acknowledge the nods and the weary greetings as the other carnies headed for their own digs.

The nights had almost always been warm and muggy. The carnival mostly played the south: Baton Rouge, Bogalusa, Hattiesburg, Vicksburg. She'd seldom been cold, which was maybe why the cold attracted her now. Cold was clean. Hot was sweaty and dirty.

Back then, back before the train wreck that was in her future,

Lystra had wanted two things: For her mother to come back. And to be able someday to take over a couple of the sideshow games. An old man named Sprinkle operated the coin toss, the dart throw, the water pistol, and the ring toss. He let his games get shabby, refusing to spring for so much as a few cans of paint.

Lystra thought she could do better. She could make the games livelier and more profitable. The key was to make them a bit easier. Let the marks take home a teddy bear occasionally; it was good advertising. Run an honest game, attract more players, pay out more in prizes—but offer more levels, more depth, and make more money in the end.

"Yeah!" Lystra said to no one. It made her smile to think how even then, even when she was a lonely seven-year-old, she was ambitious.

But yes, lonely. She had always wanted a younger sister. Someone like Plath, maybe. Someone to look up to her. Someone to talk to and play with.

Even a brother would have been welcome.

Interesting thought.

"A game within a game?" Lystra muttered under her breath.

Would it add spice? Yes. Would it complicate the overall plan? She walked it through step-by-step in her mind and concluded that it would have only a small downside risk.

It would be good to have someone to appreciate what she had accomplished. It would be good to have someone to watch it all play out with her.

"Minions," she said, and laughed. "I need minions. Yeah."

SIX

"No. Vincent is not ready to resume control." This was from Anya Violet, and spoken in a whisper. "He may never be ready."

Plath was making peanut-butter-and-jelly sandwiches in the kitchen of the new Manhattan safe house. One for herself and one for Keats. And seeing Billy's level of interest she pulled out two more slices of bread for him.

They were in the kitchen: Plath, Keats, Billy the Kid who really was a kid, and Dr. Anya Violet. Anya was of undetermined age—perhaps in her thirties, perhaps she had edged into her forties—but to Plath, at least, she seemed beautiful, sophisticated, and effortlessly sexy in a way that she decided must come only with some age and some experience.

Anya had not yet chosen a nom de guerre. She thought it was a silly affectation. Of course, she understood the thinking behind choosing the name of some mad or at least seriously unbalanced person: it signaled acceptance of the core reality for BZRK members. It signaled a break with the past. It signaled a chin-out acknowledgment of the fact that madness was very likely in their future.

She understood all that, but Dr. Anya Violet was not a child and was not interested in following the rules of the clubhouse. Nor was she sure she wanted to accept the authority of a sixteen-year-old girl. Yes, Plath was the daughter of Grey McLure, Anya's former employer, and Plath had proven herself in battle. And it had become clear that she was a bit more . . . stable . . . than Nijinsky, who had been in charge during Vincent's recovery.

But Anya was suspicious of money. She could call herself Plath, but Anya knew who Sadie was. She was rich, that's what she was. Worse yet, she'd always been rich. She'd had life handed to her. Anya would rather have seen Keats in the top job, because *there* was a boy who had never been handed anything, and Anya instinctively trusted working people. She herself had come from nothing and nowhere to earn a PhD. She shared with Keats an emotional knowledge of hard times and hard choices.

But Keats was totally loyal to Plath.

Billy was a child. Wilkes was . . . well, she was Wilkes. Nijinsky had to a great extent lost the confidence of the group. And that left two people to run things at the New York cell of BZRK: Vincent or Plath.

Plath, who saw a great deal when she paid close attention, saw all this in Anya's smoky eyes. Vincent might or might not still be damaged, but Anya loved him and would never admit he was ready to take charge again. Not if it meant risking his life and sanity.

In the matter of safe houses things had improved quite a bit. Plath had access to most of her own money now, and she had Mr. Stern and the McLure security apparatus to arrange things. So BZRK New York was quite nicely established in a five-story townhouse not far from

Columbus Circle on the Upper West Side.

They had obtained it through numerous cutouts and guys-who-knew-a-guy, and bought it for cash for nine million dollars.

Just twelve blocks away was a second safe house. This had also been purchased for cash, but this time the cutouts had been just a bit less well managed. Not so poorly managed as to seem obvious; just a few scant clues left here and there for those who were watching the movements of Plath's money.

The *fake* safe house was above a bankrupt dry cleaner. A sound system played ambient noise from within—TV, music, the sound of laughter, occasional yelling. A timer turned the lights on and off. And random people delivering handbills were hired to enter and leave the place at odd times of day and night. It wouldn't stand up to in-depth surveillance, but it would do as a diversion. It was already, according to Stern, drawing the attention of Hannah Thrum, the chairwoman of McLure Holdings, the parent company of McLure Labs. Thrum was almost certainly working for the Armstrong Twins as well, but that was all right, so long as Plath knew where all the players were.

Let Thrum follow the money. She was a numbers person. Numbers people loved to believe they saw deeper than anyone else, believing their numbers were truth. In reality, Thrum was chasing numbers like a kitten chasing a piece of string.

Plath, Keats, and Billy carried their sandwiches back to the parlor where Nijinsky, Vincent, and Wilkes waited. Anya sat beside Vincent on the couch. Plath stood, leaning back against a walnut Restoration Hardware china cabinet, bit into the sandwich, and looked over her sparse troops.

Nijinsky was a bit less elegant and less well turned out than he'd been just a few weeks ago.

Wilkes had shaved half her head and dyed the other side a sickly yellow that was only vaguely related to blonde. Wilkes—named for Annie Wilkes, the insane fan in Stephen King's *Misery*—was a tough chick, a pierced, tattooed (including a sort of down-swept flame tat under one eye), leather-and-lace teenager whose personal history strongly suggested that people not mess with her. There was a fire-damaged school in Maryland that stood witness to what happened when Wilkes lost it.

Billy the Kid: a scrawny mixed-race kid who had shot his way out of an Armstrong attack on the Washington cell of BZRK. Shot his way out, and then shot his way back in to finish off any Armstrong survivors.

Keats. The working-class London boy with impressive gaming skills and too-blue eyes. And a very nice, taut body, not that Plath should have been thinking about that at the moment. But she was; in fact, she was recalling a specific moment on the island, standing at the railing of their deck, watching the sun come up, Noah as he was then, behind her, his strong arm around her waist, drawing his forearm over her body, over her breasts, kissing the nape of her neck.

She took a breath. It was deeper and noisier than she'd intended, and she wondered if people guessed that she'd been daydreaming.

Finally, of course, there was Vincent himself. Vincent had brought Sadie into BZRK. He had basically created Plath. He'd been their fearless leader until he had lost a biot in a battle with Bug Man. To lose a biot was to lose your mind.

The biot–human link was still not understood. The mechanism that allowed the human "parent" to see through biot eyes, to move biot limbs, and to be so intimately connected with them that losing a biot was like some kind of psychic lobotomy—that mechanism, that *force*, was not understood. In fact, it had been a complete surprise when first discovered at McLure Labs by Plath's father, Grey McLure, and had remained a mystery to him to the day he had been murdered in spectacular fashion.

The effects of the brain–biot connection were plain to see. Vincent, who had once been so dead calm, so in control, had fallen into madness. And the only way to save him had been with crude intervention down in the folds of his brain.

Plath herself had done the job. She had delivered acid to sites in Vincent's brain that stored specific memories of his dead biot. She had watched through her own biot eyes as Vincent's brain cells burst and boiled and died, erasing memory, thoughts, ideas, and perhaps some piece of his personality.

After that Vincent had clawed his way back from madness. He had gone back into battle against Bug Man, and he'd won. But that did not mean Vincent was *back*.

"Okay," Plath said. "It's been a month. Things have calmed down a bit. Where do we stand?" When no one volunteered an answer, she nodded and said, "Jin?"

Nijinsky turned cold eyes up to her. He had not fared well in the last month. While Keats and Plath were both tanned and rested— well, as rested as they could be, given the fact that their boat had been blown up—Nijinsky had become increasingly frayed and ragged. His clothing was no longer perfect. His hair was at least two weeks past its optimum. He was still by any normal standard a spectacularly handsome, well-turned-out person, a tall Chinese American with a graceful way of moving and a sad, sympathetic smile.

The changes would be visible only to someone familiar with his previous level of perfection. But the signs were there, even more visible in the red-rimmed eyes, the stress lines above the bridge of his nose, the grim tightening around his mouth. And of course the sour smell of a body oozing alcohol residue through its pores.

"It's been a busy month," Nijinsky said. "Sorry you two missed it."

"Lear agreed I should disappear for a while," Plath said calmly. "I'm known."

"Yes. And Lear agreed that I should get stuck with the shit work." He shrugged and tried on an insincere smile. "Well, here's where we stand. Vincent is about seventy percent." He looked at Vincent and asked, "Fair?"

Vincent nodded. His cold gray eyes focused, then lost focus. "Fair."

"Billy is thoroughly qualified for missions down in the meat. He has two biots. Wilkes is still Wilkes, God help us all." This he said with a certain wry tone that was very much the old Nijinsky.

"What else could I be?" Wilkes asked, framing her face with her hands.

"Anya remains a bitch," Nijinsky said, trying to sound jokey about it and not succeeding. "The president is dead, long live the new guy, President Abbott. The country is freaked out, but we are still not under surveillance—as far as we can tell. The Chinese premier just had a very sudden illness, and we know he'd been compromised by the Armstrongs. So, it's possible the Chinese government is . . . aware."

"And Burnofsky?" Keats asked.

Nijinsky shrugged. He looked away, not avoiding Keats, but seeing that weirdly colored window inside his brain. He had a biot resting on Burnofsky's optic nerve. The biot was tapped into visual input from Burnofsky's right eye.

"At the moment he's working," Nijinsky said. "I can't make out what's on his monitor—I have a pretty good tap, but you know what it's like."

They all, all except Anya, did know what it was like. Tapping an optic nerve was a bit like watching an old-fashioned TV in a thunderstorm back before cable, when the picture could be wildly distorted and never entirely clear.

"Has he been in touch with the Armstrong Twins?" Plath asked.

Nijinsky nodded. He tapped a cigarette out of some exotic, foreign pack and lit it. "Four days after that ship went down in Hong Kong. By the way, Lear is sure that was an Armstrong thing. Some kind of messed-up human zoo. By that point I was done wiring Burnofsky. I sent him back in. But nothing face-to-face. Wherever the Twins are now, they aren't talking to Burnofsky in person; it's all video link."

"Do you have a biot in his ear?" Plath asked.

"No."

There was pause while everyone absorbed this. It meant Nijinsky could see what Burnofsky was seeing, but could not hear what he was hearing.

"Why not?" Plath asked, deceptively quiet.

Nijinsky blew his smoke toward her. It was not a subtle gesture. He resented being demoted and didn't mind if she knew. "Because I was using my other biots to train Billy, here."

"For a month?"

Nijinsky shook his head. "Fuck you, Plath."

Keats's eyes narrowed angrily, but Plath remained cool. "A lot has been asked of you, Jin. And you've endured a lot."

"Endured," he said, sneering at the word. "Yes, I've endured a lot. A lot of enduring has gone on."

"Why not have Anya generate a new biot and use it?"

Billy and Wilkes were watching the back-and-forth between the two, like spectators at a tennis match. Vincent was elsewhere in his mind. Keats was keeping still, irritated by Nijinsky, but accepting that this was up to Plath to handle.

"Why not generate a new biot?" Nijinsky mocked. "When you play Russian roulette, you put one bullet in the gun and spin the chamber. *Click*." He mimed shooting himself in the head. "A one-in-six chance you're dead. Two bullets? That's a one-in-three chance. Three? At that point it's fifty-fifty. You *know* why not, Plath, so don't give me that hard look. Vincent barely survived the loss of one biot. Keats's brother is shackled in a loony bin for losing two biots. You want to hear what Burnofsky's hearing? Tell Wilkes to do it. Or do it yourself, Plath."

Plath nodded. "Okay. Fair enough."

"What are we doing?" Anya asked wearily. "What is this all about anymore? The Armstrong attempt to control the president is obviously ended. And it seems the same is true of the Chinese premier. The Twins are in hiding. Burnofsky has been wired and switched sides. Bug Man is gone. What are we doing? Are we playing a game? If so, what is our next move?"

"They still have the technology," Plath said. "They will try again. In some other way. They won't give up."

"How do we know that?" Anya demanded.

"They found Keats and me. They blew up the boat that was coming to pick us up."

"Convenient, wasn't it?" Nijinsky said.

Plath didn't say anything to that, because she'd had the same thought. *Convenient.* If you wanted to push her and Keats back to New York. Say, after you'd ignored an order to get your ass back there already.

The punishment for desertion is death, isn't it? Or is that some Hollywood bullshit?

The boat had blown up, but there was no follow-up. No attack on the beach, no attack on the compound they'd been staying in. No attack as they rushed to the airport and flew away from the island.

No attack waiting for them when they refueled in Kenya or Madeira, and no attack when they'd landed at Teterboro.

Had a quick change of hair color somehow thrown off the kind of people capable of tracking her to Madagascar and then to Île Sainte-Marie? Not likely.

Just enough violence to send her running back to New York. Not as if someone was serious about killing her.

Like someone wanted her back in the game.

Get back in the game.

That had been the text from Lear. The one she'd ignored, because, why? Because she was Sadie McLure, that's why. Since when did she take orders? What was she, someone's butler suddenly? *Fuck you, Lear. I'm on a beautiful island with a beautiful boy who loves me and wears himself out trying to please me.*

For the first twenty-four hours after that she had felt liberated. Like maybe she had regained control of her life. But slowly her doubts had grown. What right did she have to blow off Lear? Lear was BZRK. Lear was the general, and she was a lowly lieutenant or whatever.

And he'd been right, hadn't he, Lear? Right that she had to get back in the game? The Armstrong Twins seemingly still lived. The nanobot technology still existed. The liberty of all humanity was still in danger.

The Armstrongs still had to be stopped. Didn't they?

"I've heard from Lear," Plath said. She wasn't sure why, but she was reluctant to tell them. Maybe because once she said it she would have to take action.

"Did he mention whether he liked the whole blonde look you have going on?" Wilkes. Of course.

"Lear says the Armstrongs have developed some kind of remote biot killer. Nature unknown. No other details. But . . ." She shook her head ruefully. "But his instructions are to destroy AFGC. Destroy their data in particular so this new technology doesn't go into use."

Long silence. Much mute staring. Biots already faced a number of potential enemies, from the slow but irritating defenses of the body itself to the much more dangerous nanobots. But nanobots could be faced, fought, and, with luck and skill, killed. The idea of a weapon that could kill in some unfathomable way, in some way that did not even allow for a fight, was terrifying. It would be push-button madness.

Finally, Nijinsky laughed, a low, slow sound weighed down by cynicism. "Well, I'm going to use that word again. *Convenient.* We're all sitting here wondering why we're still playing this game, and what do you know? Turns out the bad guys have the means to drive us all insane and then enslave the human race." He lit a second cigarette and blew the smoke insolently at Plath.

She thought about telling Nijinsky to put it out. Show him that she was back and in charge.

But was she in charge? That was not clear.

She checked Keats. He was as dubious as Nijinsky.

"Yeah," she said by way of acknowledging their doubts. "Yeah. Convenient. But I guess unless we want a visit from Caligula, we'd better . . ." She faded out, realizing what she was saying.

It was Anya who put it into words. "In the Great Patriotic War— what you call World War Two—Russians had soldiers. And behind the soldiers they had NKVD. Secret police. If a soldier complained, the NKVD shot him. If a soldier failed, the NKVD shot him. If a soldier said, 'To hell with this, I am going home,' the NKVD shot him. And then they arrested the man's family and sent them to the gulag."

"Well, they *were* fighting the Nazis," Billy piped up.

Anya snorted a derisive laugh. "Yes, murderous, evil Nazis. And who were the NKVD? Murderous, evil Communists."

"I'm confused. Which are we supposed to be?" Wilkes asked.

[ARTIFACT]

A News Item.

Wellington, NZ. Wellington Police Superintendent Thomas DuPré gave a press conference today in which he discussed the recent suicide of two Wellington Police Department officers, and the attempted suicide by a third, who remains in care at Wellington Hospital.

"All three officers reported seeing strange visions about an hour prior to their suicide attempts. They variously described these hallucinations as involving bizarre insects and strange objects."

Superintendent DuPré said all three were tested for drugs but results were negative. "It's possible that this tragic episode is simply a rather horrible coincidence."

All three incidents occurred nine days ago. The two successful and one attempted suicides were particularly brutal and appeared to be unplanned.

The investigation is ongoing.

Nothing was said publicly about the fact that the three officers, while on their way together to a soccer match a week earlier, had come across an overturned truck on the highway apparently headed to the port.

The truck had appeared to be carrying military grade weapons.

Higher authorities were called in to take over the case. And the three policemen would have nothing further to say on the matter.

[ARTIFACT]

From Deadline Hollywood:

The Academy announced today that Sandra Piper's name would remain on the ballot for the Best Actress Oscar. There had been suggestions (surely not from studios and press agents tied to competing actresses, heaven forfend!) that the actress's bizarre suicide would send a bad message to movie lovers and especially young fans. The statement reads in part, "We believe that an Academy Award is given for the work, and only for the work, and should not be affected by the tragedy that took this great talent's life."

Comments:

QxT: *Sandra Piper was a great lady and a great actress. Shame on those who are trying to prophet from her death.*

KeyAgrippa: *She was nuts. That's who we want to show off as a symbol of Hollywood?*

Book Guy: *Tragedy my ass. She was murdered. I don't know how. Yet. But I knew Sandra, we worked together on UTD. No way she killed herself, she had everything to live for.*

SEVEN

Seven thousand, two hundred and fourteen miles south and a bit east from the watery grave of the *Doll Ship*, where bloated, bleached-out bodies still fed indifferent fish, a very different sort of vessel was roaring across very different waters. The navy called it an LCAC—landing craft air cushion—a hovercraft some eighty-eight feet long and forty-seven feet wide.

This LCAC was no longer part of the U.S. Navy; it was privately owned, and it had been extensively modified with more efficient turbines, tougher skirts, and integrated deicing systems.

It was one of two in active service in Antarctic waters. The craft were used to carry large cargos ashore and, just as critically, to remove garbage, and to do so in weather that would swat a helicopter down onto the ice.

Environmentalists were determined to keep Antarctica "green," despite the fact that green was rarely seen on the ice.

The LCACs shuttled back and forth between shore and a refurbished navy-surplus amphibious assault ship now called the *Celadon*. Celadon being a shade of green. (Her sister ship was the *Shamrock*.) The LCACs were the *Jade Monkey* and the *Emerald*, again, shades of green. But the LCACs were in fact painted white and gray with splashes of rescue-orange.

The particular LCAC arriving in a whirlwind of salt spray and noise was the *Jade Monkey*, skippered by Imelda Suarez. Suarez—no one called her Imelda—had a four-person crew and a cargo of booze, diesel fuel, and a massive electrical generator covered by a tarp, as well as a climate-controlled steel container filled with potatoes, apples, fresh spinach, grapes, and oranges. The box was painted with the logo of Whole Foods, and indeed all the produce was organic.

For the old-timers the very idea that fresh fruit and meat could be almost (not quite) year-round was astonishing, and it caused quite a bit of grumbling about how easy things had gotten.

It was nearing summer in Antarctica, and there in McMurdo Sound the thermometer showed a pleasant twenty-nine degrees Fahrenheit. The wind was a noticeable but manageable eighteen knots. The sun was shining. This time of year it shone pretty nearly all day. All in all about as pleasant as you could ask for at McMurdo.

The *Jade Monkey* floated over the water and up onto gravel, its big black rubber skirts all puffed out and vibrating like a trumpet player's cheeks. Suarez powered down, and the vehicle came to rest with a disgruntled wheeze of engines and a long, slow fart as the air cushion bled out.

Imelda Suarez was twenty-eight years old, five feet seven inches tall, dark-skinned, weather-beaten but pretty in the right light. She had worked for Cathexis Inc., owner of the *Celadon* and her two LCACs, for three years, two as skipper of the *Jade Monkey*.

It was grueling, brutal, often boring, but occasionally terrifying work. Suarez had never lost a cargo, she had never lost a crewman, and she had kept that spotless record by never underestimating the A-factor. The Antarctic factor. The capacity of the most alien of all continents to complicate or obliterate the schemes of *Homo sapiens*.

Antarctica was always out to kill you.

But the advent of the Cathexis era had changed life on the ice. In the old days the bases that dotted the rim of the continent had been cut off for as much as ten months out of the year. Aircraft get a bit unsafe in high crosswinds. LCACs do, too, but these specially modified versions could make a forty-mile run from the *Celadon* in all but the worst conditions—and in emergencies, even then.

All of which was extremely useful, because McMurdo Base— MacTown, as it was known—was growing more rapidly than just about any place on Earth. There was oil under the ice and offshore. With the Middle East in turmoil even the greens admitted that oil exploration on the ice was a better option than fighting wars to maintain supplies from volatile countries.

MacTown, which had once been full of nothing but scientists, academics, and support staff—generally from cold lands like Alaska and Montana and Maine—was now home to a whole lot of people from Texas and Louisiana. The same evolution was occurring at British, Russian, Aussie, Kiwi, Chinese, Japanese, Chilean, and Argentinean bases. The effort to locate oil and develop the technology to survive the harsh environment was big, well financed, and in a hurry. And they could afford oranges that cost fifteen bucks apiece to bring in from Wellington or Tierra del Fuego.

Suarez stepped out of her cockpit, nodded at her chief who was in charge of matters from this point, stretched up onto her toes, hefted a rather heavy shoulder bag, and headed up the long gravel slope into MacTown. Solid ground, ground that was not bucking and vibrating like the deck of the *Jade Monkey*, felt oddly uneven and unsteady. She headed toward the new admin building where Cathexis Inc. had a small wing of cubicles—nothing but a bunk and an electrical outlet, really. This was her third trip of the day, and Suarez was required by company policy to grab a minimum six hours of sleep. LCACs did not want to be steered by sleepy pilots. LCACs steered by sleepy pilots had a tendency to flip over.

She was intercepted on her way up the road by a tall, not-bad-looking man with a full beard, sunglasses, and a big grin. Jim Tanner was Lockheed security. Lockheed ran McMurdo. But it was well known that Tanner was former Naval Intelligence. And it was widely assumed that he was the U.S. government's eyes and ears on the base. Or at least, one set of eyes and ears.

"Well, hello there, Suarez. Whatcha got in the bag?"

"What, this bag?" Suarez asked innocently.

"Wouldn't be contraband booze, would it?"

Suarez stopped, unzipped the bag, and pulled out a bottle of scotch. "Huh," she said. "I wonder how this got in there? And look, it has a twin. You here to help me destroy the evidence, Jim?"

Alcohol was sold at McMurdo, but it was also rationed. Nobody begrudged you a drink, but there were supposed to be limits.

"I would like nothing better." Tanner took one of the bottles, held it up to read the label. "Ah, the Macallan Sixteen. You've grown and matured, Suarez. You have grown and matured."

"If you're nice to me and let me get to sleep eventually, I'll share."

Tanner handed her back the bottle, grinned, looked away a bit sheepishly, and said, "Sadly, I am here in an official capacity."

Suarez's eyes narrowed. "Your *official* official capacity? Or your *unofficial* official capacity?"

His smile thinned out. "This will be a conversation that involves your signing a legal document promising not to disclose the nature of the conversation. The document in question is not a company document. It's a *company* document."

The company was Lockheed. The *company* was the CIA.

"What the hell did I just step in?" Suarez demanded, no longer in a joking mood.

Tanner's office was tiny—space was always at a premium in a place where Home Depot was ten thousand miles away. It was overheated, so neat that no piece of paper could be found, and seemed to have been furnished entirely with the kind of office furniture that a self-respecting Goodwill store would reject.

The document he had for her was on an iPad. If it had been printed out it would have taken up four pages. Pages full of threats and requirements and official language. The long and short of it was that if she spoke of this meeting to anyone not properly cleared for top secret or better, she would go to jail.

"I'm going to remind you that even though you have been separated from the Marine Corps, Lieutenant Suarez, the corps still owns you." Tanner turned the pad to her. She scribbled a fingernail signature and at his prompting spoke her full name to the camera.

"And now do we get to the reason for this cloak and dagger, *Captain* Tanner?"

He was behind the desk in the good chair, the one that swiveled. She had a steel-frame chair with the stuffing half blown out. The bag of booze was at her side on the floor.

"Cathexis Base," Tanner said.

"Okay. What about it?"

Cathexis Base was a facility built by Suarez's corporate masters. It was used as a transshipment point, a storage facility, a rescue facility for the *Celadon* and her sister ship. There were repair facilities for the LCACs there, as well as for the helicopters and planes Cathexis used on the ice.

"Well, let's start with this: Have you ever seen anything suspicious at Cathexis?

No, she had not.

"What about at the satellite facility. What do they call it? Forward Green? Good grief, sounds like a golf course."

"I've never been there."

Tanner nodded. "Know anyone who's ever been there?"

Suarez shrugged. "I imagine a lot of the support people have. Must have been to handle construction."

Tanner shook his head, and watched her. "No. In fact, the crews have been kept almost entirely separate. There's very little crossover. There's Cathexis Base and its people, and there's Forward Green and its people."

Suarez looked at him expectantly, waiting for some kind of clue. When all he did was look back at her, she said, "So?"

"So, it's odd."

"Okay."

He was an experienced interrogator and had mastered the trick of waiting. But Suarez had nothing to offer, so all she could do was wait as well.

He nodded as if he'd satisfied himself on some point, then leaned forward on his elbows. "Anyone at Cathexis ever suggest you might want to try piloting a new kind of hovercraft? Something faster?"

"Well, the navy already has—"

"I'm not talking about a piece of navy equipment."

"Then what *are* you talking about, because I'm tired, I need sleep, and before that I need a drink." She was bouncing one leg, a habit when she was impatient.

He opened his laptop, hit a few keys, then turned it so she could see. "The video is just seven seconds long."

The film was obviously taken from a great distance. It shook and wobbled. What it showed, or seemed to show, was a sleek, low-slung object shooting across the ice.

"Do you recognize that?"

"Do I recognize what? Something going zoom across the ice?"

He laughed. "We did a bit of enhancement and a bit of informed speculation, and the best guess from Langley is that it's a hovercraft, quite small, so not designed for cargo. There appears to be a bubble canopy large enough for one, possibly two people. Speed in excess of a hundred and twenty knots. And it appears to be armed."

"Armed?" That stopped the bouncing of her leg.

"Mmm. Armed. With a type of Russian missile, essentially an antitank weapon, although obviously it would work even better against a tractor or a Sno-Cat or a shelter."

The thing that came to her mind was obvious and a bit stupid. But she said it, anyway. "Weapons are forbidden on the ice. Nothing beyond a couple of handguns for the security people."

"Yes."

"Why would somebody need missiles? On some souped-up hovercraft?"

"That's the question," Tanner agreed. "Why would they? Speculate, Suarez."

She pushed back, tilting the hind legs of her chair. "If it's as fast as you say, it would be tough to hit from the air. White on white, going one hundred twenty knots? You'd see a hell of an infrared signature, so if you went after it in an Apache you could use the thirty mil, but an Apache's top speed is one hundred fifty knots, so you don't have much of an edge in speed."

"I knew a good pilot like yourself would see it all clearly," Tanner said. "A pilot with SEAL training, and right here close at hand. Let's have that drink, Suarez."

She hefted a bottle, unwound the capsule, and poured into paper cups. "Am I going to need it?"

"Lieutenant Imelda Suarez, I am informing you that pursuant to a special directive of the Department of Defense, you are hereby returned to active duty."

"Whether I like it or not?"

Tanner raised his cup. "Cheers."

• • •

Sailing in the San Francisco Bay in blustery weather, Francis Janklow, the CEO of Janklow/MediStat, was not as happy as he should have been. He loved his boat in the abstract, but now that he'd bought the damned thing for two million dollars he felt as if he had to use it. But the truth was, he was just not that crazy about sailing. Especially when the wind was up so that he was constantly drenched by a spray that ranged from cooling mist to fire hose.

His guests seemed to be having a good time, though. These were a senior state senator and the senator's much younger "assistant," a rival CEO, a supposed painter whom Janklow's wife was sponsoring, and of course Janklow's wife.

The boat had been his wife's idea. According to her, you could not own a waterfront property on Belvedere Island and not also own a boat of some sort, and after all Janklow had sailed as a youth.

And yet, Janklow thought glumly even as he affected many a grin in the face of the elements, he would much rather have been home with a spreadsheet on his screen and a scotch in his hand. Instead he was at the wheel, yelling instructions to the kid, Antonio, who sometimes crewed for a day.

And also seeing things. Definitely seeing things. He frowned and peered off toward the Golden Gate, open water ahead, trying to figure out just what he was seeing.

"I think I'm seeing things," Janklow said. He forced a laugh. No one heard either the remark or the laugh.

No one heard him say that it was as if a window . . . no, two windows . . . had opened in his head.

Antonio saw him stagger back from the wheel and raced back to take over.

"You okay, Mr. J.?"

"I'm . . . Nah. Nah. Yeah. Oh, shit."

And then suddenly Janklow was racing up the mast, hand over hand, like a much younger man.

Everyone saw this. The state senator's assistant yelled something and pointed. All eyes turned to look at Janklow, now thirty feet up, his sparse hair flowing in a wind that was too strong for those below to make much sense of what sounded a lot like disconnected, wild ranting.

And then Janklow fell. Although it looked very much as if he actually leapt.

He plunged straight down into the sea.

Pandemonium. All the passengers jumped up and began yelling to Antonio to *turn the boat around, turn the boat around*.

But sailboats are not so easy to turn around when under wind power. So first Antonio—without help—had to lower the sail and start the engine. Only then, a quarter mile away from Janklow, could they turn back and effect a rescue.

Janklow could be seen. He was in the water, waving his hands wildly, but more as if he was a little kid splashing in the tub.

As the boat drew up alongside, the state senator had the presence of mind to throw a life vest to Janklow, while his wife berated him for being so careless.

But Janklow just laughed; a wild, manic sound that sent chills up his wife's spine. And then, pushing himself along the side of the boat and refusing all proffered hands, Janklow went to the stern, dove down, and came up with his face shoved straight into the churning propeller.

It would be listed as an accidental death, not a suicide.

"I'm looking at the spreadsheet right now," Lystra Reid said. She had a phone propped against her ear and a pad open before her. Tiburon police officers and California Highway Patrol detectives were milling around the marina of the Tiburon Yacht Club. They had taken statements from everyone on the Janklow boat. Lystra had little enough to say, and none of it useful, and the detectives had let her go.

But rather than take off immediately, Lystra savored a bourbon rocks and split her attention between the mild chaos of the investigation and the neat order of her spreadsheets.

"Yes, I am very much aware of some of my off-book expenses, and no, I won't enlighten you further, Tom. One of the reasons I don't take the company public, yeah, yeah, is because I like to spend my money without being second-guessed. It is, after all, mine."

At the age of nine, Lystra had been sent away. Her father had finally decided that he could not raise her properly. His own business was falling on hard times; the carnival business was fading fast. Her father's act—he was a trick shooter and put on an impressive if threadbare show with guns, knives, and hatchets—no longer drew enough of a paying crowd for the carny life to make much sense.

He'd sat her down and explained it all to her. She would be going to a good, decent family that would raise her properly, with school, and friends, and all of that.

"You won't be my dad anymore?" She hadn't cried. She'd felt sick with betrayal, but she hadn't cried.

Her father, his lined face half hidden in the gloom of the Louisiana dusk, had said, "I won't be with you. I won't be seeing you, I . . . I have to find some way to make a living. But listen to me, Lystra. Listen to me. You're a very smart kid. And better than smart, you're determined. You'll do fine. And if you ever need me, really need me, life-and-death need, I'll be there."

"What about Mom? Is she dead?"

"I don't know," he said.

She knew he was lying. She couldn't recall the exact moment when it dawned on her that her father had killed her mother. But once the idea *had* dawned, certainty soon followed.

Her mother had been a bit of a party girl. That was the nicest way to put it. Lystra's mother liked a good time, and she had not found it in the life her husband gave her. She'd looked for comfort elsewhere. In booze, in drugs, in sex.

"I know," Lystra had said. Nothing else. Just those two words.

Her father had said nothing. The two of them just sat there on the broken-down lawn chairs. Then her father had poured two fingers of bourbon into a paper cup and handed it to her.

God, it had burned her throat, but she had swallowed it and not made a sound.

"Bad things happen in this life," he had said at last.

Lystra had held out her paper cup and said, "More."

He shook his head. "That taste was enough. You're still a kid."

"You killed my mother. Now you're dumping me. Okay. That's

all done. Yeah. Maybe I'll never see you again."

"Maybe."

"But if I do, you'll do whatever I ask you to do."

"Will I?" He'd seemed almost amused, but seeing the look in her eyes he had flinched, looked down, and finally poured her a second drink. "I will," he had said, and there was a sacredness to that vow.

Lystra went to live with a very nice, childless family by the name of Reid, in Tulsa, Oklahoma. She got straight As in school while barely bothering to crack a book. She wasn't just a smart kid; she was brilliant. A cold, emotionally distant, friendless-but-never-bullied kid.

But at age fourteen things began to change. Not her grades, those stayed top-notch. But at about that time Lystra began to talk to her long-distant father again. He would speak to her when she was walking through the corridors at school. He would speak to her as she sat in the Baptist church and listened to the sermon. Her lip would curl when she heard him. Her eyes would focus with inhuman intensity on the back of a man's neck until by sheer force of will she could make him turn around, uncomfortable, only to become confused when the danger he sensed turned out to be just a young girl.

Her father's voice spoke to her. And other voices as well. Angels, sometimes, though not the better sort of angel. And the voice of a girl with the odd name of Scowler.

She never told anyone about the voices; they had universally warned her not to. *Yeah, don't tell anyone we're here, they'll lock you up. Yeah.*

Then both her adoptive parents had died in a car accident. The particulars of the accident raised eyebrows but elicited sympathy.

Lystra had been sixteen at that point, just learning to drive. And despite the fact that Lystra had played various online driving games for years, she panicked while driving the real thing. She had not realized the car was in reverse. She did not notice that her parents were standing behind her, down at the bottom of the long driveway.

The police questioned her for a long time. The detectives could not quite square her story of intending to pull the car forward slowly into the open garage with the fact that the car had been in reverse and had shot at surprisingly high speed the sixty-seven feet between the rear bumper and the two Reids.

"When I realized it was in reverse, it was too late, yeah. I saw what was about to happen, and I knew what to do, but instead of hitting the brake I accidentally hit the gas pedal."

"And then?"

"I felt the impact, and my only thought was that I should pull the car forward. Yeah. Undo my mistake."

"Right. And in the process you ran over both of your parents again. That's your story. You're sticking to that?"

"How can I do otherwise? It's the truth."

No, they had not believed her. No one believed her. People who knew Lystra Ellen Alice Reid scoffed at the notion that she had panicked. Panic? Lystra, panic?

But in the end the cops couldn't prove a thing.

There wasn't a lot in the way of a social services department in Tulsa, but a shrink was tasked with testing her.

"She's a very difficult subject," he had reported. "Hard to test. Her IQ is very high—very smart, very quick—so she knows how to answer, how to avoid setting off alarm bells. But my instinct tells me she's concealing something. At times I got the impression she might be hearing voices. Phantom voices. She may just be traumatized. Or she may be schizophrenic but with enough control to hide it."

Lystra was the sole heir to a million-dollar life insurance policy that was doubled due to the fact that the death had been an accident. Double indemnity, they called it.

Two million dollars. She'd been unable to touch it until she was eighteen, and at that time other family members had petitioned the court to examine her psychologically again.

The court had found her legally sane.

The voices in her head had congratulated her on the finding.

On her eighteenth birthday, Lystra had filed papers to form the Mad Alice Holding Company. And she'd gotten her first tattoo. She'd told the tattoo artist, "I want my adoptive parents, like in this picture. But I want them to be screaming."

The tattoo artist had been reluctant, but an extra thousand dollars had cured him of all doubt.

The placement she'd chosen was strange. Her stepmother was beneath one breast, so that she seemed to be smothered by the weight of it. Her stepfather, also screaming, was beneath the other.

Once both tattoos were complete, they began to speak to her. They wept, sometimes. Other times they threatened. She heard their voices so very clearly. If she stripped off her shirt and her bra, she could see their mouths moving as they cried out in pain and despair.

But they could be useful, too, the talking tattoos. It was the dead Mr. Reid who suggested using her inheritance to buy a small, failing medical testing company outside of Washington, D.C.

So the Mad Alice Holding Company was dissolved and a successor corporation formed as an Isle of Man company, exempt from most supervision. And then, another stroke of unusual luck: a midsize competitor in the medical testing field had suffered a catastrophic hacking that had spilled the records all over the Internet.

Lystra Reid bought the stricken company and brought in the best security people around to ensure that a similar fate would never befall her. The result was a medical testing company, Directive Medical, which had never suffered a successful break-in, while—not so strangely—security problems plagued her competitors.

At the age of twenty-four, Reid controlled a third of the independent medical labs in North America, as well as significant portions of other markets around the world.

It was amazing what you could learn from data mining the health records of more than two hundred million people worldwide. You could, for example, learn that the wife of a brilliant medical researcher named Grey McLure had a rare cancer. And you could learn that this McLure fellow was suddenly in a desperate search for living cell samples. And with just a bit more work you could discover that he was also looking for a wide range of animal tissue samples for a very secret project of some sort.

Lystra hung up the phone, indifferent really to the current spreadsheet drama from her office. It didn't matter. There was no future to worry about. She swallowed the last of the bourbon and stood up to stretch. The marina was nestled between Tiburon and the adjoining Belvedere Island. Unpretentious yet extremely expensive homes rose on a cute little hill to her left and up the longer, wooded slope of Belvedere to her right. Looking south through the forest of masts, she could see San Francisco. Fog was rolling out, revealing the city, all muted pastels and off-whites.

It was all in all a beautiful location, with sailboats and ferries and container ships passing by in review. A genteel, civilized, prosperous place.

And all of it about to come to a terrifying end.

It had been good to watch Janklow go mad; he had annoyed her on more than one occasion. She wanted to get a few tastes of the madness out here in the real world—before the final chapters, which would force her to hide out and watch it as well as she could via electronic means. The personal, real-world experiences would help her to enjoy the next step.

"All done?" the waiter asked, coming to clean her table.

"Soon," she said.

EIGHT

The first thing Bug Man had asked was, "Where are we?"

Bug Man had flown on a private jet before. He wasn't indifferent to it, but he wasn't overly impressed, either. George had not told him where they were going but had retreated into a book, remaining sullen and uncommunicative.

Bug Man saw a city in the distance. It was all tan walls and terracotta roofs, a large blur extending far out in every direction, reaching beneath the jet with roads full of small cars.

"The former center of the Earth, once upon a time. The Eternal City," George had said.

"Yeah, which is what?"

George sighed. "Your education is deplorable. The Eternal City is a reference to Rome."

"Rome? That's like, Italy, right?"

George managed not to roll his eyes, but only just. "Yes, Italy, Bug Man. Pizza, pasta, wine, priests, fashion, Rome. The Coliseum," he added. "Gladiators and all of that."

"I saw the movie," Bug Man said. "Also, I played the game. Not a great game."

"No?" The plane took a little lurch as a crosswind hit it. "What makes a good game?"

Bug Man had been much more sure of his ground on this topic. He didn't know much about history, but he knew games. "A good game? That's one where you can't stop playing it, even when you're asleep. Whatever you have to do that takes you away from the game, all you're thinking about is getting back into it."

"Hard?"

"It's not about hard. Yeah, it has to be challenging. Can't be so easy it's over in five minutes, right? But it's not just about hard; otherwise, you could play online chess or work a Rubik's cube, man."

He heard the grinding of the landing gear coming down.

"Why are we in Rome?" Not that he was complaining. He'd been locked away for several days in a safe house in the emptied-out Lake District before George had come to retrieve him. He'd been about to lose his mind looking at rain falling on green hills.

"We need a good twitcher. A nanobot twitcher."

"Where'd you get nanobots? The people you work for don't do nanobots, and I am not doing any biot bullshit. I saw what that did to Vincent."

"Nanobots," George reassured him. "We came across some, and a portable controller. Compliments of a former friend of yours."

"Burnofsky?"

George laughed and didn't answer. He rolled into the nearest seat and motioned Bug Man to buckle up.

Bug Man didn't exactly miss Burnofsky. The old man was an unreliable, unpredictable, sometimes cruel degenerate. But he and

Bug Man had played a great game. The greatest game Bug Man would probably ever play.

God, that was a depressing thought. Was it all downhill from here? He supposed that would depend on just what George here had in mind.

"What do you want me for?" Bug Man asked, but the question was lost in the impact of tires on tarmac. The jet rolled down the taxiway to a waiting car.

Bug Man walked down the steps to the tarmac—it was warmer out than it should have been for this time of year. Was Rome always warm? He had no idea. The sun was setting, and all he could see were featureless hangars and repair sheds. In the distance was a Fiat sign, and beyond that a billboard for what looked like a juice drink.

"I don't speak Italian," he said.

"You won't need to," George said. "Get in the car."

Bug Man did not like that, the bossy tone. He needed to draw a line right here and now, before he was driven off to wherever. "Tell me what we're doing here, dude." When George looked evasive, Bug Man held up one hand, cutting him off. "No, man, now. Right here, right now. Enough playing around."

George nodded, as if expecting this. As if he'd have preferred to do it somewhere else, but okay, if his impatient young friend insisted.

"The Pope," George said.

"The Pope? The freaking Holy Father? *The* Pope? What about the Pope?"

"You know he's in Rome?" The question was obviously insulting, spoken as it was with more than a trace of condescension.

"What's with the Pope?"

George dropped the snarky look and got serious. "You are wanted by MI5. A word from them and every other intelligence and police agency on Earth will be looking for you. And of course, the Armstrong Twins want you dead." He stepped closer, put his face right up close to Bug Man's face, close enough that Bug Man could have told you the man's toothpaste brand. "But forget all of that, because we have a fellow named Caligula. A charming name, I'm sure you'll agree. He already knows your name. A single text from Lear to Caligula and your death is assured." He held up an index finger. "I don't mean that you will *likely* be killed. I mean that you will without the slightest doubt be killed. Caligula has never failed. *Never.*"

Bug Man swallowed. He knew the name. He knew the reputation. And he did not like the fact that Caligula knew what he was about.

"As to what you are to do, Anthony 'Bug Man' Elder, you are to retrieve a sample. A few cells. That is all. And then you will be free to go. We won't protect you, but neither will we harm you. And you'll be paid. A hundred thousand pounds."

"Cells?" Bug Man asked with a dry mouth.

"Cells. A tissue sample. From the Pope. And it must be done quickly."

"The Pope. Tissue samples." Bug Man let this sink in. George waited, expectant, curious to see whether Bug Man would put it all together.

"Jesus," Bug Man said. He let loose a short, sharp bark of a laugh. "Jesus bloody Christ on a cross."

George got a dreamy look on his face. "See, Anthony, control is so much easier when you don't require the victim to carry out complex actions. Reduce it to the binary and it's all more efficient and effective."

Bug Man nodded, seeing it—and fearing it. "You don't even need Caligula anymore. You just need a tissue sample."

George threw back his head and laughed, showing teeth that had had many encounters with dentists. "I quite like you, Anthony. I'd have done this later, not here on the tarmac, but you're such a clever boy." He pulled a small plastic bag from the inner pocket of his jacket. From it he withdrew a vial and a Q-tip. "I'll just swab the inner cheek, if you don't mind."

Bug Man did mind. He pulled away.

"Oh, it's far too late for that, Anthony. You're in. Like it or not. You haven't a friend in the world, and so many people want you dead. Turn and run and I'll let you go, but Caligula will get to you if the Armstrongs don't find you first. Now open wide."

Bug Man opened his mouth. George swabbed his inner cheek with the Q-tip and sealed it in the vial.

"We won't create the biots unless you make it necessary. You have Lear's word on that."

"*Lear's word,*" Bug Man said bitterly.

"You are not in a position to argue, Anthony. You are lost and despised and scheduled for destruction. And now, you are BZRK." He grinned and made an ironic power salute with his fist. "Death or madness, kid. Death or madness."

The Starhotels Michelangelo didn't look like much from the outside; in fact, it looked like any number of the wearily functional, '60s-era buildings that deface Rome. Inside it was moderately posh, and Bug Man was hustled into a large suite with a balcony.

The balcony had a very nice view of the dome of Saint Peter's Basilica. (And a red-trimmed Total gas station in the other direction.) The walls of Vatican City were just four hundred feet away.

There was also a nice little restaurant serving—unsurprisingly—Italian food. The TV featured the BBC and CNN International as well as other non-Italian fare, and there was WiFi, but it was a bit slow.

From here Bug Man could easily manage nanobots within Vatican City. But what he needed was a pathway. X to Y to Z to the Pope. And then back out with a dozen or so cells.

"Don't leave this room," George instructed. "Except for lunch, which you will take downstairs in the restaurant. That's when the maids will come in and clean the room. They have to come in, or it will set off alarm bells down at the desk. Normal. Everything normal."

"I can't sit in here twenty-four/seven," Bug Man argued.

"You can and you will," George said flatly. "Order all the in-room movies you like. But don't draw attention to yourself. Italian police may not be geniuses, but let's not give them a chance. Right?"

That was a depressing reminder. When would he be free to walk out in the world without being afraid? Maybe never. But never was a long time, and Bug Man was an optimist.

"So what's my path?"

"Path?"

"How do I get from here to there?"

George sat down in the easy chair. Bug Man stood looking out through the balcony's sliding glass door.

"We have access to the wafers used for the Pope's communion."

Bug Man snorted. "Are you nuts?"

"Is it a religious objection, because—?"

"It's an objection over the fact that the mouth is not a point of entry unless you want to end up riding an infallible papal turd out the far end."

George shrugged dismissively. "Surely there's some way to—"

"Have you ever seen a mouth down at the nano level? It's about as big as a valley, and it's full of massive boulders chomping, plus a tongue and spit and wind. Maybe you can grab onto a tooth and get safely up under the gums, but I'm not trying it."

"All right, there's a second way. We have access to a person who has an audience with the Pope on Tuesday. It's traditional to kiss the papal ring. Does that work for you?"

"I'm still sitting out there on a lip hoping this dude doesn't get nervous and lick them."

"It's a woman, and she's not the nervous type."

"A woman? Who?"

"Her name is Lystra Reid. Owns some clinical testing company or other. Directive Medical? Rich American." He didn't seem to approve of rich Americans. "She owns medical labs and such. A lot of them. And she's made some big contributions to an African mission the Pope is fond of."

"Is she one of your people?"

"No. But her maid has debts, and we have money. So we can get the maid to place the biot . . . sorry, nanobots in this case . . . on Ms.

Reid. You then merely have to be on her fingertips when she takes the Pope's hand, or on her lips when she kisses the ring. Then it's grab a sample and find your way out."

A loud guffaw erupted from Bug Man. He turned to look at George, feeling that he had the better of him for the first time. "You don't know much, do you? What do you think? My nanobots walk back here to the hotel? It's only a few hundred yards, maybe, but that's a hell of a long walk when you're two hundred microns long. A nanobot can't even see objects at much distance. The optics are calibrated for work down in the meat, so I wouldn't know where it was and where to make it go, even if we had a month or so to walk it back here."

"We'll find a way," George said, and yawned.

"Oh, will we . . ."

It was meant to be sarcastic dismissal, but George didn't take it that way. He clapped his hands once as if drawing the scene to a close. And in fact, he did draw the scene to a close, by leaving behind a baffled, worried—but also excited—Bug Man.

Plath and Keats arrived at the alleyway door of the McLure building after much skullduggery that made them both feel like spies. They were reasonably sure they hadn't been followed.

They were ushered into a private elevator and whisked to th
twentieth floor. It was a bit of an old-home week for Plath, not
it good. She'd been in and out of this building since chil
her last visit had begun with Anya creating Plath's bio
a massacre between McLure security men, AFGC
Caligula. Needless to say, Caligula had come out o

Mr. Stern met them in his office then led them down a guarded hallway to an unmarked door.

"So, how are you adjusting to being back in New York?" he asked them both.

"I liked the island better," Keats said.

"I can imagine. Well, let me show you what we have." Stern slid a keycard and opened the unmarked door. Inside was just a room with half a dozen workstations, each focused on a large monitor. The ambient light came from the monitors, the keypads with keys outlined in light, and softly glowing touch screens.

It had the feeling of a room that had just been emptied of people. Plath touched a coffee cup and felt that it was still warm. Stern had emptied everyone from the room for greater privacy.

He sat down and Plath and Keats pulled up chairs.

Stern tapped a few keys, then switched to a touch screen.

"You asked me for what we have on the Tulip, and specifically whether there's a data center," he said as the image of that strange building appeared. "This is the Tulip. This is a photo, obviously, taken from across the street. And this"—he swiped the screen—"is the heat signature using infrared."

The skyscraper was now a sort of layer cake of red, purple, and blue—mostly red.

"Of course we had to wait until the building was in shadow so we didn't just pick up reflected sunlight," Stern explained. "We took three readings, three different days, and this is the composite heat ⁻nature. This—"another swipe—"is the same building but shot ⁻ the north. And this is from the east. We don't have a westerly view, but we have a high degree of confidence that these heat signatures are persistent and not just one-time things."

"Okay," Plath said, making a puzzled face at Keats, who was looking intently.

"There's a lot of variation by floor," Keats said.

"Oh, obviously," Plath said, with just a little sarcasm.

"But it's all centrally air conditioned, yes?"

"It is. Normally," Stern said with unmistakable pride. "But we turned off the AC. We risked using our back door into their computer network and reset the thermostat overnight. It takes a while for the system to catch up when it's turned back on, and in the meantime we could get a picture of what's being done and where."

"Can you show the temperature readouts?" Keats asked.

Stern winked at Plath. "This one's smart." He tapped a few keys, and numbers popped up beside each floor. "You get a clearer picture off this data."

"One floor is far hotter." Keats used his finger to count the floors. The eighteenth, yes? Something is giving off a lot of heat."

"Servers, we believe," Stern said. "They have their own emergency climate control, but it's not enough to disguise the heat signature when the overall air-conditioning system is down."

"So, the eighteenth floor is where they have their main computers. Their own personal cloud," Plath said.

"That seems likely," Stern said.

"Okay, how do we get to it and destroy it?"

There it was again in Plath's head, that crystalline memory of the World Trade Center falling. It seemed almost sensuous. Had she just become used to it? Had she seen that imagery so often that it had lost its potential to shock and had now become almost balletic?

Stern sighed. He pulled up a different diagram of the building. "Those are the elevator shafts. If you see those thicker areas there, that indicates an elevator stop, a door. If you look even closer, you'll notice there are none for the eighteenth floor. And I'll spare you the suspense and just tell you that the stairs, the emergency access, also doesn't open onto eighteen. There is a single stairwell connecting eighteen to seventeen. And there's a stumpy freight elevator that goes only from seventeen to eighteen, and nowhere else. Floor seventeen, in case you were wondering, is where AFGC security lives."

"Oh," Keats said.

"Indeed. There are never fewer than ten security—TFDs as we call them: Tourists from Denver, since that's the look they put on—on that floor at any time. Another two dozen or so patrol the building or watch the entrances. They are all armed. They are mostly very well trained, many are former special forces or commandos. U.S. Marines, ex-Delta Force, Royal Marines, SAS, ex-Mossad . . . dangerous people."

"So, how do we do it?" Plath asked. "How do we get in there and destroy those servers?"

"I believe what Mr. Stern is about to tell us is that we *don't*," Keats said. "We'd have to get past ground-floor security, go up to seventeen where we would be shot at. A lot. Then somehow we'd have to reach the connecting stairwell and climb to eighteen, where we would have another fight on our hands, with forces coming from all over the building to attack our rear."

"Exactly. Now, we'd have some advantages—we can use our network access to shut down elevators, block some doors, turn off cameras, that sort of thing. But to actually have a decent chance of success? We would need a hundred men."

He laid that last fact out like a poker player showing the ace that would win the pot.

Keats snorted. "A hundred men?"

"In Midtown Manhattan. Imagine a hundred armed men appearing on the street outside the Tulip. There would be no way to avoid the police being involved, especially once bullets started to send plate glass falling down onto pedestrians."

"Isn't there some kind of . . . I don't know," Plath said, frustrated. "Some Tom Cruise kind of thing? Crawling up the side of the building?"

"The shape of the Tulip, with that suggestive bulge at the top, means that's physically impossible, even if we were insane enough to try such a stunt."

Stern turned away from the monitor with an air of finality, but Keats leaned past him and pointed at the screen. "Did you see this? Eighteen isn't the only floor that's shut off from elevators. This is, what? Thirty-four, yes?"

Stern spun back and peered closely at the monitor. "I believe you're right. But the heat signature is quite average on thirty-four, so that's not our server farm."

"No," Keats agreed. "But it's *something.*"

"In the end, as you can see, the building is effectively impregnable. Not that we would ever have participated in such a thing, anyway, but just so that you know: that server farm cannot be taken out by direct attack."

"Which means our friend Lear has ordered us to do something impossible," Keats said.

Plath looked troubled and uncertain. But she finally stood up, took Stern's hand, and thanked him.

Back on the street Plath said, "So why did Lear tell us to do the impossible?"

Keats had no answer to that.

Unless, of course, it isn't impossible.

In Plath's mind the towers fell.

BRAZIL

Lystra Reid was nowhere near when the president of Brazil was discovered naked and babbling on a street in São Paulo, apparently collecting dog feces in a Gap shopping bag.

The president was taken to a hospital, where no explanation could be found for his condition. He was diagnosed first as suffering a breakdown as a result of stress and overwork. But it soon became clear that this was no mere nervous breakdown but a complete psychotic break.

He had gone mad.

A solemn vice president assumed the office and attempted to reassure a worried nation. But halfway through her speech she appeared to become distracted.

There were, she said . . . , "*Bugs.*"

And soon after she began to weep and curse violently, and from there began to scream and had to be taken away by her chief of staff and security personnel.

LOS ANGELES

The Los Angeles County coroner, Dr. Baldur Chen, issued two different reports on the death of actress Sandra Piper. One was very thorough and public and reached the obvious conclusion: suicide.

The second was a report prepared with help from an agency in Washington. That agency sent its own pathologist to "assist." This second pathologist focused on an exceedingly careful examination of the actress's brain. Dr. Chen had never seen an autopsy that involved centimeter-by-centimeter microscopic investigation of the brain tissue.

It would have taken a much more obtuse man than Dr. Chen to fail to recognize that the agency pathologist was looking for something very specific.

Both pathologists signed off on a second, eyes-only report that dealt with this second, microscopic examination. The conclusion was that there was no evidence of nanotechnology present.

Dr. Chen was required to sign an official secrets document and was solemnly warned that he would go to a federal prison if he revealed the existence of this second report.

NINE

The Twins arrived back in New York with no more fanfare than Plath and Keats. It had been expensive, but crossing into the U.S. without a passport was possible. Not impossible. Not with enough ready cash.

They had been helped into their specially built shower, then slept for many hours until Jindal had them awakened as per their orders.

Cranky, but relieved to be home again where the environment had been shaped to their needs, they drank coffee, ate pastries, and sat in their tent-size bathrobe while Jindal gave them the rundown. This program and that business.

"We don't care about the P and Ls," Benjamin snarled after a few minutes of spreadsheets. "Do you think we give a damn about long-term profits? Have you found BZRK?"

Jindal licked his lips and rocked back on his heels. He always stood in their presence. "No, sir. Thrum's lead took us up a dead alley. She's beginning to suggest that she's being played."

"Played? Hannah Thrum?" Charles made a dubious face.

"She thinks, and sirs, I agree, maybe, that Sadie McLure and the McLure chief of security are laying a false trail to—"

"We're being played by a *teenager*?" Charles was usually the calmer brother, but this insulted his intelligence.

Benjamin slapped the table with his palm. "If we can't find them, we can still go after their allies. This chief of security. His whole department."

Jindal started to smile, almost as if he thought it was a joke. Then his smile faded. "Sir?"

Benjamin glared at him. "Never mind. Not your sort of work. No. No, get Burnofsky in here."

Jindal stiffened. He had kept Burnofsky at arm's length, suspecting, suspecting very damned strongly that the genius had been compromised by BZRK.

"Are you sure you want—"

"Get him. And get out."

Benjamin remained silent a while, judging his brother's mood. Charles, he concluded, was frustrated, but not yet ready to accept that they were entering a new phase. Charles did not yet understand that they were *losing*. In fact may already have lost.

Charles still half believed the silly cult they'd financed, Nexus Humanus, was of some use. He still seemed to think that the work of their remaining twitchers—no great prodigies among them—was just marking time, doing damage control.

"You're still trying to hide," Benjamin said aloud at last. "Our whole life, you always wanted to find a way to hide what we are."

"What we are?" Charles said a bit pompously. "What we are is two great men, who have—"

"We are freaks," Benjamin said, but not angrily. "Everywhere except on the *Doll Ship*. They've taken that from us. BZRK, the intelligence people, the police, all of them, all the forces of *the normal.* They've destroyed the one, small place where we could be. Just . . . be."

"We have this place, still," Charles said.

"Our cage. Our gilded cage."

"Yes," Charles admitted. Then he heaved a sigh. "The tide has turned, has it not, brother?"

"Yes," Benjamin said. He reached awkwardly across their body to pat his brother's chest. It was as much physical affection as they could deploy. You could not hug a man who was attached to you. "The tide has turned. The governments have become aware. In secret we had a chance. But secrecy is impossible now. They will come for us, and they will take us. They'll put us on display. They'll call it a trial, but it will be a carnival freak show. And then they'll put us in a cell until we die."

The angled mirror that let them look in each other's eye revealed that Charles was crying.

So, Benjamin thought. *Perhaps he sees at last.*

"You were too softhearted, Charles. Always. You thought you could improve them, as we did on the *Doll Ship*, and yes, it was a magnificent dream, brother. But we now face Sodom and Gomorrah, and no righteous man is to be found to justify their salvation."

The silence that followed was long.

"What," Charles asked finally, sounding exhausted, "would you have us do?"

"We tried to gently show the world the error of its ways," Benjamin said. "We tried the carrot. Now comes the stick. Now comes judgment. Now comes righteous wrath, brother. Or do we wait for our chance to star in their freak show?"

"No," Charles whispered. Then louder. "No, by God. Now comes Judgment Day. We hit them. We hit them so hard they can't stand up. And then we show them that we have worse still in store unless they submit."

Benjamin smiled. The doorbell sounded. "That would be the good Dr. Burnofsky."

In Rome, the Pope was working his way methodically through his daily audiences. He was a humble man despite the pomp of his ancient office, and he still, after many years in the job, felt a bit put off by the need to play the kingly role.

First up there was the priest who had defied death threats to keep an inoculation program going in narco country. The priest was young and cocky and brave and offered to shake the Holy Father's hand rather than kiss his ring.

Then the two Little Sisters of the Poor, one of whom had been attacked on a mission in Burma. The Pope rose from his seat to embrace them each in turn and to whisper words of encouragement. They left with tears streaming down their faces.

Then the usual collection of businesspeople and media people, all of which would culminate in the Pope getting to meet a famously good-looking actor to thank him for his charitable work. As far as the Holy Father knew the actor was not a Catholic, but he was still a great talent and this Pope rather liked the conversation of talented people.

A banker, a reporter, a union boss, an Argentinean politician (the Pope was not fond of politicians as a rule), a scientist who had discovered a way to raise sorghum crop yields dramatically, and last, before the actor, Lystra Reid, a youngish woman with tattoos peeking out from beneath her expensive clothing.

"Your Holiness," Lystra Reid said, and knelt, and kissed his ring.

And at that moment four of Bug Man's nanobots leapt from her lips, slick with lipstick, to the cold metal of what was known as the Fisherman's Ring.

A quarter mile away, Bug Man said, "And that's how the pros do it," and did a little fist pump.

The Pope's audience was broadcast via a closed-circuit station from the Vatican, and of course streamed, so Bug Man could see it all play out in the macro even as he was marveling at the unusual smoothness of the ring's gold surface.

"You're back," Burnofsky said. "I mean, welcome back."

They stared at him, unnerving him as they often did. Were they going to kill him right here, right now? Surely they must suspect that he had been wired. Maybe he should just put it out there; maybe he should just blurt it out.

Are you watching all this, Nijinsky? Or are you in my ear listening? Or are you drunk and passed out, you sad degenerate?

Burnofsky was pleased to realize that he was not afraid to die. Yet, he was afraid to die too soon. BZRK had reprogrammed him, brutally shifted his emotions, but it was crude work. Typical of the lesser BZRKers. Vincent would have done a better job. Vincent would have found a way to wire him for true loyalty. All Nijinsky had accomplished was to turn Burnofsky—for now at least—away from the bottle and the pipe. He had implanted very strong inhibitions against telling the Twins all he knew. He had turned Burnofsky's most terrible secret into a source of sickening pleasure, and oh, that had been cruel work.

But still: crude and ham-fisted. Burnofsky could no longer be said to be working for the Twins, true, but he was still working for himself, still pursuing his own agenda. Nijinsky thought his watchful biot would allow him to see and understand what Burnofsky was doing.

Foolish boy. Male model. I'm one of the great minds of the century, and you think I can't carry out my work right under your nose?

"Karl, it's good to see you," Charles lied.

Benjamin's one-eyed stare would freeze lava.

"It's good to have you gentlemen back," Burnofsky said. "I'm, um, well, sorry for your . . ."

"Defeat?" snarled Benjamin. "Are you sorry for our *defeat*?"

"Your loss," Burnofsky said, finding the right word. "I'm sorry for your loss."

"Fuck your sympathy," Benjamin snapped.

Charles intervened smoothly. "My brother and I are both grieving. You can understand our . . . impatience."

"What can I do for you?" Burnofsky asked. Benjamin's anger had sent him back in his mind to Carla. To his daughter. It had been in this room, just over there, closer to the desk. That's where he had come to them—drunk, stoned, filled with sorrow so deep and shame so dark that it would poison him as surely as a dose of strychnine. There, yes, right there he had reported to them that the deed was done and his daughter was dead.

They had said then that they were sorry for *his* loss.

He swallowed hard, trying to avoid the terrible rush of pleasure that flowed each time he recalled the murder, each time, oh, God, to enjoy it, to be excited by it . . .

For a moment he thought he might vomit. Or actually become physically aroused. Or both at once.

I will kill you, Nijinsky. I don't know how, but I will kill you.

"Massed preprogrammed attack," Charles said, trying to take control of the conversation to forestall more rage from his brother. They could still use Burnofsky, so long as they were careful. Let him reveal all to BZRK: without details it would mean nothing.

"What about a preprogrammed attack?" Burnofsky asked cautiously.

Charles smiled. "It's time we learned more about some of our . . . toys." He nodded. "Yes, Karl, we want to learn how to do it."

"You mean, how to program an attack using self-replicating nanobots? Yourselves?"

"Are we too stupid?" Benjamin demanded. "Is that what you think? Do you think we rose from where we began to all of this by being stupid?" He waved his hand to encompass all of what he'd earlier called his gilded cage.

No, by being rage-filled lunatics, Burnofsky thought. *And by having a very rich grandfather.*

"I am very well aware of your intellect," Burnofsky soothed.

"Perhaps not quite on your level, Karl," Charles said. "But as I understand it, there's an app for this."

Burnofsky's first thought was that they meant to use it against him. But no, there were so many ways they could kill him, they wouldn't be cute about it.

"Gentlemen," Burnofsky said, "if you have thirty minutes, I can teach you to use the app."

"Wake up, Anthony. You have a visitor."

Bug Man sat up fast. The lights were on. But it must still be night out beyond the shuttered windows.

George III had a cup of coffee in his hand. He gave it to Bug Man.

"What?" Bug Man said.

"Someone wants to meet you."

Bug Man was not yet fully awake, but he was getting there fast. "No one knows I'm here." Awful suspicion blossomed. "You sold me out! You mother—"

"Drink your coffee," George said, and sighed. "If I was selling you out, would I start by bringing you a cappuccino? It's full-fat milk— you're not watching your cholesterol, I hope."

Bug Man took a sip. George was trying to act cool, but he was upset. Something had disturbed his typical sangfroid.

"Put on some clothing. It's just one of my compatriots here to brief you on next steps." He was lying. He was lying and he was jumpy, very unlike his usual self.

"In the middle of the night?"

"She has an early flight." George left the room. Bug Man took another sip of coffee. A soft knock at the door.

"Yeah, George," Bug Man yelled, "I'm getting up. Damn, give a brother a few minutes to—"

The door opened. It was not George, but a white woman. Medium-tall, slender, good-looking but sharp edged. Brunette.

"Hello, Anthony. I'm sorry to barge in on you. But I have to get back to New York, so I don't have a lot of time."

She sat down on the foot of the bed, a position that made Bug Man quite uncomfortable since under the blankets he wasn't wearing anything. He was very conscious of his skinny chest and well-formed but not exactly muscular shoulders.

"Who are you?"

"My name is Lystra."

"You were the pathway."

She smiled. She tilted her head, looked closely at him, making eye contact, taking her time in responding. *Smart*, that's what he thought of her on first impression. That she was smart. And not bad if you liked older women. And she was on his bed. . . .

"I'm a lot of pathways," Lystra said.

"So, George said—"

"Do you like George?" she asked.

"Not really," Bug Man said.

"No, you wouldn't. George isn't really like us, is he?"

"Like us?"

"George is so serious. He never plays games. You and I, we like to play. We enjoy the game *as a game*."

"Do we know each other?" Bug Man asked. Alarm bells were going off in his head. He recalled George's furtive eyes.

"In a way. I've played you at different times in different games, yeah. I use several online identities. But you're better than I am.

Quicker reaction time; very, very good at taking advantage of terrain. And an amazing three-dimensional thinker. I can see why the Armstrong Twins hired you: your natural abilities, yeah, and your total lack of moral core."

Bug Man wasn't sure he liked that. On the other hand, he wasn't sure he could argue the point. Was he without a moral core? He frowned, considered it, shrugged it off—figuring that if he couldn't think of a good counterargument, maybe it meant she was right.

So he said, "Thank you. George said you weren't part of BZRK."

"Hmmm. Well, at that point I wasn't sure we should meet, you and I. Yeah. You've extracted the sample?"

"The cells? Yeah, I got the Pope's cells out. They're with my nanobots on the Pope's sleeve."

"Yes, which goes to the laundry where it will be intercepted by someone working for . . . well, *us*." She said the plural pronoun mockingly. As if it made no sense.

The alarm bells were going crazy now. Bug Man almost felt the floor tipping beneath him. Lystra laughed, almost as though she could read his mind.

"Ah, suspicion begins to form, yeah," Lystra said. "See how quick you are? That's why I like you. I'm done with you, I mean you've done what . . . *we* . . . wanted you to do. You harvested the cells. And I thought maybe, yeah . . . we . . . would just kill you now."

Bug Man froze. The playful tone was more frightening than a threat. An overt threat might ring false, might be a bluff. But this woman was not bluffing. She could have him killed.

"Here you are, though, a young man without a place to go. So very many people, yeah, want you dead."

His throat was dry, and the first words came out in a rasp. "What do you . . ." He swallowed, tried to get some moisture going.

"What do I want?" She sighed. The sigh was melodramatic and false. "Do you know the difference between us, Bug Man? Aside from the obvious—gender, age, race. We both know none of that's important. The real difference between us is that you are a superb game *player*. Whereas I am a game *designer*."

"Yeah? What game?"

"This one. Yeah. The game I call BZRK. Nanobots and biots. On the one side, twisted idealist freaks who would deprive humans of free will in order to give them all contentment. On the other hand . . ." She let it hang, then added a superfluous, "Yeah."

"That's the Twins' game," he said dully.

The not-very-convincing mask of friendliness disappeared so suddenly and so completely that it must never have been there. He had the terrifying impression that the skin on her face had shrunk so that bone and teeth and the hollows of her eye sockets were all suddenly outlined and shadowed.

Her eyes glittered. "Oh, them," she said, striving to regain her jokey tone and failing. "They have *their* game. Mine is better. More levels."

He noted that she no longer used the plural. Not *our* game. *Mine*.

She stood up suddenly. "Get dressed. I've decided. You're coming with me."

"But . . . where? Why am I—?"

"Where? Oh, places with tall buildings. New York City. And then cold, cold places. As cold as it gets this side of the grave. But what do you care, Bug Man?" She sounded weary now. "Don't you want to see how the game plays out? Don't you want to know what it was all about?"

He shook his head slowly. "Games aren't about anything. Games are just about the game."

She leaned down and laid a soft palm against his cheek. "See? That's why I like you, Anthony Bug Man. You and I are going to be friends. Or I can have George put a bullet in your head."

"Friends," he said.

And Lear smiled.

TEN

Nijinsky was shopping when it happened.

He was at Saks, the big one, the flagship store on Fifth Avenue. Christmas was coming and he had nephews. But he was shopping more for himself than for them. He liked shopping. It was a Zen thing for him. He had an eye for style, which had been useful in his life as a model but was entirely neglected in BZRK.

Saks was already in full Christmas swing, decorated in a fantasy of silver and white; the storefront windows were dioramas of highly stylized snowmen appearing in Russian-themed settings. There were delicate flights of abstract snowflakes arched across the ceiling, and a restrained seasonal soundtrack played unobtrusively.

Nijinsky lifted the leg of a pair of slacks, felt the weight of the wool, ran sensitive, knowledgeable fingertips along the crease and then inside the waistband.

And to no one he said, "What?"

He froze, just stood there, seeming to stare at a mannequin dressed in a sleek but uninspired Canali suit.

"The hell?" Nijinsky said.

"Are you finding what you're looking for?" It seemed an almost philosophical question, but of course it was just a salesperson, a woman, blonde, well put together but with tired eyes.

He stared at her now, just as blankly as he'd stared at the mannequin. "Something . . ." he said.

"Are you all right, sir?"

He was not all right. Nijinsky had four biots. One was in Burnofsky, in his eye, tapping the nerve and watching the computer upon which Burnofsky was busily typing. The others were in their crèches—holders for dormant biots—in the basement of the safe house. All were out of range, so that rather than seeing detailed pictures of what they saw, he was seeing something more like two open picture-in-picture displays with vague shapes, fuzziness, lack of detail. Like looking through a very dirty window at a poorly lit scene.

Except that now, suddenly, there was *another* window. And this one was perfectly clear.

A new biot.

He looked around then, frantic, searching for an explanation. A fit, attractive middle-aged man was trying on an Armani blazer. Two children and their nanny killing time, the kids playing tag around hanger racks. An attractive woman with ornate ink peeking out of her décolletage. Clerks. An older man; a store display designer carefully placing a hat on a mannequin.

"Sir?" the blonde saleswoman prompted.

Nijinsky shook his head. "No. I don't think I am all right."

The saleswoman said nothing to that.

And then, a second new window, as clear as the earlier one. A clear biot's-eye view of the interior of a glass tube. He could see the curvature, the texture—like stretch marks somehow—because nothing was entirely smooth down at m-sub level.

Without so much willing it as thinking it, he turned the two new biots. They moved, obeying his will. And both biots now saw his opposite: six-legged; insectoid, but with dangerous tail stingers; a spider's spinnerets; and the disturbing biot rendering of his own eyes, a nightmare twisting of his own face.

Biots. Two of them. And suddenly he understood.

He had seconds left.

"Excuse me," he said to the saleswoman. "I believe I'm about to go mad. You may want to move away." He pulled out his phone and opened his messaging app. Who? Who should he tell?

Should he even bother? Plath had pushed him aside. Why should he help her now?

He keyed in her phone number, hit the button for text, and typed.

There was a sudden rush of liquid rolling down the inside of the tube. It was no more than a droplet in the real world, but it was as big as a house in the m-sub.

"Ah," he said, as the acid engulfed both his new biots.

The next thing he said was also, "Ah," but this time he shouted it.

And the next "Ah" was screamed.

And the next twenty or so.

He broke into a run—frantic, terrified, still clutching the phone with its typed but unsent message.

"No! No! No!" he shrieked as he raced to the open escalator and threw himself down it. Threw himself, as if he was trying to fly. Arms outstretched, face forward.

He hit the steel steps, and his face exploded in blood. He climbed to his feet but was pulled off-balance by the moving stairs and pirouetted down until he landed again, hard.

But not hard enough to kill himself.

Nijinsky swung around, off the bottom of the escalator, and this time he had a plan, a mad, desperate plan, one he could barely hold on to. He tied his long scarf into a knot as he descended a second, upward-bound escalator.

People ran out of his way, bounded up the steps to avoid him. They yelled things like, "What the hell, man?" But mostly they just got out of his way.

Nijinsky knelt on the stairs. Rising, rising, and lay the end of his silk scarf on the step before him.

Five seconds.

Four.

A wild, giggling shout rose from his throat as the end of the scarf was sucked into the escalator. The shout ended abruptly as the relentless mechanism devoured the scarf, tightened it around his neck, slammed his bloody face into the steel, chewed up his left hand, cut off his air.

He could no longer speak. No longer scream. Blood filled his head, and still the noose tightened.

His windpipe was crushed. Blood now seeped from his eyes and ears. The phone fell from his fingers and lay with message unsent on the steel serrated edge of the escalator.

By the time some bright shopper thought to push the emergency-stop switch, Nijinsky was dead.

The message on Plath's phone was from Nijinsky.

It read, *2 new biots.*

But she had muted her phone and would not see the message until later because she was meeting with Stern. Again.

Plath did not ask Keats to join her this time. She would discuss the Tulip with Mr. Stern, but she would mostly be asking him what he had discovered about Lear.

Attempts to learn about Lear counted as treason within BZRK. Treason led to bad things, and she did not want to implicate Keats in that.

Of course, Keats had a biot in her brain. If he was very curious he could make the long trip out into an ear canal and listen in.

She didn't think Keats did things like that. It would be out of character. But in this new world she had entered such things had to be considered. In this new world the human body was not a singular object—it was an ecosystem. It was a Brazilian rainforest full of flora and fauna, from creepy, crawly mites to big, fat balls of pollen to Dr. Seuss–like fungal trees, to a hundred different types of bacteria, all the way down to viruses. None of it strictly human. The average human body had far more nonhuman cells than human ones, though they comprised only a fraction of the weight—about five pounds in most people.

You moved differently through the world when you truly came to accept that fact. When you knew that you were crawling, covered, congested by nonhuman life-forms. Sometimes you couldn't quite see the line between yourself and the world around you.

All about her on the sidewalk were other ecosystems, each body a similarly complex environment. Each body in turn a small part of a larger system. A system called New York. Or, more inclusively, the human race. Formerly meaningful divisions had lost some solidity.

What seemed solid in the macro was so much less so down in the meat.

The meeting with Stern followed all the rules of spy craft. They set up the meeting using text messages. They both spent an hour throwing off any possible pursuers. Their phones were off and therefore impossible to track. If she were being followed, then it was very professionally done.

And yet when Plath arrived at the steps of the public library in Bryant Park, there was a man sitting across the street in the window of a hotel café, sipping a latte and making no effort to go unnoticed.

He was middle-aged, with long graying hair and a wry, observant expression. He was dressed like a dandy—a purple velvet blazer, a top hat that sat on the counter beside him.

If he had ever had a real name, Plath didn't know it. His nom de guerre, his BZRK name, was Caligula.

Plath had seen him in action. He was a confident and extremely capable killer. He was the eighth person of whom Lear had spoken. But it was not possible for Plath to imagine giving him orders.

It was Caligula who had killed Ophelia after she was captured by the FBI. He had burned out her brain so as to leave no traces of nanotechnology behind. If Plath brought him into BZRK now—into her BZRK—Wilkes, who had been close to Ophelia, who had very nearly died beside her, might try to kill him. And that would be the end of Wilkes.

And yet, here was Plath meeting Mr. Stern to discover what he had learned in his efforts to track down the elusive personality behind BZRK. Was that why Caligula was here? Did he already know? Should she be expecting a bullet or a knife or the killer's trademark hatchet?

Could Caligula guess what they were talking about? Surely not. But he had found a way to follow her, or perhaps to follow Mr. Stern. That knowledge made her feel faint. It weakened her knees.

God, it was true: there was no escaping the man in the velvet suit. *The NKVD.* Plath had Googled it. Anya had spoken the truth. And now here was her own personal NKVD sipping a coffee and watching to see what she would do.

Or fail to do.

As Nijinksy's body was being cut loose by paramedics, Plath bought a street pretzel and a Nantucket Nectars cranberry. Stern had a coffee and an Italian sausage. They looked, perhaps, like a girl meeting her father. Or a student with her atypically tough-looking professor.

"Now that we're alone, how have you been, Sadie?"

"Getting used to being back in the world," she said, looking around at the other lunchtime diners, all somewhere between coats and sweaters on this gray day.

"It was good of you to pay the money to the boat crew who died. One of them had two young kids. Softens the blow."

"What have you found?" she asked, too cold to want to chat, and too aware of Caligula's cobra gaze.

"On the Armstrong Twins? I suspect they are in a place called Sarawak, which is in Malaysia. AFGC owns a facility in Malaysia, a rare earths mine. Rare earths are a class of rare minerals used in some sophisticated electronics components. It makes sense that AFGC would have a source."

"How likely do you think it is that they're there?"

Stern thought it over. "I'd say seventy percent. It seems consistent with what we're seeing. But it's possible they're elsewhere. It's even possible they are back in New York."

"And the *other* person you're looking for?"

Stern glanced at Caligula. "There sits the one man who might be able to take us to Lear."

"Stay away from him," Plath said too quickly.

"You're that scared of him."

"I've seen his work, Mr. Stern. The man who warned me about him doesn't scare easily." Vincent. Back when Vincent was *Vincent.* "But he was scared of Caligula."

Stern raised his cup, sipped, and said, "I have leads, nothing solid. Lear's cell number is obviously switched out daily. You gave me four such numbers. All the numbers are throwaways. Burner phones. But interestingly, two of them were purchased in odd locations."

"Odd how?"

"Well, one was bought in London; one was bought in Wellington, New Zealand; one was bought in Saint Petersburg, Russia. The last was from Punta Arenas, Chile."

"What am I not seeing in those four locations?"

"Wellington and Punta Arenas share a distinction as major jumping-off points for Antarctica."

"Antarctica. Why . . . never mind. I had another text exchange with Lear. Here's the number." She read it off to him. "Why doesn't Lear just block the number?"

"Excellent question," Stern said approvingly. "Arrogance? Or, more likely, he's deliberately leaving breadcrumbs. Either a false trail, or . . ."

"Or what?"

"Or a trail meant for the right person to follow."

A game? Was she supposed to believe that Lear was playing a game with her?

In the coffee shop, Caligula was standing up. He put on his hat, straightened it carefully, and looked directly at Sadie, who returned his gaze evenly. Then he tugged at the front brim in a slight but unmistakable acknowledgment of her, and faded from view as he moved away.

Stern caught the gesture and said, "And you're sure we shouldn't question *him*?"

"He's tight with Lear. He's Lear's attack dog. And I may need him."

"What are you planning?"

Plath shrugged. "Lear's orders. He still wants us to wipe out all AFGC data on nanotechnology. And soon."

Stern took a long pause at that. He searched her face, looking for something to reassure himself. But reassurance did not come, and now he was wary. "Have you told Lear about the practical objections to such a harebrained scheme?"

"No," Plath said. "Not yet."

She hesitated, unsure if she should go forward. Stern was an experienced interrogator—he knew when just to wait.

"It's just . . . ," Plath began. "It's just, well, I was thinking . . . a bomb of some kind?"

"A bomb? Are we back to that?" He shook his head slowly without shifting his gaze from her. When she said nothing, he said, "Sadie, please listen to me. I've been to war. I was in Iraq, and before that I was in Somalia. When you're in it, when you're scared and when you're mad and you want revenge, maybe, you find yourself thinking about doing things no human being should do. You think about crossing the line."

"Where's this line, Mr. Stern? The Armstrongs killed my father and brother. They basically killed the president of the United States, even if that's not what they intended. Burnofsky was trying to unleash self-replicating nanobots that could kill every living thing on the planet. So where's the line?"

Stern put down his coffee, carefully crumpled the paper from his sandwich, and set it aside. He wiped his hands with a napkin. Then, with a clean forefinger, he pointed at Plath's forehead. "In there." Then he pointed at her heart. "In there. That's where the line is."

It was not easy to meet his worried, penetrating eyes.

"Sadie, you need to ask yourself: Is this *you*? Are you really, truly a person planning what would look like a terrorist attack in Midtown Manhattan?"

Finally she couldn't take it and turned away. "No, of course not. But get me everything you can, okay? Everything you feel okay about giving me. I still need to find a way. . . ."

He wasn't buying it. And for a moment she was afraid he might just walk away. Then, with a pained expression, an expression of loss, he nodded his head.

ELEVEN

Saks would not release the store surveillance video. But Mr. Stern had excellent connections throughout security companies in New York. An underpaid guard, when offered ten thousand dollars in untraceable cash, decided he could in fact arrange for the video file to make its way to Mr. Stern.

He in turn passed it along to Plath. Who watched it for the third time with Keats, Wilkes, and Anya. Billy had not been asked to be present, but he was, anyway.

They decided that there was no need for Vincent to be subjected to it in his condition.

His *condition*. Fragile, that was his condition. Borderline nuts, still. High-functioning unbalanced.

"Jin lost his shit," Wilkes said on a second viewing. "Look. That's when it starts. He's fondling a pair of pants. Then that's him texting."

"'Two new biots,'" Plath said dully.

"The text was sent three minutes later," Noah pointed out. He had compared the video time code to the time signature on Plath's phone.

They watched the second part of the tape. Nijinsky hurling himself down the escalator. There was no sound. The video was decent

115

quality, but the angle was poor. They were seeing him from behind.

"Jesus Christ, how many times do we have to watch this?" Wilkes cried suddenly. She stormed off to the kitchen. Then came back with a bag of chips.

"'Two new biots,'" Keats said. "But he was *against* getting anymore."

The third segment of tape showed a distraught Nijinsky, face-on this time, kneeling, feeding his scarf into the escalator.

It went on for way too long. Nijinsky dead. People milling around helplessly. Store employees rushing over with scissors, trying to get at the scarf and cut him loose. Failing, because it was too tight, too tangled.

Eventually a security guard. Then, at last, far too late, the paramedics.

"He went crazy," Anya said. "It was deliberate. He was looking at clothing and then he was killing himself. Madness."

She wasn't thinking about Nijinsky. She was thinking about Vincent. She glanced nervously toward the stairs leading up to his room, then tried to cover the telltale gesture with a reach toward Wilkes's chips.

"New biots," Plath mused.

"Just totally lost his shit." Wilkes spoke around the crunching of a corn chip.

"Who could make a biot for him?" Keats asked. "It takes a tissue sample and the equipment." He didn't mean to single Anya out by looking at her, but she was the only one in the room with the skills, and she controlled the equipment that had been hidden in the basement of the safe house.

"It takes a tissue sample, the equipment, and the skills," Anya said. Then, angrily, "Why would I do that to Nijinsky?" She didn't wait for an answer. Everyone knew the answer. Anya sighed. "Yes, I disliked him. But I would never do this."

That earned her carefully blank looks.

"No, you listen to me, all of you. I would never. I did never. I did not do this."

All eyes were on her.

"No!" Anya cried. "No, do not do this! Suspicion will destroy us."

"What 'us'?" Wilkes asked. "Look at us. Ophelia's dead. Renfield. Vincent's out of it. Now Jin. Fucking Jin, man." She laughed her weird heh-heh-heh laugh and looked ready to cry. "We're a fucking joke."

"We stopped the Armstrongs," Keats said reasonably. "We accomplished a lot. More than we should have been able to."

Anya ignored him and instead pleaded with Plath. "Plath, you know I didn't do this. Look at me. I did not hurt Nijinsky."

Plath wanted to say something reassuring. But she couldn't quite get the words to come out. If not Anya, then who? Someone at McLure Labs? But how many people there even knew of the existence of biots? And of those, how many could make one? And of *those*, how many would use the knowledge to kill Nijinsky? Was Anya a traitor?

"I know what you are thinking." Anya's Russian accent was coming to the fore. The word came out *thinkink*. "You are wrong." *Wronk*. "It was someone else. Why would [*vwould*] I . . . ? For what reason?"

Keats said, "No one suspects you, Anya. I don't, at least. But the thing is, who else then? Not you, okay. But who?"

"I don't know," Anya pleaded. "I can think of only three others at McLure Labs with the knowledge and the access to equipment. But how would they have a tissue sample from Nijinsky?"

"He's dead now, can we call him by his real name? Shane Hwang. Not some dead, crazy Russian ballet dancer." This from Wilkes. She punched the bag of chips and sent crumbs flying. "His name was Shane fucking Hwang. I never even knew Ophelia's real name. And poor old Renfield. And when I'm dead or crazy, you people won't know me, either." The flame tattoo under her eye looked like extravagant tears. "Jesus, no one will even know me."

"Okay," Plath said, bringing silence. "I believe you, Anya. I think . . . I mean, I choose to think . . . that this is the remote biotkiller technology that Lear was talking about. Which means we are all in danger. But still, Anya, I—we—need to be able to watch you." Plath put a finger to her eye. It looked like a gesture, some kind of evil-eye, maledictory gesture. But in fact Plath had sent one of her biots racing around her own eyeball to clamber over lashes and reach the cheek.

Through her biot's eyes she could see the vast column of flesh descending like some cylindrical meteor from the sky to press a giant furrowed fingertip within a few seconds' walk.

Her biot ran beneath the vast curve, ran on until fingertip and depressed cheek met, then clambered upside down onto the finger.

"No," Anya said. "No. Nyet. Is not happening."

"I promise you, Anya, I won't lay any wire. I will not make any changes in your brain."

"Your promise," Anya sneered.

"Yes, my promise," Plath said. "I can't just let you walk away. I have to maintain surveillance." She leaned toward Anya and stretched a finger up to the older woman's eye.

Anya swallowed in a dry throat. "So you will watch me. You will tap into my eye and see everything that I see."

"It's the only way," Keats said, though he didn't sound too sure of it. He pressed his lips together and stole a worried glance at Plath, who revealed no emotion.

Look how hard she's gotten, Keats thought.

When they had first met, he'd marked her down as a spoiled little rich girl, probably a snob, who would condescend to him, look down her nose at him.

But that had not been true. She had been anything but a snob. But even then, early days, he'd noticed that effortless authority she carried with her. That was, without question, a product of wealth and privilege. Plath would admit that much. A billionaire's daughter simply had an air about her that could not be faked by a working-class kid like Keats.

Part of him was proud of her in an uncomplicated way. He wanted to say, *Well, look at you, all grown up and in charge*. But part of him was small enough to focus on their relationship rather than BZRK. He was in love with her. He believed she loved him back. But how stable could a relationship be when there was this much of a difference in their circumstances? My God, the girl basically had a private army.

Anya let Plath touch her, just below her left eye.

Plath held the contact for a few seconds as her biot scampered off and began the journey to the optic nerve.

From now until Plath let her go, Anya's sight would be shared.

Plath would see what Anya saw. In the bathroom and bedroom, too, inevitably. The idea made Keats's skin crawl, but this was BZRK.

Fighting for freedom. Saving the world.

Yeah, but hadn't they done that when they stopped the Armstrongs from controlling the president? And when they stopped Burnofsky's gray-goo scenario? Hadn't they already won?

Then how was it they were still trapped in this paranoid universe where they used the names of dead or made-up madmen? How was it that they were still taking orders from an invisible character called Lear?

The thought was out of his mouth before he could check it. "Why are we still doing this?"

Wilkes snorted. "Pretty blue eyes asks the right question. Why are we still doing this?"

"Because we haven't won yet," Plath said. But she didn't quite like that answer. "It's not over yet."

"How does it get to be over?" Keats asked. "How will we know it's over?" He had been leaning forward, now he drew back. "Look, isn't this about the knowledge, really? Once we know how to make nanobots and biots, how do we ever unlearn that? It's like nuclear bombs, isn't it. How do you stop it spreading once the technology exists?"

"When the last of us is dead, it's game over. For us. Right?" This was the first time Billy had spoken. "I mean, it's a game, right? Biots versus nanobots. Take over the world. Isn't it a game?"

"No, it's real," Plath insisted. "The Armstrong Twins are real, and we're real, and Jin was real."

"Yeah, but . . ." Billy felt the weight of disapproval. "Yeah, but games *are* real. That's what you don't get, with respect to you, Plath. Games are real to the people playing them. While they're playing."

No one said anything; after all, Billy was just a kid. But Keats couldn't shake the feeling that he'd just heard something important, that Billy had blurted out the truth. *It could be real, and dangerous, and deadly, and yet still be a game*, he thought.

When was a game over? When you lost.

Or when you won and went off in search of a new game.

Biot versus nanobot. That was the game. But now, according to Plath by way of Lear, a new level was being revealed. Something out there could kill biots remotely. Dead biots meant madness. It meant killing yourself on an escalator in Saks.

So why bother to blow up a boat? If you could generate then kill biots, then why did it seem so much like manipulation? The Armstrong Twins would not hesitate if they could kill Plath and him.

So why wasn't he dead?

Because the game was somehow more complicated than that.

The video played again, looping. Keats watched the faces watching Nijinsky. They watched in surprise as he stared and spoke to the air. Then in shock as he threw himself down the escalator. Horror as he fed the silk scarf into the mechanism that choked the life from him.

Then, Keats picked up the remote and rewound.

"Enough!" Wilkes yelled.

"Wait," Keats said. "Don't watch Jin. Watch the people around him. That woman. The one with the ink."

He advanced it in slow motion, focusing on the woman.

She pulled out her phone and glanced at it. Checking e-mail? Or checking the time?

She stole a glance at Nijinsky.

"She's looking at Jin," Keats said.

"He was a good-looking dude, maybe she—" Wilkes began, but then she fell silent, because now was the part where Nijinsky started to lose it. The people nearest were shooting him irritated or concerned looks. The woman was not. She was half smiling, watching . . . waiting.

Waiting.

"She knows," Keats said.

He cut to the next video, the horrific one showing Nijinsky on the escalator. There was a woman just a dozen steps behind him.

"Fuck! It's *her,*" Wilkes said.

Now everyone was leaning toward the screen, checking the dress, checking the shoes, the hair, comparing them to the first images.

"Yes," Plath confirmed. It's the same woman. Jin got to this place by running, then hurling himself down the escalator. And she *followed* him? What kind of person follows a crazy man?"

Now, again, Nijinsky fed the scarf into the escalator.

But this time they watched the woman behind him—the shoulders, the hair.

She stepped past and over the strangling Nijinsky. Not panicked. Calm.

She knelt by Nijinsky. Her hand shot out, took something.

"The phone," Plath said. "She took his phone. The time signatures. She sent the text."

"It's an Easter egg," Keats said. "Billy's right: it's all a game. And that woman is an Easter egg. We are *supposed* to see her."

Jindal could barely restrain himself. His first meeting with the returned Twins had ended with his being dismissed like a disappointing schoolboy. Now they would have to listen. "We have confirmation. Proof. They've hacked our network. Somehow they exploited a hole in the AmericaStrong computer system and worked their way back to us, back to core AFGC systems."

Charles saw the meat of it immediately. "Floor Thirty-Four?"

Jindal shook his head so hard he couldn't speak until he had stopped. "No, that is walled off entirely. But the good—"

"Do they have our nanobot blueprints? Our technical specs?"

"Yes. And they've been looking at this building."

"With an eye to infiltration or attack?" Charles demanded, while Benjamin remained ominously silent.

"No way to tell. But gentlemen, there's good news as well."

Charles raised his eyebrow. Benjamin glowered at Jindal, as if holding him personally responsible. "Good news?"

"The hackers have been hacked in return," Jindal said. He was giddy now, torn between excitement and fear. "We tracked them back and found a way into some of their systems."

"BZRK?"

"No. McLure Labs Security. That's who's been watching us. McLure Security. Presumably at the direction of"—Jindal hesitated, knowing the effect his next words would have on the Twins—"Sadie McLure."

"The little bitch," Benjamin spat.

"Do we know where she is?" Charles asked.

Jindal shook his head, impatient to get to the one remaining piece of good news. "No, nothing directly on BZRK. But we can now track the movements of the main McLure Security folks, and if we follow them, we'll likely find a way back to Plath herself."

"Bah," Benjamin snorted. "No time. They're planning an attack here, that's obvious. We have to hit them hard, now. Now!"

Charles looked queasy, but as Jindal watched, he could see wary acceptance grow on the wiser brother's face.

"We don't have the gunmen we used to, thanks to that disaster in Washington. But we have other means, as you know well. Massed preprogrammed attack," Benjamin said harshly.

Charles smiled faintly at that. He shrugged his shoulder. "Go ahead, Benjamin. You know you've wanted to say it ever since you came up with that name for the drones. Go ahead."

For once Benjamin did not scowl. He smiled. And said, "Locate Stern. And any other important actors in McLure Security. And as soon as you have the location and Burnofsky is ready . . . I will release the Hounds."

TWELVE

Down in the meat.

P2: soulless, mindless biot, Plath's creature, Plath's bizarro-world daughter. P2 zooming across Plath's eye, six legs stroking as Plath had learned to do, like an Olympic speed skater.

The room was dark, shades drawn, door locked, a GO AWAY Post-it note on the door. In the darkness, her eyeball—which in light could look like a frozen lake—looked like some impossibly vast jellyfish, at least here on the white.

Her eyelids—the onrushing "shore" lined with palm trees—looked less benign, more like needle-sharp teeth.

Her eyelid swept over her, rubbing across her biot back, a slight pressure, greater darkness; then it rushed away as though that row of teeth had rejected the tiny meal.

Sadie, you need to ask yourself: Is this you?

That barb stuck. It stuck, and Plath could not shake it off.

Are you really, truly a person planning what would look like a terrorist attack in Midtown Manhattan?

The World Trade Center was falling in her memory, and now there was a musical track to go with it. An old, old song, a Beatles song: "Piggies."

It added a vengeful but playful note to the video atrocity.

How had she felt about that footage the first time she had seen it, back in the classroom? She had been horrified. Sickened. She had always been that way, always capable of being outraged by terrible injustice. In school they had done a unit on World War Two, and as part of that they had done a couple days on the Holocaust. She was not Jewish. She was not part of any group that had been touched by the Holocaust, but she'd been unable to sleep afterward, unable quite to control the sickened hatred of people who could do that to other human beings.

They had watched parts of *Shoah* in class—actual first-person testimony from Holocaust survivors. She remembered vibrating with the suppressed fury she'd felt. She remembered giving up finally on any effort to control the tears.

She still felt that way when she recalled the Holocaust unit. But she no longer felt horrified by the World Trade Center. Now it was . . . what?

Beautiful, is what it was.

Is this you?

Was it really this easy to cross lines that should never be crossed? Had the stress of this unasked-for war of hers, this BZRK existence, simply washed away the part of her that cared about right and wrong?

Or. Or had she had some help?

Is. This. You?

Plath had three biots. She had sent P1 into Anya's brain. It sat now on Anya's optic nerve, looking out through Anya's left eye. It was a window open in Plath's head, showing, at the moment, a bowl of soup, a rough hunk of baguette, and three slices of sausage. Anya's hand lowered a spoon. Raised a spoon. Pause. Lower spoon. Raise spoon. Put down spoon, hands to bread, tear off a hunk, raise it toward mouth.

Plath's final biot, P3, was an enhanced model. Faster, with better sensors, stronger. It was still in the vial attached to a chain around Plath's neck, staring at nothing—a very dull TV show of curved glass wall, and not so much of that in this light.

The line is there . . .

Mr. Stern suspected she'd been caught up in something, and needed some time to think it through more calmly. Plath had different suspicions. Because, yes, she *was* thinking of attacking the Tulip. Guns blazing. Bombs blasting. The image of the Tulip disintegrating, toppling, falling to the ground in fire and smoke was almost . . . almost erotic.

And this was Plath—Sadie—who had refused when she had the chance to kill the Armstrong Twins.

She had left for Île Sainte-Marie feeling betrayed that she'd been trapped into BZRK. Feeling sickened by the violence and by what she had seen and done down in the meat. Now she was ready to launch an actual attack. To kill. To kill innocent people. Why? Was it just because Lear had told her to?

What had changed?

The benign explanation was that she had learned and matured and come to grips with grim necessity. The less benign explanation was that she had become hardened and had lost her soul.

But she feared the truth was a third possibility: that she had been wired.

How and by whom? The obvious suspect was Keats. After all, he had a biot in her brain, ostensibly protecting her from a blown aneurysm.

But why would Keats wire her? Orders from Lear? Or had he gone over to the other side? Both seemed absurd. Keats would not blindly take orders. And he would never join the people who had put his brother Alex in a mental institution.

Unless he had decided that BZRK was to blame. And wasn't that a plausible conclusion? *Wasn't* BZRK responsible, in a way?

She ran down the list of other people who might have done it. Maybe one of the McLure Security guys. Maybe one of the house servants who washed sheets and delivered food. Or maybe someone had gone to work in her brain as soon as she got back to New York. But that would mean whoever was doing it had had very little time. Which in turn meant that someone was very, very good at the job.

Someone.

But the *obvious* suspect?

She was circling the globe, around the eye that twitched beneath her, making all the minute adjustments that eyes must do. She skimmed the edge of her iris-serried ranks of gristly muscle fiber waiting to react to light, opening and closing the dark, deep hole of her pupil.

Down and around, beneath the permanent retraction point of the eyelid, so that her "sky" was now an eternal mucous membrane. Her biot skated on, slowed slightly by the claustrophobically low roof. With absolutely no ambient light, she had illumination switched on— glowing nodes built out of the DNA of exotic deep-ocean creatures.

She was in the land of muscle bundles now, massive cables seemingly fused into the melting ice of the eyeball and ascending into the dark.

And onward, farther around the globe—and now, at last, like Yggdrasil, the tree that supported the world in Norse mythology, the optic nerve rose into view.

Suddenly the world shifted wildly beneath her. Muscles jerked crazily. In the real world, the light had snapped on.

She sat up.

Keats looked at her, saw her surprise, and said, "Sorry, did I startle you?"

"No, no," she lied. "I just . . . there was a Post-it note. . . . Never mind." She could see it lying on the floor of the bright hallway. "Are you coming to bed?"

"Was kind of hoping to," he said, not wolfishly, more just a tired boy.

Plath pulled the blanket back to bare the sheets for him. He nodded at the open space, smiled at it as if it was an old friend. He stripped off his clothes while she lay back and closed her eyes, hoping he would get the message.

She tried to calm her breathing. Keats was in her brain; he would know from the pulse of blood through the aneurysm whether she was perturbed.

Keats was warm beside her. He leaned over to give her the lightest of kisses. Just a brush of lips and a whispered, "Good night."

But to her surprise Plath found herself wanting more. She pushed her fingers through his hair and pulled him close and kissed him back. In the dark, even as she crawled toward her own optic nerve, his lips were just his lips and not a parchment landscape.

He responded.

P2 began the ascent—direction was all very subjective in the meat—began climbing that tree.

He was still holding back, not quite sure whether this kiss was a prelude or just a very nice good-night. She pushed her tongue into his mouth, and now he must feel the way her pulse raced.

Up the nerve, up to the impassable membrane that guarded the brain itself. Her brain. She reared up on her four anterior legs and used the sharp pincers on her front legs to slice as small a hole as possible through the membrane. A watery liquid oozed outward.

She checked herself, inspected as well as she could her biot legs, looking for pollen, bacteria, fungus—all the things which can be so deadly if carried into the brain. She found what looked like a half-dozen tennis balls on her left rear leg and knocked them loose. Bacteria, and very much alive: one was splitting as she watched.

Keats was kissing her now, everywhere. He was no longer responding to her, but moving ahead, taking charge, setting the pace, and for once Plath let him, willingly surrendering, needing to surrender.

Her brain floated like a giant sponge, a sponge crisscrossed with throbbing arteries and veins like the tangle of rivers and tributaries in a delta. The fluid made movement slower than it was in an air environment, and her biot claws had to grab on so as not to float away.

He was inside her. His biot. Down here in these endless folds of pink flesh. At least she hoped he was, hoped he was not on her other eye spying, or worse, far worse, somewhere deeper still, laying wire.

Let it not be him. Not him. That was a betrayal she could not survive.

The tissue that was the ground could appear to be a wall, a floor, or a ceiling, depending on your perspective. The biot world was one where gravity was almost irrelevant, certainly in this liquid environment.

She was aiming for the hippocampus, a deep structure, an ancient part of the evolving brain. It was the router of the mind. If someone was wiring her, that's where they would likely start. The implanted brain-mapping imagery was a guide, though an imperfect one because no two brains were identical, and where she might expect to find a figurative gully could be a plunging valley.

In the real world her body was responding almost on its own, as though it was not connected to her, not connected to the brain upon which she now walked, the brain that was the processor of every contact between his tongue and her flesh.

Madness. She laughed. He stopped.

"No, no, no, don't stop," she said.

"You were giggling."

"Shhhh," she said, and pushed his head back to where it had been.

Toward the hippocampus, but with a stop on the way. She crept her biot forward slowly, slowly, dousing her illuminators one by one, just enough to feel her way forward to—

Light out. In the darkness of her own brain she saw his biot's light. There was his biot, not moving, just standing on the bulging basketwork he had so painstakingly constructed in order to save her life. The work had been started by her father; almost completed now by her lover.

His biot was not wiring her. It was not him.

Far away and as close as the artery that pounded beneath her feet, she felt him, felt his banked power, knew he was close to losing control, and liked that idea a great deal.

She sent her biot forward toward the hippocampus, turning lights back on as she moved away from Keats's biot.

She tripped over it before she saw it. One leg scraped across something that did not feel like flesh, something hard and sharp.

Wire.

Did Keats feel the sudden chill that went through her? He did not slow or falter. But now her mind was reeling, no longer vague and disconnected from her body and its reactions.

She had been wired.

Wait, was that a glimmer of light?

She killed her own biot's light once more and stared hard into the visual field in her brain. Into the visual field that showed her brain to her brain.

There! For just a second. Less than a second. A glimmer of light.

"Bastard," she muttered.

Keats did not hear her, he was beyond that.

The light had come from behind a pulsing vein. There was no innocent excuse. There were no light-emitting life-forms down here.

The fear rose in Plath now, competing with simmering rage. It began as a dull electrical charge in the base of her spine and fanned out from there to become nausea in her stomach and a tightened chest that felt too small to contain her air-starved lungs and pounding heart.

Who was on the other side of that vein, that vein the circumference of a subway tunnel? Who and what was back there?

Bastard, bastard, bastard, she raged, but silently.

Plath stifled her fear, and her biot plunged after the retreating nanobot. She noted that she had decided now that it was an Armstrong nanobot, not a BZRK biot, not Keats, not anyone from her side. Because that—

Wait. When had she acquired this readiness to believe the best of BZRK? Was *that* a naturally occurring thought? Or was it part of the wiring? Was that what this foe was doing right now, right now practically under her nose—finding ways to dampen her suspicion?

Again, a glimmer! It was moving away, but it evidently needed light. So did Plath, so any hope of concealment was forgotten now, any hesitation set aside with the decision to chase.

She saw him! Or at least an impression of something moving. She was gaining on him. Gaining! Which most likely meant it was a nanobot. That at least would be a relief.

Please, God, if there is a God down here in the meat, let it be the enemy, the true enemy.

Suddenly the light ahead dimmed as if it had dropped into a crevasse. She charged ahead, caught up in the chase, adrenaline flooding her system with urgency, breathing hard in her bed, trying to remain perfectly still so as not to wake Keats.

Her biot raced; she saw the dip ahead and killed her illumination, rendering herself almost invisible while using the enemy's light as a beacon.

She looked down, and there it was, waiting for her.

It was no nanobot.

She grabbed Keats's head in her hands and held it still, just inches away from her, stared into his eyes, pleading and said, "Noah, help me. Help me, Noah."

"My Stockholm lair. Yeah. Lair. Because the supervillain needs a lair, yeah?"

It was a nice hotel suite, a very nice hotel suite at the Stockholm Grand. Nice view out over the very civilized waterfront with bright-lit ferries and stately buildings. Multiple bedrooms, understated taupes and beiges and earth tones.

"It's not all that . . ." Bug Man started to say before stopping himself.

"Not so lairlike?" Lystra asked, and laughed. "Well, I have a much better lair somewhere else. Far to the south, you might say. You'll like it . . . if I let you come with me."

Bug Man stood as awkwardly as one might expect a young man to stand when threatened with death.

Lystra laughed again and waved him to a seat. He sat on leather. It made a squeaking sound that might almost have been a fart.

"That was . . . um . . . ," he said.

"Did you just fart in my presence?" She was pretending to look fierce. But Bug Man had seen her true ferocity, and this wasn't it. He relaxed a very little bit.

Lystra went to a sideboard and poured an amber liquid into two heavy crystal glasses. She handed one to Bug Man.

He sniffed and recoiled.

"It's Balcones True Blue. Lovely whiskey, that. Made with Hopi blue corn." She took a single cube of ice with a pair of silver tongs, carried it to him, and dropped it in his glass. "You taste it now. Then you keep drinking as the cube melts, which lowers the proof. The flavor evolves. Each sip will be subtly different."

Bug Man took a sip. It was fire in liquid form, and he started coughing, which made her laugh. It was a cruel laugh, and there, again, a glimpse of the harsh bone beneath soft flesh.

"My father used to let me drink whiskey with him," Lystra said. She sat down opposite Bug Man. He glanced at her bare legs. She noticed.

"You miss your little love slave?" she asked.

"Jessica? You know about . . . that?"

"Yes, of course. You're a rapist, Bug Man."

He flushed. "No, I'm not. I never forced her to do anything."

She leaned toward him, elbows on knees, drink cradled in both hands. "You programmed her. You took away her free will. You replaced it with your own. You enslaved her. And when you have sex with someone in that condition, it's rape."

He shook his head and took a drink just so he'd have an excuse not to meet her gaze.

"Rapist. Murderer. Terrorist. That's you, Bug, by the standards of the wide world, yeah."

Bug Man frowned. No, that wasn't right. "I'm . . . no. No way. I'm a gamer. I'm just playing."

"Buggy, Buggy, Buggy." She patted his knee, and he felt his flesh creep. "If you were charged in a court of law, you'd be looking at life without parole in New York. In Texas, hell, they'd execute you, yeah. Electric chair in Texas? Let me Google that." She pulled out her phone and opened the browser.

Bug Man let loose a weird giggle, and then was appalled by the sound he'd made.

"You're a very bad person. In this world. In this real world the way it is. You're a monster. Don't you know that? Damn! I was wrong." She held up her phone for him to see. "Lethal injection in Texas. The needle. That's such a weak way to die."

"I don't know what you want," Bug Man pleaded.

She didn't answer directly. Then she said, "Drink," and he drank. Then she said, "You didn't listen closely enough. I said 'In this world. In this real world the way it is.' But this isn't the only way the world could be. Is it?"

The whiskey had started a fire in his throat. And now a dangerous warmth spread from his stomach outward. He flicked his eyes up at her. She wasn't stronger than him. She wasn't armed. He could probably smash this heavy glass against the side of her head. Push her out of the window. It was, what, six floors down to the pavement? What did he have to lose if what she said about him was true?

"I sent a text just now," Lystra said.

"So what?"

"So . . . wait. Ticktock. Ticktock, yeah." She smiled. It was almost playful. "Ticky tocky."

"Lady, I think I've had it with your shi—" His mouth still moved, but no sound came out. Because just then a window opened in his brain.

"Mmmm," Lystra said, savoring it.

A second window opened in his brain. A second little TV screen with nothing in view but something that might just be an insect's leg.

"Is the third one up yet?"

A third window. This one showed all too clearly the shape he'd come to know as prey and fear as predator. A biot.

"You ever hear the phrase 'dead man's switch'?"

He had. But he felt as if he couldn't open his mouth. Fear seeped into his blood with icy fingers that outraced the warm glow of alcohol.

"A dead man's switch. They use it on subways and things like that," she explained. "If the subway conductor dies, see, he lets go of the switch and the train automatically stops, yeah. Yeah. That's me now. I'm your own personal dead man's switch. Because if my heart stops beating, guess what?"

When he didn't answer, she bared her teeth, and once again, that skeletal presence seemed to burn through her flesh. "If I die, little Bug Man, all three of your biots . . . oh, and they are *yours* now . . . die as well." She put a fist over her heart, opened it, closed it, opened it, in a mockery of sinus rhythm.

"What do you want?" he screamed, losing the last of his self-control. Then, weeping, softly repeated, "What do you want? What do you want?"

"I'm going to create a new world," she said, sitting back, dreamy now, her eyes gazing toward the French doors and the city beyond. "A whole new world. I am its god. But it's a lonely thing, being god; you could ask the real God, if he existed. He'd tell you. He created the world, and then, he was all alone with no one to talk to. He needed friends. But!" She held up a cautionary finger. "He needed friends who understood who they were, and who he was, and who held the lightning bolts, and who was there to cower and serve. He needed the love that only comes from those who are afraid. Love me, your god, or burn in hell. I'm offering the same deal as Jehovah."

"You're fucking crazy."

He flinched, expecting her to reveal that awful presence again, but instead she laughed a genuine, happy laugh. "Crazy? Nah. I'm BZRK."

THIRTEEN

Keats pulled away from her. "What's the matter?"

"Wire, Noah. Wire in my brain."

It took him a few seconds to make sense of things. "You're down in the meat?"

She nodded—distracted, scared. She pushed him off her and jumped from the bed. She grabbed at clothing. "I knew something . . . I just . . . Something was weird, so I looked."

"Why didn't you tell me? Why didn't you ask me to help?" But even as the words were out of his mouth, he knew the answer. "You thought it was me."

Plath didn't answer, her attention was elsewhere. The biot—if it was a biot, how could it be?—had disappeared, and its light along with it. Plath swung her biot left, right, shining her illumination around in the brain fluid.

Then she saw it: a fountain. Instead of water it sprayed red blood cells, the flattened lozenges that were never supposed to fly loose in the cranial fluid. The artery lay like some massive fire hose, coiled across the surface of the brain. It pulsed obscenely with every beat of her racing heart and the blood cells twirled as they flew, then arced away, scattering through the liquid.

The enemy was cutting into her artery.

"No!" she cried.

"What?" Keats demanded.

"He's cut an artery!"

"Where? Where?" Keats grabbed her shoulders, shaking her, forcing her to pay attention and answer.

"Hippocampus," she said, and Keats sent his biot racing to her.

In Plath's mind she saw the three open windows. Nothing but glass in one. A bleary view from Anya's half-closed eye of the other side of Anya's bed, empty—a slit of light coming from the bathroom. And in the final window that deadly fountain.

She sent her biot racing toward the deadly leak, clambered madly atop the artery and saw her mistake. It was not coming from the artery itself but from a much smaller vein just behind it. Still dangerous, but the pressure was less intense. Still dangerous, still potentially deadly.

And yet, had the foe wanted to kill her, it could certainly have sliced the artery. And there would be more than a few hundred cells flying. He could have done it more than once in the time available. She could right now be swimming through a blood-clouded fluid.

She had nothing to patch the hole. "Bring some fibers," Plath told Keats.

"Yes," he said tersely. He still held her shoulders. She shrugged him off, turned away, ashamed of her suspicions, ashamed to have him know.

Veins were delicate things, unlike arteries, which managed higher pressures. This vein was about as big around as the biot—translucent, like a worm that never sees sunlight—and it undulated as the blood cells jostled and pushed to make their way back to the heart.

Then she saw the bulge. Something larger than blood cells almost too large to squeeze through the vein. The enemy. It had not just punctured the vein as a distraction, it had stretched the cut to crawl inside and escape.

She could stab it right through the sausage-casing walls of the vein. She could probably kill it. But she'd be poking holes in her own vein, and the enemy—who had thus far not done anything as drastic as cut an artery—might get frantic, might start slashing from inside the vein.

"I'm almost there," Keats said.

"I'm going after him," she said, without explaining what she meant.

With her front two biot legs she pried open the elastic flesh of the vein. Blood cells pummeled her face. A white blood cell hit her, rolled down her back, and clung on. It took all her strength to push into the flow, like trying to move uphill against a rockslide.

Halfway in and the pressure shifted. Now it was cells in the vein battering her like dozens of flat stones, pushing her head and upper body after the escaping enemy. She slipped the rest of the way in and fought down the claustrophobia as the vein fitted around her like a body sock. The blood was pushing her along, pushing her toward the distant lungs where oxygen would flow to the cells and they would be fired into arteries for the outward-bound trip.

She could see nothing but blood cells, red and white, crowded all around her. Her hope was that her prey would soon cut his way out and she would be swept along with him.

But if he didn't? If he rode this all the way to the heart and the lungs? She could be lost forever in the miles and miles of blood vessels.

"No!" she said in sudden panic.

"I don't see you yet," Keats said. He had switched on the harsh overhead light so that the two of them, in various states of dress, looked sickly and frightened.

Too late to get back to her entry point, Plath knew; now she would have to cut her own way out. A second bleeder in her brain. God, she was making things worse. A risk of a second blowout that could kill her, weighed against the terror of being lost forever inside her own body.

Soon this vein would merge with another, and then any exit would cause more blood loss. She had to cut her way out now or lose her chance altogether.

She stabbed a claw into the vein wall but almost could not hold on against the pressure. Making matters worse, the cell was on her back, oozing its way like warmed Silly Putty into her shoulders, reducing the mobility of her legs. And another now attached to her left hind leg, a fat slug of a thing wrapping its mindless self around her stick-like limb.

Panic!

She slashed madly at the vein wall, heedless, cut it and felt the blood change speed and direction. Biots are not flexible, so all she could do was use her front legs to cantilever her rear out of the incision.

Suddenly the pressure was too much. Her grip failed. Her biot went tumbling end over end, no way to tell where she was, in or out of the vein.

And then, all at once, she was floating free in cerebral fluid, riding like a beach ball atop a stream of cells. She grabbed onto brain tissue and hauled herself out of the current.

From there at last she could turn around and see the damage she'd done.

The leak was twice as large as the first one. Cells were flying out in threes and fours rather than singly.

With her heart in her throat she grabbed Keats's shoulder.

"Where are you?" she demanded.

Keats took her in his arms and held her as his biot crossed into view bearing a half-dozen fibers to begin the job of yet again saving Sadie McLure from her own blood.

FOURTEEN

It was called the Gyllene Salen, the Golden Hall. It was a vast space—a long rectangle with an impossibly high ceiling, reminding some first-time visitors of a medieval cathedral decorated by Liberace.

All of one long wall was taken up by five arches opening onto a courtyard. The opposite wall was seven arches. And all of it—virtually every square inch—was covered in just under nineteen million pieces of tile, most of them gold. They depicted various characters from Swedish history—kings and saints, for the most part.

Lystra had done her homework and knew all of this. The detail added to the experience. It was a wondrous place and the perfect setting for the annual Nobel Prize ball and banquet.

At this moment on this dark December night, a handful of Nobel laureates, a slightly larger handful of previous Nobel laureates, the family and friends of said laureates, assorted VIPs and kind-of VIPs—amounting, in total, to several hundred people, all in tuxedos and evening dresses—were seated at long banquet tables loaded down with the sort of china and stemware you don't find at Bed Bath & Beyond.

This, thought Lystra, would be the point at which she would have to be very careful for her personal safety. First her immediate, physical safety—because what was coming would be violent. But more to the point, this was where the intelligence agencies of the world would focus like laser beams once the event had . . . well, played out. All the major intel powers—America, China, Japan, the UK, France, Germany, Russia—had prominent citizens here. What was coming would be an event of earthshaking impact. No one cared much what happened to a single actress or a single businessman, and no one would connect any of this to the nosy New Zealand cops who'd had to be eliminated, or to poor, conscience-wracked Nijinsky.

But the self-murder of the president of the United States, and then the sudden fatal "illness" of the Chinese leader, followed by the madness of the Brazilian president, and then this? Even the disaster in Hong Kong. Oh yes: the pennies would begin to drop. The spies and the cops and their ilk would have to be deaf, dumb, and blind not to begin to see a hand behind it all. Right now people were jumpy, worried, on edge, but they still believed the world was just sort of having a bad run of luck.

There was no luck involved. Well, she corrected herself, there was a bit of luck: the blundering Armstrong Twins had unintentionally heralded what was to come. They had provided the fanfare presaging the main event.

The Twins, poor silly buggers, were actually helping her carry out her far superior, far cooler plan.

The thought of them, those hideous freaks, imagining that they were in control. Lystra's lip curled. For a while there had been a freak show with the carnival: a bearded lady, a dwarf who dressed up like a Tolkien character, and a genetically deformed man with hands like lobster claws. They had frightened her then. The bearded lady in particular had tried to be friendly, motherly. The Human Claw, as the lobster-handed man had styled himself, was easier to handle. He just leered, the pervert, until her father had threatened to decapitate him.

Well, let the freaks think they had something. Let the Twins congratulate themselves for killing the president, blundering idiots. The penny would drop for them, too, soon.

"Girls' night tonight, boys," Lystra whispered.

She wondered if Bug Man, back at the hotel, was watching and could see her on TV. She'd told him to, and while he wasn't the obedient type, he *was* the frightened type.

The great thing about tonight was that all the king's horses and all the king's men would never suspect the end goal. They'd be waiting for some kind of blackmail demand. They'd be looking for a rational motive. The fatal weakness of rational people was that they always looked for the rational answer.

The attendees were mostly through the appetizer—a lobster-and-crab terrine with snap pea mousse, brioche, and edible flower *fantasie*—when last year's winner of the Nobel Prize in Literature, Miguel Reynaldo, stopped talking about his younger days when he was a hobo, or traveling minstrel, or whatever it was he thought he was, and stared hard at the Swedish finance minister, a dull middle-aged woman seated across from him.

"I . . . I've just had the strangest . . . But it's still there. I'm seeing . . ."

And at that point the CEO of Spotify said, "Like windows? Like there's windows in your head?"

The two men stared at each other, while those around them formed expressions of polite concern.

"Something is the matter!" This came from a second table, from a past Nobel Peace Prize winner, a man credited with saving many lives through nonviolent means—but he was not now seeming nonviolent. He had lurched to his feet, and in the process he had knocked over his very expensive glass of Champagne and caused his dinnerware to rattle and his chair to scrape.

"*Moi aussi, mais c'est bizarre, ça!*" cried a French industrialist. Then he, too, shoved back from the table as if scalded. He tried to switch to English, but it was a mangled job. "In my head things. I am see."

It spread quickly. There were a dozen tables, hundreds of well-dressed folk, and some of them, far too many of them, were now whispering urgently or shouting hysterically that something was very odd, something was not right in their heads.

"Bloody hell!" the English ambassador cried. "It's some sort of insect. Oh!"

And then versions of that in a dozen languages and multiple accented versions of English. Those not directly affected were rushing to give comfort. People shouted for doctors. The words *food poisoning* were spoken. Others said it was drugs. Someone must have spiked the *crabe et homard* with LSD.

Everyone was talking. The hall was a posh tower of Babel, volume rising, some voices trying to dominate, impose order.

Then came the first true scream. It was a soprano sound, a woman's voice. It began in terror, rose in pitch, roughened, and turned at last into a throaty animal howl.

Lystra closed her eyes and savored it. It went on for a very long time, and a smile split Lystra's face, perfect teeth shining in candlelight.

The room froze, listening, straining to see the source of this delicious scream. Already some were moving prudently toward the exits.

"God fuck you all! God fuck you all!" A deep male voice, but frantic not angry, fearful and repeating the curse over and over as the man backed away from the table, plowed into people with outstretched arms. "God fuck you allllll!"

Now the screams and cries, the roars and shouts and canine yelps broke loose in full.

Miguel Reynaldo was laughing and howling like some demented hyena, mouth so wide open it seemed his jaw must dislocate. He dug his fingernails into his face, down his forehead and cheeks, leaving bloody trails behind. Then he threw himself onto the table, twisted onto his back, shrieking all the while, kicking dinnerware and baskets of bread and glasses of sparkling water in every direction, like some great toddler having the mother of all tantrums.

And that's when things turned really ugly. Because someone—later identified as a Finnish philanthropist—came up behind the Swedish minister of finance and cut her throat ear to ear with a table knife.

And when she had sunk to the floor—gurgling, dying, spraying crimson across white linen—he kept sawing away, brushing aside her weak defensive efforts, sawing away at her trachea.

Panic!

The screams were general now as people rushed to the exits,

crushed into one another in their desperate desire to get the hell out of that room, but not all those in the crowd were behaving normally. A past Nobel laureate for physics had stripped off his clothing and was peeing on anyone within reach.

Lystra, too, began to scream and wave her hands in the air. And she grinned, widely, not only because that's what would be expected of a madwoman, but also because it was all just so wonderful.

"I bring you madness!" she yelled, and laughed, but kept a careful eye on all around her as she backed toward the nearest exit.

Back in the center of the room a man later identified as one of the world's great scientific minds was squatting on a table defecating, while around him madmen and madwomen screamed and threw things, attacked one another with cutlery and broken glass, clawed their own eyes, or simply huddled in corners yelping at imaginary spirits.

"Madness!" Lystra yelled as she reached the door.

In the space of five minutes the Nobel banquet had become a blood-splattered insane asylum.

Would Bug Man appreciate it? Would he get it? Probably not. Buggy was useful for some things, not for others. He would not be enough to occupy her own Eden. Someone smarter would be good. Someone more subtle. Someone who would chafe even more and thus be even more completely subjugated in the end.

Sadie McLure. God, the irony would be wonderful.

Not everyone was driven mad at the Golden Hall. Most were not, though it was hard to differentiate them as they ran from the hellscape splattered with blood.

Lystra Reid's gown—Prada, very chic—was already red, so the blood didn't show. However, her shoes—Christian Louboutin pumps—were absolutely ruined.

But she could not resist, as she fled the room, crying out in her pretended madness: "'As flies to wanton boys, are we to the gods. They kill us for their sport.'"

Thus did Lear quote from *King Lear* as she kicked off her shoes and ran barefoot into the cold night, laughing and twirling as snowflakes fell.

FIFTEEN

Keats handed Plath a cup of coffee. Her hands were shaking. It was morning and she'd had no sleep. They stood in the kitchen, Keats in some soccer team jersey and sweatpants; Plath in an unattractive sweater, panties, and socks.

"It's plugged. The big one." Keats sipped his own coffee and looked at her over the rim as he took a second sip.

"What?" She was confused for a moment, thinking he was talking about the coffee.

"The second hole. It's plugged. I don't think it was all that dangerous, anyway, but I've patched it, the lymphocytes are keeping it clean, and I can see clotting factor forming nicely."

"Thanks." She sent him a very serious look and added, "I don't say that enough, do I? Thanks."

"Hungry?"

She considered it. "Yes, I am."

"I'll fry some eggs and bacon. No bangers, I'm afraid. You Americans don't really do sausages very well."

"You can cook?"

He made a small laugh. "Oddly enough, I don't actually live at

Downton Abbey." Then, thinking that may have sounded resentful, he smiled and touched her shoulder. "I learned a bit of this and that. Enough to fry an egg and make toast. If we have bread." He searched the cupboards. "Yes, we do have bread. But no beans or tomato."

"Beans?"

He sighed. "The thing you Americans so proudly think of as breakfast is a sad affair compared to a proper full English breakfast. Eggs, bacon, toast, black pudding, mushrooms, beans, and a nice grilled tomato. And coffee, of course, unless you prefer tea."

"Black pudding?"

"Given your adventures tonight, it's maybe best not to discuss black pudding."

"No?"

"It's also called blood sausage."

"Ah. Yeah. Enough blood."

He set a rectangular grill on the cooktop and turned on the fire. He peeled strips of bacon from the package and started the flame beneath a sauté pan. In seconds the bacon was sizzling, and both the familiar sound and aroma made Plath's mouth water.

"Were you going to tell me?" he asked, once he had things organized and under way.

She stalled for a moment by sipping her coffee. She didn't have to tell him. But he had possibly just saved her life.

"I was planning an armed attack. I was planning to kill people. I met with Stern, without you. I asked him for . . . and he said . . ." She sighed, lost momentarily. "I never really asked myself whether it was the right thing. I have this picture in my head. . . ." She let that sentence peter out, not willing, still, to tell him everything. Not the things that would make him despise her.

He nodded. "You started to suspect you'd been wired." He sighed, turned the bacon, pushed the toast down, and used his spatula to keep the eggs from spreading out. "And you didn't tell me because you thought I might be the one doing it."

"It's the world we're in, isn't it?" she asked.

He nodded. "It's the world we're in."

"But it wasn't you." She took his hand, which after a few seconds he took back to press the spatula down on the bacon.

"Which leaves who?" he asked.

She glanced toward the door, wondering if anyone was on the other side listening. "Wilkes. Billy. Maybe even Vincent, maybe that affectless thing he's doing is just camouflage. Or it's someone else with BZRK, someone not from our group. We're just a part of it, after all."

"You're sure it was a biot, not a nanobot?"

She played the memories back. "Not a hundred percent." She tried out various values in her head. "Seventy percent sure. But if I'm planning on blowing up, um, attacking the Tulip . . . the Armstrongs wouldn't be doing that; they wouldn't be wiring *me* to kill *them*."

He served the food onto two plates, and they sat at the counter and ate, side by side, leaning so that their shoulders would touch.

Finally Keats spoke. "If you were wired, why? I mean, what you're pointing to are kind of, I don't know, moral changes."

"Have you noticed anything different with me?" she asked, afraid of the answer and covering it with transparently false nonchalance.

He thought it over while chewing bacon. "You're questioning Lear and BZRK less. I mean, maybe it's just that you've got more responsibility. But you used to be more suspicious, I guess. More critical."

She thought about that. "Yeah, maybe so.

"I'll help you look for wire."

Plath hesitated and felt herself blush. She filled her mouth with egg. If she was still wrong, if somehow Keats was the person running the biot, or at least knew about it, then he would never find any wire. It could be a way to determine his loyalty. If he found—

She cut herself off in midthought as reality dawned: there was no way to determine loyalty. Ever. Keats might be loyal today and some nano creature of either side might be wiring him to switch sides tomorrow.

"It's still inside me," she said. "Maybe it's trapped in my liver or whatever, but it's still in me." She nodded and wiped her mouth, then set her plate in the sink. "Yes," she said decisively. "The aneurysm will keep. Help me look for wire. I want to know where it all is. And help me kill this thing, whatever and whoever it is."

"And pull the wire?"

She didn't answer. She didn't answer for so long that Keats thought she must not have heard him.

"And pull the wire?" he repeated, more insistently this time.

She shook her head. "Not yet, Noah."

After that she wouldn't look at him.

The other person making an interesting discovery was Imelda Suarez. *Lieutenant* Imelda Suarez, dammit. Hopefully there was an extra paycheck to come with that.

The *Celadon*, the mother ship, had dropped anchor six miles out from Cathexis Base, hundreds of miles from McMurdo. The ice was thick and crusty here, and no way the ship could edge up to the dock, not for another month at least. She had gone ashore in the *Jade Monkey*, running easily up onto the beach and roaring along until the LCAC found its home, a hangar and refit facility they all called the Blower Barn.

As soon as she'd done the inevitable paperwork, Suarez headed toward the Office—the administrative building. Things at Cathexis Base tended to be named simply, usually by function, but with an occasional touch of wit: the Blower Barn, the Chiller (a poorly heated dorm), the Toasty (the newer, warmer dorm), the Club, the Link (the satellite dishes), the Office.

In the center of the base, acting as a sort of central park, was a glass dome raised up on a skid-mounted platform. It was seldom transparent—condensation saw to that—but it clearly housed green, living things, ranging from small elm trees to tall grasses to irises and roses. But for the most part the Andalite Dome, or AD, as it was called for some obscure reason, was more practically planted with cabbages, broccoli, romaine lettuce, carrots, and onions.

The produce wasn't anything like enough even to feed Cathexis Base, but it helped, and it was the place to go when you felt the ice start to close in on you.

As Suarez did now. Seeing the smudge of green inside the sweat-dripping bubble, she felt herself drawn to it, and decided checking in at the Office could wait. Getting into the dome was a process—you had to shed your gear and walk in wearing a T-shirt and pants alone. And you had to pass through a double airlock.

It was while in the airlock that she ran into Charlie Bronk.

"Coming or going?" he asked her.

"Just got in," she said. Bronk was a small man with a too-tough name. He was a mechanic who often worked with Suarez. They weren't friends, but they were cordial.

"I'm supposed to head out to Forward Green," he said. "One of their cats is wonky, needs a new fuel injector."

"There's no one out there can do it?"

Bronk laughed. "At Forward Green? Pff. Those are scientists and God knows what all out there. Sally Wills is the only one can turn a screwdriver, and she's on an evac to Wellington." He lowered his voice. "A psych thing. She lost her shit."

"Damn. Sally Wills? The redhead?"

Bronk nodded. "I don't suppose . . . I mean, I wouldn't ask, but it's my son's bar mitzvah and I'm missing it. I was going to Skype."

"You can't Skype from Forward Green?"

"There's no communication in or out of Forward except to here. Security."

She was on the verge of asking him why there would be secrecy, but thought better of it. That was the kind of question that might be thrown in your face some day if there was a problem. Cathexis Inc. might not be military, but when it came to secrecy, they sometimes went the military one better.

"I could do it," Suarez said with a shrug. "Of course you'll owe me. And I don't mean you cover for me on cleanup. I mean something more like you pull a shift. Three shifts."

They agreed on one shift and a round of clean-up duty. And that was how Suarez ended up on a loud chopper heading almost due south. It was a hellish ride. The wind had come up. In fact, at the halfway point the pilots discussed turning back. Antarctic weather wasn't something you took risks with.

But satellite imagery gave them a nominally clear hour before the hammer came down, so they went forward.

If Cathexis Base was businesslike and humane, Forward Green was a bizarre cross between survivalist compound and Ritz-Carlton resort. From the frosty window of the chopper she could see that the buildings were arranged in a sort of diamond around what was very certainly the only swimming pool on the continent. The pool was covered of course, and as sweaty as the Andalite Dome at Cathexis Base. It was an ostentatious symbol of wealth, because water—actual, liquid water—was one of the rarest and most expensive of commodities. It spoke of a profligate use of power—the heat to keep the pool warm, the light to make it shine, the lift capacity to bring it all together in this place.

It was built aboveground, of course—the shifting ice would have crushed anything cut into it. It was covered by a plastic roof that formed three peaks, vaguely reminiscent of the Sydney Opera House.

Suarez guessed that the power source had to be a nuclear reactor. But how had that been approved? The green movement had made peace with nuclear power, but here? On the *ice*? And in private hands?

Once she'd looked beyond that eye-popping artifact of another world, Suarez took in the rest of the place. The buildings were identical—seven three-story ski-mounted structures, with an empty slot where an eighth building might go someday.

The windows aimed out toward the ice were small, with metallic shutters that could be mechanically closed against the wind. The windows facing in, toward the pool, were larger than anything she'd ever seen before in energy-conscious Antarctica. Though they, too, were equipped with strong steel shutters.

She imagined what the place would look like locked down, with all those shutters closed. And then she noticed the four half-buried towers two hundred yards out from each point on the diamond.

"I'll be damned if those aren't gun emplacements," she muttered. Not that she saw anything like weapons.

A mile away to the south and barely visible because the wind was now blowing crystals of ice through the air was a larger structure— long, low, and unadorned—that could only be some sort of hangar.

That's where the souped-up hovercraft would be.

It hit her then full force: they didn't have anyone who could fix a fuel injector? At a facility where they were building jet-powered hovercraft? Bullshit.

She hadn't cleverly exploited an opening to reach Forward Green: she'd been lured there.

Lystra and Bug Man left Stockholm not by way of Arlanda Airport but by car, to a private airfield fifty miles out of town, out into the landscape of snow and dark pine trees.

Bug Man had only a light parka that George had supplied, in no way sufficient to deal with a Swedish winter. The run from the car to the welcoming light of the jet was enough to freeze him, but Lystra seemed indifferent, still wearing her blood-drenched red dress—though she had swapped her shoes for a pair of shearling boots. *She would look almost cute,* Bug Man thought, *if she were younger. And a whole lot less insane.*

It was warm on the plane, which took off within minutes of the door closing, soaring up into the night.

"Look!" Lystra said, and drew him out of his seat to look through the window on her side.

The sky was an eerie light show, green against black, the stars all rendered irrelevant. The green was a veil, translucent, shimmering.

"Aurora borealis," Lystra said. "The northern lights." She nodded. "We get them in the south sometimes, too. You'll see."

Bug Man watched for a while, acutely aware of her nearness. Crazy, yes. Too old for him, yes. Still . . .

She must have sensed it because she laughed, an almost girlish sound, and pushed him back to his seat.

But then she stood up, turned her back to him, and said, "Help me with the zipper."

Bug Man swallowed hard. Okay, yes, he'd thought about it. But seriously? With a woman who had his sanity and life in her hands? He'd watched the TV as instructed, and he had seen the Nobel madness. He had even seen a fleeting shot of Lystra dancing and twirling away from the carnage.

God only knew what the woman would do to him if he disappointed her.

He drew the zipper down. It snagged halfway and he had to tug at it for a bit, all the while with his nose just inches from her back.

Most of what he could see was tattooed. Blues and reds and greens.

He couldn't make out the patterns, except that most of it seemed to be faces. He saw eyes staring, mouths twisted in screams.

"Damn," he whispered, and winced, hoping she hadn't heard.

"You like my ink?"

"Uh, yeah," he said too quickly.

"Want to see more? Want to see my latest one?"

He froze. Just absolutely froze. She let her dress fall to the floor.

"Oh . . . shit," he said. There were faces on her back, on her behind, on her flanks. Not every inch was covered—maybe half of the available flesh.

More than enough. It was a horror show.

Faces. Men, women, one that might even be a child. All in agony or rage or some combination of the two.

He couldn't breathe. He did not want to see more. He did not want her to turn around.

But she did.

Slowly, slowly; savoring his fear, the fear she could hear in his raspy breathing, in the way it caught in his throat.

Her front was even more horrific. Faces from hell were staring out at him. Two were new, still healing.

She pointed to the freshest-looking one with a coyly bent finger. She was being cute. She was playing with him. But oh, God, there was no way to fake this, no way for him to force his features into anything like a pleasing expression.

"That's a man named Janklow. He didn't want to sell me his medical testing company. Because of him, yeah, the whole game was delayed."

Her breasts were just inches from him. Her eyes were the eyes of a rabid dog, focused on him with an intensity that made him tremble.

"Don't you want to know who they all are?" she asked, and the hard, sadistic voice he'd heard before had replaced the cute come-hither tone.

He managed to shake his head. No. He didn't have a single question. No, he didn't want to know. He wanted to be back in England. He wanted to be back at Tesco, shopping for his mother's onions. His fists were clenched so tight they ached.

"Sure, you want to know," she said. "These are all the ones whose lives I have taken from them."

"That actress? Do you remember, yeah? You must have read about it, seen it on TV? She dug her own eyes out with a knife. It was intense, Bug Man, very intense." She tapped the other still-healing tat, on her sculpted hip bone. America's Sweetheart in blue ink, bleeding red blood from her gouged eyes.

"What did she—"

"What did she do? Oh, she wouldn't even remember, didn't recognize me at all, why would she? I was in a hospital for a while for . . . stress?" She threw her head back and laughed. "Stress? I was crazy as a loon."

Was? Past tense? Bug Man wanted to ask. But not as much as he wanted to go on living.

"My pap and mam, that's what they had me call them. My guardians." She spit the word. "The losers my daddy dumped me on. They started talking to me after I killed them." She covered each breast with a hand, lifted them slightly so he could see the faces tattooed there. They appeared to have been crushed. Their eyes were . . .

"They would talk to me. 'Be a good girl, Lyssie. Pray to the Lord for strength, Lyssie.' Sometimes though, they would give me useful business advice." She frowned at the memory, then thankfully she turned away, walked to a narrow closet, and pulled out jeans and a sweatshirt. The sweatshirt was green with a big letter *C* over an outline of Antarctica.

Bug Man breathed a shaky sigh of relief. Ugly sweatshirt, but so much better than looking at that torture chamber on her body.

"I went crazy, yeah. Into the nuthouse with me. I was rich by then, had my businesses going pretty good, but yeah, off the deep end, yeah. Meds did nothing; they still talked to me."

Your conscience, you sick bitch, Bug Man thought.

"Not my conscience," she said, for all the world as if he'd said it out loud. He had to resist the urge to cover his mouth with his hand lest he say something to get himself killed.

"Psychotic break. Not functional. Everything falling apart . . . and he came back. Daddy. He said he would if it came to it, if, you know . . . if. I guess he thought I might eventually get weirded out over his killing my mother. Drink?"

She poured them each several fingers of bourbon. Bug Man gulped his down. He needed to pee desperately, but this was so not the time to ask to be excused.

"Nuts, yeah. So back he came, my daddy. And he said, 'I know about this man, this scientist. He's doing some weird stuff with nanotechnology. Maybe he can help. Only he refused, you see, and Daddy couldn't kill him and neither could I, because, well, he was protected."

"Burnofsky?"

"Burnofsky?" She shook her head. "But good guess. No, it was

Grey McLure. He was just starting—freaking out over his wife dying and he couldn't save her with his new toys. Then his daughter and the aneurysm, yeah. Yeah. People went crazy, though, see? Off this new thing he'd invented. This *biot!*"

The word came out in a roar that made Bug Man jump back.

"This biot. So, maybe, yeah, maybe if a dying biot would make a sane person crazy, hey. Maybe, right? Yeah? Maybe the other way, too."

"Jesus. They gave you a biot."

She nodded. "Yeah. Yeah. My very own. And then they killed it. And you know what? It worked. It *worked.* I wasn't crazy anymore."

The hell you weren't, Bug Man did not say.

"The tattoos stopped talking to me. I could cope, yeah. I could manage. Making tons of money. And then I saw it—saw the game. Saw the way I could do it. Make a whole new world, yeah."

She fell silent then, staring down into her drink.

Bug Man stood on wobbly legs and went to the bathroom. In the glaring fluorescence he stared at his own face as if staring at a ghost. He was shaking. He felt an urge to sit down and empty his bowels, but who knew what the crazy woman would do?

Oh, that's right, he told himself. *Not crazy. No, she was all cured.*

He peed and washed his hands, and having used up all his stalling tactics went back out.

Lystra Reid had not moved a muscle.

He sat down.

And unprompted she said, "Oh, and the actress? Sandra Piper? Bitch cut me off in traffic."

ARTIFACT

Plath: I need Caligula.

Lear: Name the place.

SIXTEEN

The news was all about the Nobel madness. Twenty-four hours a day. MSNBC, Fox, CNN.

Only the BBC made a connection to the bizarre case of the New Zealand cops.

Only the Web site Buzzfeed made a connection between the Nobel madness and the inexplicable suicide of Sandra Piper.

Everyone, though, connected it to the bizarre death of the American, Chinese, and Brazilian heads of state.

Fear was spreading. A sharp observer would already be able to spot a wariness in people's eyes and in their words. There was a feeling in the air.

Fear. Like the scent of smoke. Like the distant rumble of tank engines and clanking tracks. Like sirens in the night.

The theories about the cause were: food poisoning, mass hysteria, and some sort of terrorist attack using a form of nerve agent.

Only Cracked.com actually listed nanotech on its "8 Ways to Explain the Big Brain Meltdown."

There were several loops of footage that ran more or less continuously online and on TV. One was a cell-phone video of a scene of madness from inside the Golden Hall. A second showed a blood-stained woman in a party dress rushing from the hall amid a panicked crowd, then suddenly launching herself at a passing woman and biting savagely into her neck. Another showed a former American secretary of state waving madly at invisible flying enemies.

Of course there were also clips of the new president looking solemn and vowing to give the Swedish government any assistance they required. Ditto footage of the British prime minister, the French president, and a long list of folks who had no idea what was going on, all vowing to get to the bottom of it.

Rye ergot. That was the first guess. Rye ergot, a disease caused by fungus that grows on some foods and can cause symptoms similar to an LSD overdose.

Tests for rye ergot were all negative.

"Just like Nijinsky," Keats said. "It's all connected." He was watching the BBC coverage. "It's all the same bloody thing, isn't it."

He was talking to no one. Plath was out, and though a part of Keats was with her—sitting on his hands, waiting for a cue—he felt alone. Abandoned. Both here and there. Both large and small. Slumped into his chair and on edge, ready for a race. Not for the first time, he wondered mordantly what he had to fear from madness. Wasn't this already madness?

Billy was absorbed in a video game. Vincent was there, staring, almost forgotten by Keats.

Keats sat before the television, watching through his two eyes, and seeing the windows in his head, watching from other eyes. "It's all one. But who?"

The voice when it spoke surprised him. What the voice said was chilling.

"Lear," Vincent said.

Keats turned to look at him. He was still showing nothing, Vincent. A blank expression, sad eyes. Only his brow seemed to speak of any emotion; if tension can be called an emotion.

"Lear?" Keats said. "Not the Armstrong mystery weapon?"

"Games," Vincent said, as though that word should mean everything and the saying of it had exhausted him.

Keats couldn't quite think of what to say. On the one hand, this was Vincent. On the other hand, this was mad Vincent. Shattered Vincent.

Seventy percent Vincent.

"You want anything to eat?" Keats asked. "I was thinking of ordering Chinese."

"Did Lear just see it?" Vincent mused, ignoring Keats. "Or has he known all along? Should I ask him?" There was something almost like a smile on Vincent's lips. "There will be more."

Keats might have pursued it, but a few thousand feet away, his much smaller self saw that the moment was fast approaching. He readied himself to confront the lion in his den.

With Nijinsky dead, Burnofsky was off his leash. He had no way of knowing this—not yet—but there was no longer a biot in his head. Or to be more accurate, there was still a biot attached to his optic nerve, but no one was peering through those biot eyes any longer. The biot had no real brain of its own, nor did it have instincts. It continued to live, but only to live. Immobile.

Burnofsky had a Post-it note. He wrote on it: *Floor 34. Viral research.*

He held this note up in front of his eyes. Held it there for far longer than it should take to read it. But he guessed that whoever was running the biot in his head—and he believed it was Nijinsky—would not be focused on his every moment.

He was careful in the way he did this because Burnofsky knew perfectly well that his lab was under surveillance. He had come to accept that fact. Privacy was dead, anyway, particularly if you worked for the Armstrongs. But he knew the camera locations and angles. Sometimes he forgot—he had a worrying sense that his little self-inflicted wound of the other day might have been observed.

Well, the Twins had seen worse, hadn't they? They'd seen him puking his guts out. He was morally certain that they'd been watching one dark night months earlier, back before he'd been wired, when he had sat for twenty minutes with a loaded pistol in his hand trying to get up the nerve to put the barrel in his mouth and pull the trigger.

So what was a little cigarette burn, eh? Better than the opium pipe, right? Better than the vodka bottle. He wasn't drinking now, not that he'd made some lifelong decision to quit; he just wasn't drinking right now. Or snorting coke. Or smoking opium.

No, he was all cleaned up. He laid the Post-it note down in the ashtray in front of him, shielding it with his body from the hidden camera. Then he began to light a cigarette and in the process burned the note to ashes.

He drew in the smoke of his cigarette and wondered if he would get to the end of it without burning himself.

The burning was—

"Shit," he muttered. Nijinsky would think it was a reference to a *computer* virus. He wouldn't understand that Floor 34 was a crash program involving actual viruses. *Biological* viruses.

Burnofsky had only stumbled upon the information by chance. He was hiring a new engineer and happened to speak to one of the people in human resources, who smiled, told him he had plenty of available engineers, and thank God at least Burnofsky wasn't looking for a virologist.

Virologist. A scientist specializing in viruses, of course. And why was anyone at Armstrong Fancy Gifts Corporation working on biologicals of any kind?

It had to be Floor 34. Burnofsky knew most of what AFGC was into, he should have known about a biological nano program of any sort. Were they working on their own version of biots? Were they preparing to toss his nanobots aside? The possibility worried Burnofsky a bit.

As always when he was anxious, his thoughts went to opium, and then to his work, and then to Carla. And from there to the Great Forbidden Memory.

Burnofsky knew exactly what they had done to his brain. He knew. He was a scientist; he had wired many a person, done to others what had now been done unto him. He knew that tiny wires in his brain had been used to create shortcuts—sending thoughts around the usual circuitous neural pathways to hook into the most intense sensations.

In other words, he knew that Nijinsky had connected memories of his daughter's death to pleasure centers. He knew Nijinsky had made his greatest guilt into a sick and disturbing fantasy. He knew that. He could picture the wire in his own brain. He could imagine just how Nijinsky had done it.

But that changed nothing. It did not stop the physical reaction when he thought of that most awful of days.

I killed her.

And I'm thrilled.

At first he had thought of using his own nanobots to go in and rewire himself. But of course Nijinksy would see him. Burnofsky could take Nijinsky's biot—Burnofsky wasn't quite Bug Man or Vincent when it came to nano warfare, but he was confident that he could outfight Nijinsky.

But somehow . . . No.

Somehow the will to fight back always seemed to dissipate.

Was this still more wiring? Probably. If so, it was effective. He would form the desire, formulate a plan, start to get his resources in order, and then, then, then something. . . . It would all just leak away.

The answer was no. He would not finish this cigarette by putting it out in the ashtray.

He took one long, final pull on the cigarette butt—it was down to the last inch—lifted his shirt, and stabbed it into his stomach.

The pain was staggering. The smell of burned flesh was like opium, somehow, a narcotic that turned the pain into a dream, a swirling unreality.

And most of all, it took his mind off Carla. Because despite all of Nijinsky's careful work, Burnofsky felt that if he had to endure that horror-excitement one more time, he would find his gun and finally do it.

The HNDS—hover-capable nanobot deployment system—or "Hounds" were roughly triangular in shape and no bigger than a paper airplane.

The original drone architecture was under development for the U.S. military and the CIA. Stealthy, relatively quiet, wonderfully maneuverable, their only real drawback was that their range was limited to twenty miles. The military wanted a seventy-five-mile range, and the CIA weren't interested unless they could be flown at distances up to five hundred miles.

So the drones—once designated the hover-capable surveillance system (HOSS)—had been repurposed. Twenty miles might not quite be the thing for the soldiers or the spies, but it was perfectly adequate for use in massed preprogrammed attack by nanobots.

The Hounds came for Mr. Stern as he was picking up his morning bagel at Montague Street Bagels in Brooklyn. It was a short walk from his home, and the McLure Security car and driver would be waiting across the street.

There were twenty thousand self-replicating nanobots aboard the Hound piloted remotely by a tech in the bowels of the Tulip. The Twins watched on their eternal monitor. The nanobots themselves were of course not twitcher run. They had been programmed by the Twins via the app. These nanobots had been given a simple set of instructions: to multiply as soon as they encountered a source of carbon. To continue to do so for exactly forty minutes. Then to commit mechanical suicide and stop.

As Stern was crossing the sidewalk the Hound swept down Henry Street before executing a sharp right onto Montague.

Stern bit into his bagel. The cream cheese oozed from the sides and he licked a dollop before it could fall away.

And then he heard something strange. Like a ceiling fan, but with blades going very fast. He even felt the downdraft and looked up to see its source. The Hound was just six feet over his head.

The nanobots fell in a cloud, like dust.

Stern ran to the car, still clutching the bagel. The driver saw him, started to jump out to open the door for him, then saw the urgency on Stern's face, so just released the lock and started the engine.

Stern reached the door just as he began to feel a burning sensation on his scalp.

He piled into the car and yelled, "Some kind of drone!"

The driver turned around and blanched visibly. "Jesus, boss! Your head!"

Stern reached past the driver and yanked down the visor mirror. In the narrow rectangle he saw that his scalp was red with blood.

"Drive!" Stern shouted. "To McLure Labs!"

"What's happening?" the driver cried.

Stern tried to answer, but at that moment the nanobots had chewed through his cheek and were tearing into his molars, and the sound that came out of the security man was not decipherable as anything but a cry of agony.

The driver yanked the car into traffic, leaned on the horn, and forced his way past a parked UPS truck.

SEVENTEEN

Caligula found himself almost nervous. How strange. Plath was just a girl, after all.

He remembered the first time he had really met her, in a small but vicious battle at the Tulip. He'd liked her. He'd thought he saw some inner strength in her, but it had never occurred to him that she would end up running the New York cell of BZRK. Vincent had seemed bulletproof—an odd concept for Caligula to think of. But Vincent really had seemed indestructible.

For a while after Nijinsky's fall from grace Caligula thought Lear might place the burden of leadership on him. But no. Of course not. Caligula had his purpose in life, and it was not shepherding a gaggle of kids. He was useful to Lear, but only as a killer. And less and less useful at that. Lear had found other ways.

Nijinsky, poor bastard. A clean bullet would have done the job. No need for what he endured. No need for that cruelty.

He wondered what Plath would ask of him. Would she ask for his help in bringing Burnofsky in so that he could be infested with a new biot?

He hoped she would not ask him about Lear.

But of course she asked about Lear.

"It seems absurd to call each other Caligula and Plath," Plath said.

Plath had picked the meeting place, and she was waiting for him when he arrived. It was public but not: a dark booth in a dark bar. It was against the law for her even to be sitting here across from him. But there was a law for regular minors and then there was a very different law for minors who could hand a fistful of hundred-dollar bills to a concerned bartender.

It amused Caligula that she had even found this place. It was classically male, a dive bar in a pricey Manhattan neighborhood. An easy walk from the safe house, which showed caution. After all, Sadie McLure had changed her hair, but she could still be recognized if a paparazzo spotted her. She had minimized the odds of that. Smart girl.

He took in the surroundings as he did every few minutes, checking for changes in personnel, in position and posture. There were a couple of hipsters at the bar imagining themselves as latter-day Kerouacs. A tired-looking woman who was almost certainly a hooker. Three loud businessmen saying things like, "So I told him, 'That is not something I'm comfortable with.' I mean, maybe he doesn't give a shit, but I do." After a few more drinks they'd be complaining about their wives and their kids.

But that's not who Caligula watched out of the corner of his eye. It was a woman, thirty-five maybe, in an inexpensive business suit with slacks, sensible shoes, and khaki raincoat. She had brown hair cut short, but not so short as to be fashionable. She ordered something he didn't overhear but that caused the bartender to look wary. It came clear and fizzy in a tall glass: sparkling water.

If she wasn't some kind of cop, she was doing a very good impression of one. She confirmed the impression by avoiding looking at Caligula. It was a fact of life that any normal person would look at him.

Had it come to this? Were even the cops on the trail? It was one thing being shadowed by Armstrong people and by Plath's security people. It was a different matter entirely when secrecy was so compromised that FBI or intelligence or even NYPD were watching.

Things were coming to an end. One way or the other. But wasn't that what Lear wanted?

"It does seem ridiculous," Caligula allowed.

"Call me Sadie."

"Call me Caligula."

That earned him a wintry smile.

He did not lean toward her. He had not shaken her extended hand—she would understand why. Caligula might be a part of BZRK in his own way, but you simply did not trust people armed with biots. A fleeting touch was all it took to send the tiny little beasties toward his brain.

He was nursing a beer in a tall, sweating mug. He casually dragged the mug across the table, left to right, leaving a trail of water behind. A barrier to the tiny bugs.

"I never thanked you. For that first time." Plath nodded at him, a regal move that seemed natural for her. "You saved our lives."

"You're welcome," he said. And waited.

"I need you," she said.

"For?"

"Lear wants the computer servers in the Tulip destroyed."

"They'll have backups."

She shook her head. "We don't think so. They're so paranoid they keep several systems cut off from one another. We've had access to many of their networks, but some of their computers are entirely unreachable from the outside. No Internet links at all. No phone lines. They might as well be something out of the 1980s."

He nodded, accepting this as a likely fact. "It's a large building. They are well guarded. This is not a movie; I could not do it alone, or do it even with your people."

"How *could* you do it?"

"By destroying the entire building."

She stared at him. He watched her eyes. Interesting. Her pupils had expanded. A pleasure reaction. But then her eyes had narrowed, and she had drawn away. Of course: she was conflicted.

"Destroying . . ."

"There will be natural gas pipelines in the basement. If you were to fill some of the sublevels with that gas and ignite a spark, it would very likely collapse the entire structure."

"Like . . ."

"Like what, Sadie?" He knew like what. He had a pretty good idea what was being done to her. He could guess Lear's direction. But he wanted Sadie to say it.

"Like the World Trade Center. Like 9/11."

"Yes," Caligula said. "We could obliterate the building itself. It would kill everyone inside. Which is what you would want, Sadie.

You would *want* all the scientists in there to die. It would set back nanobot technology several years at least. It would be the practical end of Armstrong Fancy Gifts. By the time they recovered, someone else would have developed the same capacity. Someone perhaps a bit less . . . visionary?"

There was a TV on over the bar. It showed what every screen in the world was showing: the Nobel madness. Cut to the American president's suicide. Back to the Nobel madness. Cut to the Brazilian president.

Plath was shaking her head. "No."

"If you destroy the servers and let the scientists walk away—"

"It's not just scientists in that building. There are regular people. Clerks and janitors and people who just answer the phones." She was pleading with him to find a different answer.

"It would be mass murder. It would make you one of the greatest terrorists in history." He watched her eyes. She was repelled. She was sickened. But she was not surprised. So that idea had definitely already occurred to her.

And she did not get up and walk away.

Jesus Christ, Caligula thought, this *is the new way, the new reality.* Sixteen-year-old girls could be made into terrorists. They could be wired for mass murder.

Plath, for her part, could see it in her imagination. She could see that phallic monstrosity of a building collapsing into the fire that raged at its base.

My God, she thought, *it* could *be done.*

"We can't do that," she said. To emphasize her point, she reached most of the way across the table and pounded it with her index finger. "There have to be limits. There's a line."

"Do there? Is there?"

The table was lacquered wood. To Keats's biot eyes, it was a bit like an aerial map of someplace like Afghanistan. There were steep, deep valleys below formed by the grain of the wood. But filling in those valleys was the smooth lacquer finish. The result was a feeling like skimming along over mountains, flying at the height of the peaks.

The great problem with biots moving over large distances—distances measured in centimeters or meters rather than millimeters—was finding your way. A biot's view of the macro world was fuzzy and distorted.

Caligula felt safe on his side of the table. There were two feet separating his arm, resting on the edge of the table, from Plath's arm on the opposite side. A long run for a biot, and worse, a hard target to keep track of. Then there was the wall of water left by Caligula's deliberate dragging of his beer.

But Plath, too, had been playing games with the tabletop. Seemingly fidgeting pensively, Plath had picked up the saltshaker, picked at some dried-on food, then put it down on the table.

She put it down toward the far left end of Caligula's water obstacle.

From the point of view of Keat's biot the saltshaker was the Tower of Babel and the Empire State Building all rolled into one. He saw it as a distant shape, a feature of the landscape like some impossibly symmetrical mountain.

He saw it from there. But he also saw it through the tap he'd placed on Plath's eye using his other biot. One of Plath's own biots was standing beside him there. Plath made her biot tap Keats's creature and make a gesture meant to convey going around the saltshaker. Biots could not speak to each other, so this was a primitive but effective way to convey basic signals.

On the table surface Keats's other biot rolled farther left, moving at top speed, racing to get around the saltshaker and avoid being slowed by the water.

Had Caligula noticed? That would be the question.

Keats cleared the saltshaker tower. He spotted the wall of water off to his right but was well clear of it. Ahead, far in the distance, was a wall of indeterminate color.

Keats's first biot, K1—the one inside Plath's brain—turned awkwardly to Plath's P2 and made a gesture using two claws meant to convey that he was closing in.

In the macro Plath was dragging the conversation out to give Keats time.

Caligula drained the last of his beer and set the glass down just behind the saltshaker.

Deliberate?

Plath's P2 looked at Keats's K1. A body shake that was the equivalent of a headshake. *No, that didn't get me.*

But it had been close, very close. The glass—a rainbow-swirling object so big it looked a bit like some rainbow-hued desert mesa—came crashing down out of the sky. It sent vibration and water droplets in all directions. One of them, an Olympic pool of water, crashed behind him as he sped on.

"It is your decision," Caligula said. "Lear will insist that it be your decision."

Lear will insist, Plath thought. Never "he" or "she," always the careful gender-neutral name.

"And I will make that decision," Plath said. "But first—"

"I'm afraid that as enjoyable as this is, I must go," Caligula said.

"Is there a way for me to contact you directly?"

Caligula smiled. It was a surprisingly genuine thing, that smile. He was no comic-book villain playing a role and posturing for the camera. He smiled and meant it when he said, "Sadly, no. My orders come from Lear. My loyalty is to Lear. But Lear will respect your decision and convey it to me."

He pushed back from the table and stood.

He spoke very definitely about Lear's state of mind, it seemed to Plath. And not for the first time it occurred to her that she might have been speaking to Lear all along. *Was* Caligula Lear?

Except that there was something in the killer's eyes when he spoke of his master. There was affection, it seemed to Plath, affection and . . . not fear. No, Caligula did not fear his master. He liked Lear. He was . . . he was . . .

Proud!

It hit her so suddenly she gulped and blushed and ended up awkwardly extending a hand, which Caligula bemusedly refused.

No, Plath thought, *Caligula is not Lear.* But neither was he a mere employee.

Affection and *pride.*

Unable to sit still in the safe house, Keats had come halfway and met her on the sidewalk. With neither of them acknowledging the other, they made their way to a Starbucks. Standing in line, speaking the proper Starbucks drink formula, squeezing around a tiny round table too close to the bathroom—it was all reassuringly normal.

"Did you make it?" she asked him.

He smiled. "I grabbed his sleeve as he was standing up. I'm on his arm and heading north. In an hour I'll be seeing what Caligula sees."

"And *who* he sees," Plath added.

"So what did you two talk about?"

Just a flicker in Plath's eyes. "I told him what Stern had said about the Tulip being impregnable."

"And Caligula accepted that?"

Plath shrugged. "What else could he do? He agreed to pass it along to Lear." She frowned, formed a sentence in her head that went like this: *There's something proprietary in the way Caligula speaks about Lear. There's a relationship there. Almost father-son, I think.*

But she didn't speak it. Under the table she clenched her hands into fists. She found it difficult to talk about Lear at all. She could feel it. She could guess that it was wiring.

What she could not do was decide to rip up that wire. That felt suicidal. It felt painful, though of course it would not be.

More wiring. She'd been wired to fear ripping up the wire.

Games within games. Ever-deeper circles of hell.

Plath's phone lit up. She recognized the number. She covered one ear against the noise of steaming milk.

"Mr. Stern?"

To her surprise it was a woman's voice. "No. He's dead."

Plath froze. Then, "What?" It sounded childlike to her, her own voice. She sounded wounded.

"This is Camilla Strange. I'm . . . I mean, I was . . . Mr. Stern's second-in-command. I am now holed up at McLure Labs with reports of four of our people dead."

Plath found she was breathing hard. Audibly. "How did you know to call me?"

Was it her imagination or were there an unusual number of police sirens. Too many even for New York?

Was it her imagination, or were unflappable New Yorkers hunched a bit too tight around their lattes? Were their eyes less big-city averted and more alert-scared?

"Mr. Stern left a file to be opened in the event of his suspicious death."

"And was it suspicious? His death?"

Camilla Strange laughed humorlessly. "He seems to have been . . . eaten. Consumed. His driver brought him here, dead, with maybe a third or a half of his body gone. Muscles, viscera, organs: all eaten. Like millions of ants had been working on him. That's how he looks. Like roadkill."

"Nanobots," Plath said.

"Yes, ma'am," Camilla Strange said. "That was our thought, too. A mini gray-goo scenario. They must have been programmed in advance to replicate only so many generations. And then . . . I'm sorry, someone is . . . hold on, please."

The phone muted. Then Camilla was back. "I just sent you a piece of video."

Plath switched apps, opened the video, and turned so that Keats could see. It showed a sedan screeching to a halt at McLure Labs. A man whose entire head and shoulders seemed to be weeping blood staggered from the car, walked three steps, and fell.

"Oh, God. Oh, God. Oh, God, what is that?" The voice on the video was saying.

The picture zoomed in, and for just two seconds before focus went hazy Plath could see the dead man liquefying before her eyes.

The video ended. Blessedly no advertising had yet been attached.

"Ma'am? Ms. McLure?"

"Yes."

"You saw?"

"I saw."

"What do we—"

"Stay hidden. Stay out of it. This is out of your hands now."

Plath, shaken, hung up the phone. She excused herself to the bathroom. She vomited into the toilet bowl, fished in her bag for a mint, found three loose Tic Tacs.

War was on. If there had been any uncertainty, it was gone now. If she had entertained doubts about whose side she was on, the Armstrong Twins had made it easy.

Stern had been like an uncle. The one living remnant of her father's company. The only man she knew who'd been Grey McLure's friend.

Stern, murdered by the Twins. Her brother, murdered by the Twins. Her father . . .

She saw it again in her mind, the towers falling, and mingling with that imagery was the vivid personal memory of watching her father's jet arcing crazily out of the sky, plunging toward the stadium, the fear, the panic, the flash and heat and noise of the explosion.

If she was not in this to avenge her father and brother, why was she in it at all?

Was it all wiring now, thrusting these memories to the fore? Maybe, yes. But that didn't make it wrong, any of it.

Stern must have been in agony. . . . Grey McLure must have died in terror, not at his own extinction but at the knowledge that his son would die with him, and possibly his daughter as well.

If wire was what it took to give her strength, then okay. Okay.

She wiped her mouth, washed her hands, chewed the Tic Tacs, and thumbed a text.

ARTIFACT

Plath to Lear: *Yes.*

EIGHTEEN

The Antarctic weather came down like the wrath of God. Sixty-knot winds, subzero temperatures. Nothing was flying out of Forward Green.

It was on her third day there that Imelda Suarez decided to take a chance and see what was in the big hangar out to the south. She waited until the base boss—his actual title was Chief Executive Forward Green—had his birthday party.

Suarez had no difficulty starting up a Sno-Cat and driving off toward the south. No one saw her leave, which was not surprising in the whiteout conditions. The problem would come if for some reason she got lost or the Cat broke down. Then she would have to call for help and all hell could break loose.

In her forty-eight hours at the base Suarez had felt that this was a very different sort of place, very different from the usual Antarctic facility—even very different from Cathexis Base. The ice was a lonely and often boring place, so people tended to be friendly. People liked "new meat."

But not at Forward Green. Here she had been treated politely, properly, but not welcomed. No one had plopped down next to her at table and struck up a conversation. This despite the fact that she was an attractive woman and the gender ratio on the ice was about seven to one.

Conversations in the dining hall tended to become quieter when she was seen. Everyone was trying hard not to seem secretive, but the end result was that they just seemed more so.

Maybe it was just that Tanner had warned her to expect that something strange was going on. Maybe she was seeing what she expected to see. But that said, it was weird. It was a *very weird vibe*, as her hippie mother would have said.

The Sno-Cat is a small, tracked vehicle, like a tiny two-person tank with big windows and no cannon. The heater was blowing noisily, rattling from something stuck in the vent, and the windshield wipers were ratcheting back and forth even more noisily, but visibility was still poor. It would be all too easy to drive right past the hangar and just keep going until the gas was used up. And then she'd quite likely freeze to death. The ice was unforgiving of recklessness.

But after an anxious half hour she saw the outlines of the building in between swipes of the wipers. She kept going—no point in being coy, she had to look like she had every reason to be here.

Before stepping out of the Sno-Cat she zipped her parka all the way up, flipped her fur-lined hood forward, and tugged at the drawstrings before pulling on her huge gloves. Her dark goggles were already in place.

Suarez climbed out of the warm cab and was almost knocked over by the wind. But she was a sailor, after all, and not unaccustomed to pitching decks and bad weather, so she avoided disgracing herself. She twisted the door handle, and, sure enough, it was unlocked.

The wind—which was a battering physical force outside—became just a howling noise.

The hangar was lit only minimally, but it was still bright enough to see. And what she saw were four vehicles like the ones in the video Tanner had shown her. Three were partially dismantled, with parts strewn across wheeled steel tables.

The fourth vehicle appeared to be intact. She walked to it, torn between fascination and caution.

It was about thirty-five feet long from tip to tail, and almost as wide. It was a sort of elongated oval, a hovercraft judging by the skirts, but otherwise like no hovercraft she'd ever seen outside of a Hollywood movie.

It had a tail, almost like something you'd see on a fighter jet, but there was no horizontal plane, just a shark's fin bearing missile pods on each side. A quick count indicated six missiles total, three in each pod. She had no familiarity with the type of ordnance, but it was undoubtedly real and undoubtedly missiles and undoubtedly military in its purpose—and that fact shocked her.

Antarctica was the last place on Earth without nationalities or armies.

Before and beneath the tail was a hard plastic canopy—again like something from a fighter jet. There appeared to be two jet turbines mounted on either side, flush with the top, squat beside the canopy. The pilot would be able to see ahead and to either side by looking over the engine casings.

It was painted a marshmallow white with only a few blue accent notes here and there, plus the obligatory safety notices near the intakes and exhausts from the two jet turbine engines.

Suarez walked boldly to the hovercraft and peeked inside the canopy. The controls were more modern versions of those on her own LCAC.

"What do you think?"

The voice made her jump. It was male, high-pitched, curious not hostile. But when she turned to see its source, she was face-to-face with an assault rifle. Behind the rifle was a middle-aged man in white overalls. He was balding, had a red face and glasses. And he was not, she judged, used to pointing weapons at people.

"It looks fast," she said, trying for a nonchalant tone.

"It is," the man said with evident pride. "She'll do one sixty knots with no wind and on smooth ice."

"One sixty? And if it hits a bump?"

"Do I need to point this at you?"

She shrugged. "I'm unarmed. And I'm not up to anything. I came out here because I can't find a three-sixteenth socket wrench to save my life. I'm Imelda Suarez. I drive an LCAC. They brought me in to work on . . . well, to be honest, I think they brought me in on a bullshit excuse."

The man smiled expectantly. "And why would they bring you here on a pretext?"

"So that I would see this." She indicated the hovercraft. "So that *they* could see how I reacted. Because they need hovercraft pilots and we aren't exactly thick on the ground. There aren't a hundred left on the planet, let alone on the ice since the navy's LCACs were decommissioned."

The man lowered the gun, then set it on one of the tool carts. "I suspect you're right, Ms. Suarez. Or is it Lieutenant Suarez?"

"Not lieutenant," she said forcefully. "Semper fi and all that, but I'm no longer getting paid by Uncle Sam. Do I get to learn your name?"

"Babbington. Joseph Babbington. Doctor, if that matters to you. We expected you yesterday; that was the thinking, anyway. We were ready yesterday. I'm just an engineer. I did some of the design on the sleigh."

"The sleigh?"

He shrugged. "It's a nickname, but it stuck. 'Santa's badass sleigh,' some wit said once, and now that's what we call it." He fished a remote control from his pocket, pressed a button, and the sleigh's canopy rose. "Take a closer look."

Cautiously, very aware that the assault rifle was still near at hand, she leaned into the cockpit. She took it in with an expert eye, whistled, and said, "About twenty years ahead of my cockpit. Very nice. That's a forward-looking radar?"

"Oh, much better than that. What we have there, Lieuten . . . Ms. Suarez . . . is a computerized obstacle avoidance system technology. COAST, because, well, you know how engineers love acronyms. It senses changes in elevation—obstacles, anything over six inches above grade level—and either diverts power to the cushion to lift the sleigh clear, steers clear, or in extreme cases slows to allow the pilot to choose the course of action."

"Useful if you're shooting along at one hundred and sixty knots."

"*Vital* if you're shooting along at one hundred and sixty knots. . . . We have two qualified pilots," Babbington said, with the air of someone who was tired of playing games. "We need six total. Four primaries and two backups. You could be the third primary, if you qualify. And if you're interested."

"Since I left the military my interests have had a lot to do with what I'm paid."

Babbington searched her face for a long time. He didn't believe her. Or at least he didn't believe her yet. "The pay is three hundred thousand USD per annum."

"Jesus."

"It's a tough job. It may even be a dangerous job. And it's a job that has something in common with your military service: it demands unquestioning loyalty and obedience."

She reached in and put her hand on the yoke. They'd gone to the trouble of padding it with leather. It was like something out of a sports car.

On impulse she hopped inside, a move that required a twisting half jump, like a stunt rider mounting a running horse. She made it work.

The cockpit was snug, but there was room to the left and right, flat surfaces that even included a cup holder. The pedals felt familiar. If her LCAC was a twenty-year-old Buick, this was a brand-new Porsche. It even had a new-car smell.

It was seductive.

"Very nice," she said. "But what's it for?"

"For?"

"Dr. Babbington, I couldn't help but notice the missiles."

"Indeed."

"Why would the sleigh require missiles?"

"We're testing it for the military."

She wondered if she should let the lie go unchallenged. If she called him out, would he shoot her? No, she judged: if she failed to call bullshit, he'd know she was lying.

"That's very funny," she said. "What's the real reason?"

Babbington smiled, a nice, genuine smile. "The owner of the company is a bit . . . let's say, she's a bit unusual. She has a notion that civilization will soon collapse, and she intends to sit it out right here. But should that civilization lash out at her in its last throes, she wants to be able to defend herself."

"You work for a nut?"

"I used to work for the Pentagon, as did you. Weren't we working for nuts then? And those nuts paid rather ungenerous government salaries."

Despite herself, Suarez laughed. "Well, you got me there. What kind of range does this thing have?"

"The sleigh has a three-hundred-fifty-mile operational range. Six surface-to-surface missiles, four surface-to-air missiles just inside the engine cowling, twin thirty-caliber machine guns."

With a show of reluctance Suarez climbed out of the cockpit.

"I have to tell you, Dr. Babbington: three hundred large would be very nice. Very, very nice. But there's something else. The U.S. Navy taught me to drive hovercraft, but that was incidental to my core training."

"Which was?"

"Marines, first, as you already know. Then Sea Air Land, Doctor. Navy SEAL."

She watched his face turn gray.

She watched his eyes dart toward the assault rifle. Which was in her hands before he could move.

"This is the part where you tell me everything," she said. "This is the part where you answer all my questions, because if you don't, I shoot you, and you die."

Not a good liar, Sadie McLure.

"I told Lear no," she said.

But it was right there in her eyes.

"Then what are we going to do?" Keats asked her.

She shrugged. "I don't know. This madness, the Nobel thing, whatever happened there, that must be the secret weapon Lear wants destroyed. Right?"

He had not known what to say then. He had not known what he could safely say to her. He did not know whether the girl he loved would have him killed for turning against Lear.

It felt as if his insides were dying. Like he was a piece of fruit left out in the sun, rotting from the inside, collapsing in on himself. He felt sick.

She was wired. She knew she was wired. Yet she had refused to let him try to fix her.

The insidiousness of it. She was like a schizophrenic who knows she's supposed to take the meds but refuses to. She was becoming party to her own mind-rape.

He wanted to grab her shoulders and shake her. Everything he was to her was less important to her now than carrying out Lear's plan.

She had always held something back from him, he knew that. That was okay, he'd told himself, she just needed time. At first he'd decided the reticence was a class thing. That made him feel a bit better, really, because it was something he could understand. It was something he could defend himself from emotionally.

He still loved her. But she had never loved him, had she? And now . . . now where was Sadie McLure?

"Do you want to make love?" she asked him, that and he wanted to punch her in the face.

Not her, not *Sadie*, no, it was . . . it was whoever this person was, this reprogrammed, wired alteration of Sadie. It was this truly new creature called Plath.

"I'm tired," he said, and the relief in her eyes was almost more than he could endure.

"Yeah. Big day tomorrow," she said.

"Oh? Why?"

Her eyes flicked right—guilty, caught. She shrugged and forced a phony smile. "Aren't they all big days?"

She left, heading toward the bedroom they still shared.

Tears filled his eyes and since no one was around to see him standing there like a fool, he let the tears roll down his cheeks.

Back to New York, that's what Lystra said. "Back to New York to watch the show, yeah. A lot happening very soon. Timing. It's all in the timing, yeah."

So here they were. New York City, and damned if the tattooed madwoman didn't have an apartment a block away from the Tulip. He could look straight down Sixth Avenue and see the building. He could run for it, escape, get to the Twins and say, "I'm sorry, I'm sorry, but you don't know what this crazy bitch is doing!"

He could do that. And they'd thank him for the information and then kill him. Or Lystra would catch him and she would show him that scary face she had, the one where she seemed almost to turn into a skeleton. And then she could kill his biots and turn him loose.

Death or madness. Seriously? That's what it was down to? The three windows in his head said *yes, yes,* that was exactly the choice.

He wondered rather morbidly just what kind of crazy he would be. Stories were still leaking out of Stockholm. They said some big-deal banker found a way to hang himself from a chandelier. They said a French general was found smeared with feces, crying. They said a famous American horror novelist had run into the street and beaten a party Santa to death with a fire extinguisher.

Which crazy will you be, Anthony? he asked himself.

What escape was there? The Twins? The American government?

He stopped breathing. The answer—not a good answer, a weak, probably worthless answer—popped into his head.

Someone brilliant. Someone with mad skills. Someone who once had almost, sort of, liked Bug Man. And was just a block away.

Burnofsky.

Lystra had taken his phone. She was on her own phone right now in the adjacent room, telling her CEO, some dude named Tom, to *fire all the remaining employees, effective now, this minute, shut it all down, the whole Directive Medical shebang, stop all checks and buy more gold. Yeah. Just don't touch Cathexis.*

Burnofsky. The dude had invented nanobots. It stood to reason he'd have . . . something. But how to reach him? He knew Burnofsky's e-mail and his cell, but Bug Man had no phone.

He would have to wait until she was asleep, the monster in the next room.

Maybe I won't be a hanging-myself crazy, Bug Man thought. *Maybe I'll be a nice, gentle, shit-smeared kind of crazy.*

Somehow he was convinced that none of this would ever have happened if he'd just found the onions sooner. Gotten home.

With a chill he remembered his mother coming down with a sinus infection a year ago, give or take. She'd had tests done. Her DNA, too, might be stored somewhere on one of Lystra Reid's drives.

Her plan was now frighteningly clear. She had used her web of medical testing companies to acquire and digitize DNA from millions of people. Once you had the DNA, you could grow a biot derived in part from that DNA. The biot-DNA-donor mind link would happen—which would be disorienting all by itself. Suddenly having windows open in your mind . . . well, that was going to be disturbing.

But nothing to what came next. Lear wasn't out to disturb or unsettle people, she was out to destroy civilization. For that she needed madness. Widespread, inexplicable, irresistible madness.

So once the biots were born, she had only to kill them. An electrical surge maybe, or extreme heat or acid.

Would it really work? Would one crazy woman be able to bring the whole world crashing down?

He turned on the television; it was all he had. Al Jazeera TV had a news bulletin. He reached for the remote. He did not want to see more video of that horror show in Stockholm.

Suddenly he felt Lystra's presence and realized he was no longer hearing her from the other room. "Leave it," she said, looking toward the TV screen. "I think something kind of, yeah, big just happened."

Seven months earlier, the younger British prince had given blood in a public show of support for a National Blood Service blood drive. The NBS had been helped in their work by volunteers from Directive Medical UK.

Of course security for the Royal Family was very tight, so no one would be allowed to actually know which was his donation. It was labeled anonymously, just a numerical tracer, and sent off to the blood bank.

Except that the Directive Medical lab tech had already swapped it out with an earlier sample.

Now, as the television picture showed, the prince was in a gondola of the London Eye—the huge Ferris wheel beside the Thames—as part of an outreach to disadvantaged youth.

The gondolas were large enough to hold a couple of dozen people at once, and were in fact holding twelve specially chosen children of carefully varied ethnicities, who shrank in horror against the far end of the gondola as the prince repeatedly ran at the transparent wall and smashed his head into it.

Blood smeared the plastic. Blood completely covered the prince's face and would have rendered him unrecognizable if not for the familiar red hair.

The Eye was slowly coming around, bringing the gondola back to earth, but that footage from three minutes earlier—brutal video of the raving royal slamming himself again and again and again— was competing in one half of the screen with a live shot showing him flailing, kicking, spitting blood in every direction as appalled Royalty Protection in plainclothes and uniformed London Met police tried to get him under control.

"That was excellent," Lystra said. "You try to nail the timing, yeah, and arrange something spectacular, but wow, that was better than I'd hoped for. Yeah."

Bug Man stared in horror. "I liked that dude. He was the fun one."

"Who, the prince?" Lystra laughed. "Don't go soft on me, Bug. Much more to come. I've got three officers at a nuclear missile base near Novosibirsk. High hopes. Fingers crossed, yeah?"

And yes, she had her fingers crossed. She left and closed the door behind her.

Bug Man watched as the prince was hauled away to a waiting ambulance. "Fuck you, crazy lady. Yeah? I liked him. He was a gamer."

NINETEEN

"I need your help."

Keats to Wilkes and Billy the Kid.

Plath was asleep. He had crept silently from bed to bed waking them, holding a silencing finger to his lips.

"Anything for you, pretty blue eyes," Wilkes said, and yawned.

"Plath has been wired," he said. He knew she might wake up at any moment. No time for delicacy. "She's been wired, she knows it, but she won't pull the wires. It's got to her. We need to go in there and clean her up."

Anya was not invited. Plath had a biot in Anya. Keats badly wanted to ask Anya if she had built any more biots for Plath. But Plath might have been watching through Anya's eyes, or listening in her ear.

"You saying someone from Armstrong wired her?" Wilkes asked.

Keats hesitated. "This is lunacy. This is mad. But she saw something. Down in the meat. She doesn't think it was a nanobot. I helped her look. I didn't find anything. But I have found wire, a lot of it."

He let that sink in. "She thinks Nijinsky—" Wilkes began.

"No," Keats said. "Whatever it is, whoever's running it, it's still apparently active, so not Nijinsky. Someone else. Maybe one of you two. Maybe a traitor from some other cell."

Wilkes got up, came over to Keats, and sat down beside him. Very close, uncomfortably so. "How do we know it isn't you?" she asked. "You've had a biot in her for a long time, right? Fixing that hole in her artery or whatever? Could be you, right? And maybe you're just lying in wait for one of our biots to come crawling along and, *boom*!"

"This is kind of crazy," Billy said.

"Nah, this isn't *kind of* crazy," Wilkes said. "This is full-on crazy." She heh-heh-heh laughed and said, "This is where it all goes, right? I mean, this is where it kind of had to go, didn't it? You start playing with people's brains, man. . . . How do you know? Right? Whole world's going crazy. All those big brains. And now your prince dude."

Keats nodded tightly. "Right."

Wilkes pulled away from him. "Maybe I just transferred one of my kids to you, Keats. Just now."

"Maybe," he acknowledged.

"Maybe it's me, and if I put one of my kids into Plath, maybe that's my second one, you know? Maybe I get in there and make it worse. What's Plath doing? What's she up to? Did this wire make her soft in the head?"

"She's planning to blow up the Tulip."

"What's a tulip? A flower, right?" Billy asked.

Wilkes snorted. "It's a skyscraper in Midtown. Blow it up? What's that even mean?"

"It means that she's given the go-ahead to Caligula to blow it up. Kill everyone in it. Destroy all their labs, all their computers."

Wilkes stared at him.

"Lear told her to—" Keats began.

"Lear?" Wilkes shrilled. "Lear told her to murder all those people?"

"That was her own . . . her own solution. Maybe. Who knows? She's met with Caligula. She knows she's wired, and she knows it's wrong, but she can't, you know. . . . she can't pull the goddamned wires. We have to do it for her. And we have to find whatever is in there. Nanobot or biot, we have to find it and kill it."

"Who is doing it?" Billy asked. "I mean, who is wiring her brain to do—"

"To do what Lear wants done?" Keats asked, his voice rising. "Who is wiring her to do *exactly what Lear wants done*?"

Wilkes drew a sharp breath. "The hell," she said.

"I don't have any choice but to trust you two," Keats said. "For all I know, you're as wired as she is. Or maybe you just think it's okay. Or maybe I'm as messed up as she is and the way I see this is all wrong. But I have no choice, I have to . . . I can't . . ." He spread his hands, helpless.

"You're talking about ripping out wire that Lear or someone working for Lear put there?" Wilkes asked. "Lear's going to see that as treason. You know what that means? You know who comes to talk to you when you betray Lear? Jesus, Keats, if she's as wired up as you say, Plath'll send Caligula after you herself."

"I know!" he raged. He pushed his fingers back through his hair. "I know. I know."

No one spoke. Keats sniffed and wiped at his eyes. "This fight has changed," he said. "This isn't us against them anymore. Not that simple. I mean, doesn't there have to be some line we draw? Doesn't there have to be something we won't do, even if it means maybe we lose? And doesn't there have to be some limit on how far we'll *let* ourselves be used?"

"The Twins don't have a limit," Wilkes said.

"Neither does Lear," Keats said. "I think he's the one using biots—creating them, killing them—to drive people crazy. Sweden. The prince. The Brazilian." He waved his hand vaguely. "Probably a bunch of other stuff. The Twins, Lear, they're just two sides in the same crazy game, Wilkes."

"Yeah. And we are playable characters, right? We're game pieces."

"If we let ourselves be," Keats said.

"So now you're taking over?" Wilkes asked.

"Only until Plath is cleared. Then . . ." He shrugged. "Then we . . . I don't know."

"I'm in," Wilkes said, but her usual smart-ass smirk was gone. Her face was gray and slack. She looked far older than she could have been. "Death or madness. Right? We've always known it would come down to that."

Keats nodded. "Death or madness."

The Russian officers proved to be disappointments to Lear. A major and two lieutenants duly lost their minds as their biots died, but at the time they were not on duty. The major wandered off into the Siberian wastes and froze to death. One lieutenant was dead drunk, too incapacitated to do much of anything.

The remaining lieutenant had just finished a shift. He saw the windows opening in his mind and acted quickly. He stripped off his sidearm and threw it into the snow. Then he ran toward the medical dispensary, but lost his mind halfway there.

Naked, he charged the guarded gate of the missile silo and was arrested by security.

The lack of a nuclear event—it would have registered on seismographs—disappointed Lystra.

So she opened her laptop and scanned the list of high-value targets. She picked out the pilot of a Virgin Australia plane making the long haul from Los Angeles to Sydney.

As he approached Sydney in a few hours, his biots would be born, windows would open, and if Lystra was lucky the world would have one more thing to fear. An appetizer, so to speak, before the pasta course.

"Funny," she said. "Yeah."

She watched some old *Beavis and Butt-head* on Netflix, and fell asleep with it still playing.

Bug Man had never heard of *Beavis and Butt-head*. That would give him an excuse in case she woke up and saw him creep into her room with his heart in his throat. He could say, *I heard this on TV, didn't know what it was, so I came in and . . .*

. . . and lifted your phone.

And then you killed me, so, yeah, yeah, crazy bitch, yeah, then you killed me. The end.

Suarez had not found it necessary to threaten him much. Dr. Babbington was amenable enough once she'd made clear that she would do bad things to him if necessary. And an assault rifle was hard to argue with.

"Because society is going to crumble. That's why. She's absolutely convinced that society is about to crumble like a stale cookie."

"Who? Who are you talking about?" she had demanded.

"Jesus, you don't even know who is running this? Our lord and mistress. The owner. Of Cathexis. Lystra Reid."

"Lystra Reid? Are you sure?"

"Yes, I'm quite sure. This is only one of two *secret* facilities. This is where we create the sleighs, where we train pilots: this isn't the final level any more than Cathexis is the final level."

"There's a third base?"

A third base. Three hundred kilometers south in a small dry valley. Dry valleys are a phenomenon unique to Antarctica, places of rock and little else, where for reasons of ice drift and unusual wind patterns the ground is bare of snow.

If Lystra Reid had built a base in a dry valley, it would not be one of the McMurdo group. The McMurdo Dry Valleys were more or less permanently infested by scientists collecting rocks and drilling core samples and complaining about their grant proposals.

She pointed this out to Babbington.

"Yes, well, this dry valley is an odd duck. It's extraordinarily deep and also quite narrow—just two kilometers across at its widest point. The ice is piled high against both mountain ridges, and sooner or later, of course, the weight of all that ice will crumble the mountains and take the valley. Soon by geological standards, so within a hundred thousand years."

He laughed, obviously thinking that was a science joke. When Suarez mustered up a half smile, he seemed encouraged.

"There's actually a meltwater river there, helped by some subterranean geothermal activity, and the whole place is quite sheltered from the wind. It's a garden spot, really. The average annual temperature remains within twenty degrees of fifteen degrees Fahrenheit. So sometimes it's actually above freezing."

"Garden spot."

"Anyway, that's where the third base is." He showed her on a map.

And that was when Babbington made an ill-fated leap for the gun. In a hand-to-hand battle of SEAL vs. scientist, the outcome was not in doubt.

Babbington landed on his butt several feet from where he started.

"I'd stay there if were you," Suarez warned.

He took her advice, crossed his legs awkwardly like a kindergartener, and sat.

"I'm afraid I will have to lock you up, Dr. Babbington. I'm sure there's a tool locker somewhere. They'll find you when the party is over and when the weather clears. Do you have to use the bathroom? Because you'll be tied up for as much as a day."

Amazing, Suarez thought, *how quickly life can get weird. One minute you're driving an LCAC delivering oranges and booze and hauling away garbage, and the next minute you're beating up scientists and preparing to get yourself killed in some dry valley at the end of the world.*

She had no doubt that this Lystra Reid person was capable of killing. You don't set out to build secret bases defended by sophisticated weapons because you're peaceable by nature.

But the question in her mind was whether this whole thing, whatever was going on here, was a secret government op unknown to Tanner. Tanner was low-level; this could simply be something way above his pay grade. In which case she would earn no thanks for barging in on this third base unannounced.

But they wouldn't kill her, not if this was a government op. They'd give her a stern lecture, make her sign more threatening letters, and just maybe hire her on.

If, on the other hand, it wasn't a government op but some actual crazy woman buying missiles and building a secret lair at the frozen anus of planet Earth, well. . .

She had to tell *someone* what was up: a witness she could trust to follow up just in case Imelda Suarez was never heard from again. She glanced at the computer on a work desk.

"User password on that computer?" she asked, sliding into a chair.

Babbington shrugged. "1234ABC."

"Seriously?" She typed it in and got access to her own e-mail account. She wrote a message to her brother, Frank. Frank was with the Capitol Police. He wouldn't be cleared for this information, but she knew she could trust him.

She spent a few minutes locating a good, strong steel tool locker and pushed Babbington and a bottle of water inside.

"You okay in there?"

"Well . . ."

"You'll be fine."

Then: the sleigh.

Suarez was honest enough to admit that she was motivated in part by an almost lustful desire to drive the sleigh. It was an object of beauty. A work of art. It screamed "speed" just sitting there.

She shed her parka, stuffed it into the very minimal storage space behind the cockpit seat, and slid into the leather chair. The pedals were where they should be. The yoke was awkwardly placed by her lights, but she could live with it. The displays were elegant and wonderfully easy to read.

She closed the canopy and realized the hangar doors were shut. So she climbed back out, scrounged around until she found a remote control, and climbed back in. It was just as good the second time. She had to fight the urge to run her fingers over the displays. Beautiful. If Rolls-Royce, Tesla, and Porsche teamed up to make a hovercraft, this would be it.

There was an autopilot, but she couldn't imagine trusting herself to a computer—not at the speeds this thing moved, not on the most treacherous terrain on planet Earth. But she turned on the automated warnings as well as, after some hesitation, the impact-avoidance system that would take control if she was in immediate danger of crashing.

"You wreck this thing and your future will be very much in doubt, Imelda," she told herself.

Then, finally, she fired up the engines.

It was noisy but not deafening in the cockpit. She felt the surge of suppressed power as the twin jets throbbed. The sleigh rose on a cushion of air.

She keyed the remote, and the hangar doors slid open. Beyond the doors was whiteness, white on white as far as the eye could see.

She punched her destination into the GPS, released the cable tie-downs, and slid toward the gap at walking speed then running speed and was just hitting fifty knots by the time she blew out of the building, keyed the doors over her shoulder, and rocketed out onto the ice.

Oh, yes.

She smiled and held it at fifty knots until she had played with the controls for a while and come grudgingly to trust the forward-scanning radar.

The ice here was rippled but with no rises over eighteen inches. The sleigh's jets adjusted automatically to push more air into the cushion as she reached obstacles.

Very soon fifty began to feel slow. Boring. Despite the fact that the ice was flying by beneath her. In her rearview mirror she saw a vortex of ice crystals, a shimmery white contrail.

"Well, in for fity, in for a hundred, right?"

She punched it, and the sleigh took off like a rocket.

"Oh, yes," Suarez said. "Ah-hah-hah!"

TWENTY

Plath was still asleep when they struck.

One from Keats, two from Wilkes, two from Billy. Five busy biots raced up through her eye and into her brain.

They had planned. Wilkes and Keats would focus on ripping up wire in the places where Keats had found it. Billy would go hunting for the intruder and call for help if he found something.

"It's mostly all up in here," Keats said. "Hippocampus and some Broca's area." Amazing how quickly one could learn something as esoteric as brain architecture when life and death were involved.

The three of them were downstairs in the darkened living room. Hopefully Plath would not awaken and come down to find out why Keats was not in her bed. If she did, they would know it: arteries would start pumping faster as she woke and began to stir.

"Go ahead, Billy. But if you find something, don't fight it. Call us for help."

Billy had a Coke by his side. He was dressed in a Washington Nationals jersey many sizes too large and slumped down to look cool, with the result that he looked even younger than he was—a small, round head and solemn face in a pile of rumpled clothing. None of them had anything to do with their hands.

"There's the first wire I found," Keats said to Wilkes. Down in the meat he was pointing it out to her nearest biot.

"It's encrusted," Wilkes said. It's been there for some days at least. Maybe longer. Meaning maybe we pull the wire, but the neurons have already made it redundant."

The wire was crisp and clean, only a few molecules in circumference. But neurons had grown over and around it in places, like kudzu, vines twining sensuously around the metal of the wire.

"Maybe," Keats admitted. "But I won't have that in her brain."

That made Wilkes smile. A genuine smile, not her usual cynical leer. "Pulling it up, sir. Aye, aye, Captain. Pulling it up."

Keats saw her two biots going at it, working well together to pull up the encrusted wire. The pins were sunk deep and completely overgrown. It took two biots straining to draw them slowly out of the brain like fence posts being pulled up. They came free but were still tangled in strands of neurons.

Wilkes had to tear the strands away, breaking actual brain connections in the process. To biot "ears" they made a sound like someone squirting water through their teeth and tearing denim.

No way to know whether these were just redundant cells tracking the wire or whether they had some legitimate purpose. Was she ripping away some cherished childhood memory? Probably not, probably these connections were just reinforcing the wire, but the human brain was astoundingly complex. BZRK had very sophisticated brain mapping, but still it was largely a crapshoot.

Gee, sorry about that, Plath, I just wiped out your memory of nursery school.

Keats was doing the same around the corner. There the wire was fresher, less overgrown. His biot stood at right angles to hers in the almost gravity-free liquid environment.

In the macro Billy said, "Can I ask a question?"

"Of course," Keats replied.

"Why are we doing this?"

"Because someone has messed with Plath's head, that's why." Keats obviously thought that was the end of it. But Billy pressed. "But isn't everyone's head messed with? I mean, stuff you see, or how you were raised. Stuff people did to you."

There was something, maybe several somethings, behind that tremulous *stuff people did to you.*

But this was not the time to examine Billy's demons. "That's all natural, this is . . ." He was at a loss for words. "It's wrong, that's all."

Billy fell silent after that. But Keats could see that he wasn't convinced by Keats's halfhearted effort to justify what they were doing. Keats went on about his business, tearing out wire, pulling pins. So did Wilkes, but now she took up the same line of questioning.

"Yeah, blue eyes, but we aren't doing this with her okay anymore than whoever laid the wire down, right?" In the meat they were at right angles, here they sat facing.

"She's not able to—"

"So we're *making* her do it. Right? I mean, we're unwiring her even though she obviously isn't totally psyched about it."

"Come on, guys," Keats said. "It's not the same. Someone wired her brain. *Hacked* her brain. Took over her brain. Now we're fixing it. It's not that difficult to understand."

Wilkes began to argue, but then Billy yelled, "I see something!" His two biots had emerged from a brain fold to see a furtive shape disappear just beyond the reach of illumination.

"Nanobot?" Keats demanded.

"I don't know. I can't . . . I think it sees me. It's running! He's fast! He's got moves, he's got moves, man! 3D moves!"

"Stay with him, we'll catch up," Keats directed.

Billy was in the game now, racing as fast as his biots would go across a terrain of eerie hillocks, pulsing red worms as big as car tunnels, static sparks, and always the lethargically circulating fluid that slowed his every movement. His quarry disappeared into a shallow fold and Billy followed.

"Ahhh!"

"What?"

"Shit!"

Billy jumped out of his seat, knocking over his Coke. His fingers moved as though he was using a gamepad. His eyes seemed to dart after objects he could only see in the m-sub.

Billy's first biot was down and minus two legs on the left side before he knew what hit him. He twisted both biots to see, and there, undeniable, unmistakable, the enemy: a biot.

"It's a biot!" Billy yelled. "It's a biot-biot-biot!"

"Don't let him get away!"

"One of mine is down! I'm— he's fast!"

The alien biot had raced up a vertical surface then pushed off, somersaulted, and dropped down behind Billy's remaining mobile biot.

The foe was vertical and swimming downward. Billy made the

mistake of believing he was safe until the biot landed, but the biot spun in midfall and fastened two pincers onto Billy's eyes.

"I'm blinded!"

In the macro he instinctively rubbed his eyes, shook his head. In Billy's brain the second window was blank, showing no picture. Like a TV tuned to a dead channel.

"I see him!" Keats yelled. "Come on, Wilkes!" He grabbed her hand in excitement.

Now three biots raced to catch the intruder. But the intruder was no longer fleeing. It had taken up a position on what seemed like a vertical surface and now waited.

Keats pulled to a halt. Wilkes's two biots did the same.

"Three to one," Wilkes said. Then, "Why does that thing look familiar?" And then, "Fuck!"

Keats was already on his feet. He raced up the stairs, and without bothering to knock, opened the door to Anya and Vincent's room.

Anya was asleep.

Vincent was not.

Down in the meat Wilkes stood beside Keats. Now she and Billy both joined him in the macro, staring at Vincent, who looked at them calmly.

"You," Keats said.

Vincent didn't answer. Anya rolled over and opened her eyes.

"Billy," Keats said. "Go get Plath."

A message lit up Burnofsky's phone, but he had muted it so there was no chime.

It's Bug. Bad shit happening. Crazy bitch I think is Lear. Going to kill me and the whole damn world.

Ninety seconds later, a second message.

Are u there? Talk to me! I'm not playing.

Sixty seconds later:

Fuck! Do NOT call back. I'm using her phone. Can't wait. I'll try again later.

Bug Man had barely erased the messages and slid the phone back onto Lystra's nightstand when the alarm on that phone went off. *Zeeet! Zeeet! Zeeet!*

Bug Man leapt for the door, eased himself out even as Lystra stirred and reached blindly for the phone.

By the time she emerged he was wrapped in a blanket on the couch doing a very poor job of faking sleep.

"Get up," Lystra said, and pushed his foot. "It's time."

He pretended to yawn. "Wha—? Time for what?"

She grabbed a piece of glass fruit from a bowl on the nearby table. She hefted it in her hand, judging the weight. Then she swung it hard and fast, smashing it into Bug Man's left eye.

"AHHH!"

Her free hand was on his throat, he could feel the pressure tightening. He squirmed but did not lash out at her, did not try to hit her. She took the glass fruit—it may have been a peach—and stuffed it brutally into his mouth.

Bug Man tasted blood. She pushed harder, harder until his front teeth began to splinter. He cried out, a muffled, frantic sound, and suddenly she spun away and tossed the now-bloody fruit back in its bowl.

"Who did you text?" she asked in a conversational tone.

"Whanh?" He couldn't make sounds right, and spit splinters of teeth out onto the blanket. Tears filled his eyes, the pain but more the shock of the attack.

He felt with his tongue around the new architecture of his mouth.

"Who did you text, Buggy, come on," Lystra said. "Was it some girl?"

He seized on the idea. "Nuffing, jush shome girl back home. Jush my girlfrien'."

"Yeah, don't do that again," she said. "Now I have to password-protect my phone, and I hate that. It slows me down. Turn on the TV, go online to Vatican City feed."

He couldn't see to find the remote. Wouldn't have had any idea where to find a Vatican feed if he had, and in the end Lystra, making disparaging sounds, did it herself.

"Now watch."

Bug Man wiped tears and blood from his face and tried to focus. The Pope, but not wearing his tall Pope hat.

Bug Man knew what was coming next.

"This is your work," Lystra said approvingly. "The man is very healthy, it seems. I couldn't find a biological sample anywhere. But you got me his cells."

"My mouff . . ." He groaned and wept again, despairing. There would be no happy ending for his life: he saw that clearly now. Unmistakably. His lip was swelling. He swallowed more blood; it hadn't slowed yet. "Why 'o I haff to wash?"

"Why do you have to watch?" Lystra seemed puzzled. "I thought you'd want to see. Look! It's starting. Look at him staring around, trying to figure out where the bugs are." Then she sighed happily. "Plus, I suppose I like an audience. Genius unappreciated and all that. Get ready. This is going to be epic. It's one thing to show people they can't rely on their politicians and famous brains and all; it's another thing altogether to say even God can't stop what's coming. This will scare the hell out of people."

His Holiness the Pope stood with the benign expression the world had come to expect and love. It was a sort of half smile, eyes crinkled, hands folded in front of him.

He was bored to tears. He was often bored by these ceremonial events. Although at least this was out of doors, under a partly cloudy sky just brightening to the richer blue of early afternoon from the bright blue of morning.

The Pope sometimes walked in the streets of Rome in disguise. He disliked the fishbowl in which he was kept, always surrounded, always watched. If he was to lead the Church, then he must know its people.

Once he had gone out disguised as a priest. That had ended badly, with tourists recognizing him and crowding around him, twenty, fifty, two hundred people, a mob within seconds. His security detail had had to practically lift him and carry him through the crowd to a waiting SUV.

Then he became more creative: a toupee, jeans, and an "I heart Rome" T-shirt. He was followed on these excursions by Swiss Guards in plainclothes. He had negotiated with them to keep their distance. And they had agreed to stay at least a hundred feet away.

He was considering such a trip for the evening. What a joy it would be to find a cramped table in some little osteria, drink wine and eat antipasto, pasta, and perhaps a nice piece of fish. Watch regular people. Eavesdrop on their conversations.

Then, what? A limoncello in lieu of dessert? A walk by the river? Or succumb to the lure of the beautiful array at some well-tended gelato stand?

It might be his last excursion for a while. The world was going mad. He had been shown the footage of the British prince, the poor young man. Drugs, most likely. But contacts with intelligence agencies around the world suggested that suspicion was growing that something connected it with the self-murder of the American president, the Nobel massacre, the Brazilian president and vice president—perhaps the earlier attack on the UN in New York and even the bizarre tragedy in Hong Kong.

If it was terrorists of some sort, no one seemed to know who they were or what they wanted.

The Pope frowned, realized he was being watched by many eyes, and relaxed into his blankly beatific expression.

Yes, just as soon as he got through today's event, a *tableau vivant* of the manger scene. It was a group of Italian children, specially chosen, prepared, and rehearsed. The production was done with some of the biggest names in Italian theater, with costumes from great fashion designers. There would be music.

The Holy Father had managed to get it moved to the morning on the theory that he needed his rest in the afternoon. In fact, he needed to be back at the Vatican in plenty of time to slip out for dinner in the evening.

A small lie. He would confess it and be absolved.

He hoped the presentation was wrapping up. He didn't want to sneak a peek at the printed program or it might betray impatience. But if memory served, this was the last song, which would be followed by applause, then kind words for the child actors and singers and the adult organizers.

And then, he was out. Done by the afternoon. They'd promised him that.

Perhaps a nice piece of cod. He liked cod when it was not overdone.

Yes, the final chorus! Applause from the thousands, maybe tens of thousands of people in the square. Time to applaud, time to enlarge the benign smile, time to . . .

The Pope blinked.

Then he frowned.

What was that? What was he seeing? Some sort of . . . it looked like an insect, a bizarre insect. He was seeing it, but . . . but it was nowhere around him.

He looked around, puzzled and a little concerned. No one else seemed to see anything unusual.

And now . . . now another vision. Like a movie screen lit up inside his head, like two of them, really, and both of them showing fantastic insects.

The one insect, he could see its face. . . . He could . . . he was hallucinating. Clearly, he was hallucinating. Was it a stroke? He dreaded a stroke; his father had died at age fifty-four of a stroke.

The insect face . . . It . . .

"It's me," he said in his native Spanish.

Then, as quickly as it opened, one of the windows in his head closed. Gone.

"Ah!" he cried out. "Ah!"

He sank to his knees, and now everyone was looking at him, now the TV cameras and the phone cameras all swiveled toward him, as he cried, "Oh, oh, oh!"

The Pope began to laugh. He began to laugh and laugh and then he was screaming, he knew he was screaming, though he felt no pain.

He screamed and tore at his vestments.

The world was swirling colors, all zooming crazily around him, faces suddenly coming into focus, distorted, demonic faces.

Only when he grabbed an elderly woman's walker and began attacking the children with it did anyone try to stop him.

In the end he was hauled away by Rome police and his own plain-clothes Swiss Guards.

TWENTY-ONE

The sense of approaching doom was rising now. The country was scared. The world was scared. Glances were shielded. Heads were lowered. Shoulders hunched. Jaws tight. Voices too high or too low, too loud or whispering like a scared child.

Not as scared yet as it should be, no, not yet. But when people figured it out, the true panic would begin.

The Twins had pulled the trigger on massed preprogrammed attacks: Burnofsky had seen the footage of Stern. There would be more of that. Benjamin was in the driver's seat increasingly, and Benjamin would have his apocalypse.

But that was nothing compared to what Lear was doing.

"Of course it's Lear!" Burnofsky cried aloud, as though someone was arguing with him, as though he was fighting someone to make them understand.

Lear. What a clever, clever fellow he had turned out to be. Burnofsky saw it all now, saw the games, saw the ultimate destructive power that flowed from Grey McLure's little lifesaving creatures.

Poor old Grey. They'd been friends, he and Burnofsky. The last friend Burnofsky had had. Poor old Grey, who had gotten his panties all in a twist when he learned Burnofsky was weaponizing nanobots for the Armstrongs. A lovely idealist, old Grey. A good man who just wanted to save his sick, dying wife.

Had he ever realized the destructive potential in his creatures? Had he even an inkling of what they could do in the wrong hands?

Fucking idealists. They were ever so useful to those with evil minds.

It was all coming down, Burnofsky thought. And when it did, the Twins were going to kill him. Kill him or rewire him.

That second thing made his stomach turn. He had endured it once, was still enduring it. But like many traumas, the threat of a repeat performance was even worse. He could *not* be used this way; he couldn't be turned into some computer made of meat, rewrite, delete, up-arrow, down-arrow, parentheses, backslash. . . .

He had in some way accepted the first wiring as a sort of penance. He was a sinner, a terrible sinner, and he had deserved the punishment of having his mind crudely twisted this way and that. But not again. Not again. He had paid. Paid enough.

Not again.

Death? Death was nothing. Death was relief of pain.

That's what he had told himself while sitting in his grim apartment with a gun in his mouth. He had lacked the courage to do it. But he would die before he would let them treat him like nothing. Like *nothing.*

"I paid," he told the camera he knew was watching him. His lip curled into a vicious sneer. "I *paid!*"

His mind went inevitably to Carla, and the sickening result of that thought, the excitement, the pleasure of it. And with it the awful need to hurt himself.

He lit a cigarette. He watched the end burn a bright orange. The smoke curling, teasing the end of his nose, making his watery eyes water still more. Not tears, though. Not tears.

The Pope—that would push the Twins over the edge. They would have to realize that they were no longer the masterminds, just two more suckers playing Lear's game. And then? Benjamin wouldn't stand for it, oh, no. Lear would not take Benjamin's *Götterdämmerung* from him. Benjamin would lose it, lash out, and at last unleash the gray goo.

He would use Burnofsky for that. Yes, of course. Burnofsky would serve the Twins one last time and destroy the world before Lear could do it.

It was funny, really—despite the way his eyes watered—it was funny, funny to think that in the end it would not be a race between destruction and salvation for humanity, but a race between two different lunatics, Benjamin and Lear, both bent on annihilation.

Well. Maybe not two.

Nanobots were *his* creation, not Benjamin's. Poor old Grey had died in a fiery crash, lucky bastard, and his creations had become Lear's. But Burnofsky still lived. Would go on living, probably, until the Twins decided they had squeezed the last from him.

"They're mine," he muttered, looking at a schematic of a nanobot. "I deserve a fucking prize. Hah! I deserve the fucking Nobel, hah!" Well, that was over, wasn't it. Lear had sort of killed that whole thing, hadn't he?

There was a bottle in the desk of one of his assistants. He had seen it, but he'd never said anything about it. It wasn't his job to preach abstinence.

"It's all coming down, anyway," he muttered. "Twist me this way, twist me that way; in the end it's all death."

He watched the thoughts in his own mind, tracked them like the scientist he was. Not so easy, really, to predict the outcome of wiring, eh, Nijinsky? Poor dumb Bug Man had learned that when the president went off the rails. Not so easy.

Five minutes later the alcohol was raw in his throat and warm in his belly.

"I paid," he said. And hurt himself again with a deep, deep swig.

"Hah!" Burnofsky said. "Fuck it. Fuck it all."

His phone lay on the desk. He blinked at it. The icon for messages showed a three.

No one texted Burnofsky. In fact, he couldn't recall the last time he'd had a text.

He almost didn't look, but even carried off on a happy wave of blessed alcohol, he was still a servant to his own curiosity.

It's Bug. Bad shit happening. Crazy bitch I think is Lear. Going to kill me and the whole damn world.

Then:

Are u there? Talk to me! I'm not playing.

Then:

Fuck! Do NOT call back. I'm using her phone. Can't wait. I'll try again later.

Burnofsky stared at the messages. His first thought: *Anthony's alive still? The Twins must be slipping.*

And then, *Jesus, he's fallen in with Lear?* And that made him laugh. Of *course* Anthony would end up back in some kind of world of shit. Of course he would.

And then he saw the words *bitch* and *her.*

Okay, he told himself, tamping down his excitement. *Bitch* could be slang for anyone, male or female. And the difference between *he* and *her* could be a simple mistyped letter.

Going to kill me and the whole damned world.

The Golden Hall in Stockholm. The Brazilians. That actress. The prince. The Pope. Even that slimy prick Nijinsky, of whose death he had at last learned.

"Yes, biot madness," Burnofsky said. He gave himself a deep swig, feeling the savage joy of destruction, and the subtler pleasure of having his theory, his educated guess, ratified. He felt as if he was vibrating from the rush of discovery, the way he had when he used to make breakthroughs in the lab.

He could call the phone number back. Who would answer? Bug Man? Or Lear?

"Biot madness. Jesus Christ," he said, voice an indecipherable slur. "BZRK. It's a joke. It's a goddamned joke. " Then, pushing himself back from his desk, shaking his head, he whispered, "Ah, no, not a joke: a game."

With trembling fingers he hit the call-back button.

The number you have dialed is not a working number.

No, of course not. Lear would swap phones regularly, clever boy. Or girl. Could it really be a woman? Was a woman capable of such malice? Would a woman play this game?

He opened his browser. How did one get samples of DNA? Any hospital, sure, but these were samples from multiple countries. Who could do that?

He searched *medical testing labs*, impeded somewhat by the fact that he couldn't quite direct his fingers to hit the right keys. He came up with too many results. He added qualifiers and came up with fewer hits. Then refined the search further to focus on corporate structures.

There were only six that were privately owned and reached beyond just North America. One of them, Janklow/MediStat, had recently lost its owner in an unfortunate boating accident.

"Accident. Hah."

Among those present on the boat and giving statements to the police was another—competing—corporate titan. A woman.

Three seconds later he had a photograph looking at him from his monitor, the face of Lystra Ellen Alice Reid.

L. E. A. R.

He stared at the picture. He laughed. *My God, a pretty young woman.* That face, that serious, intelligent, attractive face hid a madness as profound as anything bubbling beneath the surface of two men so hideous they couldn't walk down the street.

Lear. Self-aware madness, then. She knew, Lear did; the creator of BZRK knew she was mad. The wicked thing. The wicked, wicked thing.

He raised his mostly empty bottle to her in a wry toast. "Nice. Very nice."

He could probably stop her. He could take this to the Twins, and *they* could probably stop her.

"I could save the world," Burnofsky said, his tone mocking.

In the old days, he might have been tempted by that. He could be a hero. A hero/murderer. A hero who had helped to cause the suicide of the president of the United States. *Right. Hero.*

He could save the world.

Or.

Or he could beat Lear to the punch and shove it in the Twins' face as well.

Hero? Sorry, Dr. Burnofsky, that role is no longer available to you. How about killer? How about destroyer of worlds?

Yeah, that position was still open.

"Why?" Keats asked it, though he knew it was foolish. How did you ask for explanations when the person you were asking might be wired himself? But he asked, anyway. "Why, Vincent?"

"I had my orders. From Lear. He gave me instructions."

Plath licked her lips, nervous, angry, but feeling as if she should be far angrier. *Knowing* she should be far angrier. But somehow the emotion didn't quite come. The rage did not rise in her. "Tell me what he instructed," she said, her voice roughened to simulate the emotion she did not feel.

"He said to wire you. To reduce your skepticism. To avoid suspicion of Lear. Or of me."

"What else?"

"Seventy percent," Wilkes snarled. "Right."

"There are . . . holes in my mind," Vincent said. "I feel them. I know something is wrong with me. That's not a lie."

"Asshole!" Wilkes said, far more furious than Plath.

Plath raised a hand to silence Wilkes. "Tell me the rest," she said to Vincent.

Anya sat beside Vincent, who seemed terribly small. She was weeping quietly, holding one of his hands in hers. Expecting him to be killed.

Plath saw herself through Anya's eye. She saw a grim-faced girl, a sixteen-year-old girl with freckles for God's sake, with stupid freckles. That picture of her finally brought the true emotion to the surface, but the emotion was disgust. Plath was disgusted with herself, with what she had become.

"Tell me what you did about the Tulip, Vincent," Plath said.

Vincent flinched and broke eye contact. "You know what I did."

"You wired the Tulip and the Twin Towers together," Plath said bitterly. "And you looped in, what? Something that would make me less questioning, something . . ."

"I wired the memories of the Towers, the Tulip, and your pleasure centers, all together," Vincent said. "They were Lear's orders. That's what he wanted. I . . ." He looked at Anya, and now Plath was looking at Vincent through her own eyes and through Anya's. "I—"

"Did you at least argue? Did you at least question?" This was Keats now, raging. "Did you not say, 'What the hell are you talking about?' Did you not say, 'How dare you?' Did you not tell Lear to *go fuck himself*?" Keats looked as if he might beat Vincent to death right then and there.

"He's been wired, too," Plath said wearily. "We burned holes in his brain to save him, but someone else saw an opportunity in that.

We never checked because . . . well, because we felt so sad and guilty. But Lear got to Vincent, Vincent got to me."

"Who would have wired Vincent?" Keats asked, but even as the words were forming, he saw the answer. "Nijinsky. It's like a disease. Lear to Nijinksy, Nijinsky to Vincent, Vincent to Plath. Like a virus."

"Vincent, walk your biot out of me," Plath ordered. "Do it now."

Vincent said nothing, just looked at her, so Wilkes dropped down beside him, clapped a friendly hand on his leg, and in a flash there was a knife in her free hand. She jabbed the point against his carotid artery. "Do what the lady says, Vincent. Or I have to kill you. Give up the one you have in her, and your others, too. It's either that or you die."

"Do it, Vincent," Anya pleaded. "For me, do it."

Half an hour later Vincent's biots were in a vial hanging from Plath's neck. Vincent, the once-invincible Vincent, was still just seventy percent. But he was one hundred percent in Plath's power.

STATE OF PLAY

Enough dots had been connected. But twenty-four hours after the day of the prince and the Pope, no one had an explanation. The prince was locked in a comfortable room in the palace and tranquilized to near coma.

His Holiness was locked in comfortable rooms at the Vatican, tied to his bed, and tranquilized to near coma.

Stockholm was fresh out of psychiatric beds in its institutions.

And then the new head of Wells Fargo bank drove her car off a bridge.

And several hours after that the Ayatollah Aliabadi was discovered amid broken glass cutting his wrists.

And the fashion model who leapt out of a tenth-floor window in Kyoto.

And the rock star who stormed offstage at a concert in Toronto, only to return a few minutes later, armed with a pistol, which he emptied into the audience, killing one and injuring four.

And the president of the World Bank who swam frantically into the Baltic Sea in freezing conditions. He was rescued but had to be confined.

It soon became hard to keep track of.

The Christmas Crazy, it was called, though it had begun earlier. The Season of Hope, as some faiths called it, had taken a very grim turn.

The world was on edge. The world was baffled and frightened but still somewhat amused, as it was only prominent people being affected by whatever bizarre syndrome was occurring.

But then a tenth-grade teacher in Larkspur, California, began attacking students with a knife. Five injured, one critically.

And a soldier at Fort Belvoir, Virginia, grabbed his AR-15 and began shooting up the officer's club. Seven dead, three critically wounded.

The word was out: listen for people who claim to suddenly be seeing things in their head. Especially if they claim to be seeing strange insects.

Grab them, restrain them immediately, or at least get the hell out of the vicinity.

All over the world events were being postponed or canceled. All over the world people eyed each other with suspicion bordering on paranoia.

Then . . . nothing. For twenty-four hours.

Some dared to hope that it—whatever *it* was—was over.

Others wondered if whoever was behind this—aliens were the top choice—was just taking a break in order to build up to something even more unsettling.

The Centers for Disease Control and counterparts all over the world were in panic mode, searching for the cause, or at least the common thread. But it was a business consultant, who worked frequently with major medical clients, who made the tentative connection on his blog.

This person, David Schiller, sixty-three, suggested that, based on limited available data, it seemed those affected were more likely than the norm to have had lab work done. Medical tests. Blood tests. Urine samples.

He wrote this up on his blog. The dozen or so readers who saw the post wrote in comments that they would be very interested to see this developed further.

Sadly Schiller was unable to post a follow-up, as six hours after he published his blog post he was arrested by Chicago police for barbecuing one of his beloved Samoyeds on a fire he built in his front yard.

His blog was hacked and deleted.

The world was frightened. On edge. Desperate for some peace or some explanation.

The world was ready.

And so was Lear.

TWENTY-TWO

"I don't know how I feel," Plath said. "I feel . . ."

"It's probably weird," Keats said.

"Hollow."

They had walked out of the safe house, both feeling that there was too little air in the place, both needing to be reassured that the outside world still existed.

They looked at each other, and Keats knew that a vast distance had opened up between them. He had wanted nothing so much as to close the much smaller distance that had persisted, even during the idyll on Île Sainte-Marie. Instead, he had dug the Grand Canyon and now looked at her across it.

She had not raged at him. She seemed too tired to be very angry that he had unwired her without permission, in fact in direct rejection of her wishes. The temperature of their conversation was cold, not hot. She stood with her hands down at her sides. Her eyes were as big as ever, but now they seemed to be looking just past him, refusing to make eye contact.

"I'm sorry," he said.

"No. You did the right thing," she said. There was no reassurance in her tone.

"Brains are complicated," Keats said pointlessly.

"Mmm. Yeah. Complicated."

"I have to ask . . ."

"What?" She frowned, wishing he would go away and let her adjust to this feeling of emptiness. She felt nauseous. She felt as if she might at some point throw up. She felt *not herself*, like this was not her body, like she was a head transplant attached to some new torso. Alien.

"I have to ask what you told Caligula."

"Caligula? Nothing. I can't text him or call him."

Keats wanted to heave a sigh of relief, but it might have seemed as if he hadn't trusted her. Then . . .

"I told Lear."

His blue eyes snapped up to hers, and his brows lowered. "Told Lear what?"

"That Caligula should do it."

"What?" He grabbed her shoulders. "You gave the go-ahead to blow up the Tulip?"

She nodded. No emotion. Yes, she had ordered up an atrocity. No emotion. Yes, she had ordered mass murder. Nothing.

"Jesus, Sadie," he said, and his voice broke.

She blinked, taken aback by his reaction. "It's okay," she said.

He released her, and now he was no longer looking at her, he was staring into the window in his mind where his biot's visual flow would be. But the images were grainy and indistinct. The distance was too great. The biot he had in Caligula's head was too far out of range for useful input.

"We have to stop him," Keats said.

"Uh-huh," she said indifferently.

What happened next was pure instinct, and he regretted it even as his hand was flying through the air, even as the flat of his palm connected with the side of her face with enough force to snap her head around and start the tears in her eyes.

When her eyes came back around there was emotion. Anger. Finally, anger.

"Listen to me," he said, regretful but determined, too. "We have to stop him."

"Don't you fucking hit me," she snarled.

"Good. You're not dead yet, are you? I'm sorry about the slap, but you sound like you're in a coma."

"And who put me there?" she demanded.

"Lear put you there!" he said. "This has all been a game for him. We wanted to stop one evil, so we never even asked questions about whether the man we served was just as bad. Or worse." He felt her attention slipping away and wanted to grab her but knew that would be wrong. So he leaned closer to her, bending down so that she could not avoid looking at him. "Madness like a bloody plague. All over. It's all *Lear*. It's Lear making biots and then killing them to drive people mad. Hundreds of dead already. The Pope went mad and attacked little children. Sadie, that's his game."

"The Pope?"

"Lear. *Lear!* And we have to stop him. We have to stop Lear!"

"The Twins," she said, sounding vague.

"Yeah, them, too," Keats said. "Come on."

He grabbed her hand and yanked her along with him.

Wilkes stood up as they burst into the living room. Billy was absorbed in his phone.

"Caligula's going to blow up the Tulip," Keats said. "We have to stop him."

"Blow up the Tulip?" Wilkes said. "I thought that—"

"Yeah, well, it's back on."

"You're going to stop Caligula?" Wilkes demanded skeptically. "You and what army, pretty blue eyes? You've seen him in action. This won't be biot war; this will be kill or get killed, with a dude who is a genius at killing!"

"We have a gun. Just one. It's—"

"It's in the drawer in the kitchen, below the silverware." This from Billy. Casual, as though it was no big thing that he knew where they'd hidden a gun. Then, "It's a Colt forty-five. Seven-round clip. One spare clip. We have a total of fourteen bullets."

"I'll do the best I can with it," Keats said, knowing in his heart that it wouldn't work, knowing—because, yes, he *had* seen Caligula work—that Caligula would kill him before he fired a shot.

Wilkes, seeing that despair, shook her head and said, "Keats, you aren't a gunman. Neither am I." She looked pointedly at Billy.

"Yeah," the young boy said. "I can do it."

"No," Keats said. He shook his head. "No. That's wrong. That's over the line."

"It is over the line." They stopped, looking back almost guiltily, to see Plath.

"This doesn't involve you," Keats said. He didn't mean it to sound angry, but it did.

Plath shook her head. "Of course it involves me, Noah. I gave the order to Caligula."

"Can you just take back the order?" Billy asked.

Plath shook her head. "That was all part of the game. Lear's game. For whatever sick reason he wanted me to choose to do it. But that doesn't mean he'll stop just because I change my mind."

She looked around at them, defiant, defying her own shame. "I . . ." She sighed and shook her head. "I don't know . . . how my brain is . . ." She sighed again. "I don't know anything, I guess. I was used. I was controlled, but then, even after you guys . . ." She made a gesture with her hand, as if she was pulling something out of her head. "I still wanted revenge, and the wiring played into that. I still wanted revenge. I guess I do even now. But yeah, what Mr. Stern told me . . . There has to be a line."

Keats saw tears flowing and his heart yearned to touch her, to take her in his arms and protect her. But that felt impossible now.

"I thought of what my dad would say," Plath said, dejectedly. "My dad, my brother . . . there still has to be some kind of limit. A line drawn." She wiped away the tears, then, resolute, said, "So we stop Caligula. But. But we give the gun to the kid."

Caligula disliked disguise, but he knew how to use it. There were two approaches. You could either become part of the background and therefore be ignored—like a janitor. Or you could pass yourself off more boldly, pretending to be someone in authority, someone who would compel obedience. For example, pretending to be a cop.

And Caligula understood diversion. He'd spent a part of his life working the carnival as a trick shooter and knife thrower, and he'd met his share of magicians. Sleight of hand was all about misdirection: look over there, not over here.

Finally he understood simple brutality.

All three were required to gain access to the subfloors of the Tulip.

He dressed as a janitor, having first determined what the AFGC janitors wore and when they worked and through which entrance they came. He gathered his long gray hair into a bun and pushed it up under a do-rag, slipped into gray-blue overalls, and, crucially, applied just enough dark makeup to be arguably Mexican. In the world as it was, a dark-skinned older man dressed as a janitor was as close to invisible as it was possible to be. It wasn't just that people didn't notice you; it was that they actively avoided making eye contact with you or noting any feature.

But timed to coincide with his fraught passage through the security station on the first subfloor, Caligula arranged a distraction in the form of a call to NYPD claiming to have seen a homeless white woman waving a knife and threatening people on the street in front of the Tulip.

The choice of a fictional white woman was important, because it in no way pointed to a theoretically Hispanic janitor. And, as well, there actually was a homeless white woman with a shopping cart on the sidewalk. Five bucks and a secret message from "aliens" in the person of Caligula had ensured her presence.

The police duly came roaring up. The security guards at the entrance duly ran to see what was happening. And the sublevel security guards duly glued themselves to their monitors and muttered jealously about *those guys upstairs who at least have something going on.*

Caligula dragged a heavy floor cleaner past without notice.

Down the stairs. One level. Two. The door was locked but was easily defeated with a six-inch segment of metal venetian blind.

The temperature went up ten degrees from stairwell to mechanical room. As mechanical rooms went it was a nice one, three stories from grated floor to pipe-crossed ceiling, with catwalks offering access to massive blowers, electrical boxes, alarm systems, and telephone and cable panels.

Everything was color coded, so it was easy to pick out the natural gas pipes from the water lines and cable conduits. *Red. An interesting choice,* Caligula thought. He might have gone with lilac. He liked lilac.

The first job was to make sure no one was down here. He walked around, looking lost with his floor cleaner until he located the engineer on duty. He was a middle-aged man, staring at an iPad propped in front of the readouts he was meant to be watching.

Caligula gave him a hello wave and a hatchet in the neck, stepping nimbly out of the way of the blood spray.

He squeezed fast-drying epoxy around the edges of the doors. He looked around, spotted a metal table, dragged it over to the door, tipped it on its side, and epoxied it across the door. Once the epoxy had hardened in twenty minutes, it would take a tank to break through. He would leave via the freight elevators, which he'd be able to watch more easily.

The next thing was to eliminate any source of spark. It wouldn't do to have the gas ignite too soon. He turned off the heating system. He decided to accept the risk of a random spark from one of the electrical panels—unlikely, given the pristine newness of the building.

Then he located the safety shutoffs that would choke off the gas in the event that the computers decided a pipe had ruptured. He jammed that useful piece of equipment with a wrench.

Which left only the last three phases: opening the flow, setting the timer on the igniting explosive, and getting the hell out of the place before it blew up.

About twenty floors above Caligula, Burnofsky worked. The beautiful thing about nanotech, he thought, was the whole nano thing itself. Nano: small. Tiny. Invisible to the human eye.

He could begin growing self-replicating nanobots within full view of the hidden cameras. A million of them looked like a couple of handfuls of dust. Blue dust, in this case, because in a moment of wracking guilt back before—before the new Burnofsky—he had given them the color of his daughter's eyes. He'd done that as a strange expiation. An homage? Was that the right word?

He was still secretive about drinking the booze. He rolled his wheeled office chair back into a blind spot, poured into an empty soda can, then rolled back into view.

Were the Twins watching? He didn't really care, so long as they didn't try to stop him.

He had ten million SRNs so far. SRNs with no limits. SRNs that would replicate and replicate, doubling in number and doubling again and again and again until there were not millions but billions, trillions, as many as there were grains of sand on all the beaches of the world.

What was the famous quote from 1984? He Googled it. He wanted to get it right. Ah, there.

If you want a picture of the future, imagine a boot stamping on a human face—forever.

Well, no, Mr. Orwell, Burnofsky thought. *If you want a picture of the future, imagine a world scoured clean of every living thing.* And more. Imagine that having taken and used all the easiest forms of carbon the SRNs keep going. They eat the steel out of buildings, the coal and oil and diamond out of the earth itself. They wouldn't just destroy all life, they would relentlessly remove all possibility that life would ever again arise to trouble an empty planet.

His eye scanned down the page of quotes from Orwell and came to rest on this: *Power is in tearing human minds to pieces and putting them together again in new shapes of your own choosing.*

Hah. Well, the Twins had tried it. The Twins, with their mad plan to unite all of humanity into one vast interconnectedness. A new world where they would be accepted. And more than accepted: esteemed, loved.

And Lear? What was young Lystra Reid's motive?

Burnofsky's own motive was clear to him now. He had done evil for ambition's sake. He had tortured himself for that evil and sought to close the eyes of the world to his shame.

Then he had been rewired so that the evil gave him pleasure. And now he would close the eyes of the world because it would bring him pleasure.

He would wait for a few more doublings. Then he would drop the force fields that held the SRNs contained and unleash the gray goo.

Then? Well, then he would go back to his old haunt, back to the China Bone. There would be time for them to prepare him a pipe. He would float on a cloud of purple opium haze and wait for the end of the world. When the nanobots reached him, well, that's when he would take a last drink and fire the heroin into his veins and leave the world behind, dying with two raised middle fingers to humanity.

Suarez wished she had music, but the cockpit was not large enough to allow her to reach for her headphones. It was just that the mad rush of sheer speed demanded some propulsive music to go along with it.

It was crazy. It was also crazy fun.

The sleigh was a dream to drive. Computer-assists and automated systems made it more like a video game than a craft moving at a hundred and fifty miles an hour. The little icon that was the sleigh on the GPS display was zooming along past . . . well, past nothing, really. This was Antarctica. There were no towns, houses, roads, or any feature, really, aside from the blur of ice and the gray blanket of hazy, overcast sky. The target was coming closer very fast, and she didn't really have much of a plan for how to approach it.

Most likely roaring in at three times freeway speeds—with jet engines screaming and ice crystals trailing a plume—was a bad idea. The smart move would probably be to park the sleigh a few miles away from the target and walk in on foot. Much more subtle that way. But on the ice one did not casually decide to abandon a vehicle that provided shelter and warmth. Not to mention a vehicle with an impressive array of weapons.

So she would try to bluff it out. Whoever she encountered would probably suspect her cover story was nonsense, but what could they do about it, really?

"People who buy illegal missiles and smuggle them onto the ice?" she said aloud. "Plenty. That's what they can do: plenty."

On the other hand, Suarez was only the third woman ever to qualify for SEALs, so she was no weakling. She was formidable.

"That's right, talk yourself into it," she muttered.

It was a good thing she had the computer navigating, because she would never have seen the dry valley. It was a rift in the ice, which at this point was a relatively sparse two hundred meters thick.

Part of her just wanted to keep shooting across the ice, but she slowed reluctantly and nosed the sleigh closer to the edge of the valley. Still she could see nothing ahead of her but ice and more ice.

"On foot it is, then," she muttered. With great reluctance she raised the canopy, unwedged herself, and managed to climb rather ungracefully out. The wind was doing thirty knots—gentle by local standards—just enough to push cold stilettos through every seam, every zipper, every opening in her parka. She pulled on her bear claw mittens, cinched the neck strap a bit tighter, and leaned into the wind to walk what seemed to be the last hundred yards.

She didn't see the edge of the precipice until she was practically on top of it.

"Whoa." Antarctica had millions of square miles of same-old,

BZRK APOCALYPSE

same-old, but hidden here and there in the largely unexplored continent there were features that would take your breath away. This was one of those times.

The ice fell away in a sheer cliff just beyond the toes of her boots. Spread out below her was a narrow valley shaped like a boat hull—pointed at the near end, rounded at the far end. Suarez's position would correspond to just off the starboard bow.

The topography was not complicated; it was effectively a big, oblong hole in the ice, maybe two kilometers long, a quarter that in width at the widest point. The floor of the valley was reddish gravel and looked like an abandoned quarry. About where the cabin would be on a yacht was a series of structures—four buildings, one quite large by polar standards, and, sure enough, under a plastic dome there was unmistakably a swimming pool.

Somebody really liked to swim.

Suarez carefully absorbed the layout. The structure with the two stubby towers would be the power plant. The largest building was some sort of hangar or factory space, unmistakably utilitarian. The third, a two-story L-shape, would be a barracks. Room for, what, fourteen, sixteen rooms plus a common space? So not a huge contingent.

And finally what looked very much like a private home, done with a reckless disregard for energy conservation, a three-story, ultra-modern, Scandinavian-looking thing with the kind of floor-to-ceiling windows you just didn't see in Antarctica, and a plastic tunnel running to the pool.

Instead of the inevitable Sno-Cats there was a pair of Audi SUVs parked outside the house, as though the occupant might have kids and pets who needed transportation to the nearest soccer field or dog park.

Craziness. Suarez had to laugh. It was nuts. And whoever had built it was nuts. They were hundreds of miles from the coast, which was to say a whole long way from even the thinnest edge of civilization. This might easily be the most isolated house on planet Earth. Sure as hell the furthest from a Starbucks.

Two helicopters lay all tied down and shipshape on a well-marked pad. One was an EC130, a species of chopper found all over the ice. But the other was an Apache, with missile pods on the stubby wings and a swivel-mounted thirty-millimeter cannon.

Who had the kind of political juice to get hold of a freaking Apache?

How had this place even been discovered? Either someone had amazing luck, or they had some amazing satellite imagery. Speaking of which, a satellite would have to be directly overhead to see the valley at all.

Suarez peered off to the far end of the valley. Was that a road? It *looked* like a road cut into the ice wall, rising at a steep grade up to the outside. Could she drive the sleigh down there? Bigger question: Could she get it back out?

The smart thing to do would be to take some pictures and get the hell out of here, get back to Tanner and let him take it from there. That was definitely the smart move.

Yes.

So Suarez, face already numb and hands getting there, climbed back into the sleigh and drove at safe speed around to the head of the road. It was definitely a road, hopefully just wide enough to allow a large truck—or the sleigh—to avoid going off the side.

"All in now," she said to herself, and sent the sleigh creeping down the incline. This proved to be as tricky as she'd thought it might be. There was no pavement, of course, just icy gravel, dropping what looked to be about one hundred meters in the course of a quarter mile, one heck of a grade. The sleigh, like any hovercraft, was not well suited to going downhill in a controlled manner and started to slide sideways almost immediately, but Suarez got the hang of it and made it to the valley floor without plunging off the side of the ice ramp.

Still no one came rushing to greet or confront her. Either would almost have been welcome merely for the purpose of ending the suspense. The sleigh was more than capable of crossing gravel, but now, down inside the rift, it was a high-strung Thoroughbred in a too-narrow paddock.

Was the whole place abandoned? Obviously anyone there would have heard, if not seen, the sleigh. You don't exactly sneak up on people when you're in a jet-powered hovercraft.

She throttled forward, creeping along at walking speed, aiming for the bizarre house—which was no less bizarre down here at eye level. The glass windows were mirrored, so Suarez could not see inside and instead saw the reflection of herself scowling from beneath the canopy.

Finally, lacking any better idea of what to do, she parked the sleigh, killed the engines, and climbed out again. There was no wind, which did not make it any warmer but did reduce the effects a bit.

Her breath rose as steam but her face, while cold, regained some of its feeling.

Now what? Ring the doorbell?

She crunched across the gravel to the door of the house. There was no bell. So she stripped off one glove and knocked.

Bad idea. The door was steel and very, very cold. Had she knocked any slower she'd have left knuckle skin behind.

No answer.

"This is insane."

The next likely target was the large—quite large—building fifty meters away.

There would presumably be a satellite phone in the buildings, or an Internet connection—some way to inform Tanner. The question was whether there would also be men and women with guns. It all had an empty but not-quite-abandoned feel.

The building was not locked. Well, why would you lock a building that was a million miles from nothing much? But it bothered her. This was all too easy.

She pushed in. Lights were on, illuminating a single large open space populated by machinery of a sleek, white-coated type. She recognized only the 3D printers, monitors, and touch screens. The other objects were not familiar, and might have been anything from manufacturing to medical gear. But one particular type of equipment predominated: a chest-height, white rectangle with inexplicable slots outlined in green light. There were a lot of those. Dozens. Maybe a hundred. These definitely were some kind of manufacturing equipment, not computers. Probably automated, given that the machines were backed too closely together to allow for people to move easily around them.

Fascinated by trying to make sense of the machines, Suarez belatedly registered the sound of armed men taking positions behind her.

Six of them. Six automatic rifles leveled at her from behind the cover of the equipment.

One of the downsides of actually being a trained fighter is that you come to accept that real life isn't Hollywood, and no one wins a fight that pits a single assault rifle against six.

"Set the gun aside. Raise your hands."

That's what she did.

TWENTY-THREE

The line of limos completely choked West 54th Street, extended back onto Seventh Avenue and then all the way up to 56th Street. Stretches, town cars, the occasional privately owned Mercedes or Tesla.

Crowds pushed against barricades manned by tolerantly amused NYPD pulling down some welcome overtime pay. Satellite trucks had been parked right on the sidewalk across from the Bow Tie Ziegfeld Theater, which all by themselves doubled the congestion.

It was not an uncommon situation. This was not New York's first big movie premiere. But even New York could not be jaded about this much star power. Every A-list actor, director, and producer was here, all of Hollywood royalty, for the premiere of the year's biggest-budget flick *Fast, Fast, Dead,* starring, among several actual human stars, a computer-generated Marilyn Monroe that was supposed to be so indistinguishable from the long-dead real thing that there'd been some speculation about whether the program might be up for an Oscar nomination.

Lystra Reid had managed an invitation for herself and a plus one. The plus one was at least ten years her junior, but this was a Hollywood crowd, and if the relatively unknown but reputed to be fabulously rich woman wanted a young, black, not terribly attractive boy toy who had clearly been on the wrong end of either a bar fight or a car accident, hey, who cared, really? The country had bigger problems.

"We're toward the back," Lystra said, guiding Bug Man in.

Despite the rocketing pain of his broken teeth and the split, swollen lips, Bug Man was enthralled. Obviously Lystra was up to something horrific, but in the meantime Bug Man played Spot the Star. Seeing a very familiar face, he said, "Man, I ufed to cruff on her when I wa' a little ki' looking a' Harry Potter," he said.

"Watching what?"

"Harry . . . Never mind." Lystra Reid was not big on popular culture, Bug Man had decided. And talking was painful and difficult, though he was adjusting to the lack of front teeth.

"I' tha' Gwynneff?" Bug Man asked, but of course Lystra was paying no attention. And the star-dense crowd was not looking at Bug Man. They were hailing old friends and talking to the roving camera crews still pushing through packed-in A-listers.

The jocularity was strained. There was not a person in the room so oblivious to all that had happened in the world that they were not nervous. Some celebrities who had initially agreed to attend had suddenly discovered that they had headaches and would need to skip the proceedings. But the ideal of "the show must go on" and the lure of cameras had kept numbers high enough to prevent organizers from canceling.

"Time to send a text," Lystra said. And when Bug Man failed to cease craning his neck to locate a particular buxom TV star, she said more pointedly, "This is going to go bad in a few minutes. So stay close to me." She laid a hand gently on his swollen cheek. "I wouldn't want anything to happen to you. And don't forget: you wouldn't want anything to happen to me."

She thumbed in a text that went to the closest cell-phone tower, from there to a satellite, and from that satellite to a touch screen almost ten thousand miles away and very far to the south.

She almost blew the timing. Another minute or two and the cameras would have turned off their lights and been hustled from the theater by security people and public relations folk.

Lystra wanted cameras. All the cameras.

The first person to cry out in a startled voice that carried even over the hubbub was a big man with a big voice who said, "I see bugs!"

Ten seconds later, another voice, female, screamed.

"Oh my God, it's like, it's like that thing in Sweden!" Lystra herself cried helpfully. "That's what *they* said. Bugs! That's what happened there! Oh my God, we're all going mad!"

"Aaaaaahhhh!" a man cried, and then more, and more, and all at once everyone in the theater seemed to realize what was happening. And what was coming.

A well-liked hunk known for starring in superhero movies started laughing and then tried to shove his entire hand into his mouth. Bug Man stared in disbelief. It was one thing knowing that something could theoretically happen. It was a whole different thing when a Marvel superhero was trying to gag himself right in front of you.

"And now we exit," Lystra said. She smiled at Bug Man. She was enjoying his amazement. She'd been right to bring him along. It would be fun to have someone to share it all with afterward. "See, this is why I've savored, yeah, a few of these events in person: video doesn't do it justice. The edge of panic. Yeah. The wild look in people's eyes."

The panic was like a herd of wildebeest smelling a lion. In a heartbeat hundreds of people surged toward the exits. A woman in an evening gown went down. She tried to stand, but someone tromped on the hem of her dress and she fell again.

Lystra and Bug Man barely made it out the door without being trampled, and she laughed as she was jostled and laughed as she was pushed hard against a door and laughed still as she spilled out onto 54th Street into the glare of lights.

They ran to get ahead of the flood, raced to get behind the cameras to watch as long as Lystra could without endangering herself too much.

A bloody Broadway star was shouting nonsense syllables. A famously beautiful actor was tearing her dress off while her director crawled on all fours making a sound like a sheep. Hollywood's favorite dad was playing with his hair, twining his fingers through it and laughing hysterically.

An Oscar-winning producer launched himself at a New York police officer, pushed him to the ground, and yanked the gun from the startled cop. The first shot struck a film critic in the chest, a fact that he found funny until he fell over dead.

"Time to get out of here. Guns are dangerous," Lystra observed.

Bug Man stared at her, looked around at the madness, and back at her. At the wild glee in her eyes.

"I know how they feel," Lystra said without even a hint of

compassion. "I've been there. I've been crazy. It's kind of . . . amazing, really."

She turned and walked quickly away, ignoring the well-dressed lunatics rushing by, dancing, twirling and attacking each other with fists and fingernails.

Bug Man followed her, because Bug Man had nowhere else to go.

The trick was to pop the natural gas pipeline in a way that would not cause a spark. Caligula was not interested in suicide.

Power saw and small explosive charge were both ruled out. And he didn't just want to open a smaller release valve—it would take forever for the gas to build up. He needed a rupture in one of the main lines. He needed the gas to come roaring in, thousands of cubic yards of it.

He had disabled the local safety cutoffs. The next cutoff covered an entire six-block area—this rupture would probably trigger it eventually, but not quickly enough.

He had brought a car jack with him, the simple, screw-type device, capable of lifting a car off the street. More than enough if he could just find the right position.

He needed a place where the pipe was rigid. Like right . . . *there* . . . where it emerged from the concrete foundation. And just two feet from that point there was a junction, a sort of flange—he wasn't exactly familiar with the terminology. Perfect. If he could just get the jack between the concrete wall and the pipe standing eight inches out from same. He pulled the jack from a bag and looked at it critically. It would be a tough squeeze. The jack, even screwed all the way down, was ten inches tall. So he either had to find another place, or he would have to chip away some of the concrete to make room.

He sighed and retrieved a chisel and a rubber mallet. Slight delay, that was all.

"He's in the basement," Keats said. "I can see what he's doing. He's chipping away at something with a chisel. There's still time."

They were outside the Tulip. In the alleyway behind. Staring at various doors—two loading bays, a smaller door, a door a few dozen yards away that was vented so probably contained electrical equipment.

No clue.

There was the front door, out on the street, but that was guarded. Their weapons were: one little kid with a Colt .45.

No. Wait. There was a second weapon: the biot in Caligula's head.

Keats could blind the killer.

Or he could maybe slice through an artery and kill or cripple Caligula.

Rewiring was not going to happen in the few minutes remaining to them. There would be no time for subtlety. And if Keats moved his biot farther into Caligula's brain, he would have to detach from the optic nerve and would no longer be able to see what Caligula was doing.

How long to blind one eye? And could he reach the other eye in time to truly stop Caligula? Or would he be better off diving down deep, finding a fat artery, and sawing away?

Keats felt sick inside. He had no plan. He had a Goth chick, a wild street kid with a gun, a biot, and Plath, who might or might not be entirely okay.

"What do we do, pretty blue eyes?" Wilkes of course, jumpy, nervous, eyes darting everywhere with manic appreciation of their hopeless plight.

The door beside the second loading bay opened. Light spilled out. A man in silhouette yelled, "Hey, move along, you three."

Before Keats could react there was a loud bang and a flash. A cry of pain. The man in silhouette was visible for a millisecond in the flash. He was younger than his voice, maybe twenty-five, uniformed. A security guard. A minimum-wage grunt with a hole in his chest that leaked dark blood onto khaki.

Billy was moving, leapt up the four concrete steps, and grabbed the door as the man fell back.

"Jesus!" Keats cried.

Wilkes was quicker, just seconds behind Billy. She grabbed the door, freeing Billy, who calmly knelt and took the dying man's gun.

Keats and Plath followed, Keats feeling as if he was in a dream. Two biot windows were open in his head, one showing the damned bulge in Plath's brain, the other watching the rise and fall, rise and fall of mallet on chisel.

Billy was already proffering the guard's pistol to Keats, butt-forward. Keats stared at it. Wilkes took it.

Keats stepped over the guard. He was crying softly and holding his wound with one hand while fumbling for his radio with the other.

He couldn't be left alive to raise the alarm.

Wilkes and Billy both looked at Keats expectantly. Waiting for his order. Plath seemed mesmerized.

On me, the responsibility, Keats thought. It had been so quick, somehow, getting to this point, the kill-or-be-killed point.

Billy must have seen the answer in Keats's eyes. He squatted and pressed the muzzle directly against the man's heart, muffling the sound as much as he could.

BANG!

And blood sprayed across Billy's face.

"It's okay," Billy said. "I did it before. Just another first-person shooter, right?"

Keats felt like throwing up. He felt a flash of fury at Plath. Shouldn't she have made the decision? Shouldn't the guilt be *hers* to bear?

The guard was motionless now. But all was not still. They were in a short hallway—barely painted drywall, weak overhead lighting, second door now opening fast, someone coming through expecting trouble, gun already leveled and—

BANG!

Head shot. A single hole drilled right in the man's forehead. The back of his head—a crust of skull and hair and something like hamburger—hit the wall and slid down, leaving a trail.

"Go," Keats said, barely audible.

Through the door, now in the wide-open space within the loading bay, boxes and crates and a chair and table and playing cards laid out, and a coffee mug, and flickering monitors.

"Basement," Keats managed to say, trying to push aside the

memory of tears rolling down a doomed man's cheeks.

One of the innocents I was trying to save, Keats thought.

Now, two of the innocents I was trying to save.

They were lost and needed light. Keats spotted a bank of light switches, crossed to them, made it halfway before his stomach sent its contents burbling out of his mouth. He threw every switch, wiped his mouth, and said, "Find a way down!"

The glare of fluorescent light had the effect of casting deep shadows that if anything made the room seem darker, with every high-piled stack of crates like a skyscraper shadowing narrow alleys.

They ran then, moved forward, the young sociopath with the name of a young sociopath leading the way. Billy moved like a cop, cover to cover, gun steadied in both hands, a goddamned gamer, a goddamned game, where would the bad guys pop up next?

"Whoa. Down here," Wilkes said, waving her own gun fecklessly toward a dark hallway.

Billy moved smoothly ahead of her. Cover. Pause. Scan. Run to cover. Pause. Scan.

A freight elevator, with buttons for up and down.

"Down," Keats said, feeling useless and now seeing flashes of his London home, so squalid and dull all his life, but now so beloved, so *needed*. To crawl into his own bed . . .

The elevator door opened on a guard with headphones in and singing along tunelessly, yet Keats recognized the song.

"Born This Way." An old Gaga tune.

Keats barely flinched when Billy put a bullet into the guard's head. The bullet must have hit just wrong because it entered the forehead and blew an exit wound out through the man's jaw.

The ricochet could have killed one of them, but no, and the man went down with such completeness that he might have been a dropped sack of garbage.

Wilkes dragged the dead man off the elevator.

Buttons. Three different sublevels. Where was Caligula? Go all the way down. Why not? Gates of hell. Keats punched the S3 button.

The elevator doors closed over smeared blood.

Billy popped the clip from the gun, counted the bullets and said, "I don't think there are upgrades or reloads in this game."

It struck Keats that if he had ever found a match for Caligula, it was this sad, sick little boy. It was not a good thought. His stomach was empty, and the smell of his vomit filled the padding-walled elevator as it dropped beneath them.

Keats had kept his place on Caligula's optic nerve. He saw the sudden cessation of hammering. The visual field swirled as Caligula moved quickly.

"He's heard us!"

"Up against the walls, hide under the blankets!" Billy yelled in high-pitched excitement.

The blankets were the padding hung to protect the elevator walls. Wilkes and Keats dived under. Too late Keats saw that Plath hadn't moved.

Billy stood waiting, gun drawn and leveled.

Keats saw Caligula rushing toward the elevator, stopping, ducking behind cover. And then the peace of the game descended on Keats. It was live-or-die time. Win-or-lose time.

All his gaming life Keats had had this other place he could go, except that he didn't quite go there as an act of deliberate choice, it would just *happen*. It would come down over him—a calm, a control, a speed of perception, an ease of decision making—blessedly blanking out fear and self-loathing.

"He'll be to your left, Billy," Keats said. "Behind a thick vertical pipe painted orange."

Billy shifted stance without a word.

"He's expecting an adult, someone tall," Keats said, still deadly calm.

Billy nodded and squatted. His head would be lower than a grown man's belly. Caligula would be quick, but he might hesitate on seeing a child.

"Wilkes. Give me your gun. As soon as the door opens, scream, really loud," Keats ordered. "Like you need help."

Caligula's eye was steady now, lid drooping just a bit, unafraid surely, confident that no one could beat him. Keats's biot was already busy sawing away at the massive optic nerve beneath its feet. Cutting, cutting, like trying to slice through a bridge cable with a hacksaw, but nerve fibers popped and coiled away, wildly whipping wires, and each taking with it a tiny part of Caligula's visual field.

The elevator stopped.

The door was loud as it opened.

Wilkes screamed, "Help! Help me! Help me!"

BANG!

BANG!

Billy and Caligula fired almost simultaneously and out came

Keats from behind the hanging blanket and fired wildly, *BANG-BANGBANG!* with bullets ricocheting off pipes.

Keats's biot sawed madly and now more shooting, and Keats was on the floor of the elevator now, crawling on his belly, aiming, squeezing off rounds, gun bucking in his hand until it banged open, out of bullets.

Billy, still standing, advanced in quickstep, running for cover, and Keats saw Caligula's eye tracking him, saw the butt of Caligula's gun as it bucked from recoil and heard the loud *BANG!* and saw Billy the Kid's neck suddenly no longer all there.

The boy fired again as arterial blood sprayed like a cut fire hose, until his head, no longer supported, fell to one side and hung limply, and Billy fell, knees hitting the floor, then onto his back and his head bounced, barely tethered. His gun twirled across the floor leaving a blood trail.

Caligula emerged from cover. He holstered his now-empty gun. Calm. No hurry. He drew his throwing hatchet, and Keats could see the killer's eye on him, on a pitiful crawling wretch, saw the way it focused on his upturned face.

Alien, the sight of his own face as he waited to die. Strange and alien. Keats knew the face, knew it was him, but how could that be? The blessed peace of action had faded, and now he was a bug, a worm waiting to be crushed by the boot of the human god.

The hatchet flew.

It grazed Keats's shoulder and clattered to the floor of the elevator.

Was Wilkes still screaming? Someone was.

Caligula blinked. Stared.

Knew. *Understood.* Because Caligula did not miss, not with gun or hatchet. He did not miss, and he knew then it could only be some fault in his vision.

Keats's biot sawed and more nerves parted.

Caligula drew a knife and bounded, like some bizarre kangaroo, rushing with unnatural speed. Keats saw the distance shorten in a heartbeat, saw the killer's focus, saw his own scared face, Wilkes's open mouth, a flash of Plath's hand pressing down on the door's Close button, and the elevator door closing too slowly.

Caligula reached the elevator when the doors were still six inches apart. He thrust in a hand to stop it.

Wilkes was on him like an animal, biting the hand, snarling, shaking her head like a terrier with a rat.

Caligula yelled in pain and rage.

Keats saw the door from the inside.

The door through Caligula's eyes.

The knife dropped from Caligula's bloody hand, but he did not withdraw, would not let the door close.

The hatchet was in Keats's hand before he knew it. He observed it through Caligula's eye, saw the killer seeing him, saw the killer track the hatchet as it went back and came down fast and hard and Caligula tried to pull the hand back now, but Wilkes still had it in her teeth and the hatchet blade hit with a cleaver-on-bone sound, barely missing Wilkes's nose and biting deep into Caligula's flesh.

Wilkes recoiled then, the hand pulled away, pumping blood from the gash.

Keats saw the doors close from both sides.

He saw the killer stare at his mangled hand, then through his own eyes saw the little pink curls of fingers on the elevator floor.

The elevator rose.

"Billy," Wilkes said. Her mouth was smeared with blood, forming a terrible rictus smile.

"Up," Keats said, and punched the button for the highest floor available, the third floor.

"What are we going to do?" Wilkes asked and there was a sob in her voice.

"Surrender," Plath said.

TWENTY-FOUR

Suarez was handcuffed. The handcuffs went through a chain that in turn went through a massive steel ring set into the wall at head height.

The wall was in a dungeon.

The dungeon was both frightening and absurd. There were mossy stone walls. There was straw on the stone floor. She'd been left with a rusty pail in which to do her business. The door was too low and made of flaking, unfinished wood. There was a narrow window, but when she dragged her chain over to it she saw that it was fake. The scene visible through the window was a matte painting of a medieval village.

"Cute," she said dryly.

It was like a movie set, or something out of a video game. Someone was having fun with the whole idea of a dungeon. Which was absurd.

The scary part came from the fact that the cuffs and chain and even the ring in the wall were all of very high-grade steel.

A man who had the bearing of a former cop or soldier, a beefy, steroided thirtysomething with a crew cut, brought her dinner after a while. The tray was plastic and flimsy, no use as a weapon. The cutlery was plastic as well, and not the good kind. Water was in a plastic bottle. Wine was in a paper cup.

Wine, because it was quite a good meal, considering the location. Better than airline food, in any event. Wine in a dungeon.

"You have a name, soldier?" Suarez asked as he set the plate carefully on the floor, five feet from where she sat.

"Yes, sir," he said reflexively. So (a) he *was* an ex-soldier, and (b) he knew that she'd been an officer.

He flushed, realizing his mistake. Then said, "You can call me Chesterfield."

"That's not your name. It's a brand of cigarette." When he did not demur, she said, "So, I'm guessing the other guards will be Marlboro and Lucky Strike?"

"Eat your food. Ma'am."

"Looks good. And I am hungry." She crawled to the food. Took a sip of the wine. "Know what the wine is?"

"It's French."

"Expensive, too, I'd guess. No point paying to ship cheap wine all the way here. Of course I'm more of a whiskey drinker."

"So's the boss."

"The boss," Suarez said pensively. "The one who thinks civilization is about to crumble so she built Crazy Town here. You're not crazy, though, right? You're just here for the money? Bad economy and all, a former serviceman has bills to pay like anyone else."

"If the boss says it's all coming down, it's all coming down. I mean, she's probably the smartest person in the world, smarter than Dr. Stephen Hawking."

Dr. Stephen Hawking? Suarez rolled that around in her head. A strange way for a guy who looked like this to put it. *Doctor?*

"Okay, well, what do you do for fun around here while you're waiting for the apocalypse?"

"It won't be an apocalypse for the people here; it will be a rebirth."

No irony in his gaze. He was dead serious. Someone had definitely sold this boy a complete bill of goods.

"Okay, which still leaves the question of what you do to pass the time?"

He shrugged, and Suarez detected a softness in him. *I'm going to try not to kill you*, she thought.

"I don't suppose there's any way I can get a shower? You know, hot water? Soap?" She mimed it for him, mimicking the movements of a bar of soap over her body, not lasciviously—that would be too obvious and set off alarm bells. Just . . . enough. She just wanted him to connect his boredom with the mental picture of a reasonably attractive woman taking a shower. Let him stew on that for a while. Activate the twin male instincts of protection and predation.

Later, when the time was right, there would be the metal pail.

"No shower," he said in a voice just a tiny bit lower than it had been. "I could maybe get you a deck of cards."

"I would be very grateful."

The explosion came as the elevator rose, an impact that knocked Keats, Plath, and Wilkes to their knees. Not an explosion that would bring down a building. Smaller.

But the elevator stopped moving, and the door did not open. The backlit buttons went dark. The overhead light snapped off, replaced by an eerie emergency light.

"He blew up the elevator doors down there," Keats said, offering his hand to Plath.

She spurned it and jumped to her feet. "We have to get out of here."

A second explosion, more distant this time. The second elevator.

"He's cutting himself off," Keats said.

"He'll die with the explosion," Plath said. Then, softly, "Maybe that was the plan all along."

Wilkes had started trying to pry open the elevator doors. Keats and Plath jumped in, jamming splintering fingernails into the gap. Slowly, inch by inch, the door opened. They were between floors, but with an open space of several feet.

Plath went through first, boosted by Keats. Then Wilkes. Together they hauled Keats after them.

They were on the ground floor—the lobby floor, polished marble. Security guards were a swarm of uniforms and plainclothes tourists from Denver, though minus the parkas. All were armed. In seconds there were a dozen weapons pointed at the three of them.

"One move and we shoot," a woman snapped.

"No need," Plath said. "I'm Sadie McLure. We need to talk to the Twins."

"And in the meantime, there's an assassin down in the basement preparing to blow this whole place up," Keats said.

Nervous glances went back and forth.

"Hey, dumb asses," Wilkes said. "Shoot us or beat us up or

whatever, but there is an honest-to-God stone-cold killer down there."

"He's wedged a car jack behind a gas pipe," Keats said. "In a few minutes high-pressure gas is going to start pouring into the basement."

"Leave his eye," Plath ordered. "Find an artery."

Keats's eyebrow shot up at the tone of command. Plath, who had seemed almost to be comatose, now sounded like her old self.

"Kill him?" Keats asked. He searched her eyes, not sure what he wanted the answer to be. In this very building Plath had refused to kill the Twins. She had refused to commit cold-blooded murder.

Many had died since then. Much had changed.

They had just ripped m-sub yards of wire from Plath's brain, and parts of her gray matter were as raw as a skinned knee. If she gave the order, who and what would be behind it? What would be her motivation? How much responsibility would she bear in the end?

And if she said—

"Kill him," Plath said.

And if she said, *Kill him,* would he obey?

"Get them up to Jindal. Cuff 'em, keep guns on them, any bullshit, shoot 'em," the woman in charge snapped.

The three remaining, active members of BZRK New York were cuffed and hustled to the main bank of elevators.

"Has he blown the pipe yet?" Plath asked Keats.

"I don't know, Keats said. "I'm no longer on the optic nerve."

Plath and Wilkes both knew this meant he had sent his biot to kill Caligula.

"And the last of the righteous succumbs to the darkness," Wilkes said mordantly, and added, "Heh-heh-heh."

• • •

Lystra Reid laughed like a mad thing, and to Bug Man's amazement actually executed a somersault, as crazy as the terrifyingly unhinged actors and producers and agents and whoever now baying like wolves in the streets of Manhattan, chased by cameras that broadcast the images all over the world.

She led the way to a limo and held the door open for Bug Man, who tumbled in, shaken.

"Jefuf Chri'!" he cried.

"No, no, no, no goddamned made-up, bullshit divinities!" Lystra yelled exultantly. "Jesus Christ and Zeus and Mohammed and whatever the hell you want, yeah, they didn't write *this* game!" She fell into the seat beside him. It was as if she was drunk or high. She was cackling. "Fuck your gods, Bug Man, I'm god now! Yeah! This is my fucking world!"

Bug Man had seen some crazy in his life. He'd spoken with the Armstrong Twins, and those boys were crazy. He'd hung out with Burnofsky, not exactly a paragon of sanity. *But*, he thought, *this chick is nuts. Once you start calling yourself "god" you're all the way into crazy.*

Berserk.

BZRK.

He was crying without quite knowing why, unless it was just some kind of overload. Too much. Too much crazy. The whole world was going crazy, and this madwoman was making sure of it.

"Wha' nef?" he asked, both to humor her and because he needed to know.

"Stop mush mouthing," Lystra snapped. "I'll tell you what next, yeah. Next, we get back to the apartment to watch the Tulip blow up," she said, and winked conspiratorially. With her hands she made a sort of finger explosion and said, "Boom! Crash! Tinkle tinkle tinkle. Woosh! Screams! Cries! It's Nine/Eleven all over, but now, yeah, the whole fucking world is going nuts! Crazy president. All the big brains? Crazy! Crazy prince. Crazy Pope! Everyone you know, yeah, is insane! And then, ah-hah-hah!"

"Then . . . what?" Bug Man asked.

"Then the Tulip comes down. And then, yeah, then, yeah, then the rest of them. Tens of thousands. Hundreds of thousands. The code is all laid in. The crèches are ready. Grow 'em, kill 'em. Grow 'em, kill 'em, yeah. Biot fucking apocalypse, Bug Man! Madness! Have you had blood drawn? Then I have your DNA, bitches. And, yeah, I have your biot. We can do sixteen thousand at a time. Sixteen thousand an hour. Day one? Three hundred eight-four thousand! A million, yeah, in sixty-two and a half hours. Everyone from big to little. Everyone from great to small. Everyone from rich to poor. The grocery clerk? Berserk! The train driver? Berserk! The guy, yeah, in a missile silo somewhere in Shitheel, Nebraska? Berserk! Cops? Berserk!"

She reeled back against the leather seat. Took a deep breath. Like she was overwhelmed by the vision in her head. "Every continent. Every country. I have twenty-nine million samples, yeah. One out of every two hundred and forty-one people on planet Earth. Berserk. Yeah."

She seemed spent. Drained. But still wondering, still amazed. "It will take seventy-five days to do them all. But it won't hold together for that long, yeah. Governments fall. Religions fail. It all comes down. Chaos. Mass insanity. The end. How many die in the end? Don't know, don't know, yeah. Maybe all of them, yeah. Whole new game then, yeah? Whole new game, right? *My* game. Adam and fucking Eve. Genghis Khan. Hitler. Stalin and Mao and what's his name? Fucking Attila. *My* game. Yeah."

The limo stopped just a block away from the Tulip. Lear bounded out with Bug Man on her heels. They raced for the elevator up to her posh apartment.

Bug Man felt a sick dread settle over him.

He didn't see where this was any kind of game. This was just plain murder. Murder on a massive scale.

Lystra was excited, fumbling the keys at first. Then she led the way to the window, tapped the remote that opened the curtains and did a game-show-model move, like she was presenting the Tulip as some sort of prize.

Then Lystra fell silent. She was thinking something over. Bug Man could practically see her arguing with herself as her head tilted slightly this way, slightly that way.

"Yeah," she said to herself, finally. "Yeah. Call him. Call him, yeah."

Keats's biot raced away from the partly cut optic nerve, six legs milling through the fluid, impeded but only slightly by sticky macrophages coming to dumbly check out the damage he had done.

It was like a wild nighttime drive down a back country road, somehow. His illumination in fact lit up very little, just the nerve and a suggestion of deeper brain ahead.

An artery, that's what he needed, and there were a lot of them in the brain. None would kill instantly; that's not the way it would work. Instead, blood would pour into the brain itself, depriving some tissue of oxygen, putting pressure on other tissue. The result would be a stroke or series of strokes and yes, maybe death, but not quickly.

Quickly enough to stop him blowing up the building? No way to know. He couldn't see through Caligula's eye anymore. Any moment could bring a fireball, a terrible shudder, and a falling floor beneath his feet.

They'd been taken to see Jindal, a worm of a man who kept rocking back on his heels, then forward onto his toes, trying to look taller than he was. He had snapped out a set of superfluous instructions to his security people, but they were already vectoring armed men toward the sublevels.

"You need to evacuate the building," Plath said.

"Hah. Just what you'd want if this were all a ruse. Just what you could be after, no? I think so. I think we'll wait until—"

The phone chirped. He grabbed it, listened, face darkening. "The freight elevators are blown. The doors are jammed. They may be booby-trapped."

"I'd bet on it," Plath said.

"Caligula was keeping the elevators to use for his own escape," Keats said, walking it through in his own mind. Elevators stopped at the loading bays, from there to the alley, and off he would go. In five minutes he could be clear of the blast and any police cordon.

Jindal's forehead creased. And he may have started to sweat just a bit.

"Evacuate the building!" Plath yelled. "We're not here because we want to die, we're trying to save innocent people!"

Innocent people, Keats noted. So there was still a Sadie somewhere inside Plath.

Jindal shook his head slowly. "If I'm wrong and the place blows up, I'm dead. If I'm wrong and I evacuated the building, the Twins will . . ." He shook his head doggedly. "There are worse things than dying."

"Yes, but none are really as permanent," Wilkes said.

"Take us to the Twins," Plath said urgently. "If you don't have the balls to make a decision, take us to the Twins!"

"*Now*, you bloody fool!" Keats added.

When Jindal still stood, frozen in indecision, Plath spun on her heel and marched for the elevator. "I've been there before. I know the way."

Four security men trained their guns on her. Plath, without turning around said, "I'm Sadie McLure. Now, you may be too gutless or stupid to make a decision, Mr. Jindal, but you know as well as I do that your bosses would throw you out of that window if you deprived them of a chance to deal with me themselves. So I'm getting on the elevator, and I'm going upstairs."

Wilkes put on a falsely cheery smile and said to Keats, "I think she's back."

Caligula had seated the jack. It was in an awkward position, and he had to turn the screw using a crowbar that could be moved only a few degrees at a time.

His vision had not deteriorated further. Which meant whoever was running the biot in his head had moved on in search of a faster way to stop him. And his hand hurt like hell. He'd used the do-rag as a makeshift bandage, but the blood had soaked through almost instantly.

Well. At this point death was a certainty. Death by brain hemorrhage or death by natural gas explosion. *Step right up, ladies and gentlemen, you pays your money, you takes your* chances.

Remembering the old carnival barker cant made him smile. They had not been so bad, those days. He turned the crowbar. It had been lonely a lot of the time, especially after he gave up his daughter. But he couldn't look at her. He couldn't.

When he'd caught his wife in bed with another man, he killed the man and then, much to his own surprise, let his wife live. He'd even forgiven her.

He had forgiven her. Their daughter had not.

His phone buzzed softly. He closed his eyes and leaned back from the jack. There was only one person who could possibly be calling him, only one person who had ever had the number.

He pulled the phone from his pocket with his good hand.

"Yes, baby," Caligula said.

"Call me Lear. How many times do I have to tell you that? Call me Lear!"

Caligula said nothing, just closed his eyes.

"Why hasn't the Tulip been blown up?"

"Well, I'm working on it," he said, feeling very weary.

"You're ruining the timing!"

"Listen, baby . . . Lear. Listen to me. This will be the last time we have a chance to talk."

"Are you arguing with me? Are you failing me? Again?"

Caligula sighed. "They tried to stop me. Plath, Keats . . . I can't get out of here. I'm going to die."

At least there was a moment of hesitation. At least there was that much. Maybe she didn't really care, but the news at least made her pause. Made her blink, perhaps, at the other end of the line.

"I guess it's karma," Lear said at last.

"What?"

"For you killing Mom. It's karma. Cosmic justice."

Caligula hung his head and for a minute could not go on. Could not speak. "Lystra. Baby. You have to know—"

"Goddamn it, you old piece of shit, call me—"

"I didn't kill her. You know I—"

"Blow it up! Blow it up!"

"—didn't take your mother's life."

"Shut up! Just shut the hell up and do it!"

"You did, Lystra. *You* killed your mother."

Heavy breathing at the other end of the line. Then, a weird, distorted voice, like a child trying to sound grown-up. A whining, almost singsong voice. "No, I didn't."

"Lystra . . ."

"*You* did. You killed her. Yeah, you killed my mother and then you gave me away."

"Baby . . ." Caligula's voice broke. He felt a sharp pain in his head. Any other time he would have thought it was just the beginning of a headache.

"How could I? I was just a little girl."

How long did he have? Minutes or seconds?

"You're right," he said at last. "You're right, ba— Lear. I did it."

"Hah! I told you so. Now, do this. Do it and all is forgiven."

He managed a slight laugh, a hoarse sound. "I don't think even God can forgive me all I've done."

"Then it's no problem, Daddy. I am god now."

She hung up the phone. Caligula knew it was true. Not about his poor, mad daughter being god. But yes, he had killed his wife, her mother. A week after they'd reconciled, he'd been drunk and angry at what he thought was a flirtation with the carny who ran the Mad Mouse ride. He'd punched her. He'd punched her hard, right in the jaw. She had fallen, unconscious, to the floor of their shabby trailer.

He'd left her there.

When he woke, raging with thirst from all the drink, filled with remorse, he'd found her still on the floor. But with her throat cut.

The bloody meat cleaver was on the floor beside her.

He had roused a sleeping Lystra from her bed and washed the red stain from her hands. Burned her bloody clothing in the fifty-five-gallon drum where the carnies burned trash and kept their hands warm on cold nights.

It was his fault she had done it. Who had taught her violence? Who had revealed his rage to the impressionable ears of a young girl?

And then, cowardly, unable to face Lystra, unable to cope with the madness that was already a part of her, he had shipped her off.

Caligula did not believe in karma. He believed in damnation. His own, and hers as well. And the damnation of the world.

He set the crowbar in place and heaved with all his might.

The pipe snapped. Whatever sound it made was obliterated by the roar of high-pressure gas gushing into the room.

He choked from the smell, reeled back, staggered to the far end of the chamber, and set the timer on the explosive device for ten minutes.

That should be enough.

TWENTY-FIVE

Sadie McLure. In person. In the flesh. And the rest of her little crew as well. Benjamin Armstrong felt disappointed. It should have been a triumph, but she was walking in under her own power, head held high.

"Someone get me a . . . a knife! Or a baseball bat! Something," Benjamin snarled.

"Benjamin," Charles chided mockingly. "There will be plenty of time for that."

"I'm going to beat her bloody and rape whatever is left of her!" Benjamin saw his own spittle flying. He felt the way Charles drew him back, restraining him, knowing Benjamin otherwise would have gone at the girl with his fist until some better weapon appeared.

More and more security men and women were arriving—by elevator, by stair—all armed, all looking to the Twins for guidance.

"The building is going to blow up," Plath said calmly.

"Of course it is," Benjamin sneered. "You know, your father was the smart one, not you, you stupid little bitch!"

"Caligula is in the basement," Keats said, striving to mirror Plath's even tone, despite the realization that one way or the other, his own time was fast running out.

He flashed on a memory of his brother Alex, chained to his cot in a mental institution in London. Mad. Utterly, terribly mad from the death of his biots. Of course, Alex had had more than one die. But at the same time, Alex had been strong.

"It's Caligula," Plath repeated.

Charles's eyes narrowed. "What is Caligula?"

"He's the one in the basement. Looks like he's rupturing a pipeline. He'll wait until the gas builds up and—"

"System!" Charles yelled. "System: show all cameras in the basement of this building!"

On the huge screen with its multitude of squares showing the Armstrong empire, five windows opened. Three were black. But two were still in operation, one trained on an instrument panel, while the other was a grainy long shot of pipes and . . .

"There!" Jindal cried, pointing. "There's someone down there. You can just see their back!"

"One of the engineers," Charles scoffed, but he didn't sound too sure of himself.

Suddenly the grainy figure reeled back, spun away from whatever he had been doing.

In Caligula's head Keats's efforts were beginning to work. Blood that had been just a single-cell spray from the throbbing artery had become a gusher, like a cartoon of an oil well. The clear cranial fluid around his biot was growing opaque with the floating Frisbees of red blood cells and the soggy sponges of white blood cells.

The force of the blood knocked his biot loose of its perch and sent it spinning, end over end. What had been a sort of narrow but calm seam of watery fluid was now a turbulent underground river.

He would not make it back to the artery.

"He's hemorrhaging," Keats said. To the Twins he explained, "I have a biot in his brain. I've cut an artery. I've damaged one optic nerve."

The camera no longer showed the man in question.

"Can you get back to his eye?" Plath asked.

She still hadn't realized . . . Keats nodded. "On my way."

"You don't give orders here!" Benjamin raged at Plath.

But his brother was no longer with him on that. Charles said, "Why would Caligula blow up the Tulip?"

Plath glanced at Keats, who seemed to her to be elsewhere. Looking through his biot's eyes, seeing a different scene altogether.

In fact, Keats's biot was racing madly back toward Caligula's eye. His biot swam and crawled, shouldered its way through the clinging platelets, the lymphocytes, the tendrils of detached neurons, floating like seaweed.

He had never moved so fast. He didn't wonder at which direction to take, which planes to use to flow through the 3D maze of Caligula's brain. The calm had come over him.

He knew what was coming for himself, but he was no longer afraid. A slight smile stretched his mouth. His eyes glistened.

He was there, in that place of peace and calm and wild, frantic action.

"Floor Thirty-Four," Plath said to Benjamin. She didn't know what Floor 34 was. Just that it was the one part of the Tulip aside from the data center that was unreachable by elevator. A guess. An intuition.

A bluff.

The silence that followed was all the confirmation necessary. Charles was shaken.

"And who sent Caligula to do this act of terrorism?" Benjamin asked, voice silky and malevolent now.

"Me," Plath said.

Charles blinked. "But . . . Surely you . . ." His tone was almost pleading.

"Lear," Wilkes said when Keats remained silent. "It was Lear. He's wired her. He got Vincent to wire her. We've cleared her brain of wire, but—"

"So now you see that we were right! Now, now with our beautiful people all dead on the *Doll Ship*, all destroyed. Now you—"

"Look, you're a piece of shit who needs to die a painful death. The two of you," Wilkes snapped. "But we do not blow up buildings full of innocent people. We're trying to stop this from happening."

Benjamin's face was a snarl. Charles was guarded, worried. It was he who said, "Jindal, get Burnofsky up here."

Keats had reached the optic nerve. He sank a probe. "I can see," he said in a dreamy, disconnected, emotionless voice. "Caligula is looking right at it. At the bomb. There's a timer."

"How much time left?" Jindal asked.

Benjamin raged at him. "Follow my brother's orders, now!"

"I have a weak picture," Keats said, speaking to Plath. "I'll try for a better one."

Jindal rapped orders to his people, then, undeterred—*Accustomed to abuse*, Keats thought—he said, "Our people will be through the door into the sublevel in a few minutes."

"How are they getting through?" Plath asked.

"They're cutting through the steel with a blowtorch and once they're in—"

"A blowtorch? Cutting into a room full of gas?" Wilkes cried. "Isn't that, uh, stupid?"

"She's right," Charles said.

"No," Plath said sharply. "No. Maybe better to blow it up now rather than wait. Less gas now. More later."

"System," Charles said. "Exterior, sublevel doors."

As one they all turned to look at the monitor. Four frames. Three showed nothing but doors. The last showed two men wearing welding helmets. The bright light of the torch caused lens flares that obscured the progress of the work.

"Seven minutes, eighteen seconds," Keats said. "I can see it now. I can see it clearly. Seven minutes and . . ." And it all came back to him. The calm of battle had run its course once his biot had reached its goal. Now Keats couldn't go on. He had run out of indifference to his own fate.

Part of him didn't want to tell Sadie. What would be gained? But he had to speak. He had to say good-bye.

"Sadie," he said.

She must have registered the sadness and gentleness in his voice. She turned to him. "Yes?"

"Sadie," he said again. "I've thought about it a lot. I've seen Alex. I know what it means. Death or madness, I . . . I guess I believe in another life, maybe. After this one. So . . ."

She stared, uncomprehending. Then a sharp intake of breath. Her eyes widened. "Oh, God."

"What?" Wilkes demanded.

"I'm getting my other biot as far from your aneurysm as possible," he said. "But you'll need to kill me. You can't have it in your head with a madman running it."

"Noah," Sadie said. Sadie, and not Plath. Sadie. "Noah . . . We have to . . ."

He took her hand in his. "We always knew it could happen."

"Order the men down there to cut straight through, forget cutting a hole, tell them just to cut all the way through in a single spot," Benjamin told Jindal.

"Better to burn than to blow up," Benjamin said. "And thus, it ends."

"You can't . . . Noah . . ."

"When Caligula burns, so will my biot, Sadie. You know what follows. It's okay."

"Noah . . ." She was in his arms, and tears were running down her face.

"Yes, of course, pity for the pretty boy, eh?" Benjamin said savagely. "Pity for poor, poor Noah. None for our people on our beautiful ship. And none for hideous freaks."

Burnofsky watched the counter on his computer monitor. The number of self-replicating nanobots had just crossed thirty-two million. The next doubling would take it to sixty-four million, then one hundred and twenty-eight. Pretty soon megabots would give way to gigabots and hence to terabots.

He laughed at that, slurred, "I made a funny," took a drink, sucked on his cigarette, and touched the butt of the pistol that was stuck into his belt.

He'd been feeding the nanobots everything he could find: stale doughnuts, candy bars from the machine down the hall, half a salami he'd found in the staff fridge. He hadn't slept in . . . how many hours? How many days? It was all kind of fuzzy.

He had the remote control in his hand. Press the button and the force field would drop. His nanobots would eat their way out into the world and from there they would never stop. They would eat their way through the building, its furnishings, and anyone dull enough to wait around.

But before they finished the Tulip they'd be carried on breezes or simply fall from chewed-through walls down onto the streets. Nearby buildings would be infested and begin the same accelerated decline and rot. The pace would accelerate as the nanobots doubled and doubled.

What would the reaction be? What would the government do? Nothing short of a nuclear weapon would stop the spread, and they would wait far too long for that. Nanobots would find their way onto ferries, cars, ships, and planes.

For the first few days the damage would be most visible at the epicenter. But then, here and there and all around the world they would appear and double and double and double.

People would flee to the woods and deserts. And they would survive for a while—maybe weeks, maybe months. In places the nanobots would consume all there was to consume and cease doubling. But by that time they would have eaten every living thing and much of the nonliving things as well.

He asked himself, where would be safe? Or at least, where would be *safest*? The coldest places, he supposed. Nanobots tended to be immobilized when things got cold enough, down to minus twenty-three Celsius or minus ten Fahrenheit. But even in the coldest lands a warm day would set them off again.

"God bless global warming," he muttered, and laughed at his own wit.

People thought they were scared now? They thought they were terrified by Lear's plague of madness? Wait until they saw their crops, their home, their car and its gas, their dogs and cats and cows and pigs, all chewed up, masticated by trillions of nanobots that did little but crap out more nanobots.

Wait until they realized how hopeless it was. How powerless they were. Wait until they saw the little sore on their ankle become a bleeding hole and endured the agony of being eaten alive, consumed, like a beetle being swarmed by fire ants. It would be like leprosy on fast forward. It would be like flesh-eating bacteria on meth.

Sure, maybe in places there would be pockets of a few scattered humans who would hold out for as long as six months. But it wouldn't matter. The nanobots would eat the algae out of the sea and every oxygen-producing plant on the land and then, inexorably, the atmosphere itself would become fatal to life.

Dirt. Water. That would be planet Earth. Just dirt and water and a vast, inconceivably vast swarm of nanobots. Mindless. Without soul or sin. Efficient, relentless, unstoppable killers without malice, without meaning, without moral judgment. Without guilt—that most destructive, weakening, sickening, disabling of emotions.

Yes, his babies would obliterate without guilt.

He pulled up the picture he'd found of Lystra Reid and gave it the finger.

"Game, set, match, Lear. Death or madness? I got a little hint for you, sweetheart. The answer is death. Death, brought to you by Karl Burnofsky."

Out in the lab he heard a disturbance: raised voices, a bustling movement, chairs scuffling. The door to his office was locked. He drew the pistol.

Someone banged hard on his door: a cop's knock.

"Damn," he said. "I'd have liked to hit a billion first."

"Burnofsky! Come out here. The bosses want you."

"I'm busy," Burnofsky yelled.

"Don't think they care, Dr. B. You've got about ten seconds."

The Twins wanted him, did they? Well, why not? It would be worth a laugh. And he had something special for them, just for them, something ever so special.

"Give me a second!" he yelled. In his desk, all the way at the back, he found the little vial he'd prepared against this very moment. He slipped it into his pocket along with the remote control that could unleash Armageddon and opened the office door for what he suspected would be the last time.

The area within the force field continued to fill with his children.

Keats had his biot back on Caligula's optic nerve. He was again seeing what the killer saw. Caligula seemed to be sitting, perhaps with his back against a wall. His legs were stretched out before him. He stared at his missing fingers, bleeding freely, unbandaged. He leaned down to rub a spot of mud from his boot, glanced at the timer—six minutes and nine seconds—then apparently coughed as his head jerked violently and his hand came up to his mouth.

Just six minutes until the natural gas flooding the basement would achieve sufficient density that a spark would bring down the entire building. The gas was invisible dynamite being stacked, ton upon ton. Caligula's eye glanced toward the ruptured pipe. He had a picture of something in his hand, a photograph of a serious little girl slumped in a busted-webbing lawn chair outside a shabby trailer. There was a Ferris wheel in the background.

Caligula coughed again and drew something out of his bag. Keats saw a small steel cylinder, a clear plastic hose smeared with Caligula's blood, and a clear plastic mask with elastic straps. It reminded him of the lecture aboard an airplane: *Should there be a sudden loss of cabin pressure* . . . Caligula pulled the mask on, and now the plastic partly filled Keats's view. Caligula was determined to wait out the—

No, he was up, up and staggering, but not toward the rupture, or toward the elevators. Keats saw a steel door. Caligula's eye went to the handle, then his hand as it touched the metal of the door.

"He knows your guys are burning through," Keats said dully.

"Jindal!" Charles yelled in response.

Jindal talked into his phone and reported, "They say they'll be through any second."

Caligula glanced back toward the bomb. Glanced at the gun in his hands. Suddenly they trembled. He seemed to be struggling to hold on to the weapon; his mutilated hand was still bleeding freely, but even the fingers on his good hand looked stiff, uncooperative.

The gun fell from his grip. The picture, too, was facedown on the floor.

"He's having a stroke," Keats reported. *Go on*, he told himself, *just keep watching. Until the end. Be the good boy. No freaking out, no last-minute pleas.* Tough, that's how his brother Alex had always been. "He's stroking out from the artery I cut."

Sadie was looking at him, her eyes ashamed, horrified.

"Not your fault," he said to her. "None of this is your fault."

"But it is," she said.

"He's picked up a crowbar. His fingers can barely hold it. He's dropped it. He's staring at it."

"For God's sake, evacuate the building!" Plath shrieked at the Twins.

Burnofsky, disheveled but animated, came in with guards on either side. His rheumy eyes sparkled. "Ah, ah, ah!" he said on spying Plath and Keats and Wilkes. "So, *that's* the panic." He seemed pleased and relieved.

"Help me get these idiots to evacuate the building," Plath pleaded. "Caligula's flooding the basement with natural gas. In six minutes this whole place goes up!"

"Is that true?" Burnofsky demanded, squinting hard at the Twins. He glanced at the monitor. The cameras in the basement had been redirected, searching for Caligula. A grainy image showed him walking, dragging one leg, then collapsing on the floor.

Keats had never been inside the brain of a dying man. There was nothing to see on the optic nerve, nothing changing in his immediate environment. But the eyelid no longer blinked as often, and it seemed to be drooping, partly obscuring the view.

If Caligula died before the explosion, then Keats would have been his killer. His biot might sit for several minutes in a dead man's brain before the explosion killed his biot and plunged him down into the dark hell of madness.

How would it feel, he wondered. How would it feel to no longer be himself?

Keats's throat was dry. His breathing was shallow. He was afraid. First would come the razor edge of madness, to be followed by an explosion that—

A brilliant flash of light from Caligula's eye.

The same bright flash filled the monitor that had been trained on Caligula. The camera aimed at the exterior where the men had been wielding the cutting torch went dead.

"They burned through!" Jindal cried.

"System," Charles yelled, his voice cracking. "Sublevel two, northeast corner stairwell cameras!"

Blank nothing, dead cameras.

"System, sublevel one, northeast corner!"

Here, too, the cameras were blank. A shudder communicated itself up the length of the Tulip to Keats's feet, like a minor earthquake. A glass fell from a shelf and shattered.

The fire killed Caligula instantly. Then it began to burn through his flesh, boiling the blood in his veins, sloughing away charred skin, burning its way to his heart, to his lungs. To his brain.

• • •

"Fire in the lobby!" Jindal reported, phone to his ear.

"They can put it out!" Burnofsky yelled. "They have to put it out!" His relief was all gone now, all gone, as his brilliant mind frantically calculated the damage that could be done to his nanobots by a burning building.

"The southwest corner stairwell is still clear," Jindal said. "Gentlemen, we have to get you out of here!" This to the Twins, who seemed paralyzed.

"Anyone who wants to live, get out of here!" Plath yelled, pulling away from Keats.

A window in Keats's mind went dark and then disappeared. Keats felt strange, very strange. Not upset. Just . . . alone . . .

"Wilkes! Run!" Plath pleaded.

"Not without you and blue eyes," Wilkes said.

. . . alone in a strange landscape.

"No one moves!" three different security men yelled at once, waving their guns in a bewildered effort to assert control.

"It blew up early," Plath said, looking to the Twins. "The explosion was only limited, but it's still burning, and there's an open gas line feeding that fire. We may still get out."

Burnofsky yelled, "System: show Burnofsky lab!"

Such strange images. Flashing pictures of his old room in London, of playing football in the alley, of the island. Of Sadie. Of the dark, looming monster that seemed now to be emerging from her, bursting from her flesh, a dark, terrible beast . . .

Burnofsky's lab was untouched. He saw assistants going about their business, clueless.

"Evacuate the building!" Charles yelled.

"No!" This came from Benjamin. Jindal stutter-stepped and stopped.

Keats saw it all. The Twins were a glowing two-headed dragon, with liquid fire bleeding from Benjamin's lips. Burnofsky melting, somehow melting, and Keats felt the laughter rise in him, rise and fill his chest and come burbling out of his mouth. He pulled against imaginary chains, yanking his arms against nonexistent restraints.

"Noah," Sadie pleaded, helpless, knowing what was happening to him, knowing that he was spiraling down.

A part of Keats—a fading, weakening remnant—watched it all from very far away, a shadow of his mind, watching himself slip, slip, slip. . . . It was all very, very clear, very, very clear to Noah, Noah like the guy with the ark, the one who liked animals, all clear, they were all devils, all of them. Mad, each of them, mad as . . . mad as . . .

A whimpering voice, Noah's own voice, but not operated by him, no, a voice mewling and laughing and crying out, "Kill me, kill me, it's what you all want, isn't it?"

In that moment, a final becalmed moment, the last sane vestiges of his mind took it all in, and his laughter was not yet the laughter of the insane, but the knowing, cynical laughter of one who sees everything clearly, if only for a single second in time.

He saw Benjamin and Charles as what they were, two rejected, despised, sad little children forever bound together, neither able to feel even a moment's freedom.

He saw Burnofsky, so desperate for redemption from suffering that he would bring down the whole world in a fit of self-loathing.

And Sadie, Sadie his love, her brain a tangled mess, wired,

unwired, but even before that crippled by a dead mother, a dead brother, a dead father, and corrupted by wealth and power and crushed by responsibility. Mad. Her, too: mad.

They were all mad. They always had been.

Crazy people had gotten their hands on deadly toys. The end was inevitable.

And me, too, he thought. As mad as any of them, believing that there could be love and honor in the midst of it.

They had all tried to armor themselves against this final moment, but their defiance had been its own lie: there was never a choice between death and madness. It was always to be both.

And then, with a strangled cry in his throat, Noah attacked.

TWENTY-SIX

Lear watched, hands behind her back, lifting herself up on the balls of her feet, bouncing with anticipation. When she first saw the fire burst from the ground-floor windows and setting a passing man alight, she let out a happy squeal.

But then, when the Tulip still stood, she clenched her fists and began to curse. "Fucking useless old man. Useless old man," she said. "Trying to say I killed her, and now look! Look!"

When Bug Man did not move from the couch, she took two long steps, reached down, grabbed the neck of his T-shirt, and dragged him to the window.

"Iff' burning," Bug Man said.

"It's not supposed to *burn*, it's supposed to explode! The gas was supposed to explode! The whole thing should be toppling over!"

The TV was on, showing a sea of flashing red lights around the theater, with cutaways to eerie vignettes of cops tackling a naked, raving rock star, or Tasering a man in a business suit carrying a severed arm, the remnants of the lunacy at the premiere.

"Blow up! Blow up, blow up, blow up, *blow up*!" Lear raged, banging the plate glass with her fists.

As if on command a huge fireball erupted from the windows of the third floor.

"It could still fall, yeah," Lear said, nodding, reassuring herself. She bent to a tripod-mounted telescope. "Can't see anything through their dark glass. Are you scared yet, you freaks? Are you wetting yourselves, you *freaks*?"

Bug Man had had enough, more than enough. He had to get away. He shot a look toward the door. Did she have guards out there? If she died, he went mad . . . if she was telling the truth about a dead man's switch . . . but there wasn't anything he could do about that, and he could not be here watching all this. He could not be with this crazy witch raving and pounding on the glass like an infuriated ape in a cage.

He stepped back, back, turned, and ran for the door. Locked.

"Really, Bug Man?" Lear asked in a mocking voice. "Really? You think you get to run away?"

"You 'ave to le' me go," he pleaded.

She ignored him and crowed wildly as another burst of orange flame billowed out from the base of the Tulip. "It'll collapse. Has to. The fire will melt the girders, has to, yeah. Damn, I want to see them when it happens."

"You coul' talk to them."

Lear's eyes lit up. She grinned. "What?"

"I know Burnofsshky's number. He' prob'ly there. He worksh late."

She grabbed Bug Man's bicep and propelled him to a laptop. "Do it! Do it and I'll . . . I'll get you new teeth. Any color you want."

Bug Man opened an app, punched in the number, and hit Connect.

Keats rushed at the Twins, hands clawing the air, animal noises coming from him.

Plath shoved Wilkes aside to put herself between Keats and his intended victims. Keats never seemed to notice her. He ran right through her, sending her sprawling.

It was on her back, stunned by the violence of his assault, that Plath—Sadie McLure—saw three security men turn, as if in slow motion, and raise their guns.

BANG! BANGBANG!

Keats twisted, turned, stood . . .

BANG! BANG!

. . . fell.

A terrible scream rose from her mouth, echoed by Wilkes as they both fell more than ran toward Keats.

"No, no, no, no, no!" Plath cried.

"You fucking assholes! You murdering assholes!" Wilkes screamed.

Keats lay on his back. Three bullets had struck him in the side of his chest, in his upper arm, in the side of his head. He was not yet dead, eyes glazing, dark blood like ink pumping from him to form a pool on the floor, his mouth working like a beached fish, gasping.

"Oh, God, Noah! Oh, God, Noah!"

He tried to speak but only managed to form a blood bubble. He grunted, the sound of a dying beast. He breathed heavily, looked at

Plath, grunted again. He blinked, just one eye, almost as if he was winking. Blood found its way out of his ears, out of his nose.

Plath tried to cradle him in her arms, tried to hold his head, but when she did, a part of his skull came away and she screamed. Wilkes, her own hands red, took Plath's hand and kept saying, "He'll be okay, he'll be okay."

A siren was screeching, up and down the scale, up and down in Plath's head, but it was only her own screams.

A cell phone rang.

Plath stared at Noah, his eyes still so blue, his eyes open, his lips no longer the parchment landscape she had seen through biot eyes, now only the lips that had kissed her. They were moving silently.

Plath's entire body was shaking. She heard nothing, and for a while she saw nothing. The world was lost to her. Only Wilkes's arms around her connected her to reality.

The sound of a phone ringing. And going to voice mail.

"I hate people who get my hopes up," Lear said. But she was distracted by a third eruption of flames. This one blew the windows out of half the lower floors. A shower of crystal fell through yellow flames, pursued by billows of smoke.

Bug Man dialed again. This time, the call was answered.

"Kind of a bad time, Anthony," Burnofsky said.

"Lear wan' to tal' to th' Twinshh," he said.

"Oh, does she?" Burnofsky said, his voice flat. "A little late for talk, I think. Hey, Anthony?"

"Wha'?"

"I never hated you, Anthony," Burnofsky said.

Bug Man had no idea how to respond to that, so he simply handed the phone to Lear after pushing the Speaker button: he wanted to hear.

"Who is this?" Lear demanded.

"Well, well, if it isn't Lystra Reid. Or should I say 'Lear'?" Burnofsky said.

"Is this one of the Twins?"

"This is Burnofsky. Dr. Burnofsky. But you can call me Karl."

"Give me the Twins."

"Well, we're all kind of busy panicking and getting ready to die," Burnofsky said. "Hey, just out of curiosity, Ms. Reid, did you ever figure out what the Twins were up to on Floor Thirty-Four?"

Burnofsky heard the silence of confusion. Then, "What are you talking about, you old fool?"

"Their secret weapon. A virus that preyed only on cobra DNA. Like the cobra DNA that forms part of the biot genome. Ironic, don't you think? They were going to obliterate all biots, and now, hah! Now you're the one killing biots."

"Shut your filthy mouth, you disgusting drunk," Charles said, now as furious as his brother.

"Oh, I'm sorry, am I embarrassing you, boys?" Burnofsky laughed. "Don't worry, the final laugh will be on Lear."

Bug Man heard shouts and cries in the background. A female voice was crying, "Noah! Noah!" Then it stopped. The line went dead.

Bug Man could see flames behind windows on the tenth and twelfth floors of the Tulip.

On the street below, the first fire engines were pulling up, but Bug Man doubted there was anything they could do. The Tulip was doomed.

"Okay," he said.

"Okay what?"

"Okay, I'm wiff you. I'm in. All the way." What alternative did he have? "So, I' goin' to tell you, Burnofshhky didn' shound righ'. Too happy. He'shh got shomething goin' on, I know tha' old fart."

Lear was curious. "What could he be up to?"

"SRNs. The gray goo."

"No," Lear said confidently. "We wired him up. Nijinsky wired him."

"And Nijinshhky's dead. So you don' know wha' going on in hi' head anymore. I wired the presiden' and guessh wha', shuicide wa' not par' of the plan for her."

Lear was pensive. She could become coldly rational when she needed to, Bug Man had learned. She would make a fascinating case for some psychiatrist some day, he thought mordantly. Or a whole hospital full of psychiatrists.

Out of her mind but still able to plan the end of the world. Then again, who else but a crazy person would even want the world to end?

"Charles, Benjamin," Jindal pleaded. "There's one stairwell still clear. But we have to go now!"

"Hundreds of steps?" Charles asked wistfully. "My brother and I, walk down hundreds of steps?"

"We can carry you," Jindal said. "We—" He stopped, because his inclusive wave, meant to indicate the security men, now included no one. The security men had fled.

Still left in the Twins' sanctum were the Twins themselves, Jindal, Wilkes, and Plath. And the gasping, dying body of Noah Cotton, the former Keats, now on his back in a wide pool of his own blood.

"Will you drag us down the stairs, faithful Jindal?" Charles said. "No, I don't think we'll allow that. Instead . . ." he shouted, "a drink, if you please!"

The building was shaking now, successive waves of it—an artificial earthquake as small explosions and gouts of flame made their way inexorably upward, floor after floor.

"The gray goo," Benjamin said. "How many SRNs do you have, Burnofsky? The flames have not reached your lab yet. Yes, better the gray goo. The best possible outcome. Apocalypse!"

"Fetch me a bottle, Jindal," Burnofsky said, "and I'll tell your bosses all about it."

Plath realized she was kneeling in Noah's blood. She was looking in horror at his brain, a pulsing pink mass that swelled out from the bullet's hole. Wilkes took her hand, but Plath felt nothing. She knew she had to look away, but it felt like abandonment to look at anything but her lover.

He had loved her. Had she ever really loved him in return? How could she know? From memories that had been tampered with, in a brain still coping with violation? That truth was no longer entirely recoverable. Nothing was. Everything that she knew and remembered, everything she felt, had to be mistrusted.

On the big monitor, cameras showed gift shops and labs,

darkened bedrooms and banks of computer servers. The Armstrong Fancy Gifts Corporation went on, largely untouched, even as its headquarters burned.

Plath seemed to make up her mind. "We're leaving," she said.

"The hell you are," Benjamin snarled.

Plath looked at him, not afraid to meet his furious gaze. "I'm going to find and kill Lear." But she made no move toward the door.

"Lear doesn't matter, not anymore," Charles said. "I'm afraid I no longer have the will to resist my brother. The self-replicating nanobots will be released. They will scour this planet, and sooner or later, they will find Lear."

Jindal had found a bottle. Burnofsky uncorked it and took a drink before offering it to the Twins. "It's not up to you, Benjamin, it's up to me." He revealed the remote control in his hand. "I push this button, and the world begins to die."

"Give it to me," Benjamin demanded. "We paid for your work. They're ours, those little machines of yours, ours!"

Burnofsky laughed. "Hitler's bunker. I've been trying to think what this reminds me of, and that's it. With the Russians closing in, there was Hitler in his underground bunker still handing out orders. Like he had an army to command. Dead man rapping out orders."

"You treacherous, degenerate—"

"Shut up," Burnofsky said. He gave them a wave, a tolerant gesture. "It's over for you boys. All over but the punishment phase."

There was an awful groan of bending metal, a shriek that was felt as much as heard. A crack split one of the floor-to-ceiling windows. The power went out. The monitor went dark.

Emergency lights came on, casting dark shadows softened only slightly by a full moon hovering just over a nearby apartment building. "Plath, now," Wilkes pleaded. "You said it. We have to go. Keats will . . . we can't help him."

But still Plath couldn't move.

"Call that number back! I'll speak with Lear!" Benjamin cried, motioning for the phone. "I want to tell her what we've done! I want Lear to know!"

Wilkes grabbed Plath's arm and began to physically pull her away.

"We? *We?*" Burnofsky demanded, erupting in fury. "*We*, you freak? We? No we. No we. Me. *Me!* I did it! They're mine and they're blue, the blue goo not the gray, and do you know why they're blue?"

He was in Benjamin's face now, gripping the remote in his hand, spit flying from his lips.

Charles and Benjamin took a step back.

"Because that was the color . . ." A sob stopped Burnofsky. "Because . . . her eyes . . ."

"Is this about your nasty little girl?" Benjamin demanded, sneering.

"Damn it, Plath. Sadie! Come on!" But now even Wilkes could not look away.

"Did you . . . ?" Burnofsky asked. "Did . . . you . . . ?" He got control of himself again, and laughed. "You make this easy. I have something for you."

Burnofsky drew a small object from his pocket. He held out a glass vial. It looked empty but for a hint of blue.

Charles knew instantly. "Get that away from us, Karl."

"These are special," Burnofsky said. "A special project I've been working on, just for the two of you."

"Someone stop him!"

"It's easy to program the SRNs with time codes, kill switches. . . . Much harder to program them for a particular, um, diet. Yes, a particular *diet*. But it's doable. I have them that can eat only steel. Others that consume only hemoglobin. Cool, huh?" Over his shoulder, he said, "Run away, Sadie. Run while you're able. I loved your dad. He was a good man. A good man. So run away. Save yourself if you can. Get far from here. You may survive for a while, until my babies come for you."

TWENTY-SEVEN

"Now! Now!" Wilkes yelled.

Plath rose from Noah's blood. Her knees and shins and hands were soaked, red.

"Noah," she whispered. She touched his face, still sweating, still gasping like a dying fish.

"Go," he said. "For me. Go."

Plath tore herself away. No way she could survive trying to carry Noah. They would both die. Someone had to live to ensure that Lear did not.

Plath and Wilkes fled the room they'd never expected to leave alive.

"What corner did he say was still clear?" Wilkes asked.

"Southwest," Plath answered. "Southwest."

"Which is . . ."

"This way." Plath led the way, first from the cathedral vastness of the Twins' lair and back out into the entryway they'd come through. She considered the elevators and rejected them. Even if they just used them to get down a few floors, there was no knowing what they'd open onto. Past the easy way out, into a stainless-steel kitchen area, through a gloomy and oppressive formal dining room that looked as if it had never been used.

They pushed out through a narrow door into a similarly narrow hallway, then followed red exit signs to what a push confirmed was a stairwell.

There was smoke in the stairwell.

"Not too bad, we can breathe," Wilkes said. "At least up here."

"No other way," Plath said, and plunged unhesitatingly down the concrete stairs.

"Great, seventy floors," Wilkes said. "Here's where it would have been a good thing to work out."

"It's all downhill," Plath said.

They ran and tumbled and occasionally tripped down the stairs, half a floor, a landing, a turn, down another flight. Over and over again.

The smoke grew thicker but not yet enough to choke them, just enough to make their throats raw and their eyes sting.

Plath was quicker, but she waited for Wilkes to catch up when she pulled too far ahead. Down and down. Then, on the fortieth floor, a woman banged back the door, took a wild-eyed look at them, and raced away as though they were trying to catch her.

Down and down and down, and by the twenty-first floor the smoke was wringing hacking coughs from their throats and watering their eyes.

A massive shock hit the building and knocked them both off their feet. Plath came up with a skinned knee and bruised forearms. Wilkes was worse off. She had twisted her ankle and could only hobble.

"You need to go on ahead," Wilkes said. "Go, go, I'll be fine."

Plath took her arm. "I left Noah. I'm not leaving you. Come on. Run now, hurt later."

They hobbled and slid and tripped, floor by floor, tears streaming down their faces. The last six floors were agony. Smoke was everywhere, searing their lungs. The heat of the fire turned the stairwell into an oven. At some point Plath simply stopped thinking, stopped even feeling anything but pain.

The last two floors were crowded with people—yelling, choking, pushing, panicking.

And all at once there was air.

Plath, still holding Wilkes by the hand, fell out onto the sidewalk and into light; rough hands grabbed her, pulled her away, a voice yelling, "Move, move, move, it's coming down!"

They staggered on, not even sure what direction they were headed, stumbling into other refugees. A fire hose was spraying blessed cold water, and only then did Plath realize that some people were on fire, their clothing smoking, their hair crisped.

Glass was everywhere on the sidewalk and streets. Red lights flashed. Smoke billowed, but was caught by a breeze that cleared most of it at street level.

A block away they stopped, gasping, and sank down onto the concrete.

"Okay?" Plath asked.

"Alive," Wilkes answered.

Plath smeared smoke from her eyes, blinked away tears and tried to look up at the Tulip.

Fire licked from windows. Smoke poured everywhere, the whole building a chimney now.

"We have to move farther."

"Can't," Wilkes gasped.

"Like hell you can't." Plath stood, hauled Wilkes to her feet and, taking the girl's weight on her shoulder, hobbled and ran with memories, too-sharp memories, of what happened when skyscrapers burned.

"Burn and fall, burn and fall," Lear crooned as she watched flames and smoke wreathe the Tulip, dividing her attention between the real-world vista from her window and the TV coverage.

It was split-screened now on the news: half showed the remaining, yet-to-be rounded up loons from the Hollywood premiere; half showed the Tulip aflame. The crawl along the bottom was all about the Plague of Madness.

"Good title, that," Lear commented. "Makes people think it can spread. Yeah. And it can, hah."

Bug Man said nothing. This was his future now. He would live or die at Lear's whim. Or she might just let him go crazy.

Three windows were open in his head. None of them showed much at the moment, just glimpses of the biots themselves. It was different than twitching nanobots, more intimate. You had only to think and the biot would move. No wonder BZRK had been so tough to beat. No wonder Vincent had ended up drooling nuts.

"Oh, look look look!" Lear pointed, as excited as a little child. "It's starting to buckle. Look! Look! You can see rebar starting to stick out the side there. My dad came through in the end, I guess."

"Your dad?"

"Yeah," she said, almost fondly. "My dad. You must have heard of Caligula. Of course that's not his real name. I gave him that nom de guerre. Caligula, yeah. Yeah."

"Caligula's your father?" He forced himself to quash the urge to say that this explained a lot.

His mouth hurt terribly. He had finally been allowed a couple ibuprofen swallowed with cold water, which had sent lightning bolts of pain shooting from his broken teeth but was already clearing up his speech. Now Bug Man was drinking raw bourbon, no ice, no water, no nothing, because it just didn't seem to matter anymore if his brain was dulled. What was he holding out for? He was owned, body and soul. He was her slave. He was her dog.

"Mmm," Lear said. "Was. Past tense. He killed my mother, you know. He tries to pretend it was me, yeah, like I could have done it. Like I could have killed her. Like I could have found her unconscious, yeah, and the cleaver, and thought . . . no. Yeah. But if I had, wouldn't I have a tattoo of her?"

Bug Man nodded wearily, as if this proved her case.

"Adoptive parents, yeah, that's different," Lear said. "You saw them."

"Yeah."

"It's going," Lear said. "It's going. Oh, this will be the best. Get me a drink. I want to toast the Armstrong Twins as they die."

"What have you done?" Charles demanded, aghast.

"Revenge is a dish best served cold," Burnofsky said. "And you know what? Even with the fire below, I feel chilly."

"Damn you, *what have you done*?" Benjamin yelled, desperation breaking his voice.

"My final work of genius," Burnofsky said. "I programmed my SRNs to respond not just to a time signature, or even a specific energy source. I programmed them with a map. A topographical program."

Charles began to scratch his chest, the place where his chest became Benjamin's.

"Yep, it will itch at first," Burnofsky said. "Then it will burn. And then, it will really start to become quite unpleasant."

"What have you done? Tell us! What have you done?"

"I've granted your secret wish," Burnofsky said. "You've lived with each other every single minute of your lives. Neither of you has ever been separate. Well, now you will be. The topography is *you*."

"What?" Charles cried. "We'll die!"

"Well, yeah," Burnofsky allowed. "But not right away. Hey, I've put a lot of thought into this. You don't think I'd make it easy for you. Has my life been easy? No, it has not." He dropped the jocular tone. "You bought my soul, you two. You bought my soul . . ."

Benjamin tore at the buttons of their tailor-made shirt, exposing pink flesh with an angry, vertical red rash in the center. He clawed at it then whinnied in horror as his fingernails came away trailing ribbons of flesh.

". . . and then you let me be mind-raped. My brain. It's all I had after I killed her, my intellect. Oh, God, and still, still, do you know what they did to me? Do you know what BZRK did? When I think of her . . ."

"They're on my back!" Charles cried.

". . . I get turned on. Did you know that's what they did to me with their wire? Crude. They thought, *Well, we will just sort of reverse polarities on old Burnofsky's brain.* Like an old *Star Trek*, did you boys—"

"I can't reach, I can't reach!" Charles cried as he flailed madly, trying to reach his back with his hand, but that had never been possible.

"Ever watch that show? They were always reversing polarities. All bullshit. But that's all Nijinsky had. Crude and cruel. A man should do penance for his crimes. A man should pay. A man should suffer, not feel pleasure."

"We don't deserve to suffer!" Charles shouted.

"No," Burnofsky drawled. "You two? No, it's not like you enslaved a ship full of people and did to them just what BZRK did to me, right? See how you're not going to win that argument?"

"We'll give you whatever you want," Charles said, and then cried out in pain and grabbed at his rear in what would in other circumstances be almost comic.

"Up your butt, are they? Right on schedule. There'll be a couple million of them by now."

"We'll give you anything! Anything!" Charles pleaded.

Burnofsky looked sick, like a man on the edge of vomiting. He stood wearily, old bones popping with the effort, and stepped closer, just out of reach of Benjamin's grasping claw of a hand. "Anything? Will you? Then give me back my little girl."

"She had to die; it was treason!" Benjamin raged. "She was a filthy, treacherous, little—"

Burnofsky punched him. It wasn't much of a punch, just enough to start the blood draining from a reddened nose.

"Give me my daughter. Give me my pride back. Give me back my own brain. Do all of that, and I'll stop them." Then, he laughed—a sudden, strange noise. "Kidding. They will carry out their programming and—"

The floor tilted suddenly, a 10 degree pitch that sent the Twins sprawling. Burnofsky staggered but remained standing.

"My apocalypse," Burnofsky said, holding the deadly remote control aloft. "Not Lear's, not yours. Mine."

"You're insane!" Charles wailed.

"You think?" He drained the last of his bottle and smacked his lips. "Who wasn't insane in this?" His eyes fell on Noah's twitching body. Noah made an incoherent sound. The tilting floor had sent the pool of blood trailing off like rivulets on a windshield. "Him, maybe. Seems like a decent kid. Maybe even sane."

The Twins were wallowing back and forth like a cockroach on its back, trying to roll over so they could stand. Noah's blood met Benjamin's elbow and soaked his shirt.

The smell of smoke had been growing more noticeable, and now it could be seen, too, pouring in from two directions as well as rushing past the windows like some gravity-defying waterfall.

The Twins were screaming now, fighting each other to scream, lungs pumping out of sync, heart hammering. Screaming as the nanobots used their flesh to create more nanobots, millions of little worker ants carving tiny slices of flesh, busy little hog butchers carving a living pig.

Against all odds, slipping in blood, their own and Noah's, the Twins managed to get to their feet.

With a sound of screeching metal and shattering glass, the Tulip sagged farther and Burnofsky staggered forward and was flattened against the glass windows. The floor now tilted up and away from him. But he still held the remote.

Then Noah began to slide, his movement lubricated by his own blood. He slid straight toward Burnofsky.

With a sound like wood being split, the window behind Burnofsky cracked but did not shatter. Burnofsky tried to push himself away, to reach something, anything he could grab, but his feet were slipping on the same blood that bore Noah's body straight toward him.

And then Noah made one desperate reach and grabbed the rolling bottle of vodka. He grabbed it and dug his heel in—slipping, sliding, but the angle helped him to rise, just a little, just enough, just enough to hurl the bottle.

The bottle smashed into the cracked window.

Burnofsky in a moment of terrible awareness pressed his thumb on the remote control, but missed the button. The remote was in his hand, but awkwardly held. He reached with his free hand to straighten it, and the window blew out.

Burnofsky went flying, flying through shattered glass, falling on his back toward the street far below. Noah had plowed into him, and for a moment the two of them were tangled in midair, grotesque acrobats trailing red.

Burnofsky fell and squeezed, but the remote was in the air beside him, falling, and his hand was held in the slippery grip of the boy with blue, blue eyes.

Madness and *death*, Noah thought. It was funny.

He laughed as the sidewalk rushed toward him and obliterated all that he was.

The Twins staggered into the hanging monitor, where Charles managed to grab on, powerful fingers gripping slippery steel and glass.

Charles Armstrong saw his face, their faces, in the hanging mirror they used to speak eye to eye.

What he saw was a grotesque head with two staring eyes and a third, lesser eye that now belonged entirely to Benjamin. Two mouths screamed. A line of blood had been drawn between those mouths, between those eyes, as the self-replicating nanobots chewed their industrious way through all that connected Charles to his brother.

The pain was unendurable. He could only scream and scream as his privates and rectum, his stomach and chest, his neck and back and now head were eaten away, faster and faster as the nanobot army multiplied. Eaten away and then cauterized as Burnofsky had planned, so that blood loss would not occur too quickly.

Charles did not feel the moment when his body began to disconnect from Benjamin's, the agony did not allow for calm consideration. But he saw, as he looked down, as he and Benjamin lowered their massive head to see, that they were now two dying men, two, connected only at the brain.

Benjamin slipped, his leg going out from beneath him, but

Charles still stood, as like a dividing cell they split slowly apart.

Then finally Charles lost his grip, and they fell onto their backs and slid toward the window.

Charles tried to scream, but his throat was gone.

They slid, consciousness fading in a hell of pain and terror as they accelerated.

Benjamin stuck out a hand and grabbed the leg of a table, but it, too, was sliding. And then, with a bump at the sill, they were in the air.

It would take them just under eight seconds to fall to the pavement. At four seconds before impact Charles saw Benjamin's body separate from his, a crudely bisected man trailing blood.

He saw Benjamin. Saw him *there*. *There!* For the first time in his life.

The Armstrong Twins hit the pavement two tenths of a second apart.

Two and a half minutes later, the Tulip came down in a catastrophic eruption of flame, smoke, steel, dust, and debris that buried Burnofsky and the Twins and Noah.

And the remote that would have destroyed the world.

TWENTY-EIGHT

Plath and Wilkes had to walk and hobble the whole way back to the safe house. The subway had been shut down. The taxis had fled the streets. They saw cars pass by, heading toward the bridge, pets and houseplants inside, household goods strapped to the roof. A hard-to-frighten city had at last been frightened.

By the time they made it they were numb with cold, lips blue, teeth chattering. Plath's tears had frozen on her cheeks. She recalled the Île Sainte-Marie, recalled where she'd been not very many days ago. A completely different world. It had been so perfect there. Warm sunshine and blue water and Noah.

They had killed him. Noah. They had killed him.

Inside the safe house at last the two girls collapsed onto the couch and shivered, burrowing beneath throw pillows in search of warmth.

Plath saw that Anya was coming to investigate the noise. In the window in her mind she saw herself through Anya's eye. She looked pitiful. Her face was smeared with smoke; her hair was thick with ash.

"What is the matter?" Anya asked. She didn't wait for an answer but ducked out to come back with blankets to pile on the frozen girls.

Then she made hot tea and helped them hold the cups until their hands could stop trembling.

"Where is Keats? Where is Billy?" Anya asked, already suspecting the answer. The TV had been on when they came in, tuned to news. On the screen the Tulip fell again and again. Hollywood and city luminaries ran wild through the streets again and again. The lurid loops played over and over again.

Plague of Madness.

An overhead shot of the Brooklyn Bridge was a river of red lights—cars fleeing the city.

"Dead," Plath said. "Both dead."

"This is Lear's doing," Anya said. "He is—"

"She," Wilkes interrupted. "Our overlord and master is a chick." Then, eyes darting suspiciously toward the stairs, said, "Get Vincent down here. Get Mr. Seventy Percent."

Anya seemed ready to argue, but acquiesced with downcast eyes.

Plath felt a wave of exhaustion that forced her eyelids down. She coughed—she'd been coughing the whole way home. The nauseating stink of smoke was in her nostrils, the taste of it in her mouth, and more came when she coughed.

Vincent arrived silently and stood with Anya by his side, looking like a man waiting for his own firing squad.

"What did you know?" Plath asked wearily.

"What do you mean?" he asked, and Wilkes was up out of her seat and swinging a fist at him, which he blocked easily. She swung again, but with less conviction, and he gently pushed her back down onto the couch.

"What did you know, Vincent?" Plath asked again with deadly, weary calm that carried absolute authority. "Did you know who Lear is?"

He blinked and shook his head. Then he leaned toward her, frowning. "Are you saying you *do* know who he is?"

"She," Wilkes said. "She, she, she. She. A sister. One of the vaginally endowed. Lystra Reid."

Vincent drew back as if frightened. "You can't do that, you can't talk about Lear. Caligula will—"

"He's dead, too," Wilkes said. "That's his work." She stabbed a finger at the TV. "He's dead. And Jin is dead. And Ophelia is dead. And Renfield is dead. And Billy is dead. Even the Twins are dead. And pretty—" She sobbed, and it was a moment before she could go on, her voice low and grating. "It's a whole big bunch of dead tonight. Now answer Plath's question, Vincent, or I swear to God I'll find some way to make you dead, too."

"I met Lear once. I didn't look at him. Her, if you say so. Maybe that explains why I was told not to turn around and look. He, she, whoever, used voice masking. I assumed it was so that later I wouldn't be able to recognize the voice."

"And did you know Lear planned to do this? To use biot madness this way?"

"No."

Plath set her teacup aside carefully. Her hands were still hard to control with any finesse. The cold seemed to have sunk deep in her, joining the cold, dead spot where Noah had been held in her thoughts. "Where do you stand, Vincent?"

He did not pretend he didn't understand. He grasped her meaning immediately. "I'm not sure I know who I am," he began.

Wilkes interrupted. "Yeah, well, welcome to the new reality. We've all been mind-fucked one way or the other." She laughed her mirthless heh-heh-heh and said, "We really are BZRK now, I guess. Crazy."

"I wish they would stop showing that," Anya said, transfixed by the TV.

"Where do you stand, Vincent?" Plath repeated.

"I have to . . ." He began, hesitated, shook his head, and continued. "I have to go back to basics. To what I believe. For a start, my name is not Vincent. It's Michael Ford."

"I'm sticking with Wilkes. It works for me."

"I'm Michael Ford," he said, almost wonderingly. Like a little kid talking about some new and amazing thing he'd just learned. "I'm Michael. I believe . . . I believe people should be free, that's why . . . I believe they should be left alone. That's why I joined BZRK."

"That's why everyone *joins*," Anya said, speaking that last word with distaste. "No one ever *joins* to do evil. It just always ends up that way."

Vincent winced as if she'd struck him.

Plath said, "Burnofsky is releasing self-replicating nanobots. Maybe they were all destroyed in the Tulip, maybe not. If he did it, if they aren't all killed, well . . . anyway, the Twins and Burnofsky are no longer the problem. Lear is the problem. And I don't think she's done. I think she'll keep at it. She wants to . . ." She shrugged. "I have no idea what she wants."

"Noah would have," Vincent said softly. "He was a gamer. This is all a game. It's been a game from the start."

Plath stared at him, thinking. He did not look away. "A game," she said finally. "And what's the point of this game?"

"Games have no point," Vincent said. "The point of the game is the game. The purpose is to play. But games have structure. They are built and written. And you can only play one at a time. Lear is wiping the board of the old game, replacing it with his . . . *her* own game."

"How do we win?"

"To win you have to understand the . . ." He shook his head. "You can't beat the game designer at her own game."

"Sure you can," Wilkes said. "I used to beat my little brother at games all the time. I'd pull the power cord out of the wall. Game over."

Before she got on her plane, Lystra Reid, Lear, punched a code into her phone and pushed Send.

The text went to the nearest cell-phone tower. The signal went from there to a central router that pushed it up to a satellite from whence it was bounced to another satellite, and still another as it wound its way south. Eventually it was picked up by a satellite dish.

From there it traveled just a few hundred feet to a computer server that recognized the code and translated it into sixteen thousand individual digital instructions that then mostly retraced the digital path of the incoming message.

Elapsed time, 3.4 seconds.

In crèches concealed in locations in several cities across North America, Europe, and Asia, DNA stew was bathed in various enzymes before receiving three micro-doses of drugs and a final jolt of electricity.

Forty-eight thousand biots—three for each of the sixteen thousand DNA signatures—came to life.

Only fifteen thousand, eight hundred and four people (a number had died since their fateful visit to a medical testing lab) saw windows open in their minds.

Of those, fewer than a third understood what it meant.

They generated more than three thousand terrified calls to 911 in the U.S. and 999 in the UK and 112 in the European Union.

"That's the first tranche," Lear said. To the pilot, she said, "Okay, we can go now."

Bug Man did not want to ask. He risked making her angry, and in this new world, where his life belonged to her, he did not want to do that. But he couldn't help himself.

"My mum?"

"By now she's thinking, 'Blimey, what's that then?'" Lear said, switching to an exaggerated British accent. "There's windows in me head, innit?"

Bug Man's throat convulsed. Tears came to his eyes, impossible to stop.

"Best to move on, Buggy," Lear said. "Get over it. Look at me. My father died tonight, and do I seem all weepy? Hey, have you decided what color teeth you want?"

"What?"

"The teeth. The teeth!" She pointed at her own. "How about green? I like green."

As the jet taxied the acid rolled toward forty-eight thousand biots.

"Hah, there we go, yeah," Lear said. "Now we're going to play."

"We know her name now. Lystra Reid," Plath said.

Anya typed it in. Instantly the computer monitor lit up with links and photos.

"I've seen her before." Wilkes frowned, then snapped her fingers. "Nijinsky. She was there when Jin died."

"Lear. She's thirtysomething, born in Bogalusa, Louisiana. Parents not listed. Schools, nope. That's about it except for later business stuff. She owns a lot of medical testing labs."

"That would make sense," Anya said.

Vincent, seemingly exhausted by his earlier conversation, remained silent.

"That's probably how she met my father. And it's how she got DNA samples."

"She will have millions of them," Anya said.

Plath looked at the best photograph of Lystra Reid. What was there in that pretty face to betray the existence of an evil, disturbed mind? Nothing. The eyes were clear, the expression open, the mouth smiling.

Plath remembered what Stern had told her. That Lear had used burner phones but without masking the callback number. One had been purchased in Tierra del Fuego. The other in New Zealand, she could not recall the city. But both had been connected to Antarctica.

"Search 'Lystra Reid' and Antarctica," she told Anya.

That earned a raised eyebrow, but the search caused a long, slow exhale. Lystra Reid had purchased a company called Cathexis.

"Pull up any articles on Cathexis Inc.," Plath instructed.

The four of them read silently. Wilkes moved her lips. Plath felt a new pang as just for a moment she thought to turn, look over her shoulder, and ask Noah what he thought.

But there was no Noah. No Noah, no Nijinsky, no Mr. Stern, and only a partial Vincent.

"Who has had any medical testing done in the last ten years?" Plath asked.

But Vincent shook his head. "Irrelevant. If we've had biots made, we're in her database."

"I have not had biots made," Anya said. "But I have been tested at one of her labs."

"So we are all vulnerable. It's possible that at any moment—"

"Great," Wilkes said. "Fine. Let me go nuts. I'll fit right in."

Plath looked to Vincent. "What will she do next?"

Vincent thought about it, eyes dark beneath his brow, mouth a grim line. "Her goal is instability. What else could it be? With her skills and her resources, if all she wanted was the whole world dead, she could have grown smallpox or anthrax in a lab somewhere. And she has nanotechnology. Why have us use biots to fight the Armstrongs? She had the upper hand all along. She could have used a lot less effort and simply obtained a sample of their DNA, grown biots for them, and inflicted biot madness."

"Okay, why didn't she?" Plath asked.

"Because she's a gamer," Vincent said with more confidence than he felt. "She wants to win, yes, but first she wants to *play*. We were Level One."

"Then we're in Level Two now." Plath nodded. "Now she drives the whole world crazy. Watches it. Shows up in person to enjoy Jin's death. Probably other events as well. She's enjoying all that."

"Sick bitch," Wilkes muttered.

"She brought me back, made me a part of it again. Why?"

Vincent shrugged. "Because you're her avatar. She wants you to go on playing. Bluebooking."

"What?"

"It's an old gaming expression. It's when a player keeps a journal of the game, but from the POV of the avatar."

"You are smart and rich and pretty," Anya suggested. "Just as she is. And alone. As she must be."

"Lear sent me to recruit you," Vincent reminded her.

"And when I was enjoying the island too much, she forced me back into the game. She even left clues for me to find that would link her to Antarctica."

"Machines do not work well at very cold temperatures," Anya said. "And nanobots are machines."

"Okay, so Antarctica because—"

"Because if the gray goo has been unleashed, it will have a hard time penetrating hundreds of miles of subzero temperatures. It's the safest place on the planet if you're worried about that."

Vincent nodded agreement. This was the most engaged Plath had seen him in a long while. Was he ready to take command again? *No. This is my game now.*

"Antarctica is also a place to ride out whatever shitstorm she's unleashed," Wilkes offered. "It's as far away as you can get without being on the moon."

"So she camps there," Vincent said. "Safe from the goo. And safe from the consequences of her own game."

"She camps. She waits. Why?"

"For Level Two to play out. So she can be there for Level Three."

"And what is Level Three?"

Vincent shook his head slowly. "Only Lear knows that. It's her game."

"And we can't beat her by playing her game," Plath concluded. "We can only pull the power cord."

"The power cord is south of here," Wilkes said.

"She will expect that," Vincent said.

"Expect it? I have a feeling it's what she wants," Plath said.

TWENTY-NINE

From New York to Tierra del Fuego was a bit over six thousand five hundred miles, which at a speed of four hundred eighty knots took eleven hours. It was not a pleasant flight for Bug Man. But he was lucky. The rest of the world was faring much worse.

During the time Bug Man was in the air eleven more tranches of forty-eight thousand biots, totaling five hundred twenty-eight thousand, were generated from stored DNA patterns. Dividing by three biots per person, that was approximately one hundred seventy-six thousand people who lost their grip on sanity.

They were concentrated in fifteen major cities for maximum disruption. New York, London, Berlin, Paris, Shanghai, Los Angeles, Tokyo, Mexico City, Moscow, Washington, Rome, Beijing, Jerusalem, Mumbai, and Sydney.

By the time Lear's plane landed at the Ushuaia's airport, Los Angeles, Jerusalem, and Berlin were burning.

The flight to the ice would be slower and in a less comfortable plane: Lear's sumptuous private jet could not land on ice. It was two thousand seven hundred miles from Ushuaia to Cathexis Base, but flying in a refurbished C-130 Hercules turboprop with a cruising speed of three hundred thirty miles an hour, it took more than eight hours. Another one hundred twenty-eight thousand people, minus those who had already passed away, were driven into madness.

These were concentrated in and around military bases in the United States, Russia, China, the United Kingdom, France, India, and Pakistan. The choice of countries was not random: each had nuclear weapons, but of those, France and the UK used only submarine-based weapons.

The first launch was from Russia, but the missile and its warhead were destroyed in flight, en route to North Dakota.

The second launch was from Pakistan. It landed in the middle of a department store in New Delhi, India, but did not explode. The madman who had fired it had not armed the warhead.

But the Indian military did not wait to consider the situation. Indian missiles flew minutes after the C-130 slid to a stop on the Cathexis Base airfield.

Fifty-two Agni-III and Agni-IV missiles flew, striking targets in Pakistan. By the time the C-130 had been refueled for the last leg of its flight, there were thirty-one million dead, a number that would double within days.

After a shorter hop and a very bumpy landing, Bug Man stumbled from the plane still wearing the T-shirt he'd been wearing in New York. His teeth, his entire mouth, and jaw hurt. He was exhausted, having been awakened repeatedly by nightmares. And now he was more cold than he would have believed possible. And standing in the whitest place on Earth.

"Where are we?"

"The bottom of the world, Buggy, the place where machines go to die. People, too."

A green Sno-Cat was tearing across the snow toward them. It roared to a stop and two men jumped out. One ran to Lystra with a full-length coat that many foxes had died to provide. The other handed a voluminous down parka to Bug Man, who shivered into it. A fur-lined hat was plopped on his head, and he was hustled into the backseat of the Sno-Cat. It wasn't exactly warm inside, but it wasn't fatally cold, either.

"How was your flight, Ms. Reid?"

"Fine, Stillers. Fine. Are all the necessary personnel in from Forward Green?"

"Yes, ma'am, all personnel, all equipment, all supplies, except for the final two sleighs, which are being prepped and will be brought here tomorrow. And we've topped off the fuel both here and at Forward Green."

"Then we are in lockdown," she said pleasantly. "Except for the final sleighs. Make sure no one shoots at them." She shook her head as if marveling at the world's unpredictability. "The world has just gone to hell in a handbasket, yeah, and we have a long year ahead of us."

Not waiting a second, Stillers keyed a radio and said, "Lockdown, lockdown. Lockdown, lockdown."

Bug Man could not quite imagine what was being locked down. It wasn't like there was a crowd standing around trying to break in. They were in the middle of a whole lot of nothing as far as he could see.

Then, as if by a miracle, the ground seemed to open up. The

Sno-Cat rounded a sharp corner, treads churning up hard-packed snow, and plunged down a long ramp into a valley. He saw buildings and an improbable house and . . .

"Is that a swimming pool?"

"Yes," Lystra said. "One of only two in Antarctica." Then, with a wistful look, she added, "I like to swim. It's a very clean sort of sport, yeah. And I look amazing in a bathing suit, yeah, if I say so myself."

Bug Man thought that was likely true, if *amazing* was the right word for a woman covered in tattoos of her victims.

"There's also an underground greenhouse. Palm trees! Palm trees in Antarctica, yeah. Yeah. We can live very well here for two years, or survive for three. If necessary. We'll see."

"Do you want to go to the office?" Stillers asked deferentially.

"No, the house. Find quarters for Bug Man, but for now he'll stay with me." She patted Bug Man's knee. "I've decided he's my good-luck charm. Oh, and tell the dentist, Dr. Whatever-the-Hell, yeah, he's got a customer. Patient. Whatever. Yeah."

Tanner was among those waiting when an unannounced flight came into McMurdo, running on fumes, or so the pilot said. Planes did not just suddenly arrive on the ice. And Tanner, like everyone else at the base, had been watching events back in the world with disbelief and anxiety turning to fear.

Tanner had called Naval Intelligence in Washington and been told that *Satan is loose among the flock, hah-hah, redrum redrum, they're listening, don't you know that?*

A call higher up the chain of command to the Pentagon had gone unanswered. Calls to USAP and Lockheed had yielded nothing.

Tanner was in summer gear—a parka over padded jeans with the big Mickey Mouse boots unlaced. He wore gloves and goggles and a light stocking cap with a Pittsburgh Pirates logo.

The plane, a C-130, a Herc in the patois, landed easily, and killed engines. Tanner reached under his parka to touch the butt of his trusty Colt .45 auto. Everyone authorized to carry a gun was carrying one. As a safety measure that would have been absurd in earlier times, Tanner had stationed an ex-sergeant with a sniper rifle on the roof of a parked truck.

The person who stepped first from the plane could not have been less likely.

"It's a girl," Tanner said.

"Yep, that's a girl." This from the station chief beside him. "Looks kind of familiar. Not some crazy pop singer, is it?"

Behind the girl came a grown woman, rather beautiful and just exotic enough to hold Tanner's eye for longer than strictly necessary. Then a girl with a strange half mohawk and a stranger tattoo below one eye. And finally a young man with dark hair, a calm expression, and an air of tension that Tanner associated with trouble.

The girl walked up without hesitation, in a hurry. She pulled off her glove and stuck out her hand. "I'm Pla— Sadie McLure."

The station chief, Joe Washington, shook her hand and glanced at Tanner.

"Sadie McLure," Tanner repeated, frowning as he tried to pull the name from memory.

"Yes. As in Grey McLure crashing a jet into a Jets game," she said.

No hint of a smile. A very serious, even grim young woman. "These are my friends. Wilkes. Dr. Anya Violet. Michael Ford."

Tanner remembered now. "What exactly are you doing here, Ms. McLure?"

Her eyes bored into him. They were eyes that belonged in a much older face. "We're here to try to stop what's happening. We're here to kill the woman responsible."

"The woman responsible? Here?" Washington wanted to laugh, but the faces before him did not look as if they were joking.

"Lystra Reid."

"Cathexis Inc.?"

"And some other businesses as well. What's happening is her doing."

The station chief had to laugh at that. "Excuse me, but I've met Lystra Reid, and she's a sharp young businesswoman. I don't know what—"

"Let them talk, Joe," Tanner said quietly.

The station chief seemed almost offended, but he nodded. "Okay. Not here. We'll drive you to my office."

An hour later Plath and Vincent, with occasional outbursts from Wilkes, had told their tale.

"To say that sounds crazy is an understatement," the station chief said.

"Do you have any proof?" Tanner asked.

Plath cocked her head and looked at him. "You know something."

Tanner smiled slightly. "Do you have proof?"

"As a matter of fact, I do," Plath said. "We thought you might be skeptical. "So here's what's going to happen. I'm going to just touch my finger to your face. Then, in a few minutes you're going to open a book at random. You'll hold the page close to your face. And I'll tell you what you're reading."

"What is that, some kind of magic trick?"

"It's the best I can do on short notice," Plath snapped. "If you like, I could blind you, or start sticking pins in your brain and giving you some amazing hallucinations."

"I'll read a book," Tanner said. Ten minutes later he was shaken and convinced.

"What do you want from us?" Washington asked. He was still skeptical, still not sure it wasn't some sort of trick, but he also knew that in matters of security, Tanner was the real boss.

"Fuel," Plath said. "And men with guns, if you have any."

"Men, I have. Guns? I could spare a couple of handguns and a hunting rifle. But Mr. Tanner here may have other means."

Tanner shifted uncomfortably, then made a decision. "Okay. Cards on the table. We've been looking at Cathexis for some time now in relation to a souped-up hovercraft they seem to have built. An *armed* hovercraft. I sent a person with some military background in to check it out. I have not heard back from her."

Vincent spoke for the first time. "You're intelligence."

Tanner gave a short nod.

"Then you have people you could call."

Tanner snorted. "Are you kidding me? With what's happening back in the world? Shit has hit the fan. Cities are burning, people are scared to death, my chain of command . . ." He threw up his hands.

"If we can prove to you that this woman is doing what we say she's doing, if we can prove to you that we can stop her, will you do all you can?" Plath asked.

Tanner thought about that for a moment and glanced at Washington, who raised his hands—palms out—in a gesture that said, *It's on you.* "Yeah," Tanner said. "You prove all that, and I will do all I can to bring down the wrath of God." Then, under his breath he added, "But it won't work."

Surreal, that was the word Bug Man had been searching for. Surreal.

He was in Antarctica, in a dry valley way below the ice, in a house, in a very expensively furnished living room, looking out of expansive windows onto a domed swimming pool, while a lunatic and mass murderer suggested he could replace the teeth she herself had broken with fangs. Green fangs.

"It would give you an original look," Lear said. "Do you know how to cook at all? My cook is busy, yeah, helping to inventory supplies. Can you fry some eggs?"

A television was on in the kitchen where Bug Man rummaged in a vast refrigerator for eggs and bacon. That much he could do. Eggs and bacon.

The television showed the BBC, but it wasn't any of the sets he'd ever seen them use. It looked a bit as if the male and female announcers were broadcasting from a concrete bomb shelter.

The crawl at the bottom of the screen was full of warnings from the army that people should stay in their homes and off the streets.

That and statements from Number 10 and acting prime minister Dermot Tricklebank, whoever that was, to the effect that *the only thing they had to fear was fear itself.*

"Hunh," Lear commented. "That's a Roosevelt quote. Shouldn't they be using Churchill?"

The stovetop was a restaurant-quality thing with massive knobs and too many burners. It took Bug Man a few anxious minutes to figure out how to work the knobs, but eventually he was able to lay six strips of bacon on a grill.

"Crispy," Lear said, pointing at the bacon.

The announcer said, *"The nuclear exchange between India and Pakistan has escalated, with at least five major Indian cities now essentially vaporized."*

"Hah," Lear said. "And don't forget the eggs. Not too runny."

"Okay."

"Winds are whipping the fire now spreading out of control through Bayswater and Notting Hill. Our reporters have seen no evidence of effective emergency response."

"It's hard to tell when an egg is done, yeah, but . . . Oh, look look look! He's setting himself on fire!"

Bug Man did not want to see that and instead focused on his work.

"Looked like a banker. Nice suit. It's interesting that a person can be mad and yet plan ahead well enough to find gas. Or *petrol*, as you would say."

Yes, Bug Man thought grimly, *who would have thought a crazy person could plan?* He turned the bacon and held down the curling tips.

"Oh, look at that! Look at that video!" This was spoken as an order not a request, so Bug Man looked. The tape showed an American Airlines 787 roaring down from the sky and smashing into a very large, gray Gothic church. The announcer said something about the cathedral at Reims.

"Not that great an explosion, though," Lear opined.

Suddenly the BBC was off the air, replaced by static.

"I knew this would be a problem," Lear said. "I avoided messing with media folks, yeah, but there's no way to stop someone cutting their power." She began flipping through channels. Static and more static. Then what appeared to be a Japanese news station with a fixed camera aimed at a woman who was giggling and stabbing her arm with broken shards of wooden chopsticks.

Al Jazeera was on, but in Arabic. A Russian station had a bespectacled, overweight man with a bottle of vodka before him on the anchor desk. He seemed to be announcing news, but his voice was slurred, and as they watched he began weeping.

"CNN! Yes! See, that's why I took it very easy on Atlanta."

Lear seemed to think she deserved some praise for her foresight.

"At this time we cannot confirm that the event in Norfolk, Virginia, was a nuclear explosion, although Norfolk is a major naval base that does handle ships carrying nuclear weapons."

"No video?" Lear moaned.

"We now have video of an oil refinery in Port Arthur, Texas, which is burning."

"I've seen oil refineries burn," Lear complained. "I've never seen a nuked city. Come on, they must have some video."

"Here you go." Bug Man plated the bacon and eggs.

"Next time drain the bacon a little better. Blot it with a paper towel."

They went into the dining room, all rich, dark wood with high-backed chairs. A chandelier hung above the table.

"It's going well, don't you think? Yeah?"

"Yes." What else could he say?

"Early stages yet." She munched thoughtfully. "I wonder if I should spread it out, you know? My first plan was to keep up the pace, sixteen thousand an hour. But what if . . . No. No, I'm sticking with the original plan. I don't want to start second-guessing myself."

No, you wouldn't want that, Bug Man thought. He wondered if his mother was still alive. Had she killed herself like so many seemed to do? Was she even now wandering the streets, raving? Maybe hurting other people? Maybe being hurt herself?

What was the point of caring? Lear had won. The world was going crazy. The human race was killing itself in an orgy of madness.

"I have some work to do," Lear said. "You stay and watch."

"I don't think—"

"That wasn't a request, yeah? Stay and watch. You know what to look for."

"I do?" Bug Man was mystified.

"The Armstrongs had self-replicating nanobots. Yeah. Maybe the fire at the Tulip got them all. Maybe not." Lear shook her head and her mouth was a grim, worried line. But she cheered up considerably when the news announced that Berlin, Germany, had been hit by a nuclear weapon.

THIRTY

The C-130 carrying Plath and her crew, as well as Tanner and seventeen ex-military volunteers from McMurdo, landed at Cathexis Base to find employees there bewildered and frightened. Their medical team had all been ordered to Forward Green a day earlier without explanation. And the Plague of Madness had spread there as well. They had seven people locked up. A dormitory had been burned to the ground, killing three.

The C-130 flew on to Forward Green. It was a cargo plane, a cavernous, incredibly noisy and very cold open space with webbing seats along both sides. Large dotted lines had been painted on the curved walls, indicating just where the propellers would chew through the fuselage should one come off in flight.

"This is their only other facility, so far as we know," Tanner said.

The plane circled, coming around into a strengthening wind. The sun was low on the horizon, as much like night as Antarctica got this time of year.

"I don't like that layout," one of the ex-soldiers said. "Those towers sure as hell look like gun emplacements."

The pilot called back over the intercom. "They are refusing to let us land." Then, a moment later, "Sir, they are warning us that they will open fire if we attempt a landing."

Tanner looked at Plath. "Well, I guess that tends to confirm your story."

He unhooked himself from his webbing seat and went forward to speak to the pilot.

Plath looked at Vincent—arms folded, eyes in shadow. At Wilkes, snoring beside her, somehow curled into a fetal ball in the webbing. And Anya, who seemed never to need sleep.

Plath had removed her biot from Anya. With apologies. They were all three now in her own head, as safe as they could be. To kill her biots you'd have to kill Plath herself. Three windows were open, as they always were, now showing slithering macrophages and twitching neurons and what were hopefully spiky balls of pollen in her eye and not bacteria.

She—

BOOOOM!

Something had smacked the C-130 a staggering blow. Tanner came tearing back from the cockpit, the back of his jacket on fire. Plath unbuckled and threw her parka over him, smothering the flames.

The plane jerked again, not as hard, but then nosed down. They were low, no more than four thousand feet up; there was little room to recover.

The nose came slowly, slowly up, but as it did the plane went into a steep turn that threw Plath into Vincent.

"Sons of bitches!" Tanner yelled.

Plath worked her hand into the webbing and held on as the plane rolled, rolled, and she hung suspended in midair while baggage and vomit flew everywhere and grown men screamed.

Wilkes was yelling something that Plath couldn't hear. "What?" she yelled.

"I said: I can't say it's been fun, Plath, but it was good knowing you!" Wilkes made a little mock-salute.

Plath reached her free arm across and took Wilkes's hand. Plath was not afraid to die, in some ways it spelled relief. But she was furious at the idea that Lear would win. "I'm not dying until I've killed that bitch!" she yelled to Wilkes, who smiled wryly and squeezed her hand.

Then, with a series of bone-shaking jerks, the plane slowly, slowly leveled off, but all the while it drifted lower.

The pilot, voice wracked with pain and fear, yelled, "Hard landing! Hard landing! Brace! Brace!"

The impact rattled Plath's spine and chipped one of her teeth as her mouth slammed shut. The webbing seat held her, but Anya was knocked from her seat and fell to the metal floor of the plane. A metallic shriek went on and on and on.

And that's when a spinning propeller—almost twenty feet from tip to tip—exploded through the flimsy fuselage, tearing Anya Violet and two of Tanner's men apart.

The plane skidded to a stop.

A giant gash made by the prop had nearly split the plane in two. Jagged metal edges were everywhere, blood and pale viscera was sprayed around the fuselage like some demented Jackson Pollock painting. A man with his leg gone at midthigh bellowed like a dying bull and tried futilely to cover the pulsing wound with his hands.

Smoke rolled back through the cargo bay, whipped away by a brutally cold wind coming through the gash.

Vincent stared at the place where Anya had been. He picked up something white and red, some unrecognizable part of her, and held it cradled on his lap.

Tanner was among the first to recover. "Get ready! They may send someone to finish us off!" He drew his pistol. It looked small and irrelevant in his hand. Dazed men responded, drawing their few weapons. One was trying to draw a gun with a hand that was no longer there. Another man gently eased him into the webbing and took the gun from him.

"You okay?" Plath asked Wilkes, and got a shaky nod in return. "Vincent?"

Vincent stared at her as if he'd never seen her before, maybe wasn't seeing her now. His shallow breathing formed a small cloud of steam.

"Anyone who can, follow me!" Tanner said. He wound his way through tangled metal to leap from the gash. Half a dozen men followed. Plath and Wilkes went to Vincent. "Come on, Vincent. Stay alive now, grieve later."

He flashed a look of pure, unadulterated fury that Plath at first thought was directed at her.

"Come on, Vincent. We have to get off this pl—"

A machine gun, sounding like a chainsaw, opened up. A line of holes appeared at the tail end of the cargo bay and walked its way forward. Metal was flying everywhere. The air stank of cordite, steel, blood, and human waste.

Plath grabbed Vincent by the jacket and yanked him to his feet as Wilkes undid his safety harness. Vincent let the gruesome body part drop, hesitated as if he might go back for it, and then Plath shoved him out onto the ice and jumped after him.

Wilkes landed on Plath, rolled off, and slithered on her belly. Plath glanced back and saw a Sno-Cat with a machine gun mounted on its roof, still firing from the far side of the wreck.

Then, with a *woosh* of searing heat, the starboard-side fuel tanks exploded, billowing out over the Sno-Cat. The man firing the machine gun was aflame, twisting, writhing, trapped somehow, and the machine gun stopped.

They were three hundred feet from the nearest building, which was one of the four gun emplacements.

"Run run run!" Tanner yelled, and led the way, slipping and staggering across the ice with the wind blessedly at his back. Plath saw immediately what he was doing. The gun tower was opening, shutters rising mechanically, revealing a long black muzzle. Tanner was trying to close the distance and get below the place where the gun could be depressed to target them.

It took twenty seconds for the shutters to open fully. Another ten seconds for the gunners to ready their weapon, and at that moment the gamble had failed. The gaggle of freezing survivors were in point-blank range.

The machine gun fired. Two rounds, killing one man instantly and hitting another in the thigh.

And then, the gun jammed.

Training took over for the ex-soldiers. They quickly closed the distance to the tower's base and began kicking at the door. One fired at the lock. The door opened and small-arms fire—a *pop! pop! pop!* sound—came from within.

Tanner, yelling obscenities, picked up a fallen body and threw it through the doorway to draw fire. He was in through the door in a flash. More gunfire as those with weapons rushed the doorway after him.

Silence descended. Tanner and his men had taken the tower.

"Come on," Plath said to Vincent and Wilkes, "we'll freeze out here!"

A second Sno-Cat was barreling toward them from the center of the compound, trailing a cloud of ice particles and steam.

The top third of the tower now rotated, bringing the machine gun to bear on the Sno-Cat, which made the fatal mistake of hesitating, slowing, and then blew apart as Tanner poured fire into it.

Plath, Wilkes, and Vincent found themselves in a bare room at the bottom of a steel spiral staircase leading up. "Wilkes, stay with Vincent."

Plath ran up the stairs to find Tanner still cursing, but also bleeding into his parka, a growing stain.

"Goddammit, goddammit, they shot me," he said as he tore off his jacket, then burrowed through layers of warmth to find a hole in his left side.

A soldier squatted to take a look. He grinned up at Tanner. "Through and through, Captain. You'll live if you don't bleed out."

"Slap on a compress, Sergeant O'Dell."

Tanner looked at Plath. "You look okay for your first firefight."

"Not my first," Plath said. "Not even my second. It's been a hell of a week." She peered out of the shooting hole as the machine gun traversed left and right. Nothing moved. The plane and the two Sno-cats burned.

"All those buildings—shuttered. Bulletproof, most likely." O'Dell, the ex-soldier who had tended Tanner's wound.

"Jesus H.," Tanner said. "It's a fortress. See what we have here. Inventory weapons and do a head count."

The bad news was that there were just six battle-ready men, plus Tanner, Plath, Vincent, and Wilkes.

The good news was delivered by O'Dell. "We have all the small arms we could want, plenty of ammo, and a dozen of these." The "these" in question were shoulder-fired antiaircraft missiles.

"I'm not familiar with those. Russian?"

"Chinese," O'Dell said. "And to answer your next question, yes, they can be fused for impact."

"Okay," Tanner said. "That is not a professional outfit out there; otherwise, they wouldn't have driven that Sno-Cat into range and then conveniently stopped. Amateurs with maybe a couple of veterans. Short-handed and poorly led, or we'd already be dead. Let's not give them time to figure anything out. Sergeant, blow some holes in that first building. Ground level if you can. We need a door."

The battle lasted two hours, by which time two more men had been killed. Plath and her friends had been given the job of ferrying wounded from the plane into the first tower while Tanner led the assault on the second.

When it was all over, they counted seven bodies of former Cathexis employees.

"A skeleton force," Tanner said. "So this was just a warm-up."

They had assembled in the dining hall and Wilkes had helpfully brewed a pot of coffee and popped open bags of chocolate chip cookies.

They were eight now, along with three wounded survivors from the plane wrapped in blankets and lying bandaged on empty steel tables. O'Dell and one other had taken a remaining Sno-Cat to what looked like a hangar that lay well outside of the main base.

"Whoever was here pulled out," Tanner said. "This place was not built for the dozen men left behind."

Vincent stood up and walked away.

"He'll be okay," Plath said, not believing it.

"He's been through a lot," Tanner said generously.

"You have no idea," Wilkes muttered as she poured mugs of coffee.

"We don't know if anyone got off a message to whoever, wherever . . . but let me just say that any skepticism about you, Ms. McLure, is officially dead and buried. We have to find wherever they went, chase them down, and stop this."

"All we've got is a Sno-Cat," a man observed. "Holds four passengers."

Vincent came back and without pre-amble said, "They left their computers on. There's another base. Farther south. A couple hundred miles."

Someone whistled low, and slow, and said, "That's a hell of a long ride in a Cat."

Then O'Dell returned. He had two prisoners, held at gunpoint. "Meet Mademoiselle Bonnard and Mr. Babbington."

"Dr. Babbington, actually."

O'Dell smacked his rifle butt into the man's spine.

"They didn't even know what was going on. They're out at the hangar out there, working on . . . well, you'll want to see this, Tanner."

"Is it a hovercraft with a jet engine and missiles?" Tanner asked wearily.

O'Dell threw up his free hand in exasperation. "You are no fun to surprise, Captain."

"We were just completing the assembly," the Frenchwoman said. "We are not dangerous. You have no need to point guns. We are engineers, just working for the company. Let us go free."

"Uh-huh," Tanner said. "Well, ma'am, you, too, *Doctor*, you now work for the U.S. Navy. You will complete your work, and if you manage to do it inside of two hours, I will not strip you both down to your underwear and send you out onto the ice."

"The sleighs are coming in," Stillers reported. He was casting questioning glances at Bug Man, wondering no doubt why his face was swollen, why his teeth were missing, and why he was wearing a bathrobe and flicking between YouTube and Twitter on the big TV monitor in Lystra Reid's living room.

"Yeah," Lear said distractedly.

"That will be the last of it," Stillers said.

"It's all coming down, Stillers. Um . . . Tell everyone good job, yeah? Yeah. Tell them all I said well done."

He nodded. "Did you want to, maybe, come over to the dining hall and speak to them?"

Lear considered the idea, shook her head almost shyly, and said, "No, I have to watch." She waved a hand toward a shaky YouTube of one of the endless array of riots in one of the endless number of burning cities. "Panic, you know. That's what gets them killed. It's like medieval, yeah? Plague. Or cholera."

She was no longer talking to Stillers, who sensed that fact and stood there stoic and awkward.

"That's the whole point. Madness leading to panic. If they just didn't panic, yeah, they'd be okay. Yeah? If they just didn't panic. But I knew they would."

"Yes, ma'am."

"Mmm. You can go, Stillers."

Stillers seemed relieved. Bug Man was not. It was better to have at least one extra person in the room in case Lear lost it again.

She flopped beside him on the couch. They had been watching together for the last few hours. Eating and watching in a bizarre parody of a girls' night at the movies. Bug Man had been half afraid she'd decide to paint his nails or talk about her love life.

"I'm glad you decided to join me, Buggy. Good old Buggy. You get it, yeah. You've been down there, down in the meat. You've been part of the game for a long time."

Bug Man did not remember choosing to be here. He remembered being blackmailed and threatened, made a party to yet another crime. If anyone ever lived to tell this story in some history book, he would be labeled as the guy who killed a president and almost killed a pope. Which was unfair. He was, at most, an accessory.

An accessory to the end of the world.

"Get us a drink, Buggy. You know, I wanted to get Sadie here, too. I thought she would be fun to have around, yeah. For a little girl-time, you know? We could talk girl stuff, yeah, that I can't talk about with you."

He poured them each a bourbon. She had said they had enough for two years, at least. He hoped that was true, because he felt he was going to need to drink an awful lot.

I'm turning into Burnofsky, he thought. *Old degenerate trying to drink away his sins. That's me now, but not old. So I can live with this for a long time. If she doesn't kill me.*

"What is that? Is that a cross? Oh, that is awesome. They're nailing that woman to a cross!"

Bug Man was sick so far down into his soul that he wished he could shut down his brain, go into some kind of coma—wake up later, maybe a lot later. He waited for the shaky video to end then navigated to the next clip.

"So Sadie, that didn't work out. But I've got you, Buggy. And it's all working," she said. "All working. Except for the self-replicating nanobots. Yeah. The goo."

"I haven't seen anything like what you're looking for," Bug Man ventured. "Just crazies, no buildings eaten up or whatever."

"Mmm. Yeah." Lear was pensive. "Probably all burned up when the Tulip came down. Burned up with the Twins. Wish I'd been able to stay to see even more of that, yeah. Yeah. Burning Armstrongs, that would have been excellent." She shrugged and sighed, disappointed. "But all it takes is one of those SRNs to survive. Just one." She bit a fingernail and added a superfluous, "Yeah."

"I'm sure—"

"Shut up!" Lear snapped. "You're not sure. I'm not sure, so you're not sure."

"Yes, ma'am."

"Gotta exterminate them, somehow. They'll just . . . just keep on. Gotta be a way to stop them."

"Race to the end of the world," Bug Man said, his tongue loosened by the whiskey. "Choose your apocalypse."

"I can't let them beat me, the Twins. Burnofsky."

An idea occurred to Bug Man. If he spoke it, he would never be able to unsay it. If she liked the idea, she would be happy with him. If not . . .

"I have an idea," he said.

"Speak it, Buggy."

"You have people's biots. You can send them a message. To the right people. I mean, you have all that cross-referenced, right? I mean, you would know which people were in the Pentagon, or maybe in Russia, wherever."

She was looking at him with the intensity of a cobra looking at a mouse. "Spit it out of that mush mouth, Bug Man."

"Okay, say you have some general, or whatever. You fire up his biots, right? He knows now what's coming. He knows he's screwed. But biots can see, right? They could see, you know, if you showed them a sign. Held up a sign in front of them."

She stared at him for a full minute, during which Bug Man wondered if he would have the strength even to resist if she decided to kill him. Did he even want to live?

Then she reached out one hand, pinched his swollen cheek, and said, "Buggy, you are a genius."

THIRTY-ONE

Plath was in the second seat of the sleigh. Tanner was driving. O'Dell was in the other sleigh, being driven by Babbington, who had been convinced to help when O'Dell shot two of his toes off and promised to keep going if he didn't.

Three more men plus Vincent and Wilkes were crammed into the Sno-Cat, trailing many miles behind.

"I still don't see a damned thing, and we're supposedly right on top of it," Tanner said. Then, "Ahhh! Shit! O'Dell, stop, stop, stop!" he yelled through his radio.

He killed the engine and fumbled for the brakes that slammed steel claws down into the ice. The sleigh went from a moderate seventy miles an hour—neither Tanner nor Babbington felt confident going any faster—to zero in five seconds. Even so, the front two feet of the sleigh were over the lip of a sharp drop-off.

"This thing have a reverse gear?" Tanner wondered. If there was, he never found it. "Okay, we get out and push it sideways."

Tanner and Plath climbed out onto the ice. Only then did they see the brightly lit compound nestled in the dry valley below.

"Under my nose," Tanner muttered. "They built this right under my nose."

"Antarctica is a big place," Plath soothed. "And Lear has a lot of money."

"Is that another swimming pool?"

O'Dell and Babbington joined them and helped manhandle the sleigh back from the lip of the cliff. Under low power, just enough to raise the weight of the sleigh from the ice, it wasn't too hard.

"There's ramp over there," O'Dell said. "But we could just sit up here and fire down into the base. Twelve missiles, fair amount of thirty-mil cannon . . ." He shrugged.

"No," Plath said. "We need to know whether this base is the place she's using to control events, or just a place to hide while the work is done elsewhere."

Tanner nodded. "Look at that slag heap over there. That's way more than you'd get from just leveling. They've dug some holes."

"Yeah, well, that base looks like it will sustain a hundred men," O'Dell argued. "I'm not seeing the gun emplacements we saw back at Forward Green. Still, we could get a very hot greeting. These sleighs aren't armored worth a damn."

Babbington took offense at that. "We needed to keep weight down, obviously. The engine is armored."

"Yeah? How about the cockpit?" O'Dell asked. "Yeah, I thought so."

"The house," Plath said.

"Yep," Tanner said. "That's the big-boss house right there. If we catch them by surprise, decapitate them—

"That chopper down there has missile launchers and a cannon," O'Dell pointed out.

Plath said, "Look, for whatever reason, Lear hasn't killed me yet.

She could have. She wanted me back in the game. She insisted I play an active role. I think . . . I think she doesn't want me dead."

"What do you have in mind?"

"I think I walk down there, knock on the door, and hope she shakes hands."

"I'm going to try to get through to some rational person, either in D.C. or Langley or any random naval vessel that might be within range. But don't count on the cavalry. You understand?"

"I do," Plath said.

He gave her an appraising look. "What are you, sixteen?"

"Yes," Plath said. "But I've packed a lot into the last few months."

He nodded. "I have a son about your age. Back in the world. Minneapolis, with my parents. I'm trying to tell myself he's okay."

Plath started to answer, stopped herself, shook her head, and finally said, "I was about to say I'm doing the same. But everyone I care about is either dead, or here with me." Noah, lying in his own blood, gasping final breaths.

She squeezed her eyes shut. There were no tears—which, she thought, was a good thing as they would have frozen.

Her father, her brother. Ophelia, Nijinsky, Anya. Billy. She saw his head fall to the side, his neck cut almost through.

At least her mother had died of natural causes. She hadn't been murdered. So much sadness, and now, the whole world was joining Plath in that sadness. That did not help. The old saying was that misery loves company. But Plath knew that misery needed hope. Misery needed to believe in a better future.

What was happening back in the world where Tanner's son lived?

Had Lear's madness killed millions, or just hundreds of thousands? Had Burnofsky's vile machines escaped to obliterate all of life?

How much could the human race stand? The dinosaurs had thrived for tens of millions of years before dying out. How many species had evolved, survived, and then at last succumbed?

Homo sapiens were, what, a million years old? And all of human civilization just a tenth of that. Had the clock run out?

Noah, lying in his own blood while the Twins raged and Burnofsky gloated.

Had she loved him? Then how could it be that she'd not told him? Too late now. Now she could only offer him more blood. More murder.

I'll kill her. For you, Noah.

"It's cold," Plath said. "Let's get this done."

"We'll drive you around to the far side, to the top of the ramp, and then stay out of sight."

Staying out of sight was an illusion. Sensors had tracked the approach of the sleighs. And now Stillers reported to Lear that the sleighs were behaving strangely. They had stopped for a while at the northern end of the valley before continuing on around to the southern entrance.

"Now they're just sitting there."

Interesting, Lear thought. Frightened employees? Was some of the biot conditioning that all her core people had been subjected to beginning to weaken?

Her eyes flicked to the TV. YouTube was still up, thankfully. Bug Man was watching a shaky video of a Tesco being looted.

"Do we have cameras on the ramp?" Lear asked.

"Yes, ma'am," Stillers said.

"Get them on-screen here." Soon a dimly lit image of the ramp opened. At first: nothing, just gravel and ice. Then, someone walking down the ramp. The person wore a heavy parka with a fur-lined hood, with dark goggles covering the upper part of the face.

"Can't see the face," Stillers said. "I'll send some guys up there."

"No." Lear smiled. "I think . . . I think maybe I can guess who this is. Yeah. Have men ready, get a sniper into position to cover my door, make sure all security personnel are armed at all times, and I'll want a handgun for myself. Do nothing unless I give the order."

Stillers nodded and went about his work.

"I believe we have company, yeah," Lear said to Bug Man. "I do not know how she did it, clever girl, but if I'm right, we'll have an old friend of yours over for a drink."

Opportunity for Suarez came with Kung Pao chicken—extra spicy, the way she liked it—brown rice, and a glass of Austrian white wine.

After so long planning what to do with a bucket as the only weapon, she was handed a golden opportunity: Chesterfield came armed.

She immediately recognized it as a Glock nine-mil with a eventeen-round clip. She had fired hundreds of rounds from a weapon essentially identical to this. All that was good, but the beautiful part from her perspective was that the standard cop holster was also very familiar, and she would be able to draw it smoothly, especially if she could get behind him.

Much better than trying to beat him down with a pee bucket.

The final piece of the puzzle was the Kung Pao. And more specifically, the peanuts.

She accepted her tray, invited him to stay so she could be sure it wasn't too spicy. She took a bite and cried, "Oh, no. No! Peanuts!"

"What's the matter?"

She put a hand to her throat and began wheezing dramatically. "Allergic . . . to . . . peanuts. I can't breathe! Help . . ." And then choking noises and a strained, whooping breathing and Chesterfield made the fatal move: he behaved like a human being, stepped in, knelt down, and in a blur of movement felt the muzzle pressed against the side of his head.

"I would honestly hate to do it," Suarez said. "You've been decent to me. But Chesterfield, I will blow your brains out if I have to. The alternative . . ."

Which was how Chesterfield ended up wearing her chains, with handcuffs added to keep him in a hog-tie position, and his own socks stuffed in his mouth with his belt wrapped tight to hold them in place.

"Can you breathe okay?" she asked him.

He nodded, and Suarez, armed with the gun, an extra clip, his radio, and his keys, opened the door to her cell very slightly and looked cautiously left and right. If there were cameras, they were not in evidence. Which did not mean they weren't there.

Nothing you can do about that but move fast, Suarez told herself. Down the hallway, which carried the ridiculous medieval dungeon theme forward. A door. She cracked it slightly. There was a sort of control room—monitors and swivel chairs and two women chatting as they watched the screens. Panic buttons were large and prominent. She winced. There was no room for error or pity.

"Hey," she said, stepping into view, and with two head shots dropped the women. One was clearly dead. The other rattled her shallow breaths in and out until Suarez covered her mouth and nose and waited for the final spasm. No point wasting ammo, and no point risking a third shot attracting attention.

Her immediate goal was simple: to find and take the sleigh she'd ridden in and get the hell out of there. But that would require some intel. She dropped into one of the dead women's seats and began cycling through the camera angles, one of which did in fact show the hallway outside her dungeon. She had been lucky they hadn't spotted her.

This monitoring station appeared to have only limited access to cameras, concentrating on the dungeon and what appeared to be extensive storerooms. Really quite impressive storerooms, too large to be in any of the aboveground buildings. She saw other people, some armed, some not. Some doing mundane tasks with iPad inventory systems, others driving forklifts, still others . . .

A man walked toward the monitoring station, holding three disposable cups and a paper sack in a recyclable cardboard holder. He might easily have been coming from a Starbucks.

"Hey, coffee!" he said as he stepped into the room. Suarez grabbed his hand, yanked him forward, slammed the door shut, and blew out his brains.

One of the coffees survived the fall, and she took a sip before getting back to her research. Surely there must be a way to break out of this limited protocol and access more cameras.

She was beginning to regret having killed all three of them—she could have used some help. But then she stumbled upon an open link that led her helpfully to a schematic of the base. The schematic had green dots for camera locations.

The first was password protected. She tried the usual combinations, and none worked. So she rifled the pockets and wallets of the dead, and finally found a tiny slip of yellow legal pad.

"Thank God for unreliable memories." Moments later: "And bingo. We are in."

The sun was just millimeters above the horizon, and the weak light left the valley in darkness. Stadium lights cast a circle of eerie orange across the main buildings, excepting the house, which cast its own warm, buttery light.

Plath was shaking with cold and fear by the time she had descended the long ramp and then crunched her way across the gravel to the house. She did not spot—indeed did not look for—the sniper who watched her through his telescopic sights.

She climbed the few stairs and stood on the porch of the impossible house belonging, she was certain, to Lystra Reid, also known as Lear.

She pulled off her glove and knocked.

The door flew open to reveal an attractive young woman wearing white yoga pants, shearling boots, and a blue down vest over a sheer white tunic.

Plath pushed up her goggles and slid back her hood.

"Oh. My. God." Lear said. "It *is* you."

"May I come in?" Plath asked, feeling an absurdity in it all that went beyond the merely surreal.

"Mmm, not just yet. First, I should tell you there's a very good shot watching you, yeah, and ready to fire at any excuse. So. Shrug off the coat, keep your hands where I can see them, and don't move." In order to emphasize her point, Lear pointed with one hand at the gun in the other.

Plath complied.

"Now, turn around slowly."

This, too, Plath did.

"Ah! There we go. You *do* have a gun. I thought you might." Lear pulled the gun from Plath's waistband and tossed it out onto the ice. It came to rest by a lawn ornament, a pink flamingo that must have been someone's idea of witty commentary on the climate.

"Now, come on and warm up," Lear said. "Bug and I are drinking excellent bourbon, would you like some?"

"Bug?"

Plath looked past Lear and saw a badly battered Bug Man, sitting on a couch and looking miserable and humiliated, and perhaps just a little hopeful.

"You two have met, right?"

"Briefly," Plath said. Then added, "I don't drink."

"Yes, you do, yeah, not a lot but on occasion," Lear said smugly. "Yeah." She handed Plath a glass. Plath took a sip, grimaced, and put the glass aside.

"If we're going to be friends, you're going to have to get into the spirit of things," Lear said, her face darkening.

So Plath picked the glass back up and followed Lear's direction to sit, sit down, take it easy, relax.

Plath sat. She saw the TV, currently on a YouTube of a burning house. Where it was she had no idea. Bug Man sat stiff and wary.

"I did it," Plath said.

"Did it?" Lear asked.

"I blew up the Tulip. I gave the order to Caligula. Then I followed the breadcrumbs here."

That had the desired effect of throwing Lear off stride. "Are you trying to tell me that—"

"Did I know it was you behind it?" Plath interrupted. "Yes. After you killed Jin it was obvious that he had failed you, somehow. Was it that he found out the reason you'd ordered him to wire Vincent?"

Lear, small smile growing. "In a way. Nijinsky hated you. He didn't like being pushed aside for some kid. So that was part of it. But yeah, he was starting to get cold feet. Developing a conscience."

"I didn't want to die choking on my own tongue on an escalator. So I didn't fight it very hard. I could have sent my own biots in to stop it all happening, my own rewiring. But I could see where it was all going."

"Oh?"

"I came to like the idea. I came to like the whole, meticulous planning of it. It was brilliant. It was genius. It's historic."

Lear's nostrils flared, and her eyes widened. "Historic?"

So, Plath noted, she liked that word. "Well, yeah," she said. She took a sip of the whiskey, suppressed the face she wanted to make, and instead said, "It gets better as you get used to it."

"Historic, yeah?" Lear prompted.

"I remember this lecture in history class. All about Genghis Khan. You know, the Mongol guy."

"I know."

No, Plath thought, Lear had not heard of the great Khan. But she didn't like admitting it. "Well, the point was that Genghis killed, like, thirty million people, no one is sure how many. Maybe twice that much. There was this one thing where he took a bunch of captured enemies, and built a platform on top of them. His own soldiers had lunch on the platform as it slowly crushed all the men beneath."

"Yes," Lear said fervently.

"But the point was, that later, like nowadays, we look back on him, Genghis, I mean, as a great historical figure. He, like, improved the economy and so on by clearing out a bunch of people who were in his way. But he killed millions."

"He changed the game. But I'm changing it more. I'm changing it all," Lear boasted. "I'm creating whole new species, yeah, to take over. I mean, you know, thanks to your dad, who was a genius. Yeah. By the way, condolences on his death, he was a great man."

Plath's mask almost dropped then. Almost. "Yes, he was."

"But we used his techniques and played around, and now we have three very interesting species. *Macro*, not micro. We'll breed them up, yeah, and then release them when the time is right. One of them can't metabolize anything but pork and human meat. Hah! Later, at the next level, yeah."

"But how are you going to watch what happens? I mean . . ." She waved a hand at the YouTube video. "How much longer is Google going to work?"

"Oh, don't worry. The satellites will work independently for a long time. And we'll start placing cameras here and there, when the time is right."

"You've thought of everything," Plath said.

Lear smiled, a shark's smile this time. "You don't really think I'm buying any of this, do you?"

"Sorry?"

"This bad-girl act. *This* Sadie McLure, indifferent to suffering. You tried to stop Caligula. I *know*. I spoke to my father before he died. That was kind of a drag. He was very useful, the old man. I was never going to bring him here, no, no, but it would have been fun watching him deal with the world I'm creating. He would have been an interesting player in the game."

Plath put her drink down again. Her hand was shaking. Lear saw it.

"The world you're creating?"

But Lear wasn't playing along anymore. "How much longer do you think you have to live, Sadie?"

Plath did not answer.

"Two ways forward for you, Sadie. The usual choice: death or madness. We have some decent twitchers here, and we could easily wire you up. Or I could be disappointed that you would just walk in here and think you could lie to me." Lear raised the pistol on her lap and leveled it at Plath.

The muzzle looked huge. *What a cliché*, some corner of Plath's mind thought. *That's what everyone who has ever stared down the wrong end of a gun thinks: oh, it's big.*

"Go ahead," Plath said.

"You don't think I will?" Lear stood up and let the down vest slide to the floor. The sheer tunic revealed shadows of the tattoo horrors beneath. Lear pointed to a spot on her belly, right where an appendix scar would be. "Right here, yeah. That's where I would tattoo your face. Maybe then you'll talk to me, yeah? They speak the truth, the tattoos do. Yeah."

"I believe you'll kill me," Plath said. "You're a mass murderer. Before you're done you'll kill more people than Genghis or Hitler. You're a sick, twisted, crazy woman playing an insane game. So yeah, I think you'll kill me."

Lear cocked her head, all the while keeping the gun aimed. "Don't you want to beg?"

Plath forced a smile of her own. A peace had descended over her. It was like what Noah had described to her, the eerie feeling of detachment and fearlessness that could come in the midst of a very challenging game. It would be over in minutes.

"I'm not afraid to die," she said. "So long as I take you with me, you foul, fucked-up psychopath."

"Hah!" Lear said. And then, the wheels began to turn in her head. Plath could see her retracing her steps. "You never touched me. Yeah, you never touched me."

"No," Plath said. "But you took my gun. As I knew you would."

Lear swallowed. She glanced at Bug Man, as if he would or could help.

"You know the anterior cerebral artery?" Plath asked. "Don't be embarrassed if you don't. I never would have, if some sick creature had not dragged me into her little BZRK game. But now, hey, I know a fair amount. Like I know that the anterior cerebral artery feeds blood to the frontal lobes. Which is where your consciousness lives."

"You're bluffing."

"Three biots, Lear. Each has a nice, long spike buried in that artery. There's blood leaking, but just a few cells, nothing fatal. It takes pressure to hold them in place. I think you may have high blood pressure, because it's a little like holding a Champagne cork in. If I keep up the pressure, leave the spikes in, well, eventually the clotting factor will seal the damage. But if I let the spikes out . . . which is what will happen if my biots are suddenly no longer being controlled . . . there will be a sudden spurt of blood. The pressure of cells forcing their way out of the holes will actually widen the holes. And since all the spikes are close together, the whole area will probably tear wide open. I know these things because of my own aneurysm. Useful."

Lear lowered the pistol and squeezed the trigger. The bang rattled the glassware.

Plath felt a terrible blow, like a crowbar against her knee. The pain was immediate. Blood gushed from the wound. Bits of white bone stuck like teeth from ripped skin.

Plath fell to her other knee and shrieked in pain.

"See, little Sadie girl, there are other ways. I don't have to kill you. I can just keep hurting you. How does it feel? Does it hurt? It's weird, yeah, but people who can face the idea of dying can't always face the idea of suffering, yeah?"

The pain was beyond belief, beyond anything Plath had ever felt before.

"See, honey, I'm not afraid to die, either. I'm afraid to fail. I'd rather die than lose the game, yeah, my game, *my goddamned game!*"

She fired again, this time into the meat of Plath's arm.

"Oh, did I get the bone on that one? Ouch, yeah? I have doctors, I have morphine, I can help, but first—"

This crash was not nearly as loud as the gunfire. Just the *crump!* sound of a bourbon bottle hitting a skull.

Lear fell sideways, and Bug Man kicked her in the stomach, then grabbed the gun from her hand.

"Shoot her," Plath cried through waves of agony and terror.

"Can't. She's got me. Biots. Some kind of dead man's switch. She dies, I lose it. So you don't kill her, either, Plath."

"My biots never got to her brain. They're only halfway up her neck."

"Hah! You bluffed the crazy bitch?"

A loud, imperious banging at the front door. Bug Man fired through it. "They won't shoot back," he said, voice high with stress. "They might kill their boss." Then he yelled, "You come in here, I shoot her! I shoot her right between the eyes!"

"That was gunfire," Tanner said. "We go in."

O'Dell threw a quick salute and ran for his sleigh. But Babbington had run off, and O'Dell had never been any sort of pilot.

"With me, Sergeant!"

Tanner fired the engine as, down below, the helicopter's rotors began to turn.

THIRTY-TWO

Suarez did not hear the gunfire in her underground position, but on the monitor she did see men rushing, guns drawn.

"Something just hit the fan," she muttered.

She had located her own sleigh. It was parked behind one of the dormitories, not hard to get to so long as no one was shooting at you.

"Hope to hell they fueled the damn thing up," she said. She grabbed the guns from the dead guards, stuck them in her waistband feeling weighed down and a little ridiculous, and raced from the room.

The dungeon theme was over, now it was bright-lit hallway, white on white. Ahead, footsteps running. A man and a woman. It took her three shots to kill them.

The hallway dead-ended, and she had to double back to find an exit. She opened it quietly, glanced around to see the warehouse she expected, and ran toward concealment behind stacked plastic crates.

"Who is that?" a voice yelled.

"The prisoner got loose!" she yelled, waited until a worried face appeared, and put a bullet through its mouth.

Running, running, one of her extra guns clattered to the floor, but she kept running. Running through her mind was that whatever had sent armed men rushing around, it wasn't her. They'd been headed somewhere else, after someone else.

Bless whoever the poor fool was, but that was not her problem.

Probably.

The sleigh came slipping and sliding, hard to control, very hard to control as Tanner raced it down the ramp. First things first: kill that chopper.

Small-arms fire popped off to his left, chipping stone from the wall to his right.

"RPG at your six!" O'Dell yelled.

The wobbly rocket arced toward them, fired from behind and below. It missed by inches and blew up against the stone wall. The sleigh was blown clear of the ramp, still a hundred feet up from the bottom of the valley.

But then the computer kicked in—roared the engines to push a tornado of air beneath the hovercraft—which slowed the descent so that rather than being fatal it was merely bone-jarring as it slammed down onto gravel.

"RPG!" O'Dell yelled again, but this time Tanner had seen it coming even before O'Dell and pushed the throttle forward. The sleigh bucked, kicked up a storm of gravel, and blew past the missile, which detonated fifty feet away.

"On that building!" O'Dell pointed and there, sure enough, were two men manhandling yet another round into the missile launcher.

"Like hell," Tanner yelled, swung the nose of the sleigh around and fired blind at the building with one of his own missiles. It struck a second-floor window and blew a hole. It did not kill the men with the RPG, but the concussion knocked them onto their backs.

"The house!" Tanner yelled. He aimed the sleigh toward it and then, at the last second, sank the brakes into gravel and the sleigh skidded sideways into a stop. O'Dell had already opened the canopy and now leapt, pistol in hand, to rush the door.

The sniper fired once, and O'Dell slammed onto his face and did not move. At the same moment the door of the house flew open and a young black kid in a bathrobe appeared, dragging Sadie by one arm.

The sniper fired and missed.

Tanner spotted the muzzle flash, and thanked whatever God watched over him that the sleigh had skidded sideways, because his weapons were pointed in the right direction. He launched a missile that blew a hole in this second structure, and while the sniper was recovering Tanner emptied his pistol at the roofline.

"Get in! Get in!"

The boy climbed in, hauling a nearly helpless Plath after him. The canopy would not close with Plath's legs sticking out, but Tanner wasn't waiting. He gunned the engine and roared away toward the ramp, firing his thirty-mil cannon continuously, causing bright-red flowers to bloom on walls, empty ground, and a couple of men.

"Get her in, get her in!"

"Can't, there's no room!" Bug Man cried, but nevertheless he hauled a screaming, bloody Plath the rest of the way into the cockpit, a tumble of limbs and hair on Bug Man's lap.

"Who are you?" Tanner demanded.

"They call me Bug Man."

"Yeah, well, listen up, Bug Man. See this? That's the throttle. That's the brake. This is the yoke. The computer will help."

"What? Why? Are you bailing out?"

"No, but you will be. There's another one of these at the top of the ramp."

Lear rose from the floor, woozy, took a stutter-step, and fell into the wall. She left a trail of blood behind.

"Fu . . . The . . . Yeah . . ." she muttered.

Her legs were jelly. Her head was going around and around and around and *oh, no.* She vomited onto the floor. Felt a little better after that. Wished she hadn't been drinking. Wished she had more sleep. Yeah. Sleep would be good. . . .

Stillers came pounding in, gun drawn. Three other men, all armed.

"Boss!"

"Di . . . get 'em?"

"They've got the sleigh, but Tara's getting airborne."

"Kill them. Kill them," Lear said, slurring where she wished she was shouting.

"Someone get the doctor!" Stillers yelled.

More voices yelling, all around her; voices yelling and walkie-talkies blasting away and something burning.

"I'm 'kay," she said. Why wouldn't her mouth work?

She felt the side of her head, then stared at her hand, red with something she couldn't bring herself to understand. "Mom?" she asked.

Slowly, slowly, her head stopped spinning. Her legs were still weak but she could stand. A white-coated doctor was doing something to her head. Someone else was putting something in her mouth. Water. Had she asked for water?

She blinked. Her father was here. What was he doing here?

She shook her head, which set off a cascade of pain. She was sitting now on a couch stained with red handprints.

Caligula. He had come around to peer at her, keeping his distance, but saying something. "She's dead, Lyssie, she's dead, and you can't ever tell anyone what you've done. . . ."

"My head," she managed to say. "Give me something. Give me something. Hurts."

She blinked and her father was gone. She blinked again and pushed herself to her feet. "Kill them! Kill them!" she cried, and this time it came out right.

"Tara's in the air," Stillers said. "She'll get them."

By sheer dumb luck more than skill the sleigh made it to the top of the ramp, weakly followed by small-arms fire that drilled a hole in the canopy and brought a whinny of fear from Bug Man.

"There it is," Tanner yelled.

"I don't know how to drive that thing!"

"Go!"

Bug Man tried to crawl out from under Plath, who was only barely moving and definitely not saying anything brilliant. There was a pool of blood on the seat that had seeped into Bug Man's bathrobe.

This as much as Tanner's shout propelled Bug Man out and onto the ice. He immediately fell down, and that fact saved his life when the sleigh he was aiming for suddenly began firing. Cannon fire blew through the engines of Tanner's sleigh, and it settled to the ground. Tanner tried to run. His legs took two more steps after the cannon cut him in half.

Bug Man screeched in terror and bolted back toward the ramp. Plath meanwhile had managed to drag herself out onto the ice and was making a red smear across it, crawling, crawling but not dead yet. *Cold, dead soon,* she thought, *not dead yet.*

In her mind there were three windows.

Three biots ran up the side of Lear's face. Blood—a jumble of red Frisbees and expiring whitish sponges—lay strewn across a landscape of flesh.

Was she even going the right direction? Which way was up? Plath saw a stream, like a mountain spring rushing down a cliff face, but the water was a landslide of blood cells.

"Okay, that's up," she told the ice that was freezing to her lip.

Up and up, following the stream, the biots raced, the newest, P3, bounding ahead.

Ahead a forest of dark hair, huge, rough-textured whips sprouting from the flesh soil.

"Mmm, left," Plath mumbled.

The biots veered left toward the falling blood, leapt atop the soft-textured, tumbling cells, running, losing ground as the current swept them, then out onto dry surface.

And yes, ahead the slope leading toward the eye, a vast lake covered then revealed, covered then revealed by blinking eyelids.

This was a road Plath had traveled before. Her biots pushed through the twitching leafless palm trees of eyelashes and leapt onto the surface of Lear's eye.

Normally biots could travel unfelt across an eyeball, but not when the biot twitcher deliberately dragged sharp claws, slicing the outer layer of the cornea.

A sky-blackening hand fell from outer space and mashed the eyelid down on Plath's biots, but it didn't matter. You could no more squash a biot with a hand than you could stomp a cockroach in plush bedroom slippers.

"That's right, Lear. Still here," Plath said. Her body was shaking with cold. She was sure she was going to die. But before she did . . .

Her biots skated hard around the orb, leaving tiny rips over the mineshaft of the pupil, racing ever faster into the dark, clambering over veins, stabbing them as she went, loosing narrow fountains of blood that sprayed up to beat against the back of Lear's eye socket.

For you, Noah. For you. It's the best I have. . . .

Ahead lay the twining cables of the optic nerve. P1 dropped back to sink a probe and try to see what Lear was seeing.

P2 ran after P3, now well ahead and already ripping and tearing its way through mucus membrane, widening an access to the brain itself.

Suarez saw the sleigh, but someone was already in the cockpit, canopy open, revving the engines. She ran flat out now. The sleigh driver saw her and seemed to be fumbling for a weapon since the sleigh was still too sluggish to move.

Suarez jumped onto the sleigh's surface and pointed her gun directly down at the driver's head. "It would be a pain in the ass to haul your dead body out of that cockpit."

The driver saw the logic of that, held up his hands, and piled out onto the ground.

"Good choice," Suarez said, and shot him in the foot.

She slammed the canopy closed and cranked the throttle, sending ice crystals and grit flying.

Across the compound she saw the chopper pulling away, rising toward the level of the ice above.

"Yeah, you just go that way, and I'll go the other," she said, and sent the sleigh hurtling toward the ramp, cannon firing at anything that crossed her path.

Babbington had grown tired of being bullied. He had run off across the ice, but when he saw O'Dell abandon the sleigh and jump in beside Tanner, he'd run back. The sleigh was warm at least. He had barely made it before the chills came on so hard that for the next twenty minutes he just shook while waiting for the cockpit heater to thaw his bones.

And then, he had shot the other sleigh.

Babbington's thoughts had been less about needing to kill Tanner than they were about not wanting to yet again be forced out into the killing cold.

His first salvo blew the engine apart.

His second tore Tanner in half. The shock of that moment froze Babbington in a very different way. He pushed away from the controls and just in front of him the helicopter, bristling with weapons, rose like an avenging god.

Cold was not worse than being blown apart. Babbington threw back the canopy to wave his arms, show his face, anything to keep the helicopter from firing, but the dragonfly-looking monster still swept toward him, nose down.

Cannon fire ripped the ice, swept by, and now Babbington was warm enough. He ran from the sleigh, ran in panic across the ice toward the ramp, waving his arms.

Suarez shot up the ramp, then swerved madly as a boy in a bathrobe came pelting down. It was perhaps the most improbable thing she had ever seen. She backed the engines, shoved brakes into gravel, threw back her canopy, and yelled, "Who the hell are you supposed to be?"

The boy, wild-eyed, dove into the cockpit beside her.

"Yeah, okay," Suarez said. "Just don't talk." She hit the throttle and Bug Man, facedown in the seat, twisted like an eel to get back upright.

The sleigh topped the crest and shot directly beneath the helicopter.

"Oh, that's not good," Suarez said.

"It' after ush!" Bug Man yelled.

The chainsaw roar of the chopper's cannon opened up, blowing a hole in the canopy, sending plastic shards everywhere. Suarez hauled the sleigh sharply left. Looked at her left hand. A two-inch piece of plastic protruded from the back of it. Her tendons were cut, her fingers slack.

Suarez pushed the throttle to full speed and said, "Hey, kid!"

"Wha? Wha? Wha?"

"Ever play video games?"

"What?"

"See that thing right there, kinda looks like a game controller? Well, that's our weapons system."

"She's in my eye!" Lear yelled. "She's in my eye!"

The doctor did not understand. Stillers did. "I'll get some of our twitchers!"

Lear's head was almost clear now, but now sheer, blind rage was clouding her thoughts. She'd been bluffed! The McLure girl hadn't had biots in her brain, but they were sure on their way there now. Still time to stop them, maybe. Somehow.

Had to be. Otherwise . . .

The nanobots could survive, the whole thing would be ruined—had to win this, had to stay alive and win this. The Twins were dead, they couldn't defeat her—dead, impossible!

"Don't kill," Plath groaned to herself. "Wire."

But Plath's own body was in spasm now, convulsing. She could no longer feel her face. Her hands blue before her, frozen to the ice.

P3 stabbed a needle into brain tissue, didn't matter where, spooled wire from its spider spinnerets as it ran, and stabbed a second pin.

"Toast!" Lear yelled.

"What? Why are you yelling toast?" the doctor asked.

Another pin, another wire and Lear felt an overwhelming urge to bite her lip.

Now P2 was in the act, stabbing and spooling, stabbing and spooling.

"She's wiring me! She's wiring me!" Lear cried.

When she wasn't stabbing pins and running wire, Plath was simply slicing through neurons and axons, plowing the soft pinkish-gray tissue.

"No!" Lear shouted. "No. No! Grah! Grah!"

Plath felt a strange warmth creeping over her. Not real, she knew. Illusion. The body shutting down. Shutting down, conserving blood warmth in her core, saying farewell to limbs.

If I didn't love you, Noah, why am I thinking of you now, now at the end?

She no longer felt the pain of her knee. Numb. Her arm still ached, but it was so very far away.

I loved that you loved me, Noah.

But still enough consciousness to stab and spool and stab again.

I loved making love to you.

"Grah, I, grah, yeah," Lear said, straining to be understood.

"She's having a stroke," the doctor said. "Look! Her left pupil is blown!"

Lear no longer saw the doctor. She saw her mother, her mother, the whore had actually slapped her across the face when she'd seen her daughter's disapproving gaze, a red welt and a sting and a humiliation.

Slap me? Slap me? SLAP ME?

I wasn't brave enough to love you, Noah.

Bitch-slap me? Me? Me? Me?

Incoherent sounds came from Lear's mouth between manic twitches. The doctor and Stillers laid her down on the floor.

"I'm giving her blood thinners," a funny, funny voice said, coming from her mother's screaming mouth, the cleaver in Lystra's hand, yeah, die yeah, slap me?

Me? Meeeee? Meeeee?

The helicopter had a top speed just ten knots slower than the sleigh. The sleigh pulled away but with painful, painful slowness.

And the sleigh was definitely not faster than cannon or missiles.

The missile grazed the cockpit with a fiery tail and exploded a hundred yards ahead. The sleigh's computers were fast, but not fast enough at one hundred sixty miles an hour to avoid the ice and stone thrown up in the explosion. It was like driving full speed in a hailstorm with golf ball–sized hail.

But the sleigh survived, rocking wildly from side to side.

"Okay, we get one shot at this, kid," Suarez said. "Be ready!"

Suarez hit the brakes. The sleigh slowed in a storm of ice particles, the helicopter roared by overhead, and Bug Man pushed the button.

The recoil was unexpected, as was the inundation of smoke and flame as the missile launched from the sleigh and curved into the sky, seeking a heat source.

The missile flew harmlessly past the helicopter—which now, ominously, turned to come back. It came on cannon blazing, blasting ice on its way to killing Suarez and Bug Man.

Suarez spun the sleigh and shot back toward the valley.

"You know there's a big giant hole up ahead there, right?" Bug Man yelled.

"Yeah. We're going to see what this toy can do."

The distance was not great. The helicopter was a half mile behind. Suarez could only hope the chopper pilot wouldn't risk firing on her own people.

Out into nothingness, out over the lip of the valley, the sleigh shot out into midair. And fell. The engines roared, trying frantically to push enough air downward to slow the descent. It worked, but not well.

The sleigh fell, faster and faster, and Suarez grunted and switched the thrust from vertical to horizontal once again.

The sleigh bolted forward and fell even more rapidly.

Ahead, a patch of blue.

Just feet from the plastic dome, Suarez kicked all the thrust back to lift. The force of it bent the dome, then the sleigh broke through the plastic and with a loud crash slammed into the pool, snapped a diving board, and rode up and over a chaise longue to stop just inches from breaking through the far end of the dome.

The engine died then and the sleigh lay inert, back half trailing in the shallow end, front end tilted up.

"I gotta get this game," Bug Man said.

Tara Longwood—the chopper pilot—gave a thumbs-up to her weapons officer and took a victory pass over the wet sleigh below.

Then she turned the helicopter back, scanning for any other targets. There was still a sleigh at the top of the cliff, but last she'd seen, the pilot, Babbington, was running like a scared rabbit.

However . . . She frowned and pointed. A green Sno-Cat sat steaming within a few yards of the sleigh.

"One of ours," the weapons officer said. "Must have just come up from Forward Green."

Tara nodded. She saw a dark-haired man climb into the sleigh's cockpit before she flew on around, circumnavigating the valley, looking for trouble.

By the time she got back to the sleigh and the Sno-Cat, she had heard a panicky babble of voices in her earpiece, coming from the ground. The dark-haired fellow in the sleigh was waving his arms, trying to attract her attention.

A young woman and another man were carrying what could only be a body toward the Sno-Cat.

Tara brought the chopper in low, ready to help ferry the wounded now that the fight was over. She landed, and the young man in the sleigh trotted toward her, seemingly unconcerned, waving as he came on.

She slid the side panel of her cockpit open. "What is this?" she asked.

And Vincent shot her in the face.

THIRTY-THREE

Plath woke slowly. She was a drowning person, fighting her way up toward air and light, but it was so far, and her arms were so heavy.

Then, all at once, she was awake. A doctor was beside her. And to her utter amazement, Vincent, Wilkes, and Bug Man were standing before her. There was also a Latino woman she had never seen before.

"Where am I?" Plath asked.

"You're still here, in the valley," Wilkes said.

Plath stared. Looked left and right. It could have been a room in any well-appointed, new hospital. She saw her leg, swathed in rigid webbing over bandages. It hurt like hell. Her arm hurt as well, but not as bad.

Her face felt raw, as if it had been sunburned. Something was wrong with the bandaged hand. She saw bandages over the stubs of her amputated little and ring finger.

Her head hurt. But she was alive.

In her mind, she saw three windows.

She took a deep breath, drank some water through a straw, answered the doctor's questions, and said, "What's happened?"

"Later," Wilkes said. "We had you brought around so that, uh . . .

there's a pretty big question, and we think we need to ask you."

"Wait. Are we—"

"We're in charge," Vincent said. "We're running this base now. Suarez here can fly a helicopter, and do a few other things, and—"

Wilkes broke in to say, "And with Lear out of the picture, all her wired-up zombies here didn't exactly know what to do."

"You've been unconscious for eighteen hours," the doctor said. "I gave you a stimulant to wake you up. But it won't last long, the pain will get worse, and you'll be better off asleep for a while longer while your body recovers. You've been through a lot."

"Why did you wake me up?" Plath asked Wilkes.

But Wilkes looked pleadingly at Bug Man. "Okay, this is some very bad shit to deal with. But the gray goo, Burnofsky's babies, we're not sure . . . I'm seeing stuff that may be caused by self-replicating nanobots. But very small scale so far. And it could be I'm wrong."

"And there's the Floor Thirty-Four virus," Vincent said. "Maybe it never escaped the Tulip. But maybe it did. The whole final tranche of Lear's victims have biots. We stopped the process before they were killed off. That's thousands of people with living biots who would suffer madness if the Floor Thirty-Four virus were to get loose."

"Not to mention all of us," Bug Man said.

"Uh-huh." Plath wanted very badly to go back to sleep, and the doctor was right; the pain from her shattered knee was stalking her.

"The thing is, there's only one way to stop the gray goo, and to make sure the Floor Thirty-Four virus never escapes," Vincent said in his dispassionate voice. "Nuclear."

"What? Wait, um, I'm lost, here. I don't exactly have an atomic bomb on me, oh, damn—Doctor, can I at least get an ibuprofen or something?"

"If it's out there and we don't stop it, the whole world dies," Wilkes said. She put her hand on Plath's forehead and held the cup so she could take another sip of water. "Bug Man has an idea."

Bug Man nodded uncertainly, not quite sure about how Plath would receive what he was about to say. "Listen, we stopped the biot crèches. The madness has stopped, but man, half the world is burning. Millions . . . you know. Nobody's in charge. But people know what it means if a window all of a sudden opens up in their head. And we still can control the crèches, we can still, you know . . ."

"Why would we?" Plath asked. Her head was throbbing. Her mouth felt like flannel, and nausea tickled the bottom of her throat.

"Because we need someone to blow up New York City," Vincent said. "Lear had good records, good data. We can pinpoint guys with access to nukes. Americans, Russians, French, Brits. And Bug Man realized that when the biots quicken—when they're born, you know—they see. And they could read. We can bring biots online, and we can show them a message."

"What message?" Plath asked.

One by one they looked to Bug Man. "Do it, or we kill your biots. Do it, or we take out your family. We explain, as much as you can, you know . . . the whole thing. But if we don't stop this, we're all dead. Us last of all, down here on the ice. But everyone. The whole human race. The whole planet."

Plath felt tears welling in her eyes. "You woke me up for this? To vote on—"

"Not a vote," Wilkes said. "We already took a vote. You're in charge, Plath. Sadie. Suarez will run security, and eventually we'll unwire some of these people, but right now, it's on you."

"Vincent?" Plath pleaded.

He looked away, ashamed. "It's on you, Plath. Whatever you decide."

In the end it was a Chinese missile that did it. The Chinese general responsible, once certain that his family was safe, tied a rope to a tree in one of his favorite countryside spots, and hanged himself.

There were very few functioning governments still left to do useful things like tally up the death toll of the Plague of Madness. But later, historical estimates would set the count at two hundred ten million, in thirty-six countries.

Four million of those had come as a consequence of Plath's order. But, in the end, Burnofsky's gray goo did not make it off Manhattan. The human race was saved. Life on planet Earth would go on.

In the weeks that followed, Plath drank much more than she should have, sitting in the living room of what had been Lear's house. She shared the house with Wilkes, Vincent, and Bug Man. She tried not to drink before lunch, but she often failed. She tried to stop, but not very hard. Wilkes made efforts to get her to move on, but the very words died on her lips when she looked into Sadie McLure's haunted eyes.

Once, and only once, had Plath gone to look at Lear.

Lear sat chained in the dungeon that had once held Suarez. Plath had asked for the door to be opened so that she could see her. See the monster. The mass murderer.

But Lear had not responded to Plath, had seemingly not noticed that she was there.

Plath stopped using that name, and reverted to Sadie. She had tried and mostly succeeded in accepting Noah's death. But she could not reconcile herself to what had happened, what she had done, to New York City.

Four months on, Wilkes found her on the floor, choking on her own vomit after drinking an entire bottle of Lear's bourbon. It was terribly clear that Sadie McLure would, sooner or later, manage to kill herself in expiation of her sins.

Wilkes would not allow that. She went to Vincent, and to Bug Man, and slowly, so very gently, the biots went to work. And little by little, Sadie McLure forgot.

TWO YEARS LATER

The woman was probably in her early fifties but looked much older. She was dressed in clean but tattered clothing, layers of it, as if she had to be ready for any sort of weather. In the pocket of her patched coat she carried a crumpled black trash bag to use as an umbrella. London was out of umbrellas.

"That's her," a street kid said, jerking his chin and holding out his hand. "That's old Mrs. Cotton."

Sadie pressed a small gold bar—no bigger than a segment of Kit Kat—into his hand and said, "If you lied to us, kid, we'll find you."

The "we" in question included seven uniformed, heavily armed men who had fanned out on both sides of the street. London had quieted since the worst of the Madness, as it was commonly called, but it was still a wild place where street gangs ruled many neighborhoods. The "we" also included Wilkes, now somewhat changed as well. She still bore the strange flame tattoo beneath one eye, but she had grown out her hair into a simple blunt cut. She was dressed in a zippered black jumpsuit and carried a machine pistol over her shoulder.

Sadie waved Wilkes back a few steps and moved closer to Mrs. Cotton, keeping pace with her.

"I'm not a danger to you, Mrs. Cotton," Sadie said. "I'm here to tell you about your son."

The woman stopped. She turned a scarred and ravaged face to Sadie. Such signs of abuse were common among the survivors of the Madness. Sadie could only imagine what this woman had endured.

"Who are you?"

"I'm Sadie McLure." The name obviously meant nothing to Mrs, Cotton, and Sadie was relieved. A lot of stories were going around the newly revived Internet. There were even ridiculous rumors that Sadie McLure had actually ordered New York City destroyed. "I knew your son."

"Alex? You were a friend of Alex?" The woman peered skeptically at Sadie.

"No, ma'am, Noah. In fact . . . we were close. I was with him at the end."

Sadie led Mrs. Cotton to a small coffee shop, a place the older woman would never have been able to afford on the starvation pension and ration coupons the shaky government was able to pay her. But Sadie had gold, and gold made many things possible.

They bought weak coffee—or at least part of the hot brew was coffee, with just a bit of wheat chaff. And they each had a biscuit.

"Were you his girlfriend?"

"Yes," Sadie said.

Silence. Nothing but the munching of the dry cookie. The sipping of coffee. Then, "How did he do? At the end?"

"Mrs. Cotton, Noah died a hero." Sadie did not elaborate. Mrs. Cotton did not seem to need it, and the truth was that Sadie's memories of Noah at the end were disjointed. Parts of what she thought she remembered seemed unrealistic. Parts of her memory seemed to fit poorly with other memories.

Wilkes stood a distance away, close enough to smell the coffee and overhear snippets of the conversation whenever the room was quiet. She had, of course, been involved in rewiring Sadie. She and Vincent had written a heroic end for Noah, an ending in which he single-handedly took down the Armstrong Twins and stopped Burnofsky.

There were elements of truth—a good wiring always rests best on a foundation of some truth. But it was still a work in progress, connecting images of Noah to heroic pictures gleaned painstakingly from Sadie's memories of movies and books.

"Your son saved the human race," Sadie said, and believed it, mostly.

Mrs. Cotton nodded grimly. "He was always a good boy."

"Yes. I loved him."

Mrs. Cotton's composure broke then, and tears filled her eyes. "I couldn't . . . I didn't know how to reach him. . . . He had this job in New York. . . ."

"It was an important job. He was an important boy. Man, actually. Because he was definitely a man by the end," Sadie said.

"I'm glad you told me this," Mrs. Cotton said, though her face was anything but happy. "Did you tell him?"

"Did I tell him what?" Sadie asked.

"Did you tell him that you loved him?"

Sadie took her hand and squeezed it gently. "Yes. I told him that I loved him. I told him that many times." Sadie glanced at Wilkes, who blushed and looked down. "He loved me, and I loved him. I think that memory is all that's kept me alive."

Sadie sat for a while longer with Noah's mother and left her with enough small gold bars to take the edge off her poverty.

She and Wilkes walked down streets that still showed the bullet holes, the fire scorches, the wreckage of the Plague of Madness. But London had suffered this badly before in its long history and knew how to put itself back together. Crews were at work. There were police on the streets. Life was slowly returning.

A century would pass before New York City could say the same.

"Now what?" Wilkes asked.

"How much of what I told that woman was true?" Sadie asked.

Wilkes met her gaze and waited, saying nothing. Finally she said, "Now what?"

They were in front of what had once been a pizza restaurant, but was now burned out and choked with rubble.

"How long has it been since you had a decent pizza, Wilkes?"

"Long, long time," Wilkes acknowledged, peering into the restaurant. "I think those ovens may still be usable. Of course someone would have to clean the place up. Get the gas working again."

"You have something better to do?" Sadie asked. She stepped over the threshold, bent down, and grabbed hold of a broken table. "Help me with this."

TWELVE YEARS LATER

Three windows were open in Sadie McLure's brain.

Her three biots sat immobile in the glass vial she wore on a chain around her neck.

When business was slow at Poet Pizza, she would sit in a corner booth with her old friends, Anthony and Wilkes. Their daughter would tease the cooks while their baby son chuckled on his father's lap.

Ten thousand miles away to the south, Michael Ford, once known as Vincent, supervised the skeleton staff that maintained what had become, in effect, a prison.

A prison with a single prisoner. Who sat in her cell, chained to the wall, screaming.

"Meeee? Meeee?"

MICHAEL GRANT likes to tell stories that will leave readers entertained, excited, and afraid to turn out the lights. He likes to make up characters who become like family members to his readers—and then kill them. He likes to take readers to places they would never have imagined but can never forget. Michael Grant has no hobbies, he doesn't take vacations, he is not particularly friendly or charitable. He just wants to grab readers and leave them wrung out, trembling, and begging for more. Which, according to just about everyone who's read a Michael Grant book, such as *BZRK*, *BZRK Reloaded*, and the Gone series, is exactly what happens. Michael is on Twitter @TheFayz, in case you want to talk to him. He lives in Marin County, California, with his wife, Katherine Applegate, their two children, and far too many pets.